ISBN 978-1-971421-00-1 (paperback)

ISBN 978-1-971421-01-8 (ebook)

First Edition

Published by Federal Pen Publishing

Phoenixville, Pennsylvania

Writing is a game of isolation, and I'm blessed to have never truly faced it on my own. Very special thanks to God, my wife, friends, family, and all of the beta readers who lent me a much-needed hand along the way.

*Most importantly, thank **you**, dear reader, for chasing your curiosity into the world of Lonnie Lovingdove.*

- Matthew Scura

THE PLIGHT OF LONNIE LOVINGDOVE

MATTHEW SCURA

FEDERAL PEN
PUBLISHING

PART ONE
IT'S ACTUALLY PRETTY SWEET

CHAPTER

ONE

As a piercing yelp echoed across the hamlet, Lonnie Lovingdove kicked off her bedsheets. She ran to the window and studied the night; the hundreds of shacks surrounding her own. Candles flickered in the windows. Laughter drifted across the smokey nightscape.

As the dog yelped again, Lonnie pulled on her cloak.

She came downstairs to find her husband Daniel carving at the hearth, right where she had left him. He grimaced as he shaved his wood block. Lonnie paused, expecting him to ask where she thought she was going after curfew, but he never looked up. With a sigh, she stepped outside.

A world of possibilities faced her—the rush of breaking rules. Her heart raced as she followed the cobblestones, listening for the dog, wondering what mysteries she might uncover. Her eyes drifted to a glowing window. At the sound of voices, Lonnie crouched beneath it, unable to leash her curiosity.

" ch," a man was saying. "I'll believe it when I see it. They give us a curfew, and then we're expected to come out and party? What the hell do we have to celebrate?"

"*We're winning the war,*" a woman answered. " They say it'll be over before the solstice."

"Of course they do. What, are they going to tell us we're losing?"

"I'd like to go to the festival."

"When did I say we aren't? We're not missing out on free pork."

"Then let's go to bed, I need . . ."

As the conversation faded out of earshot, Lonnie crawled back to the road. She had heard mention of the king's festival at work, but not the offering of pork. Her mouth watered at the idea of it. She and Daniel mostly lived off cabbage stew, and embarrassingly, she couldn't remember what pork tasted like.

But she would if she could convince Daniel to go to the festival with her.

The dog yelped again, this time closer, and Lonnie continued down the road. She shivered as the night cooled, the shadows around her dark and deep. The investigation came with an unsettling satisfaction. Perhaps sneaking out after curfew was her own form of carving; a chance to live for more than survival.

As she came to an intersection, one of the king's festival notices fluttered from a street sign. A man in rags stood before it. Tentatively, Lonnie stepped to his side.

"Good evening," she said, relieved to find an old and weathered man in place of a troublemaker. "Did you hear a dog yelping?"

The man grunted, his attention locked on the poster.

"Are you going to the festival?" Lonnie asked.

"What festival?" The man frowned as he leaned closer to the page. "Is that what this says?"

"Do you want me to read it for you?"

"You read?" the man asked, glancing at Lonnie's tattered cloak.

"My father used to have a book." She smiled as she stepped forward, lifting the page into the moonlight.

"*To the merry kingdom of Doane, in the light of a crushing victory.*

King Pollen Bane V invites all to attend a festival in celebration of the campaign's steady victory on the Eastern Front. Come prepared for feasting and camaraderie. Swine will be roasted, and there will be merriment; a party to remind us of the coming victory. Bring your appetite and bring your good wishes. Bring your sorrows and cast them to the stars.

SPECIAL NOTICE: King Pollen Bane V and Prince Pollen Bane VI will be in attendance. While the kingdom's curfew will be lifted for the night, shenanigans will not be tolerated. Any misconduct will be swiftly and severely punished.

See you at the feast!"

" It ends with a bunch of fancy signatures," Lonnie said. "I can't make them out."

The man mumbled, "pork?" and limped up the street.

Lonnie, now armed with hard proof of the free feast, turned back for home. She had pushed her luck far enough, and she needed to start working on Daniel right away if she wanted to convince him to go to the festival. Even if it meant dragging him away from the fireside, they were going to get their share of pork.

But Lonnie had barely turned around when she heard the dog bark again. She followed the sound to a dark alleyway on the other side of the street. Fast, desperate panting came from within the shadows.

"Are you a dog?" Lonnie asked. "Do you need help?" She creeped into the darkness, waving her hands before her. "Where are you?"

"Right here," a man said, whacking a stick across the back of Lonnie's head. She collapsed to find an armored kingsguard standing over her. He extended his sword to her chin. "What the hell is this?" he asked.

"I was just on my way home," Lonnie said, scrabbling to her

feet. "I'm so sorry. I was working late—the sun got away from me. I live just around the corner."

"It's after dark," the guard said. "Where's your chaperone?"

"My husband's at home. He's waiting for me right now."

"Then let's go see the bastard. Come on." The guard dragged Lonnie to her feet, again whacking her across the head.

"I heard a dog yelping. Do you know if it's—"

"Dead," the guard said. "Where do you work?"

"I'm a brick maker," Lonnie said, wincing as she glanced back to the shadowy alleyway.

"Which kiln?"

"South Doane."

"What about your husband?"

"He's a wagoner."

"What's your name?"

"Lonnie Lovingdove."

"And his?"

"Daniel Lovingdove."

"Generational peasantry?"

"Of course." Lonnie crossed her eyes as she smiled, doing her best to look stupid. "We try our best, though."

"Shut up." The guard whacked her again. "How much farther?"

"The next block. If you have more important business, I'm happy to escort myself the rest of the way home. I promise I won't—"

The next strike knocked Lonnie off her feet. She stumbled into a pile of crates, wincing as they smashed into the street. While the guard dragged her off the ground, a dozen curious faces poked out of the nearby windows. Lonnie rubbed her throbbing head as the guard steered her forward. This time, he held onto her shirt collar.

"A woman alone after curfew," he announced, lifting

Lonnie's head high. Lonnie had no choice but to face her neighbors. They looked down at her with disgust, their faces ghastly with candle-cast shadows. Heat spread across her cheeks as if she too had a candle beneath her nose. "The king is coming," the guard continued, raising his voice as more faces appeared in the windows. "If this is how you follow his laws, he might just change his mind."

"I can't breathe," Lonnie groaned.

The guard, finally satisfied, shoved her back into a walk.

"You better live on the next block, or I'll draw you back to the dungeon," he muttered.

"It's right there," Lonnie said. To her relief, Daniel stood at the door with his woodblock under his arm. He frowned at the sight of Lonnie.

"What happened?" he asked, meeting her in the street.

"I was scouting the hamlet and found your wife walking without a chaperone," the guard said. "She tells me work ran late at the South Doane brick kiln. Can you verify her claim?"

"What?" Daniel asked. "She was just home with me. What's this about, Lonnie? Running late?"

"I see," the guard said, shifting his gaze to Lonnie. "The punishment for breaking curfew is ten lashes."

"No," Lonnie gasped. "Please, sir, it was a misunderstanding."

The guard pulled back his cloak, unhitching a coil of leather from his belt. He cracked the whip and scattered the dust. Wincing, Lonnie clung to Daniel.

"What have you done?" he asked. "Lonnie, I can't save you from this."

"Save her?" The guard laughed. "You're responsible for keeping her under control. This is your lashing. Remove your shirt."

Daniel froze, his wood block dropping to the stone with a

dull clatter. A few of the watching neighbors gasped from above.

"No," Lonnie said. "*No*. Please, sir. It was my mistake. This is my punishment."

"Daniel," the guard said. "Do you wish to pass your lashings to your wife?"

Daniel faced Lonnie. With a trembling breath, he started to unfasten his tunic.

"No," Lonnie said, taking hold of him. "Please, don't do this."

"Go inside," Daniel said. He lifted his block and handed it to her. With wide, desperate eyes, he guided her into the shack.

Lonnie went cold as the door snapped shut. She turned to the window, where the curtain hid all but the sounds of her punishment.

Daniel let his tunic fall.

He grunted as he dropped to his knees.

A pungent whiff of smoke crawled up the street, as if signaling the shift in responsibility.

Lonnie jumped as the first lash cracked.

Daniel wailed, a bright echo of the whip.

The following nine lashes came like a racing thunderstorm.

TWO

When the guard left, Lonnie raced outside. Daniel lay face-down in a spreading puddle of blood. The whip had turned his flesh into mincemeat. A few of the neighbors remained gawking in their windows and Lonnie cast them a sneer. She dragged Daniel off the cobblestone and carried him straight to the hearth, where she laid him on a nest of blankets.

"I'm so sorry," she whispered.

After cleaning the lashes, Lonnie settled Daniel into the blankets and tucked his wood block beside him. She lay on his other side, hating herself for what she had done.

Her damned curiosity.

Her unnatural desire for excitement.

She had a home and a husband and general health—far more than most peasants could say. Like a fool, she had risked it all in search of a dying dog. She decided to deny herself the king's feast as punishment.

When Daniel finally woke at sunrise, Lonnie nearly dropped the kettle into the fire.

"Daniel," she said, clinging to him. "I'm so sorry. Are you okay?"

"Where's my wood?" Daniel asked, grunting as he brought himself to a seat.

"Right here." Lonnie handed him the block, wincing to see a fresh trickle of blood escaping his wounds. "You need to rest."

"I have to work." Daniel gently removed Lonnie's hands and

staggered to the hearth. He set the block on his chair, letting out a breath. "Well," he said.

"I'm sorry," Lonnie repeated. She couldn't stop herself from bursting into tears. "Daniel—"

"We're alive," he said. "And what's done is done. I have to get to the wagons, and you need to get to the kiln. We're going to be okay, Lonnie."

Lonnie followed Daniel upstairs, where she helped him dress. They said nothing for the rest of the morning. Lonnie hoped to apologize, or even rekindle some kind of passion through their encounter with the law, but Daniel took the lashing as his wood took the blade; a most minor shift in appearance.

At the kiln, Lonnie ignored the gawkers and went straight to work. Word spread fast in Doane, and everyone surely knew what had happened, but Lonnie wasn't ready to explain herself. She had no explanation. Curiosity had simply beaten her self-control. She scraped up mud and patted it flat. She slapped it into the molds and dumped them out.

When the kilnmaster announced the end of the day, Lonnie headed straight home.

As she crossed the main road, a ruckus of laughter came from the direction of the town square. Dozens of men, women, and children bustled along the dusty street for their share of pork. Lonnie could already smell it; the sweet, delicate punch of roasting swine. She put her head down and kept walking, reminding herself of the truth.

Daniel needed her.

And after the previous night, a quiet evening at the fireside would be plenty exciting.

Still, Lonnie paused, drawing one last breath of pork smoke.

She found Daniel waiting out front of their shack, sitting

atop a wagon with a mangy donkey strapped to the harness. Daniel smiled as Lonnie frowned.

"What are you doing?" she asked. "How did—"

"You know I don't like walking," Daniel said.

"They let you take a wagon?"

"I borrowed one, along with Brown Thong." Daniel gave the reins a gentle slap, drawing the donkey's stunned gaze to Lonnie. "Come on, we need to get moving." Daniel set his carving block between his feet to make room for Lonnie. Still frowning, she climbed onto the bench.

"Where are we going?" she asked.

"We're going to that festival," Daniel said. He slapped the reins and sent Brown Thong into a stumbling walk. "I've been thinking about it, and if you need excitement to keep out of trouble, then we're going to get it."

"Oh, Daniel." Lonnie wrapped her arms around him, only letting go when he gasped. "Sorry. How's your back feeling?"

"Like I don't want to get lashed again." Daniel woodenly smiled as he turned to Brown Thong.

"I feel awful," Lonnie said. "If you're not up for the festival, we can stay home. I mean it."

"No, we both could use a night out of the house. They've been working us so hard since the war started, it's just been hard to have energy for anything." Daniel handed off the reins and lifted his carving block. He let out a sigh as he went to work, scraping away toothpick-sized strips of wood. "You'll like the one once it's finished—if I can actually finish it."

"I'm sorry," Lonnie said again. "I feel terrible."

"What's done is done," Daniel said. "Try to have some fun tonight."

Lonnie relaxed as they continued toward the square. They would soon join the community in a feast to celebrate a winning war, and pork would fill their bellies. And the king and prince were coming. Perhaps she would get lucky and meet them. It would be a story to remember on all those long coming nights at the hearth.

Except Lonnie Lovingdove would never sit at the hearth again.

CHAPTER

THREE

As they neared the square, hundreds of peasants filled the streets. Daniel took over driving and pushed Brown Thong, but the peasants were too excited, and the road far too thin. He finally admitted defeat and pulled off a few blocks from the square.

"Are you okay to walk?" Lonnie asked, standing to get a better view. Crown flags waved over the mass of peasants. The undeniable scent of pork carried on the drifting smoke. It smelled incredibly sweet—as if the pigs had lived on holiday pudding.

"Go on ahead," Daniel said, his eyes back on his blobbish carving.

"Don't you want pork?" Lonnie asked.

"I'll find you when I'm finished. Go have your fun. Just be back before curfew begins. I'm sure they'll announce it."

"Thank you." Lonnie leaned over and planted a kiss on Daniel's cheek. She grinned, waiting for him to turn, but he had his wood, and his wood had him.

Lonnie gave Brown Thong a pat on the head as she moved for the square, her smile unbreakable, her hands growing clammy with excitement. She started to jog. Soon, she broke into a childish run. There were so many people; so many sights to fill the canvas of her memory. She raced through the arches and into the square.

A team of minstrels stood atop the wall, polishing their horns and tuning their mandolins. Half a dozen kingsguard

13

stood watch over a pit in the center. Thick plumes of smoke billowed out from behind them, carrying the intoxicating scent of charring flesh. The peasants stared at the smoke, laughing as they exchanged pleasantries.

Still embarrassed from her late-night adventure and ensuing lashing, Lonnie stayed back from her neighbors. She noticed a stray dog watching the smoke from the wall. Thinking of the one she had failed to save, she knelt at his side, giving his matted fur a scratch.

"I'll steal you a piece," she whispered, laughing when the dog turned and licked her cheek. "Give me another kiss and I'll steal you two pieces."

But the dog raced off. Lonnie frowned, turning as a towering kingsguard approached her. Her heart dropped with recognition.

"Well, well," he said. "I didn't expect to see you tonight. How's your partner?"

"He's recovering," Lonnie said, brushing the dust from her knee.

"Be glad he took the lashing. A wiser man would have passed it on."

"Then it's a good thing he's not wise." Lonnie winced, not meaning to slight her husband. "Do you know when they'll serve the pork?"

"Once they cook and pull it," the guard said. "The king will speak first, of course." He frowned, looking across the crowd. "Where'd that mutt go?"

"The dog?"

"Yes."

"I don't know, it's not mine."

"Of course it's not yours. It's a stray. We're ordered to exterminate them before the king arrives."

"You mean kill it?"

The guard sighed as he stared at Lonnie. He walked after the dog, and only then did Lonnie notice the dark blood drying on his sword. She took a few steps after him and stopped herself.

It was none of her business if the king ordered his guard to kill strays.

But still, the poor dog did nothing wrong, and if she could find him before the brute did, she might scare him off to live another day.

Lonnie's heart kicked, drawing her mind back to Daniel, who would be the one to suffer if she did something stupid.

But the thought of the bloody sword kept her moving—she had failed one dog already.

She politely smiled as followed the guard across the crowded square. On the other side, she had room to take a breath and reassess the situation. The guard kicked through a pile of rubble beside an archway. Lonnie winced as he stabbed into the mess. He reached down and dragged out a rat, scowling as he tossed it aside.

A bright bark came from the distance.

Both Lonnie and the guard turned.

The guard only made it a single step when a trumpet blasted. On the other side of the square, the musicians finally started playing. The peasants broke into dance, filling the twilight with laughter, and the guard took a moment to survey the flailing peasants. He shouted at an obnoxious couple. When the couple didn't respond, he marched over and made himself heard.

Lonnie used the distraction to slip through the archway. She had never walked that side of town, and the flowing music left her deaf to any barking. She searched several adjacent streets and found no sign of the dog. Figuring his disappearance completed her quest, she started back for the square.

But as she approached the arches, the dog maddeningly

returned. He kept his head down as he hunted a scent along the wall. His path would lead him back into the square, and Lonnie started to run. She decided to give him one good kick and send him on his way, but as she approached, the dog turned, his tail wagging as he ran to meet her. Lonnie took him by the scruff.

"You need to go," she said, dragging him up the street. She looked for a rope or belt to leash him with, but the streets had been swept in anticipation of the festival. Frowning, she pulled him down an alleyway.

As they approached the next crossroad, a loud, crackling wagon crossed their path. Lonnie ducked under an awning and held the dog close. The wagon passed, but others soon followed. The parade grew in size and quality, until the final vessel, one bearing the crown insignia in bright gold and green paint, rolled past the alleyway with a battalion of marching kingsguard. The dog's heart banged against Lonnie's chest. She held him tight.

Once the last straggling cart passed, Lonnie raced the dog across the street. They crossed half a dozen blocks before she found a clothesline hanging from a window. Lonnie yanked it off the wall and fastened a harness around the dog.

"This is to keep you safe," she said, cinching the knot. She stepped back to inspect her work and nodded. The dog panted as he looked up at her. Then he ran, ripping the clothes line off the wall and racing back toward the square.

Lonnie chased him, zigging and zagging across the cobblestones. She nearly twisted her ankle and slowed a little. As a final mockery of her goodwill, the dog looked over his shoulder and appeared to smile before rounding a corner. By the time Lonnie found the corner, he was gone.

"Damn," she breathed, turning to the darkening sky.

She followed the road back to the main entrance of the square. The crown's parade of wagons sat neatly parked along the wall, with a few guards standing watch. Lonnie slowed as she passed the king's massive wagon. The artisans had done a masterful job painting it, and the crest looked so clear and bright it almost glowed in the dark.

"Festival's inside," a guard grunted, stepping out of the shadow in front of Lonnie.

"Sorry," she said. She bowed and scampered through the archway. Her stomach growled at the smoke, which now lay over the dancing peasants like a heavenly cloud. She swept around the crowd and climbed a barrel near the band.

The castle staff had built a stage on the far side of the square. While empty, a large huddle of men gathered behind it. Lonnie stood on her tip toes but couldn't identify any royalty. She turned to the smoke pit, where three burly and shirtless men scraped at a mass of roasting pork. Another team worked to chop the cooked pieces.

Lonnie wiped the drool from her chin. She studied everything; the merry faces of dancing lovers, the calm professionalism of the crown musicians, the thin and starving peasants who had eyes only for the roasting pork. She wished Daniel were with her. The festival might be enough to make him realize there was more to life than trimming wood. He might see what she saw; a world of color they might never touch if they didn't take the risk of reaching out.

A quiet fell over the crowd as the music faded.

Beside Lonnie, the musicians shouldered their horns and signaled across the square. Lonnie followed the gesture, where a burly kingsguard pointed back at them. He climbed the stage and lifted a cone to lips.

"People of Doane," he called. "Please welcome Your Highness, King Pollen Bane V, and His Majesty, Prince Pollen Bane VI."

FOUR

With swishing capes and twinkling crowns, the royals climbed onto the stage in tandem. They beamed, smiling and waving, setting their hands on their hips. Lonnie and the rest of the peasants broke into riotous cheers. The overwhelming emotions left her weeping. She lifted a hand, waving, hoping they might see her and smile, but the king and prince only surveyed the crowd.

A guard stepped forward and handed the king his voice-projecting cone. The king nodded and leaned into the guard's ear. They shared a quiet word and came away laughing. Lonnie wiped her tears, desperate to know what they said.

"My people," the king shouted. The square went silent enough to hear a mouse pip. "I thank you for coming to our festival. This is a joyous occasion, and Prince Pollen and I wanted to show you just how happy we are to dine with you."

The prince lifted a hand as the people cheered. He was the opposite of his father; tall, pale, and sporting a neatly trimmed beard. When he grinned, Lonnie quickly understood why so many women fantasize over him.

"Before we feast, I'd like to give you an update," the king continued, jutting his jaw. "As you know, we're fighting a war. In fact, we're fighting for our very existence. But we're winning that war."

The crowd erupted in applause. The king and prince shared a grin before waving everyone back under control.

"Just this past week, our men have taken control of the

western front," the king continued. "We've slaughtered the enemy; we've split their heads and showed them what happens when you challenge a true kingdom. Castle Winston will not take us, and we, you're rulers, will ensure you never feel the cold prick of their steel. We're not going to stop fighting until every last drop of blood is flushed from their bodies. We're going to consume them like wildfire."

As the crowd roared, the king handed the cone to the prince. They shared another whisper and the prince came away smirking.

"My people," he called. "We've received a raven from our allies in the east. As of this morning, our cavalry is only weeks away from storming the breach of Castle Winston. When we breach, we will take no prisoners. Our men will flush out the shadow and add yet another patch to the quilt of our campaign. This land belongs to Doane, and anyone who thinks differently will soon learn that the hard way." The prince paused until the king clapped, which brought the rest of the peasants into cheer, and at last, he stepped forward and pressed his lips to the cone, speaking the words everyone in the square came to hear. "It's time we feasted. Come, and fill yourself with the fruit of life."

The butchers hoisted trays of roast pork over their heads. They carried them out of the pit, and the peasants flocked like starving beasts. At the arches, another team carried a crate of raw pork to replenish the grill, keeping the sacrificial ceremony alight. Lonnie leaped off the barrel with her stomach churning.

The crowd rioted, pushing and pulling to get their piece of pork. Lonnie scrapped along with them. Thanks to her smaller stature, she managed to weave ahead, and soon she could see the towering trays of meat. Delicious grease slopped down the cook's arms. Lonnie reached for the sky as she came within range.

"There's plenty for all," the cooks shouted, but the starving peasants didn't settle until they held fistfulls of steaming pork. Lonnie met eyes with the nearest cook and he tipped his tray. She leaped and came away with a glorious mound of meat. Drooling, delirious to hold so much delicacy, she buried her face and stuffed her cheeks.

The meat hit her tongue like a bolt of lightning. She moaned, chewing the sweet, smokey manna. The abundant fat left her sweating. She backed from the flailing elbows and found an open space by the wall. Without meaning to, she ate every last stringy piece of meat. She sighed as she leaned back. Consisting on only watery stews, it was the first time she felt sated in years.

Lonnie turned to the stage in her stupor, where the king and prince enjoyed their own share of the pork. They ate in the protection of their guards, using silver plates and forks to keep the grease from their beards. Lonnie couldn't help but stare at the prince. Even while chewing he was beautiful. She wondered what men of his status did with their evenings. Did they too carve at a fireside?

Lonnie laughed out loud. Then she frowned, realizing she still had to get a handful of pork for Daniel. Most of the crowd had been served, and as they spread out, Lonnie moved for the pit. Smoke rose in great columns over the grill. Her stomach continued to fill, leaving her feeling sick from the overdose of meat.

"Can I have some more?" she shouted, leaning toward one of the cooks. He never turned from the sizzling grill. She looked across the square, but all the silver trays had returned to the pit. "Excuse me," she called to another cook. He hardly glanced over his shoulder.

Lonnie rubbed her stomach as it began to turn. She winced, realizing she had consumed far too much food. She tried to burp, but the pain only intensified. Concerned she might vomit, she rushed out of the square. She staggered through the arch and turned to the king's entourage of wagons.

Only a single guard stood outside of the king's painted wagon, and as Lonnie's stomach clenched, she ran for the shadow behind one of the smaller carts. The pork flew from her belly. It tasted sickeningly sweet on the way out. Lonnie heaved until she ejected every last stringy piece.

She frowned as she stared at the pile of steaming vomit. The mass sent her into another dry heave. She stepped back and bumped into the wagon. As she hit the wooden frame, something knocked loose and shattered inside.

Lonnie froze, listening for running footsteps, but all remained quiet. She turned to the wagon and pulled back the canvas. An unlit oil lamp had fallen over. Cursing, she creeped around the wagon, hoping to escape before anyone caught her.

But Lonnie stopped in her tracks.

The stray dog stood just outside of the archway, sniffing along the wall. His ridiculous clothesline leash dangled from his neck; an easy grab for the murderous kingsguard. Lonnie crouched and waved for him to come, but the dog was locked onto a scent. He rushed right past her and into the shadow behind the wagon.

"No," Lonnie breathed, understanding what he wanted. She dove for the leash and missed. The dog sprinted to her vomit and went straight to work. She turned over her shoulder, expecting her nemesis kingsguard to be standing over her, but she still had time. With a desperate lunge, she dove for the leash and wrapped her fingers around it.

The dog turned with pork fat glistening across his face. Lonnie started to pull him in, but the dog turned and ran, effectively dragging her down the narrow lane between the wagons and wall. To her horror, the dog came to one of the larger wagons and leaped straight into the back.

"Get out of there," she whispered, uselessly tugging on the leash.

Only a wet, vicious chewing came in reply.

Wincing, Lonnie climbed onto the wagon, taking a last glance over her shoulder before slipping beneath the canvas. As her eyes adjusted, she found the most horrific sight of her life.

FIVE

Long tables filled each side of the wagon. Scraps of bloody meat covered them, stinking of excrement and death. Lonnie pinched her nose as she approached the rear of the cargo hold, where the dog feasted with reckless abandon.

A mountain of dismembered human bodies lay piled to the ceiling. Most of their clothes were torn off, but Lonnie recognized the crest of Castle Winston of one of their breasts: their enemies in the raging war. She swallowed her rising spit. She didn't want to make any assumptions, but a stack of silver trays lay on the table to her left. Hunks of meat eerily similar to ones she had eaten in the square lay to her right.

"Shit," she breathed, backing away from the bodies. She trembled, barely able to remain on her feet. If her stomach hadn't already evacuated she would surely spray its contents across the wagon.

"Just a little more," a man grunted from outside

Lonnie froze.

Heavy footfalls encroached.

"Just some thigh meat and a few shoulders," the man continued. "Maybe a ham, but shred it. You know the rules."

"How about you chop 'em, if you're such a professional?" another man asked, his words sharp with responsibility.

The men stopped outside of the canvas at the back of the wagon. With no other exit, Lonnie rushed to the rear, internally screaming as she dove into the pile of dismembered soldiers.

The wagon rocked as she squirmed into the depths of their cold flesh.

"What was that?" one of the guards asked. He slapped the curtain aside and light fell upon the ghastly kitchen.

Lonnie held her breath.

The cook let out a booming laugh. "Look," he said. "We've got a visitor."

"They were supposed to clear them," the guard grunted, climbing into the wagon. He drew his sword as he approached the dog, who hadn't so much as looked up from his feast.

With a quick, sharp yelp, the dog fell face-first into the meat.

Lonnie did her best not to tremble. She prayed the guard wouldn't spot her blinking eye through the small gap between tangled appendages.

The cook stepped to the guard's side, eyeing the dog. "Meaty, for a stray," he mused.

"Serve him up, then," the guard said. He raked his sword across the dog and sheathed it. "I'll stand outside to make sure we don't have any more visitors."

"I won't be long. The king said he's ready to leave, so I imagine they'll take the whole parade back shortly."

"Fucking hell," the guard said, sighing as he crouched at the body pile. He lifted a hand and splayed the filthy fingers. "How did it come to this?"

"Waste not, want not," the cook said with a shrug.

Lonnie cringed, listening to the dull, wet *twak* of the butcher's chop knife. When it came time for the dog, he simply tore the guts out and hung him on a hook. He tore the coat off in one wagon-jostling pull. With the meat neatly stacked on a pair of silver trays, he climbed back to the street.

Alone again, Lonnie lifted her head, just enough to see the guard standing beyond the waving canvas at the back of the wagon. She cursed into the cold shoulder against her lips. The scent of feces seemed to penetrate her very soul.

She wept, understanding the night had only just begun.

She wept, hoping it would not be her last.

It didn't take long for the action to begin. While hard to discern the words, Lonnie recognized the king's voice in the distance. Cheers and applause followed.

Then marching footsteps.

What sounded like a hundred men surrounding the wagons. They laughed and back-clapped. The wagon jostled, a few butchers climbed in and they started rolling. Each passing cobblestone rocked the death box. Lonnie braced herself to keep from being sifted to the bottom of the pile. To escape her fear, she contemplated her discovery.

The king and prince were feeding the kingdom with the flesh of their enemy.

She had consumed human flesh.

Her stomach locked as it clenched.

What on earth would drive the king to make such a decision?

And he and the prince had eaten it themselves.

Lonnie thought until her mind throbbed. It helped to avoid her panic, but the lingering taste of human flesh left her eternally scandalized.

The people needed to know what was happening. The peasants class already lived as slaves to the crown. Their great reward was to eat dead men in celebration of the king's campaign?

Lonnie closed her eyes as a tear fell down her cheek. She wanted to be back on the hearth, nagging Daniel as he banally carved blocks of wood into smaller blocks of wood. It felt like years ago.

And where was Daniel?

Probably sitting in the wagon with Brown Thong, wondering what was taking Lonnie so long to bring him his share of pork.

Little did he know, he had dodged an arrow. He might be the only man in Doane who hadn't participated in cannibalism.

Lonnie snarled to have her innocence stripped away. It was a raping of the soul; a virgin hand dragged into witchcraft. She wondered if the dog had found her to reveal this very mystery. Perhaps this was providence. If done right, she could escape with enough proof to show the people who their king really was.

She could start a revolution.

She could overthrow a kingdom.

The idea was all she had to keep herself from screaming. She braced herself as the wagon continued its climb through the hamlets, making a determined rise to the castle itself. Men and women cheered to the passing caravan. Their blind dedication only embittered Lonnie's newfound mission.

Eventually, the peasant's cheers were replaced with the clanking of draw bridges. The butchers in the back of the wagon started to pack up their tools, and when the wagon finally came to a stop, they climbed out and Lonnie found herself in cold darkness. She waited for as long as she could. When the decision came to either scream or climb, she pushed and slapped away the body parts.

Once free, she creeped to the end of the wagon and pulled back the canvas. She found herself in a dark, stone tunnel. A few torches lined the walls, but they were dying. Lonnie took a quiet lap around the wagon to ensure the guards were gone. The crypt-like tunnel had a staircase in its center, leading up to a large wooden door. Bright and flickering light glowed from the other side. Lonnie spat some of the taste from her mouth as she ventured up the stairs.

SIX

The entrance led into a dark corridor. Doors lined the right wall every few paces. Voices and shuffling feet came from all directions. Lonnie spied a cook's jacket hanging from the wall and slipped into it. She started down the path to her left, glancing into the open doors as she passed.

In one, a pair of men sat cleaning carrots and cabbage.

In another, a team of bakers massaged a blob of dough so massive Lonnie first mistook it for an bloated corpse.

She continued until the corridor ended at a spiral staircase. The stone had smoothed over centuries of footfall. She climbed, winding up and around the stairway until opened into a huge, columned archway. Lonnie stepped into the light and lifted her head.

A massive chandelier sat over an open ballroom. Armor and blades decorating the walls, along with tapestries, fine china, and the crown's coat of arms. Lonnie frowned as she walked along the torches lining the room. The ceiling rose so high she wondered how any man could construct such wondrous architecture.

Because there was no doubt; she had made it into the castle.

Lonnie ducked behind a column as footsteps echoed from the other side of the ballroom.

She leaned around the marble to find a kingsguard and a cook pacing toward the basement stairs.

"I don't fucking care what you want," the guard said, taking hold of the cook's shirt. "Find a few backstraps and call it a night. It's his party."

"I wasn't saying I can't," the cook said. "They take time to cook, is all."

"Then build a bigger fire." The guard nearly tossed the cook onto the stairs. He sighed, taking a moment as he faced the empty ballroom. After glancing left and right, he violently broke wind and retreated just as quickly.

Alone again, Lonnie ventured along the perimeter of the ballroom, wondering what to do. She needed some kind of proof to bring to the people.

If she decided to go through with it.

The longer she stood in the castle, the more she wanted to escape—to run home and pretend nothing had happened. The crown would kill her if they realized what she had planned.

But the sweet, salty fat still coating her tongue pushed her to keep wandering. She creeped to the open archway where the guard had come from and found an open-air courtyard. The stars shined overhead, filling the space with misty light. Lonnie turned to the tall, narrow windows at the far end of the court-yard. A flickering light glowed from within them. She moved across the grass and climbed through the hedges at the back of the yard. Wincing, she stepped onto a flower pot and leaned into one of the open windows.

She found a large feasting hall, with a table big enough for an army. Flowers and a rainbow of food covered the surface, and tall, dripping candles filled the room with a warm light. Despite these extravagances, only two men participated in the feast.

The king and prince sat parallel from one other at the ends of the table. They drank between bites of the fruit and salads. A pair of cup bearers stood nearby, as did a painter, who periodi-cally turned from his canvas to the impressive feast.

"I'm hungry," the prince said to no one in particular. He set his goblet down. "Why do we wait?"

"I'm wondering the same thing," the king said. "More juice." He lifted his glass and a cup beared skipped to his side. The king caught his arm as he began to pour. "Go and see what's taking the cook so long. We're hungry."

"Very hungry," said the prince.

"Of course," the cup bearer said. He finished his pour and rushed off. The king sat back and slapped his hands against the table.

"Well, with the east block finished, we only have a few more hamlets left to visit," he said. "I, for one, will be glad to be done with the pageantry."

"I, too," said the prince. "They're ungrateful—the whole lot of them."

"Yet they keep the wheels of the kingdom turning."

"Of course. The peasant class is critical to the crown's success."

"They do eat like animals, don't they?" the king said, snickering. "I'm surprised they didn't take a bite out of the cooks."

"They're greedy as pigs," the prince said with a laugh.

"*Watch your mouth.*" The king rose from his chair, pounding his fists into the table. "That's my people you're besmirching."

"I only meant to make a pun."

"They'll be your people one day, too. If you don't show them respect, you'll lose them before you can bear an heir."

"Our people are my greatest priority," the prince said. "I would give my life for them."

The king sat down and took a deep drink of juice. He groaned, looking over the table.

"Do I have to go up to the kitchen and cook my own dinner?" he asked, turning to the remaining cup bearer. "And you," he said, turning to the painter. "How much longer will the portrait take?"

"It's almost finished," the painter said softly. "Just adding a few details to bring it to life, my king."

"Perhaps we'll add you to the menu," the prince said. "We could cook you faster than you paint." He laughed, but as the king jumped out of his chair, he quickly sobered. "Forgive me, father."

"You speak to *my* artisan?" the king asked, marching down the tableside. He snatched a knife from a basket of bread and extended toward the prince. "You speak to my artisan and threaten to kill him? In front of your king?"

"I was only joking," the prince said, wincing as he leaned away from the blade. "Father, please."

"*We don't eat our own.*" The king leaned into the prince, setting a knee on the table. He gripped him by the hair. "The next time you suggest something so foul, I'll marry you off to Gretel Thorn."

"*Please.*" The prince broke into tears, wincing as he leaned back in his chair, hands splayed between the knife and his beautiful face. "Father, you're scaring me."

"*This is what happens when I don't get my meat.*" The king let go, grunting as he tossed the blade across the hall. It skittered over the stone and *plinked* off a column. "I want a damned backstrap," he said, turning to the ceiling in his frustration. "*Is that so much to ask for?*"

Lonnie ducked down, unable to believe her eyes. The king appeared to have gone completely mad. The biggest question was this: had he lost his mind as a result of cannibalism, or had cannibalism bloomed out of his madness? Lonnie peeked back into the window.

The king had returned to his seat, where he idly picked at a leafy salad. The prince sat still and red-cheeked. Lonnie's gaze drifted to the painter. He continued working—as if the conversation and cannibalism were perfectly normal. Lonnie focused on the back of his canvas, realizing the painting might just be the evidence she needed.

Loud foot-falls echoed into the courtyard. Lonnie turned to find a team of cooks marching down the walkway, each carrying a massive tray of gray meat. She returned to the window as they made their delivery.

The candlelight exposed the contents of the trays. Each had a mound of shredded meat, but the king's platter also had a roasted forearm and hand. Lonnie covered her mouth as the king and prince heaped meat onto their plates.

"Looks excellent," the king said, holding out the arm. "Beautifully charred." He waved to the prince and brought the hand to his mouth, giving the thumb a quick suck before stripping the flesh away. The sight of the remaining bone sent Lonnie into an unavoidable heave. She dropped to the ground to muffle the sound. A spew of bile and acid dripped from her lips.

"Excellent," said the prince. "Succulent, and sweetly salty."

"It's the taste of victory," said the king. "I only wish we weren't winning so quickly; we might be able to continue our midnight proclivity."

"We could always start another war."

"And kill innocent men for only their flesh?"

"No, I would never be so cruel."

"The biggest tragedy is letting all this meat rot. I hope the hamlets understand the gift we've given them. If we keep winning, they'll never have see a treat like this again."

Lonnie trembled as she climbed back up the wall. The king and prince took turns belching as they sucked down the last of their meat. Finally, the king tossed a napkin over his cup.

"I've been sated," he announced, letting out another screeching belch.

"As have I," said the prince. He lifted a leg and broke wind.

The king snatched an apple off the table and hurled it across the room. The prince could only guffaw as the apple exploded against his head.

"*You disgusting cunt,*" the king shouted. "Will you start shitting in front of me, too?"

Red with shame, the prince bolted from the hall. His footsteps echoed as they faded through the castle.

"Well," the king said, patting his belly as he wandered to the painter's canvas. "How are we coming? Done yet?"

"Just finished," the artisan said, giving the painting a final stroke. "How do you like it, Your Highness?" He spun the easel around. While a distance from Lonnie, she could see the talent and skill behind the artisan's hand. The painting was as true to life as her own vision. As she hoped, he had included the plate of human meat. It would serve as hard evidence against the king's cannibalism.

"Beautiful," the king said, leaning into the canvas. "I rather like this one."

"Thank you, Sire," the artisan said.

"What's this here?" The king tapped at the side of the painting.

"That's the woman in the window," the artisan said.

The king turned around before Lonnie could register the words. She locked eyes with the king and the air fizzled from her lungs.

"*Guards!*" the king shouted. He drew his dagger, running toward the hall. "Guards!"

"Shit," Lonnie said, stumbling backwards into a bush. She scrambled to her feet as the king continued shouting. As soldiers and guards raced from all directions, she broke into a mad run.

CHAPTER
SEVEN

Lonnie raced across the courtyard. She turned over her shoulder, where the king and his cupbearer sprinted in hot pursuit. Hatred glowed from the king's eyes. His cheeks puffed with desperate breaths.

"*Nab her,*" he screamed.

Lonnie rammed into the door frame as she rounded the stairs. Set raced down the steps, her heart beating so hard she feared it might burst. The king's hunting party stamped onto the stairs above her. Lonnie whimpered, running faster than her feet could manage. She slipped and tumbled. The hard stone cut against her like hammer blows, knocking her dizzy as she rolled all the way to the ground.

She sprawled across the stone and lifted her head. Through her blurring vision, she saw a team of men racing to meet her. She spat blood and wobbled to her feet. Only a single path lay before her; the open door outside of the stairwell.

She limped into the hall and slammed the door behind her. It unhelpfully banged back open. She followed the hall into a dressing chamber, where a collection of men and women huddled over a game of cards. They turned to Lonnie as she stumbled into the room.

"Who are you?" one of them asked.

"How do I get out?" Lonnie asked, turning to two doors in the back of the room. Behind her, the hall filled with the thunder of running feet. "Please, they're going to kill me."

"The door on the left," one of the women said. "Move quickly."

Lonnie gasped thanks as she ran to the door. She dragged it open to find a collection of mops and buckets.

"Grab her," the king shouted. He raced into the room with no less than twenty kingsguard. They swarmed Lonnie, who screamed and grabbed at the mops. The card players rose to get a look at her. The guards dragged her to the king, who approached her wheezing and wincing.

"Please," Lonnie said. "Your Highness."

The king massaged a stitch in his side as he studied her. He glanced at the others, who watched his every move. "Who the hell are you?" he asked, turning back to Lonnie.

"I'm just a peasant," she said.

"Is she castle staff?" the king asked.

"I've never seen her," the woman said. "I thought as much, which is why I sent her to the closet."

"That's Lonnie Lovingdove," a kingsguard said, stepping forward. "I just lashed her husband for breaking curfew last night."

"Oh, really?" the king said, a sinister pleasure rising on his face. "And what were you doing in my castle window, Lonnie Lovingdove?"

"I got lost," Lonnie said.

The room burst into laughter.

"How did you get in?" her nemesis kingsguard asked.

"I don't remember. I got sick from the pork, so I took a walk to try and settle my stomach."

"You didn't get sick from my pork," the king said. "It's impossible."

Silently, the cooks and guards shared a look that suggested it was indeed possible.

"Trespassing in the castle is a capital offense," the kingsguard said. He tugged on the apron Lonnie had stolen. "I suppose you don't remember where you found this?"

Lonnie turned to the apron and deflated.

"I'm sorry," she said. "Please, I didn't mean any harm."

"You were spying on the king and the prince," said the king. "What gives you the right? After the feast I just delivered to your village?"

"I'm ill." Lonnie turned to her feet. "I'm very ill, Your Highness. I was kicked by a donkey when I was little. My head doesn't think good. I should go home before my partner starts to worry."

"No," said the kingsguard. "You're going to the dungeon. And then you'll be drawn, and then you'll be quartered."

"I'm afraid it's the law," the king said. He turned to the kingsguard. "Go easy on the drawing. Save the tender bits up top, if you know what I mean."

"No," Lonnie gasped, helplessly fighting against her captors. "Please, I promise I won't—"

"Promise you won't *what?*" The king raised an eyebrow as he leaned forward, the fat in his beard shimmering in the torch light. "Finish that sentence."

"I promise I won't tell anyone I accidentally stumbled into the castle," Lonnie said. She turned to the dozens of faces surrounding her. They shook their heads in disappointment.

"Lock her away and start feeding her salt water," the king said. "And throw in some cinnamon. I want her well seasoned before the drawing."

The kingsguard led the way through the second door Lonnie missed, which brought them into a luscious garden outside of the castle. A dozen paths wound around tall hedges; the perfect escape Lonnie would never have. The guards dragged her through the heart of the garden, where green and golden roses bloomed in the moonlight. A delicate sweetness filled the air. Lonnie drew what might be her last fresh breath. She wept as they rushed toward a barred door. Her nemesis kingsguard unlocked it, smiling brightly as he waved her inside.

They trundled down wet stairs to the castle dungeon. Dozens of cells and cages and shackles filled the rounded prison. Lonnie took one look at the gaunt faces and soulless eyes and finally stopped fighting. She walked herself into the cell. Her roommate, a tall, skeletal old man backed into the corner. His wide eyes snapped from guard to guard.

"Someone get the salt water," the kingsguard said. He sighed. "And some cinnamon."

"He's gone mad," Lonnie said, more in defeat than argument. "You know he's gone mad."

"He's our king." The guard pushed Lonnie into the back wall, avoiding her gaze as he backed out of the cell. "We'll come for you at dawn."

"Please." Lonnie crossed the cell as another guard locked the door. "I have a husband. He'll be worried sick when I don't come home."

"His days of worrying are coming to an end." The guard locked the cell and belted the key. He smiled as he looked back at Lonnie. "Perhaps you'll see him on the other side."

"What does that mean?" Lonnie shouted. "What does that mean?" She pounded on the cell, dropping to her knees as the guard left.

"Do you really not know?" a dry voice asked from behind her.

Lonnie turned to her cell mate. He stood in the shadow, his boney arms folded across his chest. His watery eyes seemed to glow in the dark.

"Will they really kill him?" she asked.

"Does the king eat men?"

Lonnie fell to the ground. She lay in a puddle of filth,

weeping for the coming loss of her partner; cursing herself for ever leaving the warmth of the hearth. With every other spirit in the prison already broken, she alone wailed. She wept until her throat ran dry.

With her heart shattered completely, she rolled into the corner and started the wait for sunrise. At least the rocky cobblestones would make her drawing swift. She debated smashing her head against the wall and doing the job herself, but she had never been strong; only curious.

And her curiosity had only served to conjure the end of everything.

Her self pity brought on another bout of tears.

"Miss?" her cellmate asked a few moments later.

Lonnie managed to lift her head.

"May I have your salt and cinnamon?" He pointed to the glass sitting at the front of the cell.

"Take it," Lonnie mumbled.

"You're very kind." Her cellmate staggered to the glass and swept it into his slender fingers. He took a long drink and gasped. "God, it's salty," he said. "Are you sure you don't want any?"

"They're going to draw and quarter me," Lonnie said. "What's the point?"

"Well, you never quite know how these things turn out." The man forced another mouthful of saltwater down his throat.

"That's only going to make you thirstier," Lonnie said, frowning at the gaunt silhouette.

"And thinner." Her cellmate cheered the air before chugging the rest of the water. His Adam's apple danced like a bobbing buoy. He set the glass on the ground when he finished, swaying a little. "Let's hope that was enough," he said.

"Enough for what?" Lonnie asked.

Her cell mate let out a violent wretch. He doubled over,

groaning as he clutched his swollen stomach. With a scream, water gushed from his mouth. He heaved and convulsed as he ejected another spout of mucus.

"Are you all right?" Lonnie frowned as he sprayed again. The man looked possessed, writhing and bucking as he pushed more and more water from his body. By the time he collapsed onto the floor, his swollen belly had sucked back against his spine. He drew a sweeping breath as he stared up at the ceiling. Lonnie stepped over him. Blood covered his chin and chest. "Sir?" she asked, pressing her toe into his pronounced ribs.

Her cellmate's eyes shot open. He reached for her, his skeletal fingers twitching as he did.

"Get me up," he gasped. "I'm ready."

"You're not ready for anything," Lonnie said, taking his cold hand. "Should I call for help?"

"*Get me up.*" The man gasped as Lonnie pulled him onto his feet.

"You need to rest," she said, holding him steady.

"No," he breathed, swaying as he held onto her. "No, now's my chance." He managed a laugh as he turned to the prison bars. "Help me."

"Help you what? You'll never fit through."

"*Help me.*" He slapped Lonnie, if the gentle swipe could be called a slap. "I choose to fight," he breathed. "Now help me, damnit."

Lonnie guided him across the cell, where he quickly slipped an arm through the bars. He made it past his shoulder and snagged on his ribs, which even without meat were at least four inches too wide to maneuver the gap.

"You're too big," Lonnie said. "Come on, you need to rest."

"Push." Her cell mate met her eyes, a lone tear rolling into the blood on his chin. "Hold the bars and push with your feet. Push until I'm through—break the bones if you have to."

"I can't—"

"*You must.*"

Lonnie looked into the dungeon, where a few of the other prisoners watched the scene with mild interest. She took hold of the bars and set a foot against his ribs.

"Are you sure?" she asked.

"Don't stop no matter what," he said. He snaked a leg through the bars until his hips caught. As he braced himself, giving Lonnie a nod, she began to push.

EIGHT

Lonnie extended her leg and made no progress. At her cell mate's insistence, she climbed up and set both feet against his chest, using all of her strength to force him through the impossible gap. He grunted and wheezed. A bone snapped. Lonnie winced as she continued to push. Another bone snapped and her cellmate yelped.

"*More,*" he grunted.

Lonnie shifted her feet lower, closing her eyes as she gave it her all. Finally, the man shifted. Another bone snapped and he slipped four inches closer to freedom. Lonnie opened her eyes, just in time to see his ribcage slip the rest of the way through. His hips had already passed, but his head, a solid dome atop his skinny neck, would never pass the bars, no matter how much Lonnie pushed.

"Now what?" she asked.

But her cell mate slid to the ground with a final crunch. Lonnie frowned as she crouched beside him.

Three of his ribs had punctured the skin. One of them dangled by only a strip of cartilage. The man had died with a silent scream on his crimson face. Lonnie crawled away, wishing she had something in her body to vomit.

She stared at the mangled tangle of bones and skin. It served well to distract her from the following morning, when she would most certainly end up in worse condition. She had been to a quartering as a girl. Her mother, ever the stern caretaker, had wanted her to see what happened to criminals.

"Hey," someone called from across the dungeon.

Lonnie lifted her head.

"Throw me a bone," the stranger called. "Throw me one of that idiot's bones."

Lonnie ignored the call. She had destroyed her life, and she was done playing other people's games.

"Throw me a bone, damnit!" the stranger repeated. "If you want me to make a key and get us all out of here, throw me a bone you stupid wench."

Lonnie turned to her tangled cellmate; the dangling rib bone. She climbed to her feet and approached the bars. A man stood waving from across the dungeon.

"Throw me a bone," he said, nodding frantically. "That's good. Yeah, grab a nice big bone and throw it over here. I'll make a good key. I know the locks."

"Can you help me escape?" Lonnie asked.

"I swear it," the man said. "Come on, throw me a big one."

Lonnie crouched, eying the dangling rib bone. Congealed blood dripped from it like mucus. She took hold of it and pulled, thinking only of saving Daniel. Her cellmate creaked as she yanked. She gritted her teeth and twisted, this time snapping the bone free.

"Good," the stranger called. "Very good. Now throw it as hard as you can. Straight to me."

Lonnie drew back and lined up her throw. She took a breath, gripping the bone tight as she tossed it. It arched through the air and bounced off a hanging cage. It landed in the center of the dungeon, well away from anyone's reach.

"It's okay," the stranger said. "He's got plenty more. Try again. Take another one—before the guards hear us."

Lonnie sighed as she turned to her cell mate. She found another rib and pulled, but it held fast.

"*We don't have time,*" the stranger hissed. "Don't you want to live?"

At that moment, Lonnie didn't particularly value her life, but if it meant saving Daniel, she would crawl across hell. She stood tall and lifted her leg. With her eyes closed, she stomped down on her cell mate. Bones cracked and crunched. She stomped again, using the bars as a brace. This time a bone rattled free.

"Good girl," the stranger called. "Throw it lower this time. Just get it across the stone and we'll be okay."

Lonnie snatched the bone and extended her arm through the bars. She drew a breath, testing her arc. Everyone in the dungeon watched this time. She counted to three and sent the bone twirling through the air. It bounced off the stones and took a favorable hop. It clacked and flipped, skittering to a stop a few feet from the stranger's cell. He lunged an arm through the bars and swiped at it. When he failed, he retreated and sent a naked leg out, managing to pinch the rib between his toes.

"You got it?" Lonnie asked, watching as he dragged the bone into the shadow of his cell.

Soon, a dull scraping filled the dungy prison.

"How long will it take you to make a key?" Lonnie asked. "Sir?"

Only desperate scraping replied.

"I have to be out before morning. They're going to draw and quarter me." Lonnie squinted, trying to see into the dark cell. "I have to save my husband, so work fast if you can."

"Shut the fuck up," the stranger shouted.

Lonnie slunk back into her cell. She debated taking a rib to attempt her own key, but she had no idea how to do it. Unsure what to feel, she sat down, praying for a miracle.

Time passed and the scraping continued.

Lonnie wished she had a window to gauge the time. After

hours without food or drink, her skin had grown hot. She sat against the cool stone and did her best to remain hopeful, but her heart seemed stuck in a panicked run.

Still, the scraping continued.

Finally, Lonnie got up and broke a bone out of her cell mate's chest. A ghastly scent surrounded his mangled corpse. She winced as she reached around the door and fingered the keyhole. The key needed to be thin and round. Thinking of Daniel's carvings, she knelt on the floor and began to scrape. The bone left a white streak as she ground it against the stone. She pressed harder, understanding time moved against her.

"What are you doing?" her neighbor called. His scraping stopped as he leaned into his cell.

"I'm making a key," Lonnie said.

"Stop it. I'm making the key."

"You've been scraping for an hour. How long is it going to take?"

"It's going to take as long as it takes to get it right."

"Well, I can't wait. We'll see who finishes first."

"But it was my idea," her neighbor called.

Lonnie ignored him and continued scraping, slowly twirling the bone as she filed it down. The scraping resumed on the other side of the dungeon with a new vigor. They sawed back and forth in an almost cricket-like mating call. The other prisoners glanced from cell to cell as the competition heated.

"I'm almost done," her neighbor called. "Don't worry, everyone. I'll get us out of here."

"I'm almost done, too," Lonnie said. She had no idea how close she was or if her key would work, but her neighbor's abrasive need to be their savior drove her to work faster. She had the end of the rib rubbed down to the size of a paintbrush handle and started to work on giving the end of her key a tooth.

"Just a few more minutes," her neighbor said.

"Same," Lonnie called.

They scraped.

The pile of bone dust broadened.

Lonnie paused to test her key in the lock, wanting to make sure she didn't file it down too thin. She snaked her hand through the cell and poked at the keyhole.

"*Stop,*" her neighbor cried, racing to the bars of his cell. "This was my idea."

"I'm just checking," Lonnie said. "It's almost there."

The scraping intensified.

Lonnie remained on her feet and used the plating between bars to fine tune her key. She thinned the key and gave the tooth definition. Across from her, her neighbor attempted the lock, but something didn't work, because he grunted and ducked back into the shadow and continued scraping.

Lonnie gasped as her key snapped in half. Bone marrow leaked through the crack, running down her fingers like warm honey.

"I just broke my key," she shouted. "Be careful with yours."

"I knew you were going to break it," the neighbor replied. "It's a good thing I—"

A quiet-but-clear *snap* came from within his cell.

"What was that?" Lonnie asked.

"Nothing." But her neighbor's intensified breathing betrayed him.

"Did you just break your key?" one of the other prisoners asked.

"Of course I didn't," the neighbor said. "Just to be safe, throw me another bone."

Lonnie snapped off a rib and arced it across the cell. "Be careful with this one," she called. "We're running out of time."

"I've been here for six years," the neighbor said. "Don't talk to me about time."

Lonnie turned to her cell mate, wondering if she dared attempt another key.

"How do we even get out of here once the cells are open?" she asked.

A feverous scraping came in reply.

Lonnie returned to the stone and pressed her hot cheek against the wall. She closed her eyes, thinking of Daniel, praying her neighbor knew what he was doing. Time passed and the scrapping finally ended.

"Did you finish?" Lonnie asked, lifting her head.

"We'll see," the neighbor said. He appeared at his cell door and reached around, gently working his key into the lock. Lonnie could see the sweat dripping down his nose from across the dungeon. He bit his tongue as he tinkered with the lock, making a slow, tactile maneuver.

Lonnie pressed her head into the bars. She tried to curb her enthusiasm, but the tentative jailbreak promised an opportunity her heart could not ignore.

A metallic *clink* came from the neighbor's lock. He turned to Lonnie with wide eyes. Pale and trembling, he pushed his cell door open. It let out a wild squeal that woke up the rest of the prisoners. At the sight of their comrade, strutting free of his cell with only a bone in his hand, they broke into stellar cheers and laughter.

Lonnie wept at the sight of freedom; the key to her future manifest. She grinned as the neighbor approached her cell, stepping back to give him room at the lock.

But the neighbor stopped a few feet short.

"You were a fool to trust me," he said, breaking into a devilish grin. "I hope they draw you to the sea and back. And I hope you're still breathing for the quartering." He held up his key and snapped it in half. "That's what you get for trying to steal my rescue. That's what all of you get."

"You son of a bitch," Lonnie breathed.

"I'm the son of a whore," the neighbor corrected her. "And I'll see you in the depths of hell." He laughed, throwing his head back as he cackled. Lonnie slunk to her knees, unable to do anything but watch as he danced his way to the stairs. The other prisoners booed and rained hisses on him. Someone from a ceiling-mounted cage tried to piss on him and missed.

"Please," Lonnie called. "Don't leave us to die."

"Lady, sometimes you gotta save yourself," the neighbor said. He paused on the stairs, looking across the dungeon with nostalgic reverie. "Have a great rest of the night, everyone. As for me, I'm going home."

The neighbor climbed three more steps before a door at the top of the stairs snapped open.

"What the hell?" someone called down.

The neighbor jumped in his fright, grunting as he fell backwards. He tumbled and crashed all the way to the bottom of the stairs. A burly guard came running after him.

"Please," the neighbor shrieked, holding up his hands. "I was just coming to get help. My cell door stopped working."

"He broke out," Lonnie called.

A few of the other prisoners confirmed the truth, and the guard sneered as he dragged the neighbor off the ground.

"How did he escape?" the guard asked, looking across the dungeon, but no one answered. He frowned at the sight of Lonnie's crumpled cellmate. "And what hell happened to George?"

"He fell," Lonnie said.

The guard dragged the neighbor to Lonnie's cell to get a better look. He winced, leaning down to study George's mangled undercarriage.

"He fell?" he asked Lonnie.

"It was a bad fall," Lonnie said.

"You'll believe that but not me?" the neighbor asked. "Are you joking?"

"Shut up," the guard shouted. He smacked the neighbor and wrapped his hands around his chicken neck. While he choked him, Lonnie spotted the broken pieces of key hanging from his pocket. She made a quick snatch just before the guard moved to the ground, where he finished killing the escapee by stomping on his neck. "If another else breaks out," he said, still battling to catch his breath, "you get one of those." He crossed the dungeon and slammed the open cell shut.

No one said a word as the guard went down the line, checking every lock and cage. He paused as he finished at Lonnie's cell.

"Tell me the truth," he said. "What happened to George?"

"That one killed him," Lonnie said, pointing to the neighbor. "He tried to pull him through the bars."

"I swear." The guard shook his head, turning from one dead emaciated man to the other. He sighed and headed for the stairs, taking his time as she shuffled back outside.

The dungeon fell silent until the door closed with a definitive *clang*.

"That was crazy," one of the caged prisoners called out.

A few others muttered agreement.

Lonnie lifted the broken key. The end looked just long enough to do its job. She held her breath as she reached around the door and fitted the key into place. The bone felt incredibly brittle in her shaking fingers. She guided it into the lock, finding the hard resistance of the internal bolt. It was like turning a wagon wheel by hand. She pinched and twisted. She grunted, using two fingers to try and roll the bone.

"Pull it back a bit," someone called.

Lonnie slid the key back, and this time, her turn came with a pleasant *click*. She pushed the door open and her heart filled with opportunity. The second chance of escape left her panting. Every other prisoner rushed to the cell doors, their arms dangling and waving as they called for assistance.

Lonnie went to the next cell and carefully unlocked it. A short, filthy man with dried vomit running down his stomach stepped into the light. She handed him the broken key.

"Turn it slowly," she said. "Get the others out while I check the door."

"Thank you, m'lady," the man said with a hiccup. His yellow eyes suggested a long affair with fermented liquid. As he went to work on the next cell, Lonnie creeped to the stairs, eying the long, ascending rise into the outside door.

Her heart pulsed as she climbed. The idea of having her neck stomped quickened her pace. As she came to the door, she gave it a gentle push to find it barred from the outside.

"Damn," she breathed. She turned around, where half a

dozen gangly prisoners gathered at the bottom of the stairs. She swept back down to meet them. "It's barred from outside," she said. "Is there any other way out?"

"I might know a way," an old woman said. She smiled toothlessly, her gums the same washed-out gray of the potato sack she wore as a dress. "Everyone go hide in your cells. Close the doors. Give me that key."

"What?" Lonnie asked.

"Trust me." The old woman, who looked anything but trustworthy, took the key nub and started to climb the stairs. As the other prisoners rushed back into their cells, Lonnie did too, realizing she had little choice. She closed her door as the woman climbed out of sight.

A loud, desperate knock came from the stairwell.

The old woman lifted her potato sack and she scurried back down the stairs.

"What the hell?" the guard shouted as the door banged open. He came running after her, his face red as he sneered.

The old woman ran into her open cell. Grunting, the guard raced after her. As soon as he entered, the old woman took hold of the cell bars and kicked him into the back of the cell. While he rolled, she ran outside, locking the cell just as he rammed into the door.

"You damned wench," the guard shouted.

The old woman laughed and stomped the bone key into dust. Every prisoner broke into cheers as they raced out of their cells, surrounding the trapped guard. Lonnie couldn't help but grin as she stepped over to take in the sight.

"I'll break your necks," the guard said. While everyone laughed, he lifted the keys from his belt and shoved one into the lock.

"Run," Lonnie shouted, racing for the stairs. She flew up

them two at a time and stepped onto dewy grass, facing the stars; the rimming red of a sunrise kissing the castle walls. The other prisoners fanned in all directions across the yard. As guards began to shout from above, Lonnie ran with them, searching for a path that ended in life.

CHAPTER
TEN

Lonnie followed a high wall of hedges. She ran with the reckless abandon of a child, her sprained ankle long forgotten. Only Daniel filled the page of her mind; she still had time to save him. If her luck continued, they had a chance to escape and start over together, as they should have done long ago.

At the end of the hedge, Lonnie found a staircase that led to the castle wall. She wound around the stairs and climbed straight up. Below, the escapees scrambled through the court-yard like rats.

And they weren't alone. A dozen guards chased after them with swords drawn. Several had already been caught. The grass drank their running blood.

Lonnie turned ahead as she mounted the castle wall. A few guards stood along the outpost, shouting directions to the runners below. One spotted Lonnie and drew his sword. He smiled as he creeped forward, shifting the sword from hand to hand.

"You're trapped," he said. "You want it in the chest or the belly?"

Lonnie dove head-first over the wall. She let out a sigh to find a moat below. Her body slapped against the water as she landed, knocking the wind out of her. She gasped and flailed to get to the bank. By the time she made it onto her feet, she could somewhat breath. She turned to the wall to find a pair of archers training their bows on her.

With a yelp, Lonnie broke back into a sprint. Several arrows flew over her shoulder and she moved into a zig-zag. She ran down the winding yard and found cobblestone.

As she came into the hamlet surrounding the castle, she slowed, not wanting to draw attention. She did her best to wring out her hair as she moved toward one of the private stables at the end of a king's driveway. She found three horses inside. One had a bit, so she hopped on his back.

The ride to Doane took an hour. Lonnie kept her head down until she rode past the village square. A massive mound of left-over pork lay in a pile outside of the archway. Rats and strays lay beside it, their bellies swollen and glistening with fat. Lonnie's nausea returned, but her body was so empty all she could manage was a timid wretch.

She kicked the horse into a gallop with home in sight. The wagon Daniel borrowed sat out front of their shack, along with Brown Thong, who chewed on a shirt from the neighbor's clothes line. Lonnie dropped off the horse and didn't care as it took off running for the castle. She ran into the house, her heart sinking to find the door broken open.

"Daniel?" she called, facing the hearth; the empty rocking chair. She moved for the stairs with a lump rising in her throat. "Daniel, I'm back." She climbed the stairs one step at a time. The energy felt wrong, and part of her knew she shouldn't go any further.

She pressed the bedroom door open and stepped inside.

"Daniel," she cried, almost laughing to see him safely in bed. But she dove onto the mattress to find his body hard as stone. "Daniel?" Lonnie took his hand, but the cold flesh confessed to the realization of her nightmare.

Daniel's eyes were slightly open, his face a buttery shade of yellow. Lonnie pulled the covers back and burst into tears.

A noose wrapped her partner's neck. Skin bulged in a purple

band around it. Lonnie fell to her knees, pressing her head into the mattress. She wailed. Her panic and fear swirled into a dagger. The blade looped around, pointing to its keeper with cold accusation.

This is your doing, Lonnie Lovingdove.

Lonnie reached for Daniel's hand. She frowned to find a smooth stone beneath it.

But it wasn't a stone. Daniel's final carving lay in his hand, and this time, he had managed to finish.

Lonnie lifted the lumpy heart. Daniel had carved their initials across its center. The carving was rough and unfinished, and Lonnie wondered if Daniel had added their initials in his last moments of life: a final message.

Until death do us part, Lonnie Lovingdove.

Lonnie fell to her knees. She heaved and shouted and screamed. Her body quivered, the pain so great and fierce she debated taking the noose from Daniel's neck and joining him in whatever came next.

But Lonnie Lovingdove was too timid for poetic suicide. She would go into the wilderness, where time would pull the noose for her. It would only take a few days to finish drying out. Perhaps a bear or a wolf would find her and consume what remained of her spirit.

A spirit who kills that it once loved.

Lonnie stilled as she turned the carving in her hand, running her thumb over Daniel's name. She had always viewed their relationship as in-progress—a slow-blooming flower nowhere near its final form, but the crude carving echoed the reality. They would never have the opportunity to polish the edges. They would never know what they might have been.

Lonnie found Daniel's carving knife on the floor and lifted it, studying the sharp blade. She set it and the carving on the bed as she rose. Her eyes filled with tears as she looked down at Daniel. He looked so tiny in his death.

"I'm sorry," she whispered, climbing into bed with him, wrapping her arms around him. She planted a wooden kiss on his cheek. "I didn't mean for any of this to happen. I just wanted to feel something. I'm so—"

A stampede of horses galloped down the street, their hoof-falls echoing like thunder.

Lonnie stiffened as she turned to the window. She creeped out of bed and crawled beneath the windowsill, leaning out just in time to see a kingsguard stop at the corner. As he nailed a notice to the post, Lonnie turned to the sky, gasping to find the sun halfway home. In her mourning, the day had shifted into late afternoon.

She rolled the carving and knife into a clean dress and stepped to the door, taking one last look at her husband.

"I'm so sorry," she breathed, trembling as she pulled the door closed. She moved downstairs; never again to live the banal existence of the Lovingdoves. She paused in the living room; the hearth never to kindle another argument. Thinking of Daniel, she collected a handful of ashes from the pit and smeared them across her forehead.

She stepped outside and turned to the sign at the end of the street. In a final bow to her curiosity, she ventured to the post.

The sheet of canvas contained a sloppy drawing of her own face. It was the same disgusted grimace she made in the window at the castle. Beneath the painting, a proclamation went out to the kingdom.

"*Wanted dead and alive: Lonnie Lovingdove. For crimes of high treason. Do not trust this woman. Bring her to the castle for a valuable reward. Your king, Pollen Bane V.*"

Lonnie shouldered her dress with Daniel's heart and blade.

Broken, both inside and out, she followed the winding path out of the East Doane, where a wicked forest led into the Seregile Mountains.

PART TWO
EVERYONE BENDS TO THE WIND. EVENTUALLY

CHAPTER

ELEVEN

Lonnie followed the cobblestone until it shifted to sand. There, she crossed fields until trees rose up and the path turned to soil. She jumped and turned at every little sound. A croaking frog left her screaming. A squirrel, popping up on a fallen tree, left her stumbling into a pricker bush. She shivered as night fell upon the forest. The glowing eyes behind the trees left her panting. Her skin burned with dehydration. Her lips cracked and blistered.

She finally gave up on death and knelt at a stream, where she drank until she grew nauseous. In the dark, and all alone, she set her hands around Daniel's heart and brought it to her chest. She wept and recounted her mistakes; the foolish decisions that left her empty in the cold.

Heavy footsteps came through the brush.

Lonnie froze as something big and heavy bumbled behind her. The creature sniffed and let out a grunt. Lonnie shook so bad the heart fell from her hands. She sucked in a breath, turning as a massive brown bear stepped to her side.

The grizzly sniffed at her hair and coughed. With a grunt, it took a few steps down stream. Lonnie dared a glance as it began to drink, the bear apparently in no mood to eat a rotten woman.

A curious, rotten cannibal, she corrected. *One who might as well have hanged her husband.*

Lonnie wept as she knelt beside the bear. She leaned into the mud and waited for him to consume her. Sadly, he only wanted water and soon continued into the brush. She lay back on the forest floor and listened to the passing stream. Her head ached, her body itched, and her heart burned in phantom pains of the love she shared with Daniel.

Still, exhaustion had its way with her, and the next thing she knew a warm bath of sunlight kissed her awake.

She rolled back to the steam and dipped her lips into the cool, trickling water. Her stomach accepted it more readily and she filled herself. She sat in the mud and tried her best to think of nothing; to pour out the kettle of her emotions.

But Lonnie was not a man, and her mind would not shut off.

She wept until every last nerve in her body went numb. Finally, she lay back on the ground and wondered if she could drink enough water to make herself pee.

"I see a broken soul," a man said.

Lonnie launched into a seat, snatching Daniel's heart as she searched for the speaker.

"Who's there?" she called, finding only trees and shrubbery.

"You poor thing," the man continued. "You've had your heart broken, too. Oh, my dear sweet creature."

Lonnie turned to the sky, shielding her eyes from the sun. A slim, incredibly hairy man sat on a tree limb. Naked but for thick swatches of body hair, he looked down at Lonnie with humiliating pity, his blackened feet swaying beside the tree's trunk.

"Who are you?" Lonnie asked. "Why are you watching me?"

"I felt you," the man said. He swept his long, dark hair over his shoulders. "I felt you all the way from the Shrine. What is your name, broken one?"

"Lonnie Lovingdove. Who are you? And what's the Shrine?"

The naked man grinned, again brushing his hair back. "Once they called me Henry Smith. Now, I am Lahn Doe Meelay. Do you know what that means?"

"How would I?" Lonnie asked.

"Lahn Doe Meelay is Shrinian, and it translates to *Master of God's King*." Lahn stood on the tree limb, his great phallus protruding like a zealous boil. He walked along the limb, balancing with his arms as it thinned. Lonnie climbed to her feet as the bow began to bend. Lahn Doe Meelay walked all the way to the leaves. As the bow flexed to the ground, he stepped off and let it neatly swish back to the sky.

"Who are you?" Lonnie asked. "Why are you naked?"

"I'm the man who will set you free, Lonnie Lovingdove," Lahn said. He met her, offering a soft, pale hand. "May I mend your broken heart? May I pour the pieces of your soul into a furnace, where the flames can build you back anew?"

"I don't know." Lonnie tried very hard to keep her eyes from the man's enormous phallus. "What does that even mean?"

"*Look at you.*" Lahn's voice softened, the words falling on a harsh whisper as he leaned into her face, his bright eyes finally drawing her attention. "*I can feel the pain churning through you. You've suffered great loss. You've lost everything.*"

Lonnie's mouth tightened as she battled her tears. Lahn set his hand on her shoulder. The heat of it made her gasp.

"Let me fix you, Lonnie Lovingdove. Let me show you a new way of life."

Lonnie whimpered, wrapping her arms around Lahn as she broke into tears. "*I'm in so much pain,*" she breathed. "*I've done so much wrong.*"

"But the greater the pain, the stronger you'll be." Lahn smiled, wiping Lonnie's tears with a strand of his hair. It smelled of coconut and honey. "Come with me to the Shrine."

Unable to speak, Lonnie took Lahn's hand, and together they moved through the forest.

CHAPTER
TWELVE

L ahn led Lonnie along a mossy path. They crossed miles, stooping beneath fallen trees and across streams, making their way toward the ridge of the Seregile Mountains. The bright and sunny day left the forest glowing in dazzling shades of green and yellow. Lonnie mechanically followed her naked leader, feeling definitively hollow.

"What is the Shrine?" she asked.

"It is the womb of enchantment," Lahn said, smirking as he turned over his shoulder. "But you're not ready to enter. No, not yet."

"Then where are we going? I'm very tired."

"To reach the sky, we must first face ourselves. Hush now, Lonnie Lovingdove. Lahn Doe Meelay has you under his wing."

They stopped at the next stream and Lahn made her drink. He slipped into the woods to relieve himself, and then they resumed the march, now making a vertical climb into the rockier terrain at the mountain's summit. The extended hike kept the dread from Lonnie's body, but her mind insisted on tracing the shadow of her mistakes. She held Daniel's heart against her belly. Every once in a while she felt emotion enough to cry, and she did so quietly for fear of Lahn's judgment. She couldn't help but find his new name rather blasphemous. She had many questions for him, but knew better than to ask. The fact she still remained curious after all the pain her curiosity had caused made her angry. Thankfully, the rage pushed out her fear and depression.

"And so we begin," Lahn said as he crested a steep section of the mountainside. He extended his hand, pulling Lonnie onto a perfectly circular swath of grass. A broad, square stone sat in the center. Seven smaller stones surrounded it. Lahn led Lonnie forward.

"Is this the Shrine?" Lonnie asked.

"Nay," Lahn said. "This is a door; where snakes shed their skin; where fools don the cap of divinity." Lahn climbed onto the center stone and surveyed the valley. Lonnie started to climb after him and he gently pushed her back. "Not yet," he said, setting his hands on his hips. Lonnie had forgotten he was naked and turned from his eye-level phallus.

"What are we doing?" she asked. "I'd like to eat, if there's food. I haven't eaten—"

"Right on time," Lahn said, beaming as he turned. "You're not hungry by chance, Lonnie Lovingdove. This place has put an inextinguishable lust for sustenance into your belly."

"I also haven't eaten since—"

"Hush. Let the forces feel you. They must search your shattered soul to know what it once was; to know what it must become."

Lonnie turned to the mountains as the breeze grew into a wind. She stilled, letting her hair and tattered dress billow under its invisible fingers. The wind braced her. She lifted her arms and let out a breath. Lahn stepped behind her and pressed his body into hers. He interlaced their fingers, holding her tight as the wind wicked heat from her flesh.

"Do you feel it?" he whispered.

Lonnie had several ways of answering the question, but settled for a simple, "Yes."

"You are welcomed with open arms, Lonnie Lovingdove. Now, you will have your feast." Lahn let go of Lonnie and crossed the circle of grass. He knelt, his buttocks flexing as he dug a small box from the earth. Lonnie met him at the center stone. The box, a smooth and onyx beauty, held only two items. Lahn lifted the fat, blue and red mushroom and held it out to Lonnie.

"A mushroom?" Lonnie asked. "I was hoping you might—"

"This is food for the soul," Lahn said. "Eat, Lonnie Loving-dove. Eat every last spore." He placed the warm mushroom in Lonnie's hand and took hold of the other item, a bright and perfectly spherical grapefruit. "Do you have a knife?" he asked.

Lonnie's eyes widened, and Lahn laughed. She unraveled her shirt and handed him Daniel's carving knife.

"Do you still think we met by chance?" he asked, sliding the blade through the heart of the grapefruit. Juice dripped from the rind and Lahn caught it before it could touch the stone. "Consume your mushroom," he said. "Eat, and then you must drink."

Lonnie took a breath, never one to enjoy a raw mushroom, and stuffed the fleshy fungus into her mouth. It exploded with a bitter tang. She chewed quickly, swallowing it mostly whole. When Lahn handed her half of the grapefruit, she squeezed it into her mouth and sucked the rind dry.

"You have just lost your name," Lahn said, taking the empty rind. "Soon, you will lose your mind, and when you return, we'll have what you need to rebuild."

"What do you mean?" Lonnie asked. "Aren't we going to the Shrine?"

Lahn grinned and Lonnie frowned. His mouth looked to have two hundred teeth stuffed into it. A great pulse of fear moved through Lonnie's chest. She drew a trembling breath as she stepped back. The wind rose up, pushing with the force of a tidal wave. She set her feet in the grass and leaned into it. Lahn laughed as he sucked on the other half of the grapefruit.

"Fight all you want," he said. "But everyone bends to the wind, eventually."

Lonnie twitched as a shock of heat zapped through her head. The world seemed to expand and contract. She screamed just before everything returned to normal.

"What's happening to me?" she asked.

"This is only the mist before the rain," Lahn said. He grinned once more, and this time a single, nasty tooth filled his mouth. Lonnie screamed as dread took hold of her guts. She swayed and the world twisted, the color saturating to a level that left her squinting. Lahn came up behind her and began unbuttoning her dress. "Stop," Lonnie said. "Please."

"But this is Lonnie Lovingdove's dress," Lahn said. "And you're no longer Lonnie Lovingdove."

"Who am I?" The words bounced and echoed through her mind.

Lonnie lifted her arms as Lahn dragged the dress down her body. Naked, and battered in wind, she folded her arms across her chest.

"Who are you, you ask?" Lahn said. "We're about to find out."

All at once, the sky shifted to a deep, royal shade of purple. Lonnie lifted her head and stopped breathing. The clouds twisted and danced with one another. She laughed, spotting a bunny rabbit and a dog—a dog which closely resembled the mutt in the hamlet square.

The dog sparked a memory that daisy-chained the traumatic life story of the woman formerly known as Lonnie Lovingdove.

Lonnie whelped as the sky shifted to dark, sinister red. The world turned upside down and she fell flat against the earth. A deep, booming rumble came from beneath it; it was the Fist of Eternal Suffering, breaking a special tunnel to meet her.

Lonnie screamed as her mind unraveled.

She tasted the coconut and honey in Lahn's hair.

She heard the mushroom dancing in her belly.

Somewhere in the distance, Lahn laughed with great passion. His laughter fell upon her like freezing rain. Lonnie blinked and couldn't find a difference between dark and light. Her mind swirled like stewing cabbage. She could see the spoon, twirling and mixing sense into fantasy. She had just enough brain power to make a final realization: whatever spell Lahn had cast upon her would be the last.

She clawed at the earth and staggered to her feet.

The earth slipped its tongue between her toes.

She started to run, but Lahn caught her by the wrist.

"No," he said, taking hold of her. Their combining flesh created a spark of heat. "This is only a wave. The monsoon is coming, and you must remain with the stone if you want to see the other side."

Lonnie froze, turning across the world of blurring fear and color. The wind swept back into a gale, and this time, it brought her to her knees. She scrabbled across the grass. As she began to convulse, her mind stripped clear of all function. She found Daniel's heart in a cushion of grass. She pulled it into her naked belly and wrapped herself around it.

THIRTEEN

As day drifted to night, the mushroom beat upon Lonnie like a hammer. The unraveling fantasy danced between dream and grotesque nightmare. She gaped and moaned as the mushroom gifted her odd moments of sentience.

Brown Thong galloped across the meadow. His tail twirled like a water wheel, throwing ribbons of green and gold in his wake.

Lonnie screamed as a rusted spike broke through the earth between her legs.

A collection of naked children stepped over her, one kneeling to wipe the foam from her lips. Lonnie gripped a boy's hand as she saw Daniel in his face. She tried to scream, unable to face the child she could never give her partner.

Through it all, the Fist of Eternal Suffering never stopped pounding the ground beneath her.

A torrent of rats scurried down the mountainside. They climbed onto the stone monolith and offered trays of gray, shredded long pork. Their smiles were so sincere Lonnie laughed.

The sky turned black and fire sprung through the growing cracks in the earth. Lonnie lifted her head, unable to help her curiosity. She found the eye of the Fist of Eternal Suffering and went completely stiff. Foam sprayed from her gaping lips. A thousand thoughts bounced across her mind and wove into a single thread—she could taste the color of its tapestry. The thread came with an epiphany that caused Lonnie to draw a sweeping breath.

I am not to be trusted.

She sat, turning to the monolith. A tall man stood upon it, wearing a bright blue tunic. His face had a strange configuration, the mouth round and nose flat. Lonnie squinted as she studied him. The face was not a man's, but a monkey's. A regal monkey. Lonnie could feel the wisdom and power behind the man-ape's knowing eyes. He stared at her with an eternal judgment, and her epiphany returned with translation.

You cannot trust yourself.

—and that is okay.

He will show you the path to redemption.

For the first time in hours—or days, for she had lost all sense of physical time—Lonnie felt a spark of relief. She stared at the monkey, terrified of breaking their gazing contest. He stood so still he might be stone but for his rising chest. The sun crossed the sky at his back. Lonnie stared until her eyes ran dry. The monkey's gaze hardened, ever so slightly, and a rush of terror finally beat her back into submission.

She fell back to grass, biting into her cheeks until a coppery glue mucked her mouth shut.

FOURTEEN

Lonnie woke up shivering. Her body ached, feeling every abused muscle over the days and nights of her flight. She sat in the dewy grass and realized she still remained naked. Her mind felt like mush, but it was hers again to control. She drew a weak breath and looked across the clearing.

"Lahn?" she asked. The word came out as a gravely caw. She broke into a coughing fit and winced at the tension in her stomach. Below her, on the other side of the mountain valley, the sun moved for its bedding, painting the sky in a glorious sunset. After the extended fantasy, it might as well be black and white.

She climbed to her feet after the sunset. The wind continued pulling away her heat, and she could hardly walk. She needed water and food. Afraid of pushing her voice, she took a slow lap around the platform. Lahn seemed to have left her. She turned to the mountain above, where the stone rose all the way into the firmament.

Something sparkled in the dirt a hundred or so feet up the mountainside. Lonnie couldn't make it out. She frowned, taking a few steps forward, but as she set foot on the ascending path, her body locked.

You cannot be trusted.

She cowered, covering her bare breasts as she turned to the stone; where the man-ape had met her. Terror traced a cold finger down her spine. She turned in a circle, panicking and sure someone watched her.

But only the grass and wind proved the world remained in motion.

Lonnie hunched and made her way to the monolithic stone in the center of the clearing. She knelt and huddled against it, hiding from the wind; hiding from the world. She could not trust herself. She needed to wait for him to come back.

So she remained until sunrise.

When warm, golden light bestowed her with heat, she lifted her arms in greeting to the day. A laugh fell from her cracked lips. She set her hands on the stone, feeling the rising heat.

"We meet again," Lahn said.

Lonnie swept around, cowering to find him standing behind her. She brushed her hair in front of her breasts and covered her vagina. Lahn grinned.

"And we meet for the first time, too," he said, taking a step forward. He wrapped a hand around Lonnie's chin, gently lifting her gaze. "What did you see?" he whispered. "*Who* did you see?"

"A man-ape," Lonnie breathed. "A man-ape in blue."

Lahn pressed his forehead into Lonnie's. "And what did this man-ape tell you?"

"I cannot trust myself. I'm to trust . . . *he.*"

"He is me," Lahn said, his breath sweet with milk. "And I have your name."

"My name?" Lonnie cowered, but Lahn held her in place.

"*Peet Doe Munk.*" He smiled, sweeping his hair over his shoulder. "Tail of the Monkey."

"Tail of the Monkey?" Lonnie asked. "And you're Master of God's King?"

"Come, Peet." Lahn took Lonnie by the hand, leading her away from the stone; to the path leading up the mountainside. "It's time we go home."

"Home?" Lonnie asked. "I can't go—"

"To the Shrine," Lahn said. "To the womb, dear Peet." He wore a dark satchel that Lonnie hadn't noticed in his abundance of hair. As they walked, he handed her a bowl of water and a handful of nuts. "For your strength," he said with the offering.

"Are they normal nuts?" Lonnie asked.

Lahn slapped her so hard she fell to the ground.

"I'm sorry," Lonnie said.

"You are never to question me," Lahn said. "Yes, you can no longer trust yourself, but I am not yourself. I am your new mind; I am the one who's come to save you. A vision of the Munk is the highest of gifts, and to disobey the vision is to disobey a god."

"I'm sorry," Lonnie repeated, trembling as she climbed back to her feet. "I'm so tired and hungry."

"And I am offering you food." Lahn knelt, extending the handful of nuts. "Eat, Peet. Eat and come with me to the Shrine. The others desperately await your arrival."

Lonnie's head burned with questions, but instead of following her curiosity, she ate.

"Good, Peet," Lahn said. He smiled and pulled her back onto the trail. "Come. This is only the beginning."

They climbed the mountain in a winding pattern, making the steep ascent quite manageable—even in Lonnie's state of extreme starvation. She followed Lahn's footsteps like a child, and in a way it was the truth of the situation; she might finally have a father who cared for her tomorrow.

After an hour of climbing, they came onto a dirt path that followed the ridge. Lahn quickened their pace. Lonnie lifted her head as the scent of smoke. They rounded a long bend in the path and came to a tall, wicker wall. A strange band of symbols had been woven into the top of the archway. Lonnie almost asked what they said, but her still-burning cheek reminded her to keep quiet.

"Welcome to the Shrine," Lahn said, unwinding a cord that held the gate shut. He pulled on the slack and dragged the gate open. Lonnie took his hand, and trembling, Tail of the Monkey followed Master of God's King into the Shrine.

FIFTEEN

A large clearing expanded within the round, wicker wall. Small mud huts sat like massive piles of dung across the outskirts. A massive fire pit breathed smoke from the center of the clearing, with a series of poles rising around it. The clearing had been carved out of the mountain, leaving a tall wall of dark mud and stone to Lonnie's right. Symbols and runes covered the wall. They swirled in spirals and hooked arrows, all leading to a tall door at the center. Two burning torches hung from pikes at each side of the door.

"What do you say, Peet?" Lahn asked. He smirked, nodding for her to speak.

"It's not what I expected," Lonnie said.

"Would you like to meet the family?" Lahn didn't wait for an answer and stepped forward, cupping his hands around his mouth. "My lovely ladies and gentlemen," he cried. "Come into the sun and meet your sister."

Naked, wide-eyed men and women began to crawl from the small openings in the mud huts. They scratched at their arms and twitched a little as they began making their way across the clearing. A rush of fear came out of nowhere and Lonnie too began to twitch. She hid herself behind Lahn, peering over his shoulder at the odd collection of on-coming strangers.

"Don't be afraid," Lahn said, pulling Lonnie to his side. He locked his hand into hers and dragged her forward. "Everyone, this is Peet Doe Munk. Say hello."

"Hello," they all mumbled, awkwardly smiling as their eyes flickered from Lahn to Lonnie.

"Hi," Lonnie whispered. She tried to not feel naked in the crowd of other naked humans, but she had only abandoned her clothes the day before. She brought her arm across her breasts and Lahn slapped it back down.

"Peet is hungry, and I've promised her a feast," he said. "Let's show her how we dine at the Shrine."

The people scurried off, the men rushing to a larger mud hut at the rear of camp, while the women went to the firepit. Lahn pulled Lonnie after the women.

"All rescues," he explained, waving to the family. "All brought to me by the Munk."

"They seem nice," Lonnie said.

"They're still healing. The rebuilding of the heart and soul takes time."

"How long does it usually take?"

Lahn sneered at Lonnie's use of a question, going as far as raising a fist, but he thought twice and laughed.

"The mind follows the heart, Peet."

He led her to the firepit, where the men dropped off bales of wood and straw. The women went to work rekindling the flames. Everyone had the same, anxious tremor. They all couldn't stop glancing at Lahn.

"Peet has just returned from her meeting with the Munk," he said. "She needs water and a chair."

"Yes, Lahn Doe Meelay," one of the men said, nodding fervently as he limped off. Lonnie couldn't help but notice the men were all hideous. Compared to Lahn, whose supple skin and effervescent charisma left him beaming, they might as well be bridge trolls.

"I must now leave you," Lahn announced. "I'm going fishing."

The women all stiffened, wincing as they turned to Lahn.

"Don't fear," he said. "I'll be back before you know it. While I'm gone, I want everyone to welcome Peet into the family and show her how we live. Perhaps I'll return with another. The Munk has blessed us this month, and I feel he's preparing us for something great. Kisses, everyone."

The girls, with gigantic, frantic eyes, glanced at Lonnie as they each crept forward and kissed Lahn on the cheek. When they finished, he turned to Lonnie, who realized he expected her to kiss him, too.

"Oh," she said, pressing her cracked lips to Lahn's cheek.

"Thank you, Peet," he said, giving her rump a slap. "I'll see you all soon. If you hear the Hundledun, blow the horn and get into the huts. Fear not; *he will not hurt you.*"

Lahn marched across the Shrine, playfully tossing his hair back as he moved for the gate. Everyone remained still as he drew the wicker gate shut on his way out. Lonnie, unable to contain herself, turned to the younger girl beside her.

"What's the Hundledun?" she asked.

The girl, who looked to be in her early twenties, stiffened as she turned to Lonnie. "We're not supposed to speak of it," she whispered, her eyes flashing to the wicker gate. Everyone's eyes were on the wicker gate. It wiggled as Lahn fastened the rope on the other side. Lonnie turned with them, wondering if something out of the ordinary might happen. Her heart raced as her mind explored ideas of what a Hundledun might be.

"I'll check," one of the women said. She held up a hand as she walked toward the gate, her limp pronounced.

"What's your name?" Lonnie asked the younger girl. "I'm Lon—Peet Doe Munk."

"I know," the girl said. "I'm Fest Doe Raymo."

"That's pretty. What does it mean?"

"Mother of God's Keeper. I imagine you know your name's meaning."

"Tail of the Monkey." Lonnie frowned as Fest raised an eyebrow. "I'm not in love with it," she admitted. "Is it possible to change names?"

"I don't think so. And we better stop speaking." Fest pointed across the Shrine, where the woman had finally limped to the gate. She gave the gate a tug to ensure Lahn had properly locked it and then made her way to the wall of symbols, where she started to climb.

"What's she doing?" Lonnie asked. "Who is she?"

"She's checking," Fest said. "And that's Grit Mey Afron."

"What does that name mean?"

"Master of Death's Keeper."

"That's a nice one." Lonnie began to like her name even less as she watched Grit finally scale the wall to a place where she could peer over the top of it. She surveyed for a moment and began the slow and tedious climb back to the ground. "What's she checking?" Lonnie asked.

"She's looking for the Hundledun," Fest said, lowering her voice. As if knowing Lonnie was about to ask for more information, she joined the others in tending the fire.

Lonnie sighed and looked across the Shrine. The men stood huddled on the far side of the fire pit. A few jumped as Lonnie caught them staring at her. The rest of the women either watched Grit or absentmindedly fed sticks into the rising fire. Lonnie surveyed the long, saggy wicker fence surrounding the Shrine. She doubted it could stop a half-interested man, let alone a Hundledun.

Fest had begun fastening a long metal pole to the one of the posts rising around the pit. Lonnie ventured to her side.

"What's that?" she asked. Fest jumped out of fright.

"You're not supposed to ask questions," she said, cinching the knot. "This is the spit for dinner."

"Sorry," Lonnie said. "I mostly think in questions. And the Shrine is a curious place."

"You'll learn." Fest swung the spit across the fire and scurried to the other side to fasten it. Lonnie, wondering if the other women might be more hospitable, turned to the woman who had scaled the wall to look for the Hundedun. Fest had called her Grit.

Grit studied the fire tending with crossed arms, her face stern and wrinkled. She turned straight to Lonnie as she made her approach.

"Hi," Lonnie said, offering a hand. Grit didn't bother to look at it. "It's nice to meet you. My name is Peet."

"I heard. Welcome." Grit spoke with the sincerity of a tax collector, and Lonnie decided against asking her any questions.

"I'm sure whatever you're cooking for dinner will be delicious," she said. "And I'm glad the Hundledun—whatever that might be—is not close by." Lonnie nodded, pleased with her anti-questions.

But Grit only scratched beneath her naked breast and scowled a little deeper. She finally turned to Lonnie, giving her body a disproving once-over. "We'll talk while we eat," she said. "Until then, close your mouth."

Lonnie cowered a little, unused to women making such commandments. She joined the perimeter of half-crazed Shrine residents and tried to remember why she had come; the devastating curiosity that destroyed her entire life. It helped to play through the story of her past, where all questions were already answered.

Her stomach dropped when she realized she left Daniel's heart at the mushroom platform. Without the carving, she had only vapor to remember him, and that would not be enough.

"Fest," she said, rushing to her side. "I have to run back down the hill. I forgot something at the stones."

Fest nearly dropped the string of wild flowers in her hands. "You can't leave," she whispered.

"I need to get my carving."

"You'll die if you leave. You can't climb the mountain without Lahn, and the Hundledun—he'll suck your soul out of your flesh. It's impossible, Peet. You'd never make it through the fence."

"It's made of wicker. I could bend a hole right through it."

"I can't help but notice you're not working," Grit said, stepping beside Lonnie and Fest. "I expect you're about to tell me what's so important."

"Peet wanted to know where to relieve herself," Fest said. "I just informed her to step behind a hut."

"Grit," Lonnie said. "I have a problem. I left a very important carving at the stones where I met the Munk. I need to run and fetch it."

"That's not how things work here," Grit said. "Once you come in, you don't go back out."

"I need my carving."

"If you left it at the stones, then the Munk intended for you to leave it at the stones. This is a womb, and we take nothing with us."

"When will Lahn be back?" Lonnie asked.

Grit punched Lonnie in the nose. She fell backwards, landing on a hard stick. Blood ran down her lips. Wide-eyed, she stared up at Grit.

"You will not ask questions here," she said. "Any information you need will be given to you. Lahn Doe Meelay is our mind. Questions are his indulgence, not ours."

"I'm sorry," Lonnie said, staggering back to her feet. She blushed as everyone's frantic eyes locked on her.

"Stay out of the way," Grit said, taking up the string of flowers and thrusting it into Fest's belly.

Lonnie wiped the blood from her mouth as she stepped back, hating how everyone continued staring at her. Her extreme hunger brought her attention to the spit, but it appeared dinner would consist of several roasted strings of wild flowers. She wanted to cry but feared it might earn her another punch. She hoped Lahn might be more sympathetic to her need for Daniel's heart.

A short while later, for the wildflowers did not take long to cook, Grit pulled the lines and handed everyone a handful of crispy pedals. Lonnie followed the group to a small circle of dirt. They sat, and after demolishing the miniscule rations, Grit turned to Lonnie.

"Tell us how you came here and why the Monk gave you your name," she said. "If you please us, we will do the same."

SIXTEEN

Lonnie gave an abridged version of her story, leaving out the details of which kingdom she came from and which king fed his people human meat. Desperate for sympathy, she embellished Daniel's death, claiming he had breathed his last breath in her arms. He told her to run before the king could kill her, and so she did.

"I was in the woods, weeping," Lonnie said. Her new family hunched crossed-legged around her with wide eyes. "That's where Lahn Doe Meelay found me. He brought me to the stones, where I ate the mushroom and lost my mind. The Munk came at the end of the vision, but he didn't give me the name; Lahn did. He never explained what it means."

"Tail of the Monkey is rather self-explanatory," Grit said. She smiled, leading a few of the others into mimicked glee.

"Tell me, then," Lonnie said, getting the hang of question-less questioning. "I enjoy learning the meaning of names."

"You're a searching appendage," Grit said. "You drag on the ground, you venture where you don't belong, and if you were removed from the body, very little would change. Humanity lost its tail for good reason. You are a relic of old; a weight better off shed."

Lonnie winced, the words hitting her like daggers. "Tell me what your name means," she said.

"I am Grit Mey Afron, Master of Death's Maker. It's a very honorable name, with an extremely complicated meaning. Give me a moment to find words you'll understand." Grit scratched at her chin, turning to the darkening sky.

Lonnie decided she hated Grit Mey Afron. She did her best to embody the rest of the circle's eerie calm while she waited for the meaning.

"As master of Death's maker, I am a step above the realm of mortality," Grit began. "I control the place where such concepts are very literally conceived. But it's more than that. I am directly in charge of the mother, and the mother who can bring death into life can also bring far greater change into reality."

"Interesting," Lonnie said, trying her best to be impressed. "It must be complicated to manage so many high-level positions. You're master of Death's maker, Fest is mother of God's Keeper, and Lahn is Master of God's King. It makes me wonder who is at the top of the chain."

"A reasonable thought for a monkey's tail," Grit said. "But it's all very simple; in our physical bodies, Lahn Doe Meelay is our keeper. We do as he commands and prepare for the future he authors."

"I would be interested to know more of your names," Lonnie said, turning across the pale collection of runaways.

"Only speak if you're comfortable," Grit said. "Your identity is yours to reveal."

"I am Rep Din Chow," a woman said after a moment, finding a nervous smile. "It means Fountain of Spirit Fuel. I spent my life working the fields for slave masters. If only they could see what I've become." Rep twitched as she looked across the circle, her mouth shifting from a smile to a sneer.

"Gab Nay Bey," another woman offered. "The Mind of Nine Gods."

"Cul Bee Slip," a man said. "The Spirit of Perfect Destiny."

"Deep Vol Bang," a woman said, trembling as she climbed to her feet. "The Queen of God's Father."

A man rose to speak, brushing flower pedal crumbs out of his pubic hair. He smiled, twitching as he briefly made eye contact with Lonnie. He opened his mouth to speak just as a thunderous *boom* came from the other side of the mount.

Everyone screamed and dropped face-down on the dirt. Lonnie turned to the wall of runic symbols.

"What was that?" she asked.

"No questions," Fest mumbled into the dirt. She dragged Lonnie down with her. "Be still—it's the Hundledun."

"What is the Hundledun? Can it hurt us?"

"*No questions,*" Fest hissed.

Lonnie's heart raced as another great *bang* crashed in the distance. It sounded like thunder, but the clap of its expulsion penetrated through her flesh like an arrow.

"Someone tell me what that is," Lonnie demanded.

"It's the Hundledun," a man gasped.

"I know it's the Hundledun," Lonnie said. "Tell me what a Hundedun is."

"The sworn enemy of the Munk," Grit said. "He comes when he senses disobedience. We must have angered the Munk, who's allowed him to come. Think lovely thoughts. Think of your name; think of the power you hold inside yourself."

Lonnie had a hard time believing any of it, but the Hundledun continued to boom away, and there was no denying the power and scale of a being who could make such a ruckus.

"*We're going to die,*" a man said, climbing to his feet. He panted, twirling in a frantic circle as he took off running for the gate.

"Don't," Fest shouted after him. But the man kept running.

"Swang," Grit screamed. She rose as she called after him. Lonnie turned, watching Swang's flailing arms and legs sprint for the gate. The booming continued from beyond the mountain, rumbling the earth so severely the spit fell from the fire pit.

"It's not safe," Swang shouted. He crashed into the wicker gate and began pulling on it. A last clap of the Hundledun's boom came from beyond the mountain, and then a terrible click-clacking. Lonnie turned to find a boulder bouncing down the mountainside. She pressed her face into the dirt as the boulder dropped onto Swang.

No one said a word in the newfound silence. Finally, Grit kneeled, setting a hand on Lonnie and Fest's backs.

"We're okay," she said. "We're okay, everyone. The Munk saw our obedience and pushed the Hundledun out. Well done." She cautiously climbed to her feet, as did the rest of the camp. Lonnie trembled right along with them as she rose and faced the gate.

"Oh, Swang," Fest said, covering her mouth.

"His disobedience nearly cost all of us our lives," Grit said. "Let's clean up before Lahn returns." She led the family to the gate. They gathered around Swang's body, each taking a moment to gasp as they faced the damage.

The boulder had split his head in two before planting it in the ground. It took a pike and nearly an hour to pry him loose. With the body released, the men dragged him to the rear of the Shrine. Lonnie frowned to find a crowded graveyard hidden behind the mud huts. What looked to be a hundred stones marked the deceased members of the family. Even more disturbing, someone had pre-dug half a dozen additional graves. The men dropped Swang into the nearest hole and began hand-shoveling dirt over top of him. Lonnie stepped to Fest's side.

"That was crazy," she said, eyeing the other graves. "This looks like a lot of disobedience. I guess they all died the same way."

"Oh, no," Fest said. "The Hundledun has many weapons. Swang's death came rather easily, as far as a Shrine death goes."

"I'll speak," Grit said, stepping to the head of the grave. "We never like to see a brother go, but disobedience comes with a price. Swang Doe Moan has sinned and paid that price. I hope his sacrifice will strengthen us as we bring a new sister into his place." Grit knelt and tossed a handful of soil into the grave. She nodded before joining the others.

"Swang Doe Moan was a pretty name," Lonnie said to Fest. "Tell me what it means."

"It meant Dung of the Morning," Fest said. "It's strange; the Hundledun seems to only come for the weaker names."

Lonnie shivered, imagining she must have the weakest name on the mountain. It placed a tremendous fear in her heart and she made a vow to herself; she must learn to obey.

"You should say something," Grit said. Lonnie turned, realizing she was talking to her.

"I didn't know Swang," Lonnie said.

"Yes, but you've been asking all kinds of questions, and I can't help but think the Hundledun came looking for you. I suggest you say something for Swang."

Lonnie glanced at Fest, who nodded. She stepped to the open grave, where Swang's crushed head still remained half-exposed in the dirt.

"Swang should have been braver," Lonnie said, unsure how to eulogize a man she had never spoken to. "He ran quickly before his death. He died just as quickly. I'm sure some will miss him."

"That's enough," Grit said. "It's time for bed. Everyone, get into your huts. Lahn will be back in the morning and we need to rest. I believe we're going on a mission tomorrow. Boys, get to bed as soon as Swang is underground."

The girls all brightened with the order to go into hiding.

They gave each other a hug and merry goodnights before prancing off to their glorified gopher holes. Lonnie caught Fest's arm before she could run off.

"Where do I sleep?" she asked. "Sorry. I mean, tell me where to sleep."

"Usually, a new member digs their own hut," Fest said. She surveyed the mounds of dirt. "Since it's so late, you can just sleep in Swang's hut."

"I wonder if Grit might have a problem with that."

"Don't be so scared of Grit. She's not Lahn." Fest gave Lonnie an unexpected hug and jogged off.

Lonnie, with many things to puzzle, made her way to the men's huts. She had no way of telling which one belonged to Swang, so she waited, watching the men finish filling Swang's grave. The cloudy sky had shifted to a dark gray by then. Lonnie stood back by the wicker fence as the men finally crawled into bed. The only unoccupied hut sat on the far end, and with a head overflowing with questions, she crawled inside, hoping sleep might grant her some answers.

But maddeningly, once inside Swang's hut, Lonnie stumbled upon a mystery that only offered more questions.

CHAPTER

SEVENTEEN

Lonnie could hardly kneel in Swang's tiny hut. A thin blanket lay across the back side, with a smooth rock for a pillow. Lonnie crawled onto the blanket and tried to get comfortable. As something poked her back, she rolled over to find a few wooden boards buried in the dirt. She slid her finger between them, realizing they covered a hidden compartment.

Lonnie frowned, turning to the hut's entrance.

She worked one of the boards out and set it aside. Without light, she ran her hands into the dark compartment to investigate. She found a tightly rolled scroll in the corner. The scroll looked to be a dozen feet long, and Swang had written over every inch of it. Lonnie crawled to the hut's entrance for light.

"Why can't we ask questions? What's so bad about wanting information? If Lahn Doe Meelay wants to lead us, why can't we ask him for advice? Why are all the women so nasty? Why can't I wear a tunic? Is it possible to leave this place? Can I have sex with family members?"

Lonnie drew out another few feet of Swang's question diary. It vindicated her to know he too wanted answers, but it also terrified her. The Hundledun had come for Swang because of his weakness, and she and Swang not only shared weak names, they shared a vehement proclivity for curiosity. She scrolled a few more feet through the diary.

"Why is Lahn so much nicer to the girls? Why can't we eat good food? How do they expect me to look as handsome as Lahn if they

only feed me flowers? Would it be so insane to let me wear a loin-cloth? Am I allowed to pleasure myself? What would Lahn really do if I left? Is the Hundledun a woman? Does my wife ever wonder where I went? Are Lahn's missions crazy, or am I? What makes a man crazy? Is wanting to hide your penis crazy? Does anyone else hate pooping in front of the family? Why does poop smell bad even when you only eat flowers?"

Lonnie could see Lahn's mind unraveling in the quality of his handwriting. She moved to the end of the scroll, where the ink looked hardly a day old.

"Why is my name Dung of the Morning? Why does Lahn only give cool names to the ones who never die? What does the Hundledun kill us so often? What does the Hundledun's name mean? How come Grit can't die? If Lahn died, who would take care of us? Would the others listen if I tried to take control? Why am I so weak? Why am I cursed? Why is my name Dung of the Morning? Why is the new girl so ugly? How long will it take for the Hundledun to kill Peet Doe Munk? Is her name weaker than mine? Should I try to run before it can kill me so it has no choice but to kill Peet? Why can't Lahn find a pretty girl for once? Am I the only one who doesn't trust the Munk? Should I leave if I know I don't belong here? Am I scared to run away? Would it be that bad if I just made a break for it? What if this is my final question? What if this is? Or this? How does Lahn expect us to be loyal if we can't have sex within the family?"

Lonnie rolled up the scroll with trembling fingers, feeling filthy for reading such intimate thoughts. The questions were both insulting and fascinating, but there was one silver lining: Swang might have been more curious than her.

But she had only been barred from asking questions for a day.

What would she start doing after a week?

How long would it take before she had a scroll of her own?

How soon would the Hundledun take to see her weakness and decide she needed a rock through the skull?

"Stop it," Lonnie commanded her mind, stuffing the scroll back into the hidden compartment.

Within seconds, a great boom came from the other side of the mountain. Lonnie froze, trembling as the ground shook beneath her. She slid the board back in place and flapped the blanket over it. She lay back and closed her eyes. The tremor stilled and she let her breath out. Her mind tensed, a thousand questions begging to enter the ether. She drew shallow and frantic breaths as she shut them out. Her skin moistened under the effort. She tried to think confident thoughts.

The Munk had met her. He saw something worth saving, and he brought Lahn to fulfill that mission.

Lonnie jumped as the boards settled beneath her. Trembling, she climbed out of bed and dug up the scroll, gently lifting it as if the words might infect her with leprosy. After a glance across the Shrine, she crawled into the night, quickly making her way to the fire pit.

She tossed Swang's poisonous thoughts into the coals and watched them burn. With wide, frantic eyes, she surveyed the night, hoping the offering might be enough to save her. She nervously scratched at her hip before slouching back across the grass. Inside the hut, she lay down and thought of statements and exclamations.

You are here for a reason.

You cannot trust your mind.

Lahn wants to help you.

The Munk wants to help you.

The Hundledun won't hurt you if you behave.

Your name is weak, but accurate.

Perhaps you can get a new one when you cut the curiosity from your heart.

Lonnie didn't feel good, but she felt safe enough to close her eyes. She lay back on the stone pillow and let starvation drag her to sleep.

EIGHTEEN

"Come to life, my lovely lads and ladies!"

Lonnie woke with a numb face. She lifted her head from the rock pillow, wincing at the daylight. She crawled to the hut's entrance to find Lahn standing before the smoldering fire pit. He looked fresh, his hair clean and fluffy. His belly also looked healthily bloated. He cupped his hands and called out again.

"We have a mission today," he shouted, laughing as he surveyed the Shrine. "Well, come on."

Lonnie, still shaken by Swang's scroll, trembled as she rose into the daylight. Lahn found her and his gaze immediately hardened. Lonnie nearly fell over backwards as he marched across the grass.

"You slept with *Swang*?" he snarled. "One night, and you—"

"No," Lonnie said. "Swang's dead."

"*What?*" Lahn turned to the graveyard. The fresh grave soothed his anger. "What happened? Speak to me, Peet."

"The Hundledun dropped a rock on his head. I'm sorry, I thought it would be okay if—"

"It is," Lahn said, taking her into his arms. "Everything is going to be okay, my dear, sweet Peet."

Over Lahn's shoulder, Lonnie found the rest of the family gawking at her. She blushed and tried to hide in his hair.

"It's always when we least expect it," Lahn said, turning to them. "It's always *who* we least suspect. Thank the Munk no one else was hurt." He took Lonnie's hand and led her to the fire pit, where the others gathered. "I've just learned Swang was lost to the Hundledun. I'm so sorry I wasn't here. Is everyone else okay?"

"We're fine," Grit said. "Swang brought about his own death. He tried to run, so the Munk allowed the Hundledun to take him."

"We've grown careless," Lahn said, guiding Lonnie to a seat. "We come to this place to rebuild ourselves, yet our brothers continue to fall. Swang refused to give his old self away, and he's paid the ultimate price for his greed. We all need to learn from this. Fest, what do we learn?"

"An untrained mind is poison," she said, swallowing a lump as she looked across the family. "If we don't heal them, the poison will kill us."

"Grit? What do we learn?"

"The Munk is always watching," Grit said.

"Peet, what have you learned?" Lahn asked.

"Questions are bad," Lonnie said.

"But why are questions bad?"

"I don't know."

Lahn sighed and turned to the dwindled fire, shaking his head. "She doesn't know," he said, surveying the family. "Can anyone tell Peet why questions are bad?"

Grit happily raised her hand. "Questions aren't bad," she said. Lonnie expected Lahn to slap her, but he only nodded. "If a soft mind goes exploring, it will create evidence for stupidity. Until the heart and soul are rebuilt, questions are as dangerous as witchcraft."

Fest twitched beside Lonnie, her eyes wide as she set her gaze on the ground.

"In this place," Lahn said, crouching to level himself with

the rest of the family, "I am your mind. I alone know what you need to know. If you don't trust me to give you the knowledge you need when you need it, then go ahead and run; see what the Hundedun thinks of your plans. Go on—anyone is free to leave. Walk through that gate with your pride and questions and see how long you live. Perhaps the Hundledun will tell you why he does what he does before he kills you."

Grit laughed, and when Lahn laughed, every member of the family broke into an anxious chuckle. Lonnie too laughed, but she felt very little humor in the situation. Her entire body trembled with a level of fear she had never felt before. It penetrated her, firing into every nerve.

"Despite our loss, the day is beautiful," Lahn said. "We will not dwell on Swang and his mistakes. I promised a mission, and you're going to have your mission. Take a few minutes and we'll get moving. Peet, come with me."

Lahn took Lonnie's hand and led her toward the wall, where the runes and symbols blended into the morning shadow. He slowed as they approached the mountainside door. The lamps had gone out, but their fragrant oil filled the air with a deep scent of patchouli.

"Do you know what this door is?" Lahn asked, pulling a key from his shoulder bag.

"No," Lonnie said.

"The Munk built this door nearly three hundred years ago. How do I know this, you might wonder? Well, I know the Munk built this door because I watched him build it."

Lonnie twitched as questions populated her mind. She turned from the door to Lahn. "I didn't realize you were so old," she said.

"I look young because I've lived a righteous life," Lahn said. "I recently turned six hundred and fourteen years old. It's why I'm so wise."

"I've never heard of someone so old."

"That's because there aren't many of us around." Lahn smiled, the gentle wrinkles around his eyes mimicking those of a man no older than forty.

"I'd be interested in hearing more about the door," Lonnie said.

"This is no door; it's a portal to the other side, where I personally meet with the Munk. It's where I learn your names. It's where I make peace and secure our protection from the Hundledun."

Lonnie frowned, unable to transform her many questions into statements.

"I'm going to get a few things for the mission," Lahn said, turning to the door. "This won't take long."

"I'm excited to see the other side," Lonnie said.

"No, no. You'll be staying out here. No one goes into the portal but me." Lahn unlocked the door and pulled it open.

Lonnie peered through the gap as Lahn slipped inside. She only saw black before he snapped the door shut. Frowning, she turned back to camp, where Fest met her gaze from across the firepit. They shared a mutual confusion. Lonnie shivered as she looked up at the wall; the runes the Munk had carved three hundred years ago, when Lahn had been a mere three hundred and fourteen. So many questions danced within her mind. She shivered to keep them inside.

When Lahn returned, he carried a large crate across his naked belly. He waved a finger for Lonnie to follow him back to the firepit. Everyone else seemed to understand the drill, because they all lined up by the time Lahn arrived.

"You're protected," he said, opening the crate and handing out wreaths of flowers. The women put them on their heads, while the men slid them up their arms. Lonnie felt quite silly as she fit the halo on top of her head.

"This doesn't seem like the strongest form of protection," she mumbled to Fest.

"It's to protect our minds," Fest said. She lowered her voice and added, "although, I don't think it does anything."

"This way," Lahn called, setting his own crown of flowers upon his head. His wreath held triple the amount of flowers of everyone else's. The flowers spilled all the way to his supple buttocks. He led them to the rear of the Shrine, where a smaller door in the wicker fence allowed access to the other side of the mountain. Lahn opened the gate and led everyone onto a narrow path.

Lonnie stayed in the rear with Fest, hoping to dig more information out of here. She waited until they made it a few minutes outside of camp.

"I'm interested to know when Lahn will explain what exactly all this means," Lonnie said. "You must have some answers."

"We need to be careful," Fest said. "I don't always believe Lahn has our best interest at heart."

"Explain that further."

"He's strange, and often rude. Everyone has strict rules to follow but him."

"I know," Lonnie said. "It's crazy."

"Shh." Fest cowered a little. "We can't be heard talking like this."

"I'll be quiet, but please, tell me more. I've never heard of the Munk or a Hundledun. Tell me what the Hundledun looks like. You must have seen him by now."

"No one has ever seen it," Fest said. "That's part of what concerns me. It's so big and powerful, and it knows exactly where the Shrine is, but somehow it never hurts us unless someone starts asking questions or tries to run away."

"Lahn told me he's six hundred years old," Lonnie said. "I don't believe that's possible."

"It isn't."

"You sound very confident."

"In my past life, I was a witch," Fest whispered. "I can tell you with absolution that it's impossible. Even if he made it to one hundred, his hair wouldn't be half that luscious."

"If Lahn lies about his age, he probably lies about other things," Lonnie said. "It's curious how so many people follow his every command. Tell me how long you've been here."

"Only a week," Fest said. "A very long week."

"Tell me why you left your home and came with him."

"The town grew tired of my spell work. I was more or less chased out. I got lost in the forest and Lahn found me. He offered me a mushroom and I stupidly ate it. It poisoned me and I saw strange visions. It scared me to death. I saw the Munk. Lahn told me he could help me fix my life so I came to the Shrine, but I don't believe him—not after the last week."

"I find it strange you've stayed if you don't trust Lahn," Lonnie said.

"I'd leave right now if it weren't for the Hundledun," Fest said. "I saw the Munk in my visions; everyone does, so he must be real. And the Hundledun must be real, too, because Swang is the fifth person to be killed while trying to run since I arrived."

"The Shrine makes me sick with questions," Lonnie said. "It's very annoying that such a curious place forbids the one thing it creates."

"I'd like to go into the portal," Fest said. "I think we'll find all the answers we need behind that door."

"Maybe we should take a look."

"We need Lahn's key."

"Maybe we should steal it."

"If we're wrong, we might die."

"If we don't do anything, I'm going to lose my mind."

"Same," Fest said, letting out a breath. "We'll continue this conversation later. It looks like the mission's about to begin."

Lonnie turned ahead, where their path led into a mountain-top village. She gaped at the tall, wooden structures poking into the sky. It looked like a kingdom fallen from the clouds. Fest took her hand as they followed the trail into the misty village.

NINETEEN

A tall, wooden fence wrapped the mountain-top village. Lahn led the family through the gate and gave everyone a moment to take in the scene.

A huddle of stores and tall buildings welcomed visitors into the beautiful hideaway. Three paths stretched out across the village, winding with the mountain's humping spine. The architects clustered the buildings in every possible space. When they ran out of ground they built up, where rope bridges connected the towers. Odd trees added a splash of green to the overwhelming assembly of brown timber.

A few shop keepers peered through their windows at the collection of naked visitors. The dozen or so pedestrians took one look and quickly went on their way.

"Come," Lahn called, waving everyone into a huddle. Once all anxious heads were pressed together, he wrapped his arms around them. "We're here to share the good news. If we're lucky, we'll find some new members for the family. Everyone, pair-up and make your way through the village. Tell the people of the peace you've found at the Shrine. Tell them all are welcome if the Munk accepts them. We'll meet back here for lunch."

"Let's pair-up," Fest said, turning to Lonnie.

"No, I want Peet with me," Lahn said. "This is her first mission." He took Lonnie's hand and dragged her to his side. "Fest, you go with Grit. Everyone else, find your partner. No girls and boys together."

Soon, the frazzled collection of naked men and women stood in same-sex pairs. Lonnie couldn't help but feel incredibly ridiculous with her lack of clothing and flowery head dress. She wished she had longer flowers like Lahn to hide her breasts.

Lahn pulled Lonnie down the path on the right, which sloped up into a grove of clustered homes.

"Missions are an important part of our work," he explained as they headed for the first door. "It's difficult to give one's self up, as you saw with Swang. We have a bit of one-step-forward-and-two-steps-back to deal with."

Lonnie, unable to verbalize her confusion without a question, stood silent as Lahn knocked on the door.

An older man answered. He blinked and looked from Lahn to Lonnie, his eyebrows rising into his hairline. "What the devil is this?" he asked.

"Sir, I formally invite you to give up your life and explore happiness," Lahn said. He grinned in his charming way, but the man only frowned.

"What does that mean?" he asked.

"We have a community on the mountain. If you'll give up your worldly possessions, we can show you a better way of life."

"I'm happy here, thanks." The old man stepped back before slamming the door. Lahn laughed.

"Thankfully, the rotten eggs announce themselves," he said, pulling Lonnie down the path. "Come on, we've got a lot of ground to cover."

They went down the lane and invited dozens of confused and frightened men and women to exchange their lives for naked enlightenment at the Shrine, but no one accepted the offer. Lonnie wondered what she would have said if Lahn came knocking on her door in Doane.

Frowning, she realized she knew exactly what she would

have done. She would have laughed and thrown the door in his face.

She trembled, feeling more and more naked.

How exactly had he convinced her to come with him?

Had she lost her mind?

And if so, when?

When Daniel died?

When the poisonous mushroom boiled her brain?

It was all of it, she realized, her heart beating harder by the second. *He knew I was weak and dragged me in like a lost child.*

She looked across the village, wanting to break free and run to the nearest tailor's shop.

But Lahn held her hand tightly. She had a sinking feeling they were paired for this exact eventuality. The locals stared as they continued through the village. Many laughed, and they had every right to do so.

A nervous sweat broke across her back as she turned to Lahn; his beautiful, convincing face. If Lahn hadn't been so handsome she would have certainly run from him in the woods. He called to her from the bough of a tree, for God's sake.

The fact she hadn't run proved her insanity.

Which must be exactly why he chose to proselytize sans clothes. Anyone who could look past his nudity already had one foot in the door.

"I don't feel well," Lonnie said. "I'd like to go back to the gate and rest."

"We'll be done soon, Peet," Lahn said, giving her hand a squeeze. "You're just hungry." They crossed a wooded path and came into the last cul-de-sac of homes. Lonnie spotted Grit and Fest on an adjacent trail. Fest looked to be just as troubled. Grit too held fast to her hand, dragging her around as Lahn did Lonnie.

Lonnie shivered, wondering if someone had overheard their

conversation on the trail. She needed to talk with Fest immediately. If they wanted to escape, it would be together, and the sooner the better.

Finally, after Lahn failed to convince the last of the mountain's residents to follow him and the Munk, he escorted Lonnie back to the main gate. Most of the others had returned and stood nervously waiting. To Lonnie's surprise, a pale, extremely thin woman had joined the party. She wore a heavy wool shirt and pants, anxiously rubbing at her sleeves as Lahn approached.

"I see we have a new friend," Lahn said, offering his hand to the woman. He took her trembling hand and massaged it. "What do they call you?"

"Kimberly Arthur," she said. Her voice had an ugly throatiness to it.

"Are you prepared to leave everything behind and come with us?"

"I don't have anything left to leave. My husband and son have been killed."

"Then let's get you home," Lahn said, pulling her closer. As he hugged Kimberly, he waved for Grit. "Get the others back," he said. "I'm going to take Kimberly to the stones for her initiation. I'll be home as soon as I can."

"Right," Grit said, turning to the rest of the huddle. "Let's get moving. We'll eat lunch back at the Shrine." Lahn pulled Grit aside for a private word, whispering violently into her ear. Grit nodded as she turned to Lonnie. When Lahn released her she took Lonnie's hand. "Fest," she called, extending her other hand. "Come on. I want to walk with you two."

"I'd rather walk with my hands free," Lonnie said. "It helps me balance."

"If you trip, I'll catch you," Grit said. "Fest, let's go."

Lonnie sighed as they wandered out of the village and onto

the open path along the mountain ridge. She felt strong enough to break Grit's grip and make a run for it, but Lahn and Kimberly walked only a few dozen yards behind the family, and she didn't dare try to outrun him. She and Fest shared a glance during the walk, in which they conveyed seven words with only the desperation of their eyes.

We're going to do something dangerous tonight.

It stirred Lonnie with a new energy. Instead of twitching, she stood a little taller. Fest too seemed to be gaining confidence. She stopped twirling her hair and neatly swung her free hand at her side. Lonnie used the walking time to make a mental to-do list.

She wanted to peek into the portal.

She needed to escape.

She wanted to know the truth of the Munk and Hundledun.

She needed to get Daniel's heart back from the stones.

When they made it back to the Shrine, Lonnie sat with the others at the fire pit, nodding as Fest took a seat beside her. Grit went off to close the wicker gate and Lonnie leaned into Fest's ear.

"We need to get out of here immediately," she whispered. "Tell me the best time to do it."

"At night," Fest whispered back. "Once everyone's in bed. If we're quiet, they won't even know we're gone."

"What about the Hundledun?"

"What about it?"

"What if it's real and tries to kill us?"

"What choice do we have?"

"Stop it," the man beside Lonnie said. He swallowed a lump as she nervously rocked onto his knees. "You're asking questions. I heard you."

"We were just talking," Lonnie said.

"*I heard you.* Those were questions."

"Tell me what's going on," Grit said, rushing back to the circle of naked impotents.

"They were asking questions," the man said, his hand trembling as he pointed to Lonnie and Fest.

"No we weren't," Fest said. "He misheard us."

"They'll bring the Hundledun, Grit." The man drew a shaky breath. "I heard them. They were whispering questions back and forth. They'll bring the Hundledun—I swear they will."

"Fest, move to the other side of the fire," Grit said. "Peet, stand up."

Lonnie rose as Fest scampered off. Grit took Lonnie by the wrist and dragged her toward the mountainside door.

"You're hurting my arm," Lonnie said.

"And you deserve every bit of it," Grit said. She doubled her grip and pulled harder, forcing Lonnie into an embarrassing half-run. "Apparently, the mushroom didn't take with you," she said. "Since you arrived, we've had nothing but trouble. But we're going to fix that."

"What do you mean?" Lonnie asked.

Grit slapped her so fast it barely registered.

"You ask another question and you'll be eating three." Grit thrust Lonnie into the wall of runes. As Lonnie crumbled, malnourished to the point of dizziness, Grit pulled a box from within the wall and held out a pair of fat, red and blue mushrooms.

"No," Lonnie said, scrabbling backwards.

"Yes," Grit said, catching her by the ankle. "You're going back to the Munk. Perhaps this time you'll learn." She pinned Lonnie, forcing her onto her back. Lonnie screamed for help and Grit shoved the mushrooms into her mouth. "Chew," she hissed, covering Lonnie's mouth. "Chew or you're going to choke."

Lonnie bucked and kicked to little effect. With tears

streaming down her cheeks, she chewed, coating her mouth with the bitter, horrible juice of the poisonous mushrooms. Only after her throat bobbed with acceptance did Grit release her.

"I'll lose my mind with two," Lonnie said, gasping to breath. "It's going to kill me."

"Very likely," Grit said. "But if you survive, you might finally be ready to listen. Get up. We have a few minutes before you start to go."

She dragged Lonnie off the ground, leading her back to the fire pit. Everyone avoided Lonnie's gaze as she sat on the dirt. Grit smiled and walked around the circle of trembling men and women, stopping as she came behind Fest.

"This is going to be interesting," Grit said. With incredible speed, she yanked Fest's hair and cocked her head back. As Fest screamed, Grit stuffed a pair of mushrooms into her mouth. "You're both going back," she said, covering Fest's mouth to make her chew. "This is a lesson for the rest of you." Grit swept a finger across the shaking family. "Lahn has given me a promotion in his absence. Anyone who shows signs of anything but blind obedience will go straight back to the Munk. You can either learn from watching Peet and Fest's journey, or you can join them."

No one said a word, and after Fest swallowed her mushrooms, Grit nodded. She set the spit back over the fire and turned to the men.

"Gather flowers if you want to eat. Ladies, build us an inferno."

Lonnie and Fest locked eyes from across the pit; their lips stained blue with the mushroom's poisonous blood. They shared the same seven silent words, and their execution would be very different from the original thought.

We're going to do something dangerous tonight.

TWENTY

Lonnie tried her best to stay calm and not think about the trouble brewing in her belly, but the family watched her and Fest like they might spontaneously combust. Everyone twitched and trembled except for Grit. She calmly handed everyone their serving of smoked flowers. As Lonnie ate, she wondered if the equivalent of goat food would be her final meal on earth.

As the fire crackled, Lonnie turned to the dancing flames. A strange pressure started in her head. Her vision blurred for just a second. She turned to Fest, who grinned back at her.

"Do you feel it?" Lonnie asked.

Grit slapped her in the back of the head and hissed, "no questions."

"Yes," Fest replied. She laughed, bold and brightly. "I'm feeling all kinds of things."

Lonnie's left arm involuntarily twitched. She drew a quaking breath as her chest tightened. Again, Fest let out a joyous laugh. She stared into the flames with wide and glistening eyes.

"Peet, look at them all," she said.

"Stop talking," Grit said.

"Tell me what to look at," Lonnie said. She blocked Grit's incoming slap, desperate to know what Fest found so funny. Her mind seemed to be on a precipice. At any moment she might scream and lose total control, but she also had a mad desire to understand Fest's untimely pleasure. "Fest, tell me what you're seeing."

"The dancing elves," Fest said, giggling. "They're on the logs—digging out the embers."

"Stop this," Grit shouted. "Everyone but Fest and Peet get into your huts." She rose, slapping and shoving the rest of the family to their feet. "I said, go."

As the rest of the family raced off to the huts, Fest walked around the fire, grinning as she sat right beside Lonnie.

"There," she whispered, pointing into the flames. "Don't you see it?"

"No questions," Grit screamed. She swung her fist at Fest, but Lonnie again caught it out of the air.

"Go away," she said.

"Yes," Fest said. "You're being annoying."

"I'm in charge," Grit hissed. "No one tells me what to do."

"Or what?" Lonnie asked.

"Yeah," Fest said. "What are you going to do?"

Grit screamed as she dove at Lonnie. She crashed into her and they tumbled back, rolling into the fire's heat. Lonnie's mind surged with a strange vein of pleasure in the ruckus. She easily defended Grit's flurry of punches. Fest laughed so hard it brought Lonnie to laughter.

"Fest, stop it," she said. "I'm trying to fight."

"Oh, just finish it," Fest said. She rose and began unfastening the spit. Grit, still draped over Lonnie but far from in control of the fight, turned to her and gasped.

"Help," she cried. "Everyone, come out and help me."

"No one likes you," Lonnie said. She blocked a punch and rolled on top of Grit. "You're just as crazy as Lahn. How long have you been here? Do you seriously believe in any of this?"

"Watch out," Fest said. She held the iron spit held over her head, the sharp tip aimed at Grit. "Peet, move so I can kill her."

"Please," Grit said. "Please, don't. I'll stop. You can do whatever you want."

"Yeah?" Fest raised an eyebrow before breaking into laughter. "You are so weird."

"You're going to bring the Hundledun," Grit said. "He'll come and kill us all if you don't stop."

"But I've been thinking questions all day," Lonnie said. "Why hasn't he already come?" She paused as she glanced at the fire. Finally, she saw the elves working to strip the embers from the logs. They were a jolly troupe, whistling while they worked. One of their pants sagged to reveal a butt crack. Lonnie burst into laughter. "I see them," she said. "I see the elves."

"Help," Grit screamed again. "They're going to kill me!"

This time, the family poked their heads from the mud huts. As they timidly crawled out, looking like pale horse dung, Lonnie and Fest both howled with laughter. Lonnie felt light enough to float into the clouds.

"This isn't like the last mushroom," she said to Fest.

"It feels great," Fest agreed. "Lonnie, can you please step back? I want to kill her."

"The Hundledun will come," Grit said. "For the rest of the family's sake, please; spare me!"

"Fine." Fest tossed the spit aside. "But you need to fuck off. I'm leaving the Shrine, and so is Peet."

"My name is Lonnie Lovingdove," Lonnie said.

"*Lonnie* and I are leaving. Come on, Lonnie. My name is Bally Beauregard, by the way."

"It's a pleasure to meet you, Bally." Lonnie gave Bally a tight hug. Her hair smelled of peaches and cream. "Do you want to peek into the portal before we go?"

"Don't we need a key?"

"Can't we just break it open?"

"Let's see." Bally led the way to the cliff wall. Above them, the evening sky darkened, shifting into magnificent shades of purple and green. Lonnie found her poisoning enchanting with a partner to share the experience. She and Bally came to the door and gave the handle a turn. "How do we break it?" Bally asked.

"We could hit it with a rock," Lonnie said. She looked through the grass, but her eyes wandered to the carved symbols in the wall. They swirled and danced as if made of living flesh. Lonnie slapped Bally's arm and she turned to the vision. Together, they drifted into a parallel trance.

"Whoa," Bally whispered.

The sky darkened and they continued staring. Lonnie couldn't move; the symbols seemed to be trying to tell her something, but she couldn't quite break the code. Her mind throbbed like a beating heart as the mushrooms began to take deeper hold.

"We should get moving," she said. "I think this is going to get stronger."

"Yeah," Bally said.

Behind them, feet slapped across the grass. Lonnie waited until she couldn't ignore and finally turned.

Grit had the spit in her hands, running full speed at Lonnie. Her teeth flashed as she closed the gap. Lonnie simply stepped aside and let Grit ram the spit into the door. As Grit crashed with her momentum, Bally turned, frowning.

"You are so fucking *annoying*," she said. "Give me that." She pulled the spit from the door and brought it over her head. As Grit screamed, Bally thrust the spear straight through her chest. Grit kicked and gurgled for her last minute of life.

"Wait," Lonnie said. "We can use the spit to break the door open."

"What?" Bally asked, her attention back on the twirling symbols in the wall. "Oh, yeah. Go for it."

Lonnie twisted and tugged the bloody spit free. She shoved it into the gap between the door and mountain, grunting as she put pressure on.

"Help me," she commanded.

Bally started to push on the spit. The door creaked under their strain. A long, twisting crack spread through its center.

A rumbling boom came from the other side of the mountain. The rest of the family, who watched the violent scene in trembling horror from the fireside, started to whimper.

"That was loud," Lonnie said. She turned to the wall, lifting her gaze to the rainbow sky above.

"Really loud," Bally said.

Another rumble shook the ground. Lonnie and Bally held onto one another to stay afoot. They met each other's gaze as a tremendous *bang* rattled the mountain. The door itself started to tremble.

"That sounds like the Hundledun," Bally whispered.

"Shit," Lonnie whispered.

TWENTY-ONE

Ultimate pleasure shifted into penetrating fear. Lonnie and Bally ran from the wall, racing for the safety of the fire. A great *click-clacking* came from behind them. Lonnie turned just in time to see a boulder tumbling down the mountain. She tackled Bally out of the way.

Gasping, they sat up, just as the boulder bowled down three of the family members.

"Damn," Bally said. "They're dead."

"Watch out!" Lonnie jumped to her feet at the sound of another rock. In the twilight, and with strange patterns swirling across her vision, she struggled to find the racing stone.

Bally dove into her and they rolled through the grass. A massive, gray stone rumbled past them like a runaway bull. Lonnie turned as it crushed four more family members.

"You need to dive out of the way," she shouted at them. The dozen or so remaining men and women went running for their huts. "We better get out of here," Lonnie said.

"Do you still want to look in the door?" Bally asked.

"Yeah, but—"

"Come on. Just watch for the rocks." Bally led the way back. They dodged two more boulders, and once at the door, they realized the rocks had too much momentum to drop straight onto their heads. "Let's be quick," Bally said as she propped the spit back into the door. Lonnie stepped to her side and they rocked and pushed. The door groaned, the crack spreading in long fingers across the door. Finally, it burst open with a satis-fying *pop*.

Lonnie blinked to see through the swirling patterns in her vision. She pulled the door the rest of the way open, squinting into the dark cavern inside the mountain. A sensation of hope filled her spirit. She gasped as a breath of sweet, summery air flowed out of the nothing before her.

"Someone's singing," Bally said. "Do you hear it?"

Lonnie frowned, turning an ear to the cavern. It took a minute, but she too heard the singing. The soft voice trilled through notes of a minor melody. It sang in a language Lonnie couldn't understand. Each word pushed a fresh breath from the cavern. Lonnie turned to Bally.

"Should we go in?" she asked.

"We didn't break it open to smell it," Bally said. She stepped forward, creeping into the black void of the mountain's heart. Lonnie followed her with a head full of wondrous music.

"Look," Lonnie said. "Someone's coming." She pulled Bally back, leaning over her shoulder.

A dark form appeared from the dark end of the tunnel. Lonnie squinted, unable to make out any details.

"It looks like a man," Bally said. As the cavern filled with the scent of coconut, Lonnie gasped.

"It smells like Lahn," she said. "Lahn, is that you?"

The approaching form said nothing.

"He's trying to trick us," Bally said. "I'll get a torch." She raced back outside, leaving Lonnie alone with the stranger.

Lonnie swayed as a spell of dizziness took over her body. She steadied herself on the cavern's walls. Nausea and terror gripped her. The singing had stopped, leaving only the soft padding of feet on the hard-packed dirt. Lonnie swallowed as the approaching man's form grew with his approach.

"Lahn?" she called.

A bright light splashed onto the walls from behind her. She turned, expecting the sun to come hurtling into the cavern and crush her.

But Bally tripped into her, holding up a flaming stick. "The torch," she said. She stepped beside Lonnie and extended the flame into the cavern. Lonnie squinted as she snuggled into Bally's side. The stranger marched without fear of the light.

Both women let out a gasp as the Munk himself stepped forward. He wore a green tunic, with white and yellow flowers woven across his breast and arms. The light flashed in his narrow eyes.

"Are you real, or is this the mushrooms?" Lonnie asked.

"Why haven't you killed the Hundledun already?" Bally asked. "He's a menace."

The Munk stopped five feet before them. He scowled as he looked from Lonnie to Bally. Lonnie glanced to his hands, shivering at the dark fur covering his fingers. A spike of fear came into her as the Munk turned his hand to reveal a long, crooked blade.

"He's got a knife," she whispered to Bally.

"Who are you?" Bally asked. "What gives you the right to torture all of these poor people?" She stepped forward, paying no mind to the knife. "Look at you. You dress like a priest, and you're not even a real monkey. Oh my God. Lonnie, I just figured it out."

"What?" Lonnie asked.

"It's Lahn. He's been wearing a mask." Bally laughed, her mind seemingly determined to make light of the mushrooms. "Is this your game? Scare us into being your little pets? I bet the Hundledun is just you rolling rocks down the mountain. Come to think of it, it conveniently never attacks when you're in the Shrine. Go on, Lahn. Take off that mask. We know it's you."

The Munk's face shifted, his eyes so big and glistening

Lonnie still couldn't laugh it off. He lunged forward and swung his blade into Bally.

But Bally ducked aside and parried a fist into the Munk's nose. With a grunt, he fell flat on the floor. Lonnie and Bally stepped over him as blood dribbled from his snout.

"Take that silly mask off," Bally said. She crouched and helplessly tugged at the Munk's neck. Grunting, she tore his tunic open to find a chest covered in fine, dark fur. "Oh," she said, frowning as she turned to Lonnie. "Mr. Munk?" she asked, giving him a soft tap on the chest.

"How hard did you hit him?" Lonnie asked.

"As hard as I could," Bally said.

Lonnie pressed her ear to the Munk's chest, unable to find a heartbeat. She jumped as the knife fell from his hand with a dull thump.

"Well." Bally lifted the knife and turned to the dark corridor. "Should we go into the portal? I don't think we have to worry about the Munk."

"He was real," Lonnie said, her own heart taking up the Munk's missing beats. Her vision filled with flashes of red patterns. "Shit. That means the portal is real."

"Yes, so are we—?"

"I'm scared."

"Of what? We don't know what's in it. Lahn goes through all the time, so it can't be dangerous." Bally picked up her torch and started walking, moving with a curious excitement. "Come on, Lonnie."

Lonnie could hardly breathe. She turned from Bally to the Munk, who seemed to be withering away before her eyes. His face shrank and started to wrinkle. The hair molted from his chest and fluttered with the breeze, twirling into barber's shavings across Lonnie's feet.

"I think we should go," she called to Bally.

"Oh, don't be such a chicken," Bally shouted.

But the mountain rumbled, trembling and shaking so hard dirt fell from the cavern's wall. It knocked Lonnie to her knees. She turned to Bally, whose face finally shifted from glee to reasonable fright.

"We shouldn't be in here," Lonnie said.

"I guess not," Bally said, rushing back to meet her. By the time she met Lonnie, the Munk had shriveled to a wrinkled skin. The rumbling and booming only deepened with the Munk's disintegration. As rocks and great clods of dirt broke loose from the cavern, Lonnie and Bally fled for the door.

"My heart's going to explode," Lonnie shouted.

"Mine, too," Bally said, although she laughed as she said it. They raced the last dozen feet and dove back into the Shrine. As they sat, they turned just in time to see the cavern completely collapse. The symbols and runes in the mountain wall began the crumble. They fell in a soily rain and misted Lonnie, who led Bally back from the wall.

"We need to get out of here," she said. "If the Munk was real, then—"

"*The Hundledun!*" Lahn screamed. He came charging up the path, the wicker gate left open in his panic. Rocks and stones dropped from the mountain around him. He looked incredibly brave and handsome as he spotted Lonnie and Bally. "We're not safe," he cried. "We have to—"

A great log fell from the sky. In Lonnie's mushroom poisoning, it seemed to float for a full minute before crashing down on Lahn. The impact broke their beautifully naked leader's spine and he fell to the ground twitching. A streak of green lightning splashed the scene with horrific clarity.

Lonnie took Bally's hand and they raced for the gate. Stones continued to rain, but the runaways kept to the wall, where only mud and dirt could reach them. Both women ran for their lives. They stopped when they came to Lahn, who twitched and groaned in agony.

"Please," he hissed. "Peet, call the Munk and get help. You have to stop the Hundledun."

"I might have killed the Munk," Bally said. "I'm sorry, Lahn, but we have to go." She dragged Lonnie onward, leading her through the gate and onto the trembling mountainside. The quaking ground left Lonnie stumbling. She turned over her shoulder as another bolt of lightning flashed. The entire mountain top lit up, and there, on the very peak stood a crooked beast so big and horrendous Lonnie's feet came out from under her.

She rolled and tumbled down the mountainside. Bally shouted and chased after her. It took a full minute to come to a stop. Lonnie gasped as she rolled to her hands and knees, frowning to find seven fingers on each of her hands.

"Are you all right?" Bally asked. She skidded to her knees beside Lonnie.

"I saw the Hundledun," Lonnie said. "He's real and he's on the mountain."

"Then we should keep running."

A chain of thunder boomed from above. Lonnie turned as lightning flashed. The Hundledun's gargantuan form moved for them. It crashed down the mountain with terrifying speed. Lonnie grasped onto Bally and they screamed, both falling to the ground as the Hundledun swept over them.

It stood taller than a house, with a body wrapped in waxy flesh. Its head drifted toward them like a shattered rock; the eyes as big as moons. The monstrous jaw drew open to reveal three rows of thick, rotting teeth. Lonnie breathed so fast she grew lightheaded. Purple and yellow spirals flashed in her peripheral vision.

The Hundledun let out a long, guttural growl. It slapped a

hand against the earth and leaned forward, misting the runaways with breath so full of rot and piss Lonnie gagged.

"We're on your side," Bally shouted. She dropped Lonnie's hand and stood, meeting the Hundledun face-to-face. "Don't you understand? We've killed the Munk for you. Lahn's dying, and so are most of the others. The Shrine is crumbling."

The Hundledun lifted his head, turning over his shoulder.

"Go and see," Bally said. "The Munk's in the cave, so you'll have to dig him out, but he's there. I killed him myself. With one punch, too."

The Hundledun roared as he turned back to Bally, pressed his oozing nose into her belly.

"Get the hell off me," Bally said, giving him a slap. "I'm so sick of this. Come on, Lonnie, we're leaving." She dragged Lonnie off the ground, not bothering to give the Hundledun a second glance as she started back down the trail. Lonnie, ever curious, couldn't help but turn back.

The Hundledun sat in a squat on the mountainside, frowning as it turned from the Shrine to the women who destroyed it.

"We better run," Bally said. "Just to be safe."

So they ran, as fast as they could manage with the mushroom poisoning growing ever stronger. Lonnie could hardly see through the swirling patterns and creatures in her vision. For a while a pack of horse-legged turtles joined their flight down the mountain. When the turtles ran on, a team of wheeled demons took their place. They fled with graceful symmetry, laughing as they mocked her.

"You'll never get back," one shouted, throwing a handful of fire at her feet. "No one comes back from this."

"Your mind was mush before the mush," another said. "Now it's simply soup."

"Make them stop," Lonnie shouted, but Bally was in deep

conversation with an invisible ally on her other side. She laughed and laughed as they sprinted through the night. Lonnie finally closed her eyes, hoping the mushroom's poison would be enough to keep her on her feet.

It worked until it didn't. Lonnie took an unexpected short step and crashed flat on her face. She gasped as the wind fell from her lungs. Bally crumpled beside her. They lay for a while catching their breath. Lonnie lost the ability to think and worked her mouth like a puppet for a few minutes. Her arms and legs kicked and flailed without her consent. She found a glimpse of sanity and screamed.

Bally laughed beside her.

"It's here," she said. "I Know it's here. I feel it. Help me look."

"For what?" Lonnie asked. She tried to stand and rolled back to the ground. An iron spike shot through the earth between her legs. She screamed, rolling her head to find Bally.

Bally stood before the stone monolith. She set a wooden crate upon it, laughing as she broke the top open, throwing splinters of wood aside. Lonnie crawled after her using only her toes and fingertips.

"Lonnie," Bally said. "I've got it." She lifted a trim, pointy stick over her head. The end sparked with a purple ember. "And it remembers," she cried, breaking into a cackle so fierce Lonnie stopped crawling.

"Help," Lonnie mumbled into the earth. A great song, played by a thousand beasts came through the dirt. It plucked on her heartstrings and rattled her soul.

"I believe this belongs to you," Bally said, crouching beside Lonnie. She grinned, her skin pale and sweaty, her face filled with wrinkles that hadn't existed before. Lonnie tried to back away but Bally took her hands and set Daniel's wooden heart carving between them.

PART THREE
LET'S DO SOMETHING FUN

TWENTY-TWO

Lonnie woke in the middle of a rainstorm. Her brain tingled with aftershocks of the mushroom poison, and she hardly had the strength to keep her eyes open. She groaned as the rain beat upon her. Each drop sent a shockwave of pain and pleasure through her body. She closed her eyes and tried to go back to merciful sleep.

It didn't work.

For two days Lonnie lay on the ground and groaned. As she regained control of her fingers she played with the grass, but the rest of her body remained useless. Every once in a while she heard a troubled grunt from somewhere nearby.

Her memory came and went. Sometimes she replayed the insanity of her escape from the Shrine, and sometimes she thought she was a rock, enjoying a tiny piece of eternity on the Seregile Mountainside.

On the third day, her brain snapped with a spark of heat so frightening she remembered how to scream. Panting, she surged upright, her mouth slack as she looked across the platform of stones.

Bally lay not three feet beside her. Her eyes were wide, her lips bouncing like a dying fish in the grass. Lonnie tentatively shifted to her knees, paranoid she would lose control of her body. But she managed to stand, and once standing, it didn't take too much effort to walk to Bally.

"Alive?" Lonnie mumbled.

Bally nodded, her face locked in a permanent turmoil.

"Stuck?" Lonnie waved to Bally's body, and she nodded again. "I got loose. You might too." Lonnie winced from the pain of speaking. She coughed, sending a fistful of blood through her lips. It filled her with terror, and the terror brought on a flash of patterns; swirling designs not unlike those carved by the Munk three hundred years before.

Lonnie turned across the platform, her panic easing at the sight of Daniel's heart. She grunted as she shuffled toward the carving. While slightly swollen from the rain, it remained intact. Lonnie burst into tears as she lay on the grass and held it against her belly. It served to heal her; the warmth of Daniel's soul touching her despite the poison in her veins.

Bally screeched like a bird of prey as she lurched upright. Lonnie turned, her mind going blank at the sight of her naked companion.

"Food," Bally groaned. She bobbed in her weakness. "Need . . . a . . . lot . . . of . . . food."

"Yes." Even without a mind, Lonnie's body knew enough to agree. "How?"

Bally stiffened, searching the grass around her. She rolled to her hands and knees and crawled. With a desperate snort, she lifted her stubby stick. She grinned as she held it. Lonnie wondered if it too might be a carving from a lover, and the thought brought her back into herself.

"We . . . need food," she said. "And water."

"The woods." Bally pointed her stick down the mountain, where the canopy of forest spread like a great quilt. They wobbled to their feet and met each other.

"I'm not well," Lonnie admitted.

"Aye," Bally agreed. She lazily waved to the woods again, and with a nod, Lonnie followed.

They shuffled their way down the mountain. Every muscle in Lonnie's body throbbed. Physical movement reinvigorated the mushroom poison, but Lonnie had become accustomed to it. She blinked until the flashing colors faded from her vision. As they came into the trees, she felt an enormous relief to be out of the sun. Three days of naked sunbathing had left her raw and shockingly pink.

"Water," Bally said as she caught up with Lonnie.

"Where?" Lonnie asked.

"Don't know. Just need."

Lonnie had enough sense to know water ran down hill, so she led them deeper into the forest, searching for denser patches of greenery. They found a stream an hour later. Both escapees dropped to their bellies at its edge. With desperate greed, they dunked their heads and drank all their stomachs could hold. Lonnie rolled to her back as the water seeped into her body.

"It's fighting the mushrooms," she said, managing a smile. "It's pushing them out."

"Good." Bally remained on her belly, determined to keep filling herself.

They camped beside the stream for the rest of the day, drinking and drinking. Lonnie finally had to make water by sunset. She released a ghastly splash of urine across a patch of elephant ears. As she shivered, groaning as she squatted, her body flushed with a warm comfort. Her mind still shifted in the aftermath of its tremendous poisoning, but she could see through to her old self.

"I'm getting better," she said as she stumbled back into camp. Bally had finally rolled to her back, with both hands folded across her swollen belly. She lifted a thumb in reply. "Do you have any ideas for finding food?" Lonnie asked. "Or should we wait until the morning?"

"We need to do something fun," Bally said. "We deserve some fun after all we've been through."

"Okay. But what about food?" Lonnie winced as she slunk back to the cool mud. "You can't have fun when you're this hungry."

"Then we should sleep. We might find some flowers to eat, but we're going to have to leave the forest to find real food. Where did you say you're from?"

"Doane," Lonnie said.

"That's only a day's walk."

"But the king wants to kill me. That's why I ran away in the first place. They put up signs with my portrait."

"But they don't know me," Bally said. "I could go in and get food for us."

"It's too risky," Lonnie said. "Where are you from?" She turned to Bally, her attention settling on the carved stick in her hand. In her dawning sanity, she realized it might be a wand. "Aren't you some kind of witch? Can you do a spell to make food?"

"Conjuring is a fairytale for children. I'm from East Ballick. And they drove me out of town, too. Although, they really just suggested I leave."

"Then let's go to East Ballick. We'll get food and figure out what to do next."

"You know," Bally said, grinning as she rolled to face Lonnie. "We could have a lot of fun in East Ballick. They're scared to death of me."

"What did you do to scare them?"

"Whatever I wanted, really."

"What kind of magic can you do? I've never seen it in person, aside from whatever just happened at the Shrine. King Pollock doesn't allow it in the kingdom. He declared it unnatural and dangerous."

"The same king who eats people?" Bally asked.

"Him and his son, *Prince Pollen Bane VI.*"

"Sounds like a real cunt." Bally lifted her wand, raking patterns in the air over her head. "My magic is different," she said, flicking her wrist. A purple spark shot from the tip of the twiggy wand. It arced across the twilight dim and sizzled out in the stream. "I'm a bit destructive."

"What do you mean?" Lonnie asked.

"Have you ever met a witch?"

"Just you."

"Well, most witches spend their time trading potions and healings for whatever they can get. We're born with a deep connection to the other side."

"What's the other side?"

"It's like where the Munk came from, I guess. I don't know, I've never been. Do you know the legend of the first witch?"

"No." Lonnie leaned up on her elbows.

"According to the legend, the very first witch figured out a way to make a deal with the dead. She traded her afterlife in exchange for power in this world. It was the first of many witch trades."

"Is that how all witches get their powers?"

"Of course not. Who in their right mind would want that? The first witch made a generational deal. Supposedly, anyone born a witch is a descendant of hers, so whether they like it or not, they're in on the deal."

"So you won't have an afterlife?"

"I don't know," Bally said, blushing a little. "I don't like to think about it. I'm a witch, so if the legend is true, then yes, but it could just be a fairy tale."

"That's not fair," Lonnie said.

"Well, even if it is true, it's not all bad. It's pretty fun being a witch."

"How?"

"Why don't I just show you?"

"Okay."

"I'll show you in East Ballick. We'll have fun." Bally smiled as she rolled onto her belly, slurping a few mouthfuls of water. "I need food before I start performing magic. And clothes. I hate being naked."

"I want clothes, too," Lonnie said. "I had an extra dress with me, but Lahn must have hidden it after I ate the first mushroom."

"We'll get beautiful dresses in East Ballick," Bally said. "There's an excellent seamstress. I promise this much: we're going to have fun."

The women fell into a peaceful silence with the thought of covering their bodies in cotton. Lonnie still felt the occasional zip and zap of the mushroom poison, but every passing hour brought back more of herself. As her curiosity slowly stirred back into a frenzy, she found herself desperate to see Bally's magic in action.

Thankfully, it didn't take long.

TWENTY-THREE

The next morning, the women filled their bellies and headed east, following the sunrise through the forest. Lonnie's mind felt close to normal, and she smiled as they walked, thinking of how lucky they were to have escaped the Munk and Lahn and the Hundledun. Bally scowled with concentration. After an hour, she verbalized her thoughts.

"So you were married?" she asked.

"I was," Lonnie said. "Before the king killed my partner."

"What was it like?"

"Well." Lonnie didn't want to speak ill of the dead, or besmirch the rekindled love she had for Daniel in his passing, but Bally looked truly curious. "It was fun when we were young, but it became very boring after a while. We both worked all day, so we only spent the evenings together. He liked to carve beside the fire. I usually watched."

"That doesn't sound fun."

"It wasn't. I've always been adventurous, and I tried to get him to go out into the city with me, but all he wanted to do was sit in his damn chair and whittle away wood blocks."

"Why didn't you just go out?"

"The king ordered a curfew. The one time I snuck out I got caught and they lashed Daniel for it. That was the night before they killed him."

"Your king sounds like a massive cunt," Bally said. "Did he really trick the whole village into eating human meat?"

"Everyone who went to the festival," Lonnie said, her mouth tingling with memory of the salty meat.

"What did it taste like?"

"I don't like to think about it."

"It's not like you chose to eat it. Was it any good?"

"It tasted like very salty pork. It was cooked well, so there's that."

"You liked it," Bally said, grinning.

"I threw everything up as soon as I knew what it was," Lonnie said. "It was the most disgusting thing I've ever done in my life."

"I'd eat some right now if we had it." Bally set a hand to her belly, which currently resided in the shadow of her ribcage. "How far are we from the edge of the forest?"

"I don't know. I've never been to East Ballick."

They fell back into silence for a while. As the sun rose to center-sky, they fell on their instincts to keep their path eastward. Mercifully, they passed a few more streams which gave them something to put inside their stomachs.

As they continued through the woods, Lonnie asked, "do you think Lahn was really six hundred years old?"

"I guess he was," Bally said. "I mean, the Munk and the Hundledun were real. I just wish we had gone into the portal."

"It would have been dangerous."

"Yes, but if I'm the descendant of the first witch and live under her generational curse, I might have been able to barter my way out of it."

"You would have given up your powers?"

"I don't know, but I certainly would have appreciated the option."

"It's crazy how easily you killed the Munk."

"One punch," Bally said, grinning.

"Did you use magic?"

"I can't do magic without my wand. That was pure rage. And the mushrooms, I guess."

"How did we ever go along with all that? I should have ran when Lahn offered me the first mushroom."

"It's simple: we were sad and alone. People will believe anything when they're sad enough."

"What do you think happened to the others after we left?" Lonnie asked.

"I'm sure the Hundledun killed them, if they survived all the rocks."

"It's so sad."

"Those idiots got what they deserved. Some of them lived there for years."

"But the Munk and Hundledun were real. You said yourself that Lahn was probably six hundred years old."

"So? We've gone about our lives just fine before we wandered into their bubble of lunacy. I killed their great protector with one punch. How does someone hundreds of years old, from another realm, get bested by an ex-witch?"

"I guess he wasn't that smart," Lonnie said.

"The Munk might have been the dumbest one on the mountain."

"I wonder what happened to that poor girl who just joined. She must have been just starting her poisoning when it all came down."

"She's probably still running through the woods," Bally said, laughing. "If she's lucky, she took her clothes with her."

"Why couldn't we ask questions? That's what I really want to know."

"I thought it was kind of nice. But then again, I don't usually ask many questions. You, though—you can't stop."

"I'm curious by nature," Lonnie said.

"Hold on." Bally froze, turning from left to right. She

approached a great tree and set her hand upon its bark, sniffing the air.

"What is it?" Lonnie asked.

"Smoke." Bally swept through the brush, moving in a limpish run. Lonnie followed as fast as her emaciated body would allow. They struggled through the foliage until they came into a clearing, where a lone house sat like something out of a painting. Smoke drifted from the chimney, coughing out dark wisps of delightful smoke. A clothes line ran from the house, holding a collection of burly pants and jackets.

"What do you think?" Lonnie asked. "I don't see any women's clothes."

"That's a good thing," Bally said as she walked into the clearing.

"Why is that good?"

"Because if they don't see women too often, they'll be quite pleased to find two naked ones. At the least they'll feed us, and at best we'll have our clothes."

"What if they want to hurt us, or . . ."

"I killed the Munk with one punch," Bally said.

"Fair enough." Lonnie drew a breath as they crossed the clearing, hoping Bally's defensive abilities matched her confidence. Still, she did her best to drape her hair over her breasts.

TWENTY-FOUR

As they neared the house, the smell of burning oak came with a welcome companion: stew and wild game. Lonnie and Bally practically ran the last few paces to the door. They brushed the dirt from each other and Bally knocked. Lonnie huddled behind her.

But no one answered their knock. After repeating the wrap, they took a lap around both sides of the home, meeting at the clothes line.

"Help me up," Bally said, reaching for the line. Lonnie took a nervous glance to the curtained windows and pushed Bally up the wall. She drew the line and ripped half of the clothes free.

"They're huge," Lonnie said, lifting a pair of pants that could fit a party of women.

"It's something," Bally said. She pulled one of the giant shirts over her head and rolled the sleeves up. It made an ugly dress, but the beggars could not be choosers.

Once Lonnie dressed, Bally led the way back to the front door. She knocked again, frowning as the call went unanswered.

"Hello?" she called, leaning into a dark window. "See if the door is unlocked."

Lonnie pressed the latch and pushed. The door groaned on the hinge, squealing in the clearing like a tortured cat. Bally pushed past Lonnie and led the way inside.

The house opened into a dim kitchen with a large fireplace, where a kettle boiled over a bed of coals. Lonnie didn't pay attention to anything but the scent of meat and sustenance. She and Bally raced to the hearth and peered over the stew, finding a dark, bubbling brew.

"Bowls," Bally said, turning to the kitchen. "Big ones." She dug through the cupboard and came away with two large, wooden bowls. She snagged a ladle from the wash bucket and returned to the fire. "Hold this," she said, thrusting the bowls into Lonnie's hands. Before Lonnie had a good grip she started ladling the strew into the bowls. She scooped with greed, drawing big chunks of game and potatoes from the bottom of the pot. Lonnie's mouth watered as her bowl ran over. She only came out of her trance when the boiling broth dripped across her toes.

"Damn," she said, stepping back. "Come on, it's full enough."

They spilled a trail of stew across the floor and set the bowls on the table. With desperation, they blew onto the incredibly hot stew. Steam and soon-to-be-wonderful memories drifted into the air. Lonnie dipped a finger into the broth and yelped. As she sucked on her burned finger, the salty, delectable stew left her sweating.

"Let's find something else while it cools," Bally said, turning to the cupboard. She climbed onto the counter and ransacked the place, finding nothing in the way of sustenance. Lonnie took a moment to peer out the door. She glanced across the clearing, relieved to find it empty.

"Did you find anything?" she asked, turning back to Bally.

"Flour," Bally said. She dropped a sack on the counter. "But no water."

"Would it cool down the stew?"

"Let's see." Bally dumped the sack on the table between their bowls. Without ceremony, she poured her stew across the flour, leaning in as it hydrated into a brown slurry. Bally went to work massaging the rest of the flour into it. After a minute she had a mass of ugly paste.

But it was cooler than hot, and both women went to work shoving great plugs of it into their mouths. They scraped every last bit off the table. By the time they finished, Lonnie's stew had cooled, and they took turns sucking it straight from the bowl.

"More," Bally said, grabbing the empty bowls. "Get the ladle."

"I'm pretty full," Lonnie said. But she took up the ladle and refilled the bowls. Her body trembled with a belly full of food. She felt sick and lightheaded, but strength started to etch its way across her body. By the time they finished their second bowls, they were both lost in a fit of giggles.

"It's drowning out the last of that mushroom haze," Bally mused, patting her belly as she sat back. "I think starving was making it worse."

"I'll be happy to never eat another mushroom again," Lonnie said. She let out an uncontrollable belch and covered her mouth. Bally laughed.

"Nice," she said, tapping her finger onto a missed spot of flour. She sucked it clean. "We had amazing luck finding this place."

"No kidding. Clothes and food?"

"Now we just need a bed." Bally turned over her shoulder, eyeing the door leading into the back of the house. "Interested in a quick nap?"

"I could sleep for three days after that stew," Lonnie said. "But whoever lives here is coming home, and they're big." Lonnie lifted the slack of her dress-shirt, which even after the feast could accommodate a few more people. "We should move on."

"We'll just take a peek," Bally said. "Come on." She groaned as she slipped off her chair and made her way to the back door. Lonnie could barely keep her eyes open as she followed. She wanted to argue and push for a swift retreat, but Bally didn't give her a chance.

The door dragged across the floor as she pushed it open. The only light in the room came from a small tear in the curtain, which allowed a beam of golden light to expose a massive, perfectly dressed bed in the center of the room. Bally and Lonnie wandered forward without a word, their sagging heads confessing the truth of their situation.

"He might come home," Lonnie said as she pulled back the covers.

"It's inevitable," Bally said. She climbed into bed, giving her pillow a few punches before settling into it. "No one who makes stew like that would leave it for long."

"He might not like to come home and find our mess." Lonnie pulled the cushy, pine-scented covers over them. "Even if we are half-naked."

"I don't imagine anyone would be happy to see what we've done." Bally dropped her head into the pillow, stretching out beneath the covers. "This bed must be stuffed with feathers," she said, massaging the mattress.

"Or cotton," Lonnie said. "I've heard kings sleep on cotton."

Bally laughed and said something. Lonnie laughed and mumbled nonsense back to her.

They slept without dreams.

When Lonnie opened her eyes, she couldn't see anything but the flickering firelight from the open doorway. She winced at her stomach ache. Beside her, Bally snored with disturbing depth. Lonnie sat up and listened, paranoid they may not be alone, but only the cracking fire could be heard. She lay back down and decided they shouldn't press their luck.

And then she woke up again, this time hungry.

"Bally?" she asked, slapping across the blankets.

"Quiet," Bally whispered, pressing a hand over Lonnie's lips. "Someone's here."

Lonnie's haze burned off and she stared at the open door.

A shadow crossed the firelight, accompanied by heavy footfalls. The stranger frantically paced across the kitchen.

"We need to get out of here," Lonnie whispered. "Before he finds us."

"Just wait," Bally said, holding up a finger. She held her wand in the other hand, and wanting a talisman of her own, Lonnie took Daniel's carving from the night stand.

The stranger grunted with annoyance.

A loud bang followed.

Lonnie slid her legs over the side of the bed, turning to the bedroom window.

"Wait," Bally said, taking hold of her arm.

"He's going to find us," Lonnie said. "He's getting angry, and he sounds huge."

"There's one more thing I need from him." Bally whipped the covers off. "Come on. This shouldn't take long."

"What are you going to do?" Lonnie trembled as she climbed out of bed. She took hold of Bally. "This is insane. What are—?"

"Be quiet," Bally hissed. "Just let me do the talking. You'll thank me later." She led the way to the bedroom door, giving her frazzled hair a quick hand-combing, and stepped into the kitchen. Lonnie squeezed Daniel's carving tight, with no other choice but to follow.

TWENTY-FIVE

Lonnie stepped to Bally's side and faced the man they had robbed. He stood nearly eight feet tall. His arms were so massive they looked like veined tree trucks. He hadn't noticed them in his confusion; he stood at the table with a barrel of what looked to be beer, frowning as he stared at the mess from their floury confection.

"Hey," Bally said.

The man stiffened, but didn't turn.

"We made a bit of a mess," Bally continued. "We were hungry, and the door was open."

"I just cleaned the place . . ." The mountainous man turned, his face lined with age, his hair spotted with gray. "Are those my shirts?"

"They are," Bally said. "We were cold and needed clothes."

"I just washed them . . ." A great misery filled the man's eyes. "Why didn't you ask me first? I'm a kind man. I would have offered it."

"You weren't home and we didn't feel like waiting."

"I have a job. I needed to work."

"I'm sorry," Lonnie said. "We just escaped a camp and were starving. They left us with nothing. Your stew saved our lives."

"Did you like it?" the man asked. "Was the seasoning okay?"

"It was delicious." Lonnie smiled as the man did, but Bally cast her a dangerous glare. "What?" Lonnie whispered.

"He's *mine*," Bally hissed. She walked into the kitchen,

glancing over the dribbles of soup and spillage. "Do you live alone?" she asked the stranger.

"Well," he said, turning to the fire. "I suppose I do, now that Angela's gone."

"Was she your wife? I saw the portrait in the bedroom."

"She was. We were married for forty years." The man took a drink from his barrel. He shifted into a seat at the table, hunching forward with a terrible despair. "We were married for forty beautiful years."

"I'm sorry," Lonnie said. "I recently lost my husband. My name is Lonnie."

"I'm Kegan," the man said. "I'm sorry to hear about your widowage. It's nice to know I'm not alone."

Bally stepped beside Lonnie and slipped a hand around her back. She pinched her skin, hard enough to let Lonnie know she was displeased with her.

"What?" Lonnie asked.

"*Let me have him*," Bally said. She turned, the severity of her gaze sending Lonnie back a step. "So, Kegan," she continued, approaching the table. "Did you and Angela have any children?"

Kagan sighed, slumping back into the table. "We wanted to, and we tried. It just never happened."

Lonnie, sharing a similar regret, wanted to run up and hug Kegan, but Bally's animosity left her immobile.

"So it's just you here?" Bally asked. "Living all alone? Cooking bad stew and eating it all by yourself?"

"Yes," Kagan whispered. "I'm worried I may be too old to find anyone."

"You're also freakishly big." Bally leaned into the table, looking like a child in the shadow of Kegan. Her vulgarity left Lonnie speechless.

"I know what I am," the giant man said. He let out a long

breath, his face breaking as he turned to Bally. "Why have you come to torture me?"

"I'm simply an agent of truth," Bally said.

"What truth?"

"You're past your happiness, Kegan. I'm sorry, but I can't lie to you. You're alone and you'll remain so. This home is only haunted by the ghosts of your past. Working and cooking will never bring back Angela. Was that her recipe?"

"Twas," Kegan breathed, sniffing back tears. "I thought I had it right this time . . ."

"It tasted like bath water. Is that what you want Angela to see—you bastardizing the food she once made out of love? You're just fooling yourself."

"I know." Kagan glanced at Lonnie with a horrendous guilt in his eyes. Lonnie almost burst into tears then and there, but Bally turned with wide eyes and gritted teeth, and the direction was clear.

"We're going to leave you now," Bally said, facing Kegan.

"Please," he breathed. "Don't let me be alone. I can try to make the stew again."

"You and I both know that's not going to happen." Bally shook her head as she surveyed the home. "I'm sorry we ever came. This place is so cold. And lifeless."

Finally, Kagan could contain his misery no longer and burst into tears, pounding the table with a fist as he wailed. To Lonnie's surprise, Bally swept to his side, actually climbing up into his lap.

"Oh, it's okay," she said, wrapping her arms around his neck. "Let it out. It's okay."

Kegan howled, with great tears streaming down his cheeks. Bally quickly wiped them away. As she began sucking the tears off her fingers, Lonnie frowned. She thought it was a mistake until Bally did it again, and again, and again. Bally shifted to her knees and pressed her cheek to Kegan's. He wept inconsolably as he held her. Bally licked the tears straight from his cheek.

Lonnie turned away, unable to make sense of the disturbing scene. She walked to the door and took one last look, making awkward eye contact with Bally as she licked Kegan's cheek. Bally's eyes were fierce and alive. Her greed and energy left Lonnie terrified.

Lonnie ran out the door and faced the moon, her heart pounding, her head spinning with curious disgust. Inside the house, Kagan continued to wail.

Lonnie didn't understand Bally's game, and she didn't need to. She took off running across the clearing. To see her newfound friend fizzle into a maniacal bitch hurt on multiple levels, and in the wake of the mushroom poisoning, she couldn't handle the emotional overload.

But just as she made it to the tree line, a shout came from the house. Lonnie turned to find Bally's silhouette in Kegan's door frame.

"Lonnie," Bally shouted. "Wait."

Lonnie ignored the call and fled. She tripped over twigs and foliage, desperate to escape the insanity. A few minutes into the run she snagged on a bramble and nearly fell. In the tussle, Daniel's carving slipped out of her hands and tumbled into the shadow.

"Lonnie," Bally called, her voice closing in.

"No," Lonnie breathed, crawling through the leaves, swatting for the smooth piece of wood. She found it tucked against a fallen tree limb. Just as she slipped it under her arm, Bally crashed through the brush beside her.

TWENTY-SIX

"Lonnie," Bally said, panting to catch her breath. "Let me explain." Her wand glowed, underlighting her face with a ghastly shade of purple.

"Leave me alone," Lonnie said as she broke back into a run. She could barely see in the mid-night forest, but Bally had no problem keeping pace.

"Stop this," she said. "Lonnie, let me explain. Everything will make sense. I had to do it."

"Why?" Lonnie snapped. She turned, angry enough to punch Bally in the nose. "Why were you so nasty to him? His soup was good. He was nice."

"I didn't have a choice," Bally said. She tried to take Lonnie's hands but Lonnie backed off. "Fine." she sighed, shaking her head. "I had to charge my magic, okay? We're going to need it if we're going into East Ballick."

"What the hell does that even mean? You crushed his soul."

"I needed him to weep. I didn't ask for my magic, and I certainly didn't make the rules of it. But they are what they are. I need tears to do what I can do."

"So you talk a stranger to the edge of self-annihilation?" Lonnie asked. "You could have asked me. I cry every time I think of Daniel."

"It only works with male tears," Bally said.

"What the hell kind of magic do you do?"

"*Occumancy.*"

"What does that mean?"

"I'll show you as soon as we get to East Ballick—I don't want to waste it here."

"No." Lonnie gritted her teeth, unable to entertain any more lunacy. "I'm sorry, but I can't do this. That was horrible."

"Do you think I like it?" Bally asked.

"Actually, yes. I do. You acted like you were drinking fine wine off his face."

"*I was born this way*. Do you know how much shame I feel every time I have to charge? Why do you think I gave up my clothes and wand to live at the Shrine? Lonnie, I need a friend. Please, don't leave me like everyone else." Bally broke into tears, her wand swinging low at her side. "*Please*. We were supposed to go out and have fun together."

"I'm just trying to survive," Lonnie said. "I can't handle this."

"You didn't even see what actually happened. After Kegan cried, we talked. I told him it's going to get better. I told him the soup was incredible."

"Are you lying?"

"No. He felt better after having a good cry. Sometimes it helps."

"I don't know," Lonnie turned to the woods, the dark, endless Seregile woods. "I'm trying very hard to escape my trouble."

"And destiny put us together for a reason," Bally said. "Kegan told me the way to East Ballick. We're only a few hour's walk. We can be there by sunrise, and once we get into town I'll show you what Occumancy is. We'll have the most fun you've ever had in your life. I promise, Lonnie. You just have to trust me."

Lonnie sighed, turning back to Bally. Nothing wholesome could come of an ability that required male tears to engage, but her curiosity roared like a bonfire. She met Bally and looked her in the manic eyes.

"Did you really tell Kegan his stew was good?" she asked.

"Of course I did," Bally said. "We were laughing before I realized you ran off."

"And you know how to get to East Ballick?"

"We'll be there by sunrise."

Lonnie turned to Daniel's carving, wondering what he might say if advising such a decision.

"I can give you a last word with him," Bally said, setting her hand on the carving. "Come with me and I can show you many great things."

"I just want to be happy again," Lonnie whispered. "But every step I take only makes my pain worse."

"That's why you're going to follow me. Let me show you what fun is. We'll have the adventure of a lifetime. I promise, you'll never be the same."

"East Ballick?"

"East Ballick." Bally smiled, offering her hand.

Reluctantly, Lonnie took hold of it and they walked.

They moved through the moonlit woods in silent contemplation. Lonnie had an incredible amount of energy after eating real food and sleeping in a cozy bed. They effortlessly crossed miles before the sun rose. When it did, breaking dawn and illuminating the forest, Lonnie spotted golden wheat fields beyond the trees. She and Bally raced into the sun.

"Do you know where we are?" Lonnie asked. She turned across the field, where wheat stretched endlessly in every direction.

"We're almost home," Bally said. "East Ballick is fertile, and we have some of the largest crops on the entire continent. Come on."

They ran through the wheat until they tired. Bally ripped a

few stalks from the soil and scraped the wheat from the chaff. She grinned, stuffing it into her mouth. She pulled another handful and passed it to Lonnie.

"I just eat it?" Lonnie asked.

"It's like bread," Bally said. She laughed, her face bright and full of life in the sun. The animalistic tear-drinker of the night had left her, and Lonnie grew curious, turning to her wand.

"Can you show me your magic now?"

"We're going to need it in town, but yes." Bally lifted her wand, the tip permanently alight with a tiny, purple glow. "I'll show you a quick trick. Stand still."

Lonnie stopped, her hands trembling as she faced Bally. Bally looked her straight in the eyes and the manic glint returned to her gaze. She smirked, cocking her head as she lifted her wand.

"Is this going to hurt?" Lonnie asked.

"That depends," Bally said. "I'll keep it light, for your first time." She lifted her wand between them. As the tip flashed bright green, Lonnie couldn't help but turn to it. "Up here," Bally said. "Look at me, Lonnie."

Lonnie lifted her gaze and screamed.

The Munk stood before her, his sinister scowl as menacing as ever; his eyes both massive and narrow. He snarled as he stepped forward.

"You killed me," he breathed. But the voice was soft and feminine. He broke into a strange grin, and then began howling with laughter. Lonnie stumbled back in fear of the mushroom poisoning reinfecting her mind.

Or worse, leaving a permanent ripple.

"Lonnie," Bally said, still laughing. The Munk's anamorphic face shifted into Bally's and Lonnie frowned, blinking against the strangeness of it. "Did you see him?"

"What the hell just happened?" Lonnie asked.

"Occumancy." Bally gave her a little wave as she laughed. "Do you understand?"

"You can shapeshift?"

"No, that's impossible," Bally said. "Occumancy is the art of fooling the eyes. Basically, I can make others see whatever I want them to see. I can change myself, or make them see others as something they're not. It's endless fun, really."

"So, if someone else just watched us, they would have only seen you as you, and not the Munk?" Lonnie asked.

"Yes. Unless they looked at my wand while I cast the spell. I can also create phantoms, but it takes a lot more energy."

"And human tears give you energy?"

"*Male* human tears," Bally said, shrugging. "Now do you understand why we're going to have fun?"

"Not really."

"Then allow me to show you. I'm the unofficial queen of East Ballick."

"It's a very strange ability," Lonnie said, thinking through the applications. "What do you do with it?"

"It depends on what I want," Bally said. "You'll see." She extended her hand, and with a growing desire to see Occumancy in action, Lonnie took it, marching alongside her strange, witchy friend to East Ballick.

CHAPTER
TWENTY-SEVEN

The city of East Ballick rose like a mirage out of the wheat. With tall, yellow-brick buildings, the city had an air of wealth about it. It stretched far and wide across flat plains. Hundreds of villagers moved about the dirt roads on horseback. Everyone dressed well, which suggested the peasant class was either well hidden or had ascended their birthright.

Bally led Lonnie down the main street and took in the sights with a nostalgic glow about her. It didn't take long for Lonnie to realize quite a few of the passersby recognized Bally. Some quickly moved to the other side of the street, and others made abrupt turns into the nearest alleyway. One old man dropped his pipe and gaped as he pointed at Bally, backing into the wall, his jaw bouncing in silent confoundment.

"Good to see you again, Larry," Bally said, giving him a sweeping bow. She cackled and waved Lonnie down a side street. "Did I tell you we have a great seamstress?" she asked. "What do you say we get out of these rags?" She tugged on Kegan's massive shirt.

"Okay," Lonnie said. "But I don't have any money."

"We have Occumancy," Bally said. "In East Ballick, it's as good as gold." She led the way to a long building with a raised entrance, where dresses and swatches of fabric hung in the open windows.

They barely stepped foot inside when the shopkeeper let out a shriek. The old woman cowered, holding out a needle as Bally approached the counter.

"*Love Eater*," the woman breathed. "You leave this place."

"My friend and I need new dresses," Bally said, surveying the merchandise. "The sooner we have what we need, the sooner we'll be on our way." She set her hand on the counter, revealing the glowing wand.

"Take what you want and go," the woman said. "Please."

"Thank you." Bally smiled, turning over her shoulder to Lonnie. "You heard her; take whatever you like. Find a nice travel bag for that carving, too."

"Are you sure?" Lonnie asked the troubled shopkeeper.

The old woman glanced from Bally to Lonnie and nodded, a crazed desperation in her eyes.

"Come on." Bally led Lonnie down an aisle of bright, summery dresses. They browsed for a while, holding the dresses up, laughing at the pomposity of some of the designs. Lonnie finally settled on a trendy green dress with gold trim. She picked out a slip and matching travel bag, and with the shopkeeper's blessing, changed behind a curtain in the back of the shop.

"What do you think?" she asked as she stepped out.

"It's strange to see you look so good," Bally said. She grinned, holding up two dresses. "What do you think? Blue or white?"

"Black would suit you," the shopkeeper mumbled.

"What was that?" Bally asked.

"I said that would suit you," the shopkeeper amended. "The blue."

"What do you think, Lonnie? The blue one?"

"I like it," Lonnie said. "Anything beats that horrendous shirt you're wearing."

"I'll try them both." Bally carried the dresses to the back, nearly bouncing in her glee.

Lonnie glanced at the shopkeeper, who anxiously worked

on her sewing. Her hands trembled so badly she made little progress. Lonnie made her way to the desk.

"It's free," the woman said, barely looking up from her work. "Just take it and be gone."

"Thank you," Lonnie said. "Your dresses are beautiful."

The woman nodded, taking a peek at the back of the shop. "What the devil are you doing with the Love Eater?" she asked. "Has she got you under a spell?"

"Bally's my friend," Lonnie said.

"Then you're crazy and a fool." The woman poked the needle into her thumb and hissed. "You take what you need and leave," she said, sucking on the blood. "I don't want any trouble."

Lonnie slinked from the counter and busied herself by studying the jackets, which looked to be as carefully constructed as everything else in the old woman's shop. She tried on a lovely overcoat and swished it around.

"Yes," Bally said from behind her. "You are definitely taking that."

Lonnie turned to find her once-naked friend in the blue dress, which favorably hugged her thin body. She did a little twirl and giggled as she reigned the swishing dress tails in.

"You like it?" she asked.

"It's beautiful," Lonnie said.

"Good. Then I just need a jacket and we'll be on our way." Bally found one that matched the style of Lonnie's, and with the satisfaction of spoiled princesses, they left the seamstresses shop.

"Why was that woman so afraid of you?" Lonnie asked.

"I'm kind of a big deal here," Bally said. She tucked her wand into her shiny new travel bag. "Fear is a sign of respect."

"Why did she call you the Love Eater?"

As Bally scowled, Lonnie half expected Bally to march back

into the shop and take retribution, but she only laughed. "Did she really?" she asked. "I haven't heard that one in a long time."

"What does it mean?"

"I don't really know. Come on, we need wine."

"It's still morning," Lonnie said.

"Then we'll get food and wine." Bally led Lonnie back to the main street, where the pedestrians greeted the newly tailored women with polite nods and winks. A few women noticed Bally and turned away in disgust. One man turned bright red and tripped over a picket fence.

"Can you please tell me why everyone is scared of you?" Lonnie asked.

"I'll tell you everything once we have some wine," Bally said. "And not everyone hates me. Come on, I'll show you." She waved Lonnie into a tavern, where a midday crowd settled in for lunch. They took a table in the back of the dining room with a helpful wall to hide them from the rest of the public.

"How are we going to pay for this?" Lonnie asked, turning to the large menu carved into the wall behind the bar.

"You don't get it, do you?" Bally asked. "I've never paid for anything in my life. You need to relax."

"I'm not used to this kind of place." Lonnie, who had considered it a blessing to eat more than once a day, had never set foot in a tavern. She and Daniel barely made enough money to pay for their shack, and her new outfit was a luxury of unfathomable depth.

"Ladies," a man said as he came to the table, smiling brightly. He froze when he recognized Bally. The color shifted from his cheeks. "*Love Eater,*" he breathed, clutching his shirt. "*The demon herself.*"

"I'll eat your children," Bally said, rising from the table. "I'll boil and mash them into a sausage."

"Demon!" the man cried, but he laughed, gasping and

wheezing as he pulled Bally into an embrace. "When the devil did you get back?" he asked. "I thought you were off on your vision quest?"

"I realized I'm better suited to society," Bally said, giving him a kiss on the cheek. "Derek, this is Lonnie Lovingdove, my friend."

"Lonnie, it's a pleasure to meet you." Derek offered his hand, and when Lonnie took it, he planted a whiskery kiss on top. "Welcome."

"Thank you," Lonnie said, still recovering from the faux missgreeting.

"What do you need, Bally?" Derek asked.

"We're pretty well starved," Bally said. "And we want a good barrel of wine."

"Do you have your wand?"

"It's right here." Bally lifted it, and at the sight of the glowing tip, Derek began to sweat. His eyes shifted to Bally's; the purple light aglow within them.

"Shall we transact?" he asked.

"Yes," Bally said. "Lonnie, pick what you want from the menu. I'll be right back." She and Derek headed into a door in the back of the bar. As Lonnie's mind turned with horrible ideas of what transactions one might make with an Occumancer, she focused on the menu to distract herself.

The King's pie sounded good at first glance, but a salty memory turned her off the idea. She settled on the mashed potatoes and boiled calf's meat. Her eyes shifted to the backroom as time continued to pass. She began to worry Bally might be in trouble. Then she feared Derek might be in worse trouble.

But they both returned laughing, Bally slapping Derek as he whispered something in her ear. They returned to the table as if nothing had happened. Lonnie couldn't help but notice the tip of Bally's wand still glowed with a hint of green.

"Did you decide what you want?" Bally asked.

"The mashed potatoes and calf's meat," Lonnie said. "And wine, I guess."

"Oh, you'll have wine," Derek said. "A barrel of East Ballick's darkest red. It's thick as honey, and almost as sweet. Bally, what do you want, Love?"

"The potatoes and calf sound fine." Bally sat back as Derek headed to the kitchen. She drew a breath and rested against the booth, smiling as she found Lonnie's puzzled gaze. "What?" she asked.

"What just happened?" Lonnie asked. "What did you two do?"

"I gave Derek something he can't get from anyone else. I promise, you'll understand everything by tomorrow morning. We'll be rich as kings by then."

"Does that mean we're going to steal again?"

"No, and what did we steal? That old hag gave us these clothes. You need to relax, Lonnie. Didn't you say you always wanted to go out on adventures?"

"Yes, but—"

"Then open your eyes. You're standing at the steps of an adventure you won't ever have again. You don't know what's going to happen, but it's going to be crazy. Just embrace it and have fun."

"You're right," Lonnie said, taking the travel bag off her shoulder. "I dreamed of being free all my life. I can't tell you how many times I sat at the hearth pinching my legs until I left marks; wanting to scream out of boredom. It's just . . . I miss Daniel. I feel so guilty for what happened to him."

"You didn't kill him," Bally said. "Your disgusting cunt of a king and his prince did, the man-eaters. You need to stop blaming yourself."

"The wine," Derek said, grinning as he carried a belly-sized barrel to the table. He plopped it down and hammered a tap into the bunghole. While he filled two tall glasses with thick, near-black liquid, Bally kicked Lonnie beneath the table. She grinned so hard her face aged by decades. Lonnie anxiously smiled back.

"To the Love Eater," Bally said, taking her glass.

"Cheers," Lonnie said. She lifted the glass and filled her mouth with a wine so strong and sweet she shivered. "Wow," she breathed, her breath already saturated with the alcohol. She looked up to find Bally's glass upside down, the last dregs of wine spiraling into her gullet.

Wanting to feel just a touch of Bally's freedom, Lonnie forced herself to chug the rest of her wine. Her belly rumbled with a fiery heat as she set the glass down. She burped and the candle on the table erupted with flame.

"Excuse me," Lonnie said, covering her mouth.

Bally took their empty glasses and proceeded to refill them. As she handed Lonnie's back, she leaned in, whispering toxic fumes into her ear.

"And so begins our adventure."

CHAPTER

TWENTY-EIGHT

The food came a few minutes later, but as the wine worked its way into Lonnie's blood, she found it hard to eat. Every panic and worry flushed straight out of her mind. She laughed, enjoying the way the world wobbled beneath her. Bally smiled like a Cheshire cat.

"Now you're starting to get it," she said, taking a bite of the boiled calf. "You have to eat, though. We've got a long night ahead of us, and it's barely noon."

"I'll try," Lonnie said. "I like this wine. A lot." She took another good swig, the thick juice melting another band of worry from her mind. "I didn't ever get to drink back home. Sometimes Daniel got a small bottle of wine from his slave master as a gift, but it was usually piss. This is good."

"The blood of grapes," Bally said, lifting her glass to the light. "A million berries slaughtered for a night of inebriated freedom."

"That was beautiful."

"It's on the barrel." Bally laughed, slapping her wand against the wine keg. "All right, eat up. We have a lot of work to do."

"What kind of work?" Lonnie shoved a few forkfuls of mashed potatoes into her mouth, pleasantly surprised to find the mush seasoned.

"Enough with the fucking questions," Bally said. "For the rest of the day, you're going back to Shrine rules. Don't worry, don't fret, just enjoy the ride and know that I have your best interest in mind."

"Fine," Lonnie said, pleased with the idea. She took another drink of the syrupy wine. "I'm excited to see what happens."

"As am I."

They spent another hour in the tavern and managed to not only clear their plates, but also split a generous serving of peach pie. Lonnie felt slightly sick from all the sugar, but once they were back outside, taking turns lugging the barrel of wine up the street, an overwhelming sense of confidence took over. She started to laugh as pedestrians leaped at the sight of Bally.

"Do you have any family?" Lonnie asked. "Are there other witches in East Ballick?"

"Thankfully, it's just me," Bally said. She had been carrying the wine, and starting to stagger under its weight, handed it back to Lonnie. "We need to get a cart or something," she muttered.

"And a horse," Lonnie said.

"Now you're thinking, and I know just the place." Bally cut down the next alleyway. A few blocks later they came to a small stable, where Bally opened the gate and led Lonnie into the barn. They found a grizzled old man with a hoof in his hands and a mouth full of tac. He froze at the sight of Bally.

"You're back," he mumbled, spitting the tac out. He let the horse wander off as he rose. "You said you were leaving for good."

"I thought I was," Bally said. "It's hard to quit East Ballick."

"It's been hard to quit you," the man said. He turned to Lonnie, frowning. "Who's this?"

"Lonnie Lovingdove, meet Bronson."

"Hi," Lonnie said, stumbling a little as she stepped forward to shake his hand. "I'm a friend of Bally's."

"Okay." Bronson nodded, turning back to Bally. "So what can I do for you?"

"We're going back to work tonight," Bally said. "I have a big barrel of wine, so I need a cart and some kind of beast to drag it. It's going to be a long night."

"Well." Bronson frowned, surveying the dim barn. "I might be able to find something, but—"

"I'm charged," Bally said. "Just tell me what and I'll take care of it."

Bronson's hands trembled as he glanced at the door.

"Is your wife home?"

"She's shopping."

"Then what are we waiting for?"

"I'm supposed to be a good boy. I told her I was done after you left." Despite his words, Bronson headed to the back of the barn, dragging a small cart out of one of the stalls. He hammered in some of the loose nails and gave it a few turns. "Are you okay with a pony?"

"As long as it's cute," Bally said. While Bronson went out into the gated yard, she leaned down and drew a mouthful of wine from the tap. At her insistence, Lonnie topped up as well.

"I'm trying really hard not to ask what we're doing here," Lonnie said. "It's difficult."

"You'll learn soon enough," Bally said. "I told you all witches are traders at heart. I just so happen to sell one of the more valuable experiences."

Bronson returned with a small, golden pony. The horse walked with a bubbly gait. Lonnie couldn't help but pet the little creature as Bronson hitched it to the wagon.

"What's her name?" she asked, running her fingers through the fluffy mane.

"Patrice," Bronson said. "She's a good girl. Just give her some water and rest when you can, because she's not much of a worker." He cinched down the mount and stepped back, setting his foot on the cart. It buckled but remained level. "Do you have a strap for that wine?" he asked.

"No." Bally heaved the barrel up on the cart, and Bronson fashioned a tie-down. "Now, what can I give you, my friend?" she asked as she stepped back, lifting her wand.

Bronson breathed heavily and glanced at the door.

"Can she leave?" he asked, tipping his head toward Lonnie.

"No, Lonnie's my friend. Just tell me what you want. She's not going to judge you, right Lonnie?"

"Of course not," Lonnie said. She smiled, her arm still wrapped around the pony.

"Fine." Bronson walked to the door and leaned out, surveying the streets with the care of a city watchman. Finally, with still-trembling fingers, he returned to Bally. "My neighbor's wife, Jessica," he mumbled. "She's what I want."

"Easy enough," Bally said. "And where shall I put her?"

Bronson swallowed a lump as he glanced at Lonnie. He skulked off to the stalls and returned with a white and dark-spotted mare. He steadied the horse and waved to it, unable to verbalize the instructions. Bally held back a smirk as she drew her wand.

"You'll have a few days," she said. "Do what you will with them. Lonnie, look away."

Lonnie turned to the ground and a flash of green light illuminated the dirt. Bronson grunted, and then he gasped.

"*Jessica*," he breathed. The green light fell away and Lonnie lifted her head, frowning to find Bronson nose to nose with the mare. "Oh, how I've longed for this day."

Bally stepped back and pulled Lonnie with her. Bronson ran his hands over the horse's back, his eyes wide, his mouth slack. He came to the horse's tail and let out a long-held breath.

"Thanks," Bally said, taking the pony by the reign. "Remember, your wife's coming home at some point."

"Jessica," Bronson breathed, wiggling out of his pants. Bally dragged Lonnie back outside.

"Is he . . ." Lonnie turned from the barn to Bally. They burst into thunderous laughter.

They fell to the ground, howling and pounding the earth. Tears fell from their eyes as the white mare whinnied. Bally finally rose and helped Lonnie off the ground.

They took Patrice's lead and made a quick retreat. Lonnie's head hurt from so much joy. The harder she tried to make sense of the logic, the funnier it became.

"He's insane," she said. "Does he really think that horse is his neighbor's wife?"

"As far as his eyes are concerned, she is," Bally said. She squatted at the wine barrel and took a long drink. Feeling a bit thirsty, Lonnie did the same.

"Is that what you did to Derek?" she asked. "Is that how we paid for the wine?"

"Derek?" Bally asked. She winced. "Of course not, Derek's a friend. I just sucked his cock."

"But your wand was green."

"I may have turned myself into a beautiful maiden before I sucked said cock."

The women fell back to the ground as they laughed. When Lonnie composed herself, she crawled to the barrel, taking a sip from the wine barrel. She sat on the ground and pondered the improbable uses of Occumancy. When Bally first explained it, she thought of it only as a tool for deception and fear, but there were endless possibilities.

"So you can make me see anyone?" Lonnie asked.

"No," Bally said. "I can only make you see anyone you've seen before—at least as you remember them. I can also make you see anything in your mind. It takes less power to transform someone, but I can also conjure a vision."

"Can you turn into my mother?"

"Of all the people in your head, you want to see your mother?" Bally asked. "What about your husband? Don't you want to say goodbye to him?"

"Daniel?" Lonnie frowned, wondering if she could handle such a vision. The idea sounded intriguing, but it also seemed in horrible taste. Yet it would only be a trick—Bally reskinned as her partner. "No," she said. "I don't think I could handle it."

"Then your mother? When did she die?"

"When I was a teenager."

"I'll give it a shot, but don't get all clingy and kissy. Think of it more like a portrait than a visit." Bally lifted her wand, waiting for Lonnie's permission.

Lonnie nodded and stared at the dull purple ember glowing at the tip of the wand. It brightened and flashed blinding green. Lonnie finally turned away as her eyes began to ache. She blinked through the haze and turned to Bally.

But Bally had gone away.

Her mother, all wrinkles and judgment, stood before her in the road. Bally tried to make her smile, but Lonnie's mother had never smiled.

Lonnie knelt at the wine and drew a mouthful. She hiccuped as she came back to her feet, facing her mother with both fear and a strange sense of excitement.

"Hello, you wretched old *thing,*" she started. "Remember Daniel? Well, I married him. We lived together and had a wonderful life. Dad went on to remarry and finally found happiness. We had to burn your old bed and clothes, because nothing would wash out your stink."

"Wow," Lonnie's mother said. "So you hated her?"

"Oh, hate isn't strong enough for what I feel for you,"

Lonnie continued. "You beat me and made me feel ugly and stupid. You pushed me out of the house any chance you had, but guess what? I survived. You made me strong and adventurous."

"I'm sorry."

"No, you're not. You were never sorry for anything you did. I hope whatever hole you're rotting in is infested with worms and rats. I hope they eat your eyes and shit in your mouth. Your death was a gift for all of humanity." Lonnie stepped forward, her body thrumming with decades of pent-up resentment. The wine served to stoke the internal flames into an inferno. "It's a good thing you died before I grew up, because I would have killed you myself. I would have shoved a pike up your ass and pulled your legs until it came out your ear. I would have cut your belly open and knitted your innards into a quilt. I would have cut that crooked nose off your face and fed it to a dog. You disgusting, wretched cunt."

"That's enough," Lonnie's mother said. She waved the wand and Bally returned, her face shifting out of the horrific mask that was Lonnie's mother.

Lonnie hyperventilated, her body trembling from the expulsion of filth.

"That was new," Bally said, brushing past Lonnie for the wine. "Usually when someone wants to see a dead friend, they tell them how much they miss them."

"My mother wasn't a friend," Lonnie said.

"Are you all right?"

"Actually, I feel better than I have in days." Lonnie smiled, crouching with Bally to take another drink. Patrice let out a musical toot and they laughed. "I'm sorry if that was weird," Lonnie said. "I was never strong enough to stand up to her when she was alive."

"I'm glad I could help," Bally said. She went back for another drink and frowned, lifting her wand.

"What?" Lonnie asked.

"I need to refuel my Occumancy."

"Male tears?"

"Yes."

"Do you have someone in mind?"

"You're damn right I do. Come on—take Patrice's lead."

"Who is it?" Lonnie asked.

"Wouldn't you like to know?" Bally grinned, her teeth stained bright purple from the wine. "I told you, we're playing by Shrine rules; you have to figure it out as we go."

CHAPTER

TWENTY-NINE

Bally led the growing caravan back to the main street, where they headed deeper into East Ballick. The buildings grew taller in the center of the city. Lonnie felt unabashedly free. No kingsguard leered on the corners looking for reasons to arrest her. There didn't seem to be a single peasant or slave in the entire city.

For every block they passed, at least one person recognized Bally. Lonnie found it incredible that one woman could obtain such infamy. She turned to Bally with a newfound admiration as they marched through the afternoon heat. While slightly insane, she had a gift for making life incredibly interesting. The fact she called Lonnie her friend helped to settle any concerns of treachery.

"We're going a long way," Lonnie said, following the Shrine style of questionless prodding. "I imagine we're getting close to your source of male tears."

"Maybe we are," Bally said. "Maybe we're not." She grinned, walking with a wine-induced sloppiness. Lonnie could only laugh, guessing she was twice as drunk as Bally.

They crossed another mile until Patrice's panting became unignorable. Lonnie spotted a trough outside a tavern and led the pony to water. While she desperately drank, Lonnie swept some of the foamy sweat from her hind quarters.

"I've spent a few nights in here," Bally said, turning to the tavern. "Long and very wild nights."

"Let's go in," Lonnie said. "I'm hungry again."

"We'll get food soon, but first I want tears. They're stronger on an empty stomach." Bally gave Patrice another minute of drinking and took the lead, dragging the exhausted pony back onto the road. They walked another half a mile before Bally stopped outside of a tall, visibly crooked building. It looked like it might tip over at any moment.

"This is interesting," Lonnie said, realizing the building had no windows.

"It's the orphanage," Bally said. "They built it like that to protect the children from child snatchers."

"Is there a problem with child snatchers in East Ballick?"

"Not when they build the orphanage like this. Come on." Bally opened the front door without knocking. She waved for Lonnie to follow, so she did.

The orphanage was hot, and Lonnie immediately began to sweat. Only a few candles illuminated the ghastly building. A pair of cracked rocking chairs concluded the front room's decor. Bally led the way onto a staircase, which wound up the building's center.

As they ascended, a ruckus of laughter and merriment came from overhead. For the first time since drinking the wine, a touch of worry came into Lonnie's chest.

"Whose tears are you here to drink?" she asked. As if in echo of her question, a young boy shrieked, his pleasure infectious.

"Shrine rules," Bally said, grinning as they continued to the next floor. They climbed four stories before finally stepping into a hallway. The heat left Lonnie so heavy she clung to the railing. Screams and laughter came from a door at the end of the hall, and Bally moved straight for it.

"I feel a slight concern if you're going to do what I think you're going to do," Lonnie said, struggling to keep up.

"I'll be using Occumancy," Bally said. "Please close your

eyes once we get inside." She took the door latch, turning to Lonnie. "You know what? Close them now—just to be safe."

Lonnie squeezed her eyes shut as the door creaked open. A ruckus of cheers and stomping feet raced across the room. The children laughed and screamed with delight as Bally stepped forward.

A soft flash of green leaked through Lonnie's eyelids. She turned around, hoping she hadn't been infected with the Occumancy spell.

"Did you miss me?" Bally shouted. She laughed as the children continued squealing. "Lonnie, you can look now."

Lonnie opened her eyes to find three dozen children packed in a huddle around Bally, each one desperately fighting to get a hold of her. They stared at her with a love so pure and honest Lonnie almost melted into the floor.

"I can't stay long," Bally said, squeezing and kissing the children. "Oh, I missed you all so much." She organized the children to ensure each one had a turn to greet her. Lonnie couldn't believe her eyes.

"What are they seeing?" she asked.

"Hush," Bally said, hugging a group of the filthy orphans. "I'm so glad all of you are okay. Have your keepers been taking good care of you? Have you been getting enough food?"

The children more or less agreed, and Bally nodded, smiling as she returned to her feet.

"And where are your keepers?" she asked.

"Upstairs," one young boy said, pointing back into the hall.

"Good. Right where they should be, yes?" Bally laughed as the children cheered. "I'm going to have a word with them. You all behave. And have some fun. This is your house, right?"

The children broke back into cheers and proceeded to race around the room, laughing with reckless abandon. Bally gave them a last wave before shutting the door.

"That was beautiful," Lonnie said. "What did you turn yourself into? What did they see?"

"I always come to them as Happy Snout," Bally said.

"What's Happy Snout?"

"The biggest, fluffiest teddy bear to ever live and breathe." Bally drew a satisfied breath through her nose, turning to the stairs as they continued back down the hall. "I have a heart for the orphans. Once upon a time, I lived here. It wasn't always like this."

"You're an orphan?" Lonnie asked.

"We're all orphans, eventually. But yes, whatever witch birthed me dumped me off on the doorstep. I lived in this hell until I gained my powers. Now I check in to make sure the kids are okay, and the keepers are . . . behaving." Bally started up the stairs, her wand already in hand. The heat and wine left Lonnie dizzy as she climbed after her.

"Then whose tears are you going to drink?" she asked.

"Shrine rules." Bally took Lonnie up the last two flights of stairs, where they came to a single wooden door. "Again, I'll ask you to keep your eyes closed until I say it's safe."

Lonnie turned around and closed her eyes.

The door squealed open.

"*Love Eater,*" a man screamed. Feet raced across the floor, this time in flight. A woman gasped and fell to the ground. It sounded like someone overturned a table.

"No," Bally shouted. "You look at me. *You look at me or I'll drag you to hell.*"

The room fell silent but for troubled breathing.

"Father Gale, so nice to see you," Bally said. "And you too, Sister Beth. Brothers Michael and Kyle, you haven't aged a day."

"You were only here a week ago," one of the men said. "We've done nothing to the children, Bally. They've had everything they want. We've been very good and very sweet."

"That's lovely to hear," Bally said. "Eyes up, everyone."

"Please," a man said. "Bally, you don't need to do this."

"I don't need to do anything."

A flash of green light painted the hall. Lonnie squeezed her eyes as tight as she could, but the light seemed to be far greater than Bally's previous spells.

As the men and women broke into terrified screams, Bally gave Lonnie a slap on the arm.

"It's safe," she said.

Lonnie ventured into the room after Bally. Three fat, sweaty men knelt on the floor, trembling as they held their hands out to Bally, pitifully attempting to ward her off. The women were already in tears, covering their faces with their hands.

"*Look at me,*" Bally commanded. "Pick up your fucking faces and *look at me.*"

The keepers stared on with terror as Bally met them, running her hand along one of the men's oily faces. He burst into tears and tried to turn away. Bally took hold of his face and feasted, lapping up his tears with a pleasure that left Lonnie slightly nauseous. She slipped back into the hall.

Bally spat nasty, sinful words. Her presence alone drove the keepers into a deep panic, but she wanted more, and she expertly talked them into a misery Lonnie had never considered possible.

"They'll stay for a month," Bally informed the keepers. "If you don't keep up the good work, I'll give them permission to stay *forever.*"

"No," a man gasped. "We promise, the children will have everything they want—they already do!"

"Then keep it that way." Bally stepped into the hall, bouncing her eyebrows at Lonnie before thrusting the door shut. "That'll do," she said, extending a hand to the stairs. "After you."

"What did you show them?" Lonnie asked.

"Many things. I projected, and my projections are still there. They'll fizzle out in a few days, but they don't need to know that."

"What did you project?"

"You really don't want to know," Bally said. "They were my keepers once upon a time. They used to torture and harass me. Now, I torture and harass them. I've drunk gallons of their tears over the years."

"Have you ever thought of saving tears?" Lonnie asked.

"What do you mean?" Bally frowned as they wound down the stairs.

"Like collecting a whole bunch of tears in a jar. You could carry them with you and not have to force someone to cry every time you need power."

Bally continued frowning as she walked off the stairs. She led Lonnie into the front room, her face twisted in thought.

"What's wrong?" Lonnie asked.

"You—" Bally froze midthought, pausing in the front doorway. The sun cast her scrawny frame in silhouette. "I feel so stupid," she said, swaying as she leaned into the door frame.

"What?" Lonnie came to her side, also swaying heavily under the weight of the wine.

"That's the smartest idea I've ever heard. It's unlimited power." Bally caught hold of Lonnie's shoulders, her eyes wide and frantic. "You're a genius, Lonnie."

"It seems pretty obvious," Lonnie said.

"We have to eat something." Bally turned to Patrice, who huddled against the porch railing in a futile attempt to shade herself from the sun. "We have work to do."

"Are we going to collect a jar of tears?"

"Oh, we're going to do more than that, you beautiful, curious genius. Come on."

THIRTY

Bally nearly ran up the main street, continuing their quest for the center of East Ballick. The buildings rose like yellow-bricked mountains against the afternoon sun. Lonnie chased after her with the lead, almost dragging the exhausted pony along. Patrice huffed and puffed as if she had been riding for days.

"Bally," Lonnie called. "Patrice is getting tired."

"Then we'll get a new horse," Bally said. "*Come on.*" She continued her mad dash for another six blocks, where they finally stopped outside of the biggest tavern Lonnie had ever seen. It looked to be renovated out of an old hall of worship, with tall, stained-glass windows. Even from outside, the building buzzed with conversation. Lonnie barely had time to tie Patrice out front. She raced up the stairs after Bally, who threw the double-hinged doors open.

A hundred or so men and women filled the tavern's dining room, where prim waiters carried platters of food and drink between the tables. Everyone turned to the obnoxious intruder, and judging by their horrified stares, all were acquainted with the Love Eater.

A tall, weathered proprietor stepped out from behind the bar and approached them, waving for everyone to stay calm. He politely smiled as he met Bally.

"We were told you left town," he said, keeping his voice low. "We don't want any trouble."

"I'm not here for trouble," Bally said. "I need to speak with the men."

"The men are enjoying their food in the company of their wives. All of us would prefer it if you don't disturb the dinner service. Please," he added, glancing at the glowing wand in Bally's hand. "We're just trying to enjoy some peace."

"Then we'll eat something, too," Bally said. "Come on, Lonnie."

The barkeeper stepped back, looking less than pleased as Bally and Lonnie surveyed the still-frozen dining room. They settled into the only open table, which happened to be in the center of the room. Everyone around them did their best to stare at their plates.

"What's the plan?" Lonnie whispered.

"We'll eat something to keep up our energy," Bally said. "After that, I'm going to speak with the men." She flagged down a waiter and ordered a bottle of wine and rice-fried pork.

"Are you going to ask the men for their tears?" Lonnie asked.

"What do you think?" Bally said. Dark bags had formed under her eyes after hours of marching and drinking. She grimaced as she turned to the bar. "Are you bringing that wine, or do I have to get it myself?" she shouted.

The room, which had worked up the courage to resume conversation, fell silent again.

"Sorry," a man called from the bar. "It's coming now."

Bally shook her head as she sat back. She winked at Lonnie, fighting a smile as the waiter carried the bottle to the table. Bally snatched it from his hand and yanked the cork out. She drank half the bottle and handed it to Lonnie, who took a few sips.

"Finish it," Bally said.

"I need to eat or I'm going to pass out," Lonnie said.

Bally groaned and grabbed the bottle, gurgling and gulping

as she finished it. She set it on the table and stared at the empty glass.

"Is that for tears?" Lonnie asked, her mind feeling incredibly slow as the wine continued to drag her into a stupor.

"No, it's for collecting piss," Bally said, rolling her eyes. She said nothing until the food came, and even then she only broke her silence to command Lonnie to eat. "We have a long night ahead of us," she said. "Thanks to your idea, it'll be extra long."

Lonnie focused on the chunks of pork and filled herself, which didn't take long. Before the Shrine she had little appetite, and after days of near-starvation, she had little capacity in her stomach. She did feel better with food in her belly. It soaked up some of the wine and gave her enough strength to sit without slouching.

"Okay," Bally shouted, pushing back her chair. She climbed onto the table and faced the room, which stared up at her in pale, anxious terror. "If you have a vagina, get outside."

While a violent bout of soft-spoken arguments broke out across the restaurant, a majority of the women happily rushed outside. The arguments ended with the rest of the women throwing down their napkins and storming after them. With the room wholly male, and all eyes on Bally, she smiled.

"Most of you know me," she started. "If you don't, I'm the Love Eater; the Witch of East Ballick. I'm here to ask for your help. Lonnie, stand up."

Lonnie, jumping out of her daze, sheepishly climbed onto the table.

"What do you want me to do?" she asked.

"This is Lonnie Lovingdove," Bally said, wrapping an arm around her. "She's my best friend, and this afternoon, she gave me the best idea ever. But I need all of your help to do it."

"What do we get?" a nearby man asked.

"I want to do what we used to do," Bally said. "But this

time, the trade is simple: you give me a nice bout of tears, and I'll give you whatever you want to see—turn whoever you want into whatever you want." She tipped her head to the door, which seemed to bring energy back into the room. "I'll turn your wives into the princesses of your dreams. Or the fattest hags you've ever rolled down a staircase. As long as I get your tears, I don't give a damn."

"What if we don't want to?" someone shouted from the back. "*My wife* just so happens to be beautiful." He crossed his arms, proudly glancing across the room.

"If you want to play games, I'll turn your beautiful wife into your father for the rest of your life," Bally said. Gasps and groans broke across the room. "Or we can all work together and get whatever we want."

"I've never cried," a man said from behind Bally. "Even if I wanted to, there's no way I could force—"

Bally lifted her wand and leaped off the table, holding it in front of the man's face. "Everyone close your eyes but him," she cooed.

Lonnie closed her eyes with the rest of the room. A dull flash of green clouded the black of her eyelids.

A blood curdling scream filled the air. Lonnie opened her eyes to find the man leaning back in his chair, desperately batting at the air. He moaned and trembled. Bally leaned closer, bringing her forehead to his.

"The bottle," she hissed, grasping at the air over her shoulder.

Lonnie realized she was talking to her and climbed off the table. She snatched the bottle and handed it to Bally, who set it below the trembling man's nose.

"It's still not enough," he breathed. "I can't cry—"

Bally pulled her hair over her shoulders. The man screamed and kicked back, sending his chair crashing to the ground. As he broke into deep, moaning sobs, Bally sat on his chest and began collecting the precious tears. The rest of the men scowled as if watching a public raping.

Finally, the man ran out of emotional energy and fell still, his hands gently trembling as his sides. Bally rose and passed the bottle to Lonnie.

"Now you get to see whatever you want," she said, smiling. "What do you want to see, good sir?"

The man pushed himself to a seat, blinking as he looked across the room. He cleared his throat and let out a breath. Bally knelt beside him, licking the last moisture from his cheek.

"Anything, anywhere," she said. "Please, let me give you this gift."

"Well," the man said. "I'd like it if my wife could . . ." He leaned into Bally's ear to whisper the rest of his wish. When he came away, an anxious giddiness filled his puffy face.

"Everyone who isn't him, close your eyes," Bally said. She lifted the wand and Lonnie averted her gaze. When the green flash settled, Lonnie found the man back on his feet. He sheepishly tucked his shirt in and brushed the dust from his pants. As if the terribly public humiliation had never happened, he gave Bally a quick nod and left the tavern.

"Are you going to do that to all of us?" a man called from the crowd.

"Well, it doesn't have to be so sinister," Bally said. "In fact, let's get some wine going in here. We can make a party out of this, yes? Everyone, let's get drunk. I'm just as happy to drink tears of joy."

A hesitant cheer went across the room. Lonnie felt ready for another drink. She turned as the waiters carried barrels of wine out from behind the bar. They set them on tables around the room and dispensed glasses.

"Lonnie," Bally called. "Go outside and find a musician. Let's make this a proper party."

"Sure," Lonnie said. "Where do I find a musician?"

"Someone help her." Bally climbed off the table and began tapping the first keg of wine. "She's a windowed slave from Doane, so be polite."

Lonnie winced to be broken down so honestly, but a handsome man stepped to her side and offered a hand.

"I'll help you," he said. "Come on, I know the perfect place."

Lonnie took the stranger's strong, tanned hand and followed him to the door.

THIRTY-ONE

Outside, the expelled women all stared at the tavern with crossed arms and tapping toes. They scowled at Lonnie and her escort, who pulled her down the front steps.

"I'm Jack," he said, leading her through the crowd.

"I'm Lonnie Lovingdove," Lonnie said. "Thanks for—"

"You *tell* me," a woman shouted. Lonnie jumped, turning to find the man who had been terrified to tears once again on the ground, this time with his wife as the aggressor. "You tell me what she did," the woman continued, beating him with her travel bag. "Who is she?"

"She didn't do anything," the man said. "You're you, just as beautiful as the day I met you."

His wife, with a bulbous nose and objectively hideous face, only beat him harder.

"You kissed me," she screamed. "Since when do we kiss—let alone in public?"

"Come on," Jack said, dragging Lonnie across the street. Once they were clear of the fight, they broke into laughter. "I have a feeling this is going to be a wild night," he said.

"It's been a wild day," Lonnie said. "Do you know Bally?"

"The Love Eater? We all know her. She's haunted East Ballick since she escaped the orphanage. The men aren't as scared of her as the women, although I don't think anyone missed her. How do you know her?"

"I just met her the other day. We were in a cult together, but we escaped."

"Do you want me to rescue you?" Jack asked. "I could take you away and hide you in a nice little castle in the middle of the forest."

"Yes," Lonnie said, but as Jack burst into laughter, she realized he was joking. She grinned toothily and slapped his arm. "You're really funny," she said with a giggle.

"Yes, but not as funny as what's going to happen at that tavern. Let's make this quick—I don't want to miss anything." Jack led her into an empty concert hall. They climbed a staircase in the lobby and moved through a small apartment complex above the auditorium. Jack knocked on every door and recruited a team of half-drunk musicians, promising them unlimited wine and frivolity in exchange for their music.

Lonnie did her best to focus; the wine left her head clouded, and her body maddeningly sloppy. She almost fell down the stairs on the way back outside.

"Easy," Jack said, laughing as he caught her. "Do you want me to carry you?"

"Yes," Lonnie said. But when Jack laughed and didn't pick her up, she blushed. "That was funny," she said, forcing another laugh.

"Oh, shit." Jack froze, staring across the road.

Three other men had emerged from the tavern, and the women had them on the ground, flogging them with their shoes.

"Why are they so mad?" Lonnie asked. Before Jack could answer, an idea came to her, and she started to jog, meeting the crowd. "Hey," she called, but the women were screaming so loud they couldn't hear her.

"Hey," Jack bellowed, this time drawing their attention. With shoes raised, the women turned to Jack, who pointed to Lonnie. "Go ahead," he mumbled.

"I just wanted to say I have an idea," Lonnie said. She

swayed, unused to so many people paying attention to her. Her heart threw a striking punch at her ribs.

"What?" a woman asked. She held her husband by the ear, who looked to Lonnie for mercy.

"Why don't you go inside, too?" Lonnie said. "Bally can cast spells on all of you. And we have wine. Come get drunk and have fun."

"Lonnie," Jack said, taking her arm. "That's not a good—"

"You know what?" a woman called, turning to the others. "She's right. Why do they get to have all the fun? My Robert's face is mincemeat. I'd like to kiss him and like it for once."

As the concept of first-person Occumancy swept through the women, their wrinkled scowls began to melt. They broke into frantic banter. When they came to their conclusion, they put their shoes on and turned to Lonnie.

"But will the Love Eater do it?" they asked.

"If you let her harvest their tears," Lonnie said, "then yes."

"She can have his blood if you can give my Robert a knight's body," one woman called, and as the others laughed, so began the procession into the tavern.

"You're dangerous," Jack said. He laughed, wrapping his arm over Lonnie's shoulder. "Come on, let's see how this plays out."

Lonnie followed the women into the tavern, which created quite a scene for the rest of the room's occupants. The men guiltily looked from their wives to Bally, who was fast at working collecting tears from a bawling fat man. The dining hall stunk of wine and sweat. Lonnie crossed the room to explain her idea to Bally, hoping she wouldn't be too upset with the invitation.

"Good, you fat little scum stain," Bally hissed, scooping tears off the man's cheek. He frowned with such severity his face looked like a melting lump of clay. Nearly an inch of salty tears filled the bottom of the wine bottle.

"Bally," Lonnie said, stepping beside her.

Bally turned, her eyes crazed and bloodshot. Dark dribbles of wine stained the whole of her chin purple. "What?" she snapped.

"The women are back," Lonnie said. "I invited them inside. They were beating the men, so I told them you could give them spells, too. They want to change the way the men look. They'll cooperate if you help them."

"I don't need them," Bally said, grabbing her subject's nipple through his shirt. As he cried out, she scooped another tear into the bottle.

"I think everyone will be happier if you do it this way," Lonnie said. "Maybe you can do a spell for all of them at once or something."

"That takes a lot of energy."

"You have a room full of men ready to give you their tears."

Bally turned, her greasy hair matted into thin strands across her forehead. She studied the room with calculated eyes. Finally, she grunted, nodding to Lonnie.

"Tell them to line up and think about what they want," she said. "Tell them to choose wisely, cause I'm not doing any do-overs."

Lonnie thanked Bally and returned to the women, who anxiously stood by the door.

"Well?" one of the bolder women asked.

"She'll do it," Lonnie said. "She said to drink as much wine as you want, and think about who you want your partners to look like. It can be literally anything. Or anyone. Just pick a winner, because you only get one spell."

The women mused on this, the fat man still weeping inconsolably from the other side of the room. Lonnie helped herself to a tall glass of wine. She drank most of it in one go and winced, her head swimming with alcohol. The room seemed to be spinning. She sat in a chair, wobbling as Jack sat next to her. He set his hand on her thigh.

"You're quite something," he said, smiling as he scooted closer.

"You have a wife," Lonnie said. She slapped his hand off.

"No, I don't." Jack sobered, his fierce eyes meeting Lonnie's. "At least not yet."

"I already have a partner." But as Lonnie said the reflexive words, she realized they were no longer reflective. A sharp pain pushed through the numbing wine. "I mean I used to have a partner," she whispered. "And I loved him very much."

"Forgive me," Jack said. "I didn't know. I only meant to say I like you, Lonnie Lovingdove. Please, forgive me."

Lonnie burst into tears. With no other option, she fell into Jack's arms, pressing her face into the heat of his chest. She wept and he consoled her. The wine dug deeper into her blood. She finally cried herself out and sat back, feeling completely empty.

"I'm not usually like this," she said, glad to see she hadn't scared Jack off. "I've had a terrible last few days."

"But tonight's a new night," Jack said. "And it's still very young." He lifted Lonnie to her feet, guiding her across the room.

"Where are we going?" Lonnie asked. Around them, the men and women re-congregated, now speaking in friendly conversation as they gathered over wine. It helped to drown out Bally's vicious tear extraction.

"I'd like to dance with you," Jack said, grinning as he pushed his belly into Lonnie's.

"You can't dance without music," Lonnie said.

But before she even finished the words, the musicians struck up a beautiful, sweeping waltz.

And Jack moved wonderfully. He led Lonnie, taking her across the room, where others cleared tables to join them in the dance. By the time the song finished half of the room was slow-dancing. Candles glowed around them and filled the air with smoke, adding a pleasant acidity to the bittersweet wine. Lonnie moved with a newfound freedom; the wine finally leaving her with a clear mind.

She laughed, staring into Jack's bright, startling eyes. They danced three more waltzes before Bally climbed onto a table, shouting for control of the room.

"No," she shrieked, her hair a frizzled and greasy mess from all the spellwork. "This is not that kind of party. Play something lively or shove those harps up your ass."

The band, who seemed used to harsh reviews, shrugged and counted off their next song.

Bally grinned as they broke into a raucous tune, the beat pushing everyone into a drunken jig. She turned and found Lonnie, who also grinned, tipping her head to her handsome partner. Bally nodded, lifting a half-filled bottle of tears.

If the party had ended there, Lonnie might have called it one of the greatest nights of her life.

THIRTY-TWO

Lonnie danced until she could no longer pretend to be sober. She fell into a chair and found an abandoned glass of wine. While Jack ran off to the bathroom, she looked across the wondrous party, rather proud of her handy work.

The men and women had come together in a starling show of fraternity. With wine-stained lips, they laughed and danced, their energy rising as the wine barrels emptied. Some told stories and howled with a delight only found through intoxication. Other couples kissed, as if youths in their first throes of passion.

Lonnie smirked, realizing they may indeed be seeing each other's false faces for the first time. Her laughter increased as the candles burned down and the passion ignited. Men threw their wives against the wall, kissing them, pulling up their dresses to expose their ankles. One man unbuttoned his shirt to expose a fish-white belly.

"I'm gonna get meat," Jack mumbled from somewhere behind Lonnie. "Do you like it burned?"

Lonnie mumbled something and waved him off, her laughter dying out as a couple climbed onto a table, their clothes falling like wilted petals. They stripped completely naked and caressed one another. A crowd greedily gathered around them. Lonnie climbed onto her table, knocking a glass of wine over. She looked over the crowd and covered her mouth; the man and wife began making love—for all the world to see.

Even stranger, the other couples took the lewd expression

as an excuse to break into their own copulation. The room grew hot. Scents of musk and bodily fluid soon washed away the sweet wine and smoke. Though the wine blurred her vision, Lonnie gaped as she studied the scene. She had heard stories of royal orgies and debauchery, but to see it; a dozen couples making love in the presence of their neighbors—she blushed so hard she grew lightheaded.

As she wandered the edge of the table it tipped, sending her crashing to the ground. Bottles shattered and chairs clattered across the floor. Lonnie staggered to her feet. She walked a crooked line, searching for Bally. She found her in the center of the room, catching the tears of a man in emotional agony.

"Bally," Lonnie shouted, crashing into her shoulder. "There's a problem."

"What?" Bally grunted. She turned, looking a hundred years old.

"They're having *sex*," Lonnie said, whispering the last word. "Everyone's starting to do it—right here in the tavern—without clothes."

"So what?" Bally's gaze drifted to the ceiling, her tongue sliding across her mouth like a desperate lizard.

"Are you all right?" Lonnie asked.

Bally didn't react.

"Are you okay?" Lonnie gave her a gentle shake, and Bally jumped back to animation. She stared at Lonnie wide-eyed. "Bally, you're scaring me—this whole party is scaring me."

"But the tears," Bally said. She grinned as she held up the wine bottle. The tears reached just shy of the cork. "It's harder than I thought, but *look*. By the time we're done here, I'll have three bottles."

"I'm feeling sick," Lonnie said.

"Then drink some wine." Bally turned, finding her glass on the table. "Drink this. You'll feel better."

"Are you sure?" Lonnie took the wine, feeling sicker just by holding the greasy glass.

Bally answered by pressing the glass to Lonnie's lips.

Things got blurry after that.

And quickly.

THIRTY-THREE

Lonnie stood atop a table with Jack holding her steady. She laughed so hard tears fell down her cheek.

Across from her, a man and his wife made love like dogs. They grunted and spasmed against one another. A dozen others watched the breeding with wine sloshing out of their glasses. They cheered as the husband thrust. Beyond them, four other couples entangled in an equally spasmodic orgy.

Lonnie squinted to keep her vision from blurring. The sight of such intense passion put a strange longing in her belly. She turned to Jack, who held her upper thighs tightly.

CHAPTER

THIRTY-FOUR

Lonnie sat in deep conversation with an old, big-boned woman named Naples. The woman had wandered into the party late, and while disgusted by the debauchery, she confessed to Lonnie she had no other place to go; no friends or family to spend her time with. They talked for an hour before Lonnie had an idea.

"I don't think I could make the journey," Naples said. "No horse can carry me. And what if I don't like him? What if he's cruel? What if he thinks I'm as ugly as I really am?"

"Stop that," Lonnie said, slapping Naples' hand. "He's a wonderful man who will accept you for the beautiful soul you are. I can feel your energy. I know you as well as anyone I've ever known in my life. You'll love him, and he'll love you."

"I don't even know his name," Naples said.

"His name is Kegan, and he's waiting for you. Go to him."

"What if I can't find him?"

"You came into the tavern for a reason; you met me for a reason. This is divine providence, Naples. This is destiny. Find Kegan and tell him I sent you. Go and start the rest of your life."

"I don't even know your name," Naples said.

CHAPTER

THIRTY-FIVE

Lonnie sat alone on the bar, wobbling as the room swayed. She held a glass of piss-warm wine and pondered whether she should drink it.

A scream brought her attention to a nearby table.

Bally, her skin gray and wrinkled to the storybook complexion of a witch, twitched and staggered as she danced on top of the table. She lifted a bottle of tears and chugged. When she stopped for air she belched, turning to the ceiling and howling like a wolf. She lifted her wand and screamed.

Lonnie closed her eyes just before the flash of blinding green.

"*Change partners,*" Bally shrieked.

The drunkards crashed across the bar like stampeding bulls. With one eye squinted, Lonnie watched the mass of naked men and women shuffled like a deck of sweaty cards.

THIRTY-SIX

Bally's magic started with a soft yellowish-green, and then burst into the full-fledged emerald strike of Occumancy. Lonnie would always think of it as ripening lightning. She almost closed her eyes in time for every spell.

Almost.

THIRTY-SEVEN

Lonnie woke pinned to the wall, with Jack against her, his whiskered chin grinding into her neck. She blinked and pushed him off. Jack stared at her, his shirt unbuttoned, his hairy belly heaving with labored breaths.

THIRTY-EIGHT

Lonnie stared at the tip of Bally's wand. She had never been so close to it. The wood had been made with a deft hand; intricate carvings and symbols encircling tiny crystals wedged into the tip. Bally's hand wrapped it like a white claw, her knuckles stained purple with wine. Lonnie gasped as the crystal glowed with a soft, yellowish-green light. The hair on the back of her neck rose and the world turned a brilliant shade of emerald green.

THIRTY-NINE

And then, oh happy days, she lay with Daniel—her partner, the only man she could truly love. He kissed her and she held him tight. They lay on a bed of seat cushions in the corner of the tavern. The candles had burned out long ago. They lay in shadow, with bodies humping and groaning in the haze around them.

Lonnie wrapped her hands around Daniel's neck, unable to verbalize her pleasure of having him back. He smiled in his shy, wooden way, and leaned down to kiss her breasts. Lonnie moaned as she lay back. Daniel pulled her dress the rest of the way off and met her nose-to-nose.

"I love you," he breathed, stealing a quick kiss.

"I love you, too," Lonnie said.

But she frowned as he entered her. His penis felt much smaller than she remembered.

PART FOUR
WHEN IN DOUBT, IMMOLATE

FORTY

Lonnie woke with her head pounding. The world seemed to be spinning beneath her. She could barely move as she opened her eyes, wincing to find the sun beaming down at her.

Trees passed overhead.

Bright clouds swirled in a turbulent wind.

Lonnie rolled her head, finding a long stone fence passing at her side. She wobbled as she floated across whatever the hell path she lay upon. Finally, she pushed herself to a seat and found herself on the back of a small cart.

Bally squatted at the front, mechanically whipping Patrice, who struggled forward as if moving through quicksand. A sheet of foamy sweat covered the pony's tiny body. Lonnie tried to speak but her mouth was too dry. She sat back against a pyramid of wine kegs, wincing at her throbbing headache. Her mind could do little but interpret the passing countryside.

She lay in her stupor for what felt like hours before the nausea finally subdued her. Retching, she rolled to her belly and vomited into the dust. The thin vomit came out in sprays of purple. Lonnie heaved until her body had nothing left. She gasped, her arms dangling over the side of the bobbling cart.

"Lonnie?" Bally asked. Her voice came with a harsh rasp.

"Water," Lonnie mumbled, just as gravely.

"Soon." Bally tossed a folded blanket at her. It rolled over Lonnie's shoulder before dropping into the road. The tangled blue cotton soon became a strange shape on the horizon.

And then it was gone.

FORTY-ONE

Lonnie woke as water splashed across her face. She jumped back, rolling all the way off the other side of the cart. She landed in a small creek.

"Stop," Bally cried.

Patrice let out a strangled whinny and the rolling wheels finally stopped grinding.

Lonnie pushed herself out of the cool water. Bally stood looking down at her, the sun leaving her in shadow.

"Did you jump or fall?" she asked.

"Fell," Lonnie breathed. She lowered herself back into the creek, the cool water an incredible pleasure to her burning flesh. She drew a mouthful and forced it down her cracked throat.

"Well," Bally said, hopping off the cart. "There's your water." She came alongside Lonnie and extended her hand. Lonnie took a last drink and came up, slumping on the bank of the stream. She turned to Bally, who looked like a corpse. She sipped from a glass of wine, her bloodshot eyes and colorless flesh horrendous in the daylight.

"What happened?" Lonnie mumbled.

"What do you remember?" Bally asked.

"Nothing."

"Probably for the best."

"It hurts."

"What hurts?"

Lonnie waved a hand across her body.

"Wine," Bally said, handing her the glass. "It's the only cure for this kind of thing. Just take it slow."

Lonnie took the glass and studied the dark syrup; the lip-stains decorating the rim like snow frost. She drank a mouthful and detested the tingling sensation. But her headache loosened at once, so she drank a little more.

"What the hell happened?" she asked. "Where are we?"

"We had a good harvest," Bally said. She opened her jacket, revealing three bottles of clear liquid dangling from a rope around her neck. As she met Lonnie's eyes, she grinned, her teeth so blackened by wine they might as well be missing. "It was a productive party."

"I can still smell the sex." Lonnie sniffed a handful of her dress and gagged. She took another sip of wine and managed to hold it in. "Where are we?" She turned to the creek, realizing they were not in the woods but some kind of aqueduct in a stone courtyard.

"Do you not remember?" Bally asked.

"Remember what?"

"You really did get drunk, didn't you?" Bally cackled, clapping her on the back.

Lonnie stared at the wall, starting to recognize the cuts of stone. Her stomach dropped and she grew hot all over again. With a gasp, she jumped to her feet and tried to run. She nearly crashed head-first into the cart and fell back to the ground.

"No," she breathed, climbing the wagon wheel. "We can't—"

"You seriously don't remember?" Bally heaved Lonnie onto her feet. "We were talking after the party. You were telling me—"

"We're in *Doane*," Lonnie said, breathing so hard she actually did vomit again. She wiped her chin and took Bally by the shirt. "*You brought me back to Doane?*"

"It was your idea," Bally said. "You told me we should visit and have some fun."

"They'll kill me. They have portraits of me across the entire kingdom. How did we even get into the city? We have to leave. They'll kill—"

"*Calm down.*" Bally took her firmly by the shoulders. "This was your idea. You seriously don't remember? You told me how handsome Prince Pollen Bane is, and I said I wanted to meet him. You told me we should go, so we did. You fell asleep after we set out, and now you're telling me you don't remember anything?"

"I drank half a barrel of wine last night," Lonnie said. "No, I don't remember. We have to leave. If they recognize—"

"That's not going to happen," Bally said, tapping her want to the necklace of jarred tears. "I've been Occumancing everyone who even glances at us. As far as they can see, we're two ugly little wenches out to see the kingdom."

"This is insane."

"Well, it was your idea." Bally took her glass to the barrel and quickly filled it. She let out a long and frustrated breath. "I can't believe you think I'd let them catch you," she said, shaking her head.

"I'm sorry," Lonnie said. "I seriously can't remember anything. I can't even think straight from all the wine."

"I told you; you need to drink again to fix yourself."

"I don't want to keep drinking."

"Just a few glasses and you'll be straightened out. I prom-ise." Bally dug a glass from a bag and filled it, handing the warm wine to Lonnie. "You said we'd have fun in Doane."

"Well, I was drunk," Lonnie said, sipping the wine. "I don't know why on earth I would have suggested we come back here."

"Because we can walk free, thanks to these tears." Bally

grinned, jingling the bottles. "We don't have to stay long. We'll just slip into the castle so I can see how handsome the prince is."

"The castle?" Lonnie frowned, taking another drink. It not only cured her headache but brought her back to full-on drunk. She swayed as she finished the glass. "This is like a bad dream," she said, turning to Patrice. The teeny pony glanced back, meeting her gaze as if thinking the same thing. "I seriously wanted to bring you here?"

"You wouldn't stop going on about the prince," Bally said. "'*Oh, he's so handsome and sweet. Everyone in the village wants him. You HAVE to see him, Bally. You have to see how handsome and sweet he is.*' I finally agreed just to shut you up."

Lonnie laughed, finally free of her panic. "That party was insane," she said. "I've never done anything like that."

"It feels good to cut loose, doesn't it?"

"From what I can remember, yeah."

"Then let's have one more run of it," Bally said. "Let's meet that handsome prince and play some games with him. He'll never know who we are or what we're doing."

"What kind of games?"

"The kind they write into the history books." Bally laughed, and with the wine surging back through her veins, Lonnie laughed, too. They were soon back on the road, driving for the castle, with wine in their hands and mirth painting their smiles. Lonnie could almost remember suggesting the idea of visiting the prince.

Ahead of them, as Patrice huffed and puffed her way up the hillside, a twin trail of blood ran from the horse's tiny nose.

CHAPTER

FORTY-TWO

Just to be safe, Lonnie wrapped a blanket around her head to keep her face hidden. Once they passed a few knights and no one recognized her, she began to relax, finding an unexpected nostalgia for Doane. The city had never given her much, but it would always be home. She had met Daniel and began their courtship in the city square. She had built a home and found a safe and predictable life.

"I used to work there," Lonnie said, tightening her shroud as they came upon the east brick kiln. Slaves and workers littered the sandy field. Bally held up her wand as they passed, the tip glowing with brilliance. Lonnie stared at the faces of her former co-workers and wondered if anyone noticed her absence.

Then she saw the massive painting of her face on the post outside of the kiln. The artist had given her the same guilty expression she wore in the window at the castle; the day she caught a mad king eating human meat. A whole list of charges and warnings accompanied the painting, but Lonnie couldn't read it from the road. She shivered as her foreman stared her straight in the eyes and didn't recognize her.

"Looks like a shit job," Bally said, whipping Patrice. "What did you do?"

"I formed the bricks," Lonnie said. "You slap mud into the mold and they take it to the kiln."

"Well, maybe your escape was for the best. There has to be a thousand better jobs."

"Well, yeah. But I lost Daniel." Lonnie patted across her shoulder, panicking to realize she didn't have his carving. "Bally," she breathed. "I don't have my bag."

"Here," Bally said, dragging it out from under the bench. "You were insistent we didn't forget it."

Lonnie tugged the bag open and lifted the carving, hugging the smooth wood tight. Drops of wine stained the section below her and Daniel's initials, but it remained in her possession, and that was all she needed. Smiling, she drank more wine, feeling quite content despite the insanity of their destination.

"How far are we?" Bally asked. She glanced back at Lonnie, still looking painfully haggard.

"It's a few more miles," Lonnie said. "We'll see it soon." She leaned forward, studying Bally's face.

"What?" Bally grimaced, making her all the more ugly.

"You don't look so good."

"It'll come back." Bally turned to Patrice as she combed her greasy hair into her face. "It's from the nocturnal spell work."

"What do you mean?"

"You're only supposed to do Occumancy during the day, when the black part of your eye is small. It protects me from the spells. At night, your eyes are wide open. Everytime I cast a spell at night it takes a piece of me. I cast a lot of spells last night."

"So you're going to stay like this?" Lonnie asked.

"No, it comes back after a while. That was the one good thing from my week at the Shrine; I looked great, didn't I?" Bally smiled, turning to Lonnie, but her gruesome complexion made it hard to smile back.

"You did," Lonnie said. She turned ahead, where one of the castle turrets rose over the hillside. Her hand shook a little as she brought the wine back to her lips." We're almost there," she said, pointing out the turret.

"Excellent," Bally said. "This is going to be fun."

"You know, they don't just let people into the castle."

"Oh, but we're not arriving as any old people."

"What do you mean?"

"Shrine rules," Bally said, grinning. "Remember that?"

"No questions," Lonnie mumbled, nodding.

So they ascended the hillside, Patrice trembling with each step. Lonnie drank a few more glasses of wine and felt properly wasted by the time they moved for the gates. Bally lifted her wand as they rolled up the drawbridge. The gatekeeper stepped out with a crossbow in hand. He stared at the glowing wand, but as he turned to Bally and Lonnie, his frown melted into a grin.

"Good day, fair ladies," he said, resting an arm on the cart. "What business do you have with the crown?"

"I'm Princess Casper," Bally said, waving to Lonnie. "And this is Lady Pine. We've come to meet with Prince Pollen Bane VI."

"Welcome. Is the prince expecting you?"

"No, we've come to surprise him." Bally smiled, tucking a greasy strand of hair behind her ear. "May we cross the bridge? We've come a long way, and our steed is in need of feed and watering."

The gate keeper glanced at Patrice. "I've never seen such a big horse," he marveled. "Sure thing, Your Highness. I'll draw the gate and have a messenger inform the prince of your arrival. Please wait until the bridge is fully drawn."

Bally gave Lonnie a smug glance as the gate chains began to clatter. Soon, the cart rumbled over the planks, coming into a welcome party at the castle gates. Lonnie kept her shroud tight as Bally lifted her wand. The party stared at the glowing tip with wonder, all smiling when they finally turned to the royal guests. Lonnie froze to find her nemesis kingsguard in the procession. She stopped breathing as he met her eyes. When he smiled, she drank the last of her wine.

"Your Highnesses," a man in a fluffy fur coat said, stepping forward. "I am Walter Thomas, Lord High Steward of Castle Doane. I welcome and thank you for coming. Prince Pollen Bane VI has been informed of your visit and is quite pleased to meet you."

"Thank you, Lord Thomas," Bally said, throwing on a poor impression of noble air. "May we visit the royal baths before we meet the prince? Our journey has been long and hard, and we desire to wash before our union with His Highness."

"Of course," Lord Thomas said. "Stablemaster Braun, please take this steed to be fed and watered. Princess, I'll escort you to the baths myself."

While the stablemaster dragged Patrice to be fed and watered, Lonnie and Bally climbed off the cart and followed Lord Thomas into the castle. Lonnie's nemesis kingsguard walked with them, putting a flutter back into her heart.

"May I take your luggage?" he asked Lonnie, motioning to her shoulder bag with Daniel's carving.

"No, thank you," she said. "These are my personal effects."

"Of course." The kingsguard stared at Lonnie a little longer than she liked. "Where did you say you come from?" he asked.

"Perhaps this ring will answer your questions," Bally said, extending her naked hand.

"I've never seen such jewels," the kingsguard said. "They're incredible."

"We come from a place of wealth. We're also very tired, so if you don't mind, we'd like to save our energy for the prince."

"Lord Thomas, make sure the princess and Lady have whatever they need." The kingsguard marched ahead, taking one last glance at Lonnie before rounding a corner.

"This is insane," Lonnie whispered. "That one knows me and wants to kill me."

"You're crazy," Bally said. "This is fun; haven't you always wanted to be a princess?"

"Of course, but . . ." Lonnie slowed as they came upon a massive portrait of her face outside of the guard's station. Bally smiled, seemingly amused by Lonnie's infamy. Lord Thomas stopped up and admired it, too.

"Lonnie Lovingdove," he said. "A peasant who not only attempted to murder the king, but also caused quite a stir in the dungeon."

"Is castle security lacking?" Bally asked, raising an eyebrow.

"Of course not. The king was never in danger, and we expect to capture Lonnie Lovingdove any day now. Her punishment will be one for the history books. The king has hired a whole army of torturers to make an example of her. Hopefully you'll be around to see it, if you're into that kind of thing."

"We'd be quite interested," Bally said. "She might be closer than you think."

A lump rose in Lonnie's throat. She elbowed Bally in the ribs as they continued down the hall.

"What the hell?" she whispered.

"I have an idea," Bally said. "If this goes like I think it will, we're going to fix every one of your problems today."

FORTY-THREE

"Every perfume and amenity awaits you inside," Lord Thomas said as they came to the stone entrance of the baths. "If you need any assistance, call out and an attendant will be at your side."

"Some wine and food would be nice," Bally said.

"Of course," Lord Thomas said. "Do you like pork?"

"*No*," Lonnie said. "No meat, just vegetables and fruit."

"Of course. I'll have a servant bring you a platter." While Lord Thomas bowed and headed down the hall, Bally led Lonnie into the royal baths.

A series of large, bubbling pools filled the cavernous room. Candles flickered from the walls with heat, waving against the rising steam. It smelled of lavender and citrus. Bally shucked out of her dress. Lonnie frowned, drunk but not enough to be fully at ease.

"What did you mean when you said you're going to fix every one of my problems?" she asked.

Bally moaned as lowered his skeletal body into the water. "You have to get in here," she breathed.

"Bally," Lonnie said. "What did—"

"I'm Princess Casper, Lady Pine. You seem to have grown confused through our travels." Bally cast a nasty scowl at Lonnie, pointing to her ears. "Come into this tub and rest your mind."

Shamed, Lonnie climbed out of her dress and into the warm

tub. The tension melted from her spirit as she sunk into the heat, the steam rising and coating her face. She washed herself. The heat amplified the wine and brought her to the point of physical melting.

"This is crazy," she breathed, rolling her head to Bally.

"Yeah," Bally said.

Soon, a servant delivered a platter of bright vegetables and fruit. She also brought a pitcher of wine and communion cups. She frowned as she looked down at Bally and Lonnie.

"What?" Bally asked. "Oh, shit," she said, lifting her wand. It flashed bright green and the servant blinked.

"I'm sorry," the servant said. "Forgive me for staring."

"Get out," Bally said.

The servant nodded before scampering out of the baths.

"You can't forget to Occumance," Lonnie said. "You heard what they're going to do to me."

"Not if I have anything to say about it," Bally said.

"And why not?" Lonnie snatched a handful of cherry tomatoes and broccoli. The food tasted strange on her pickled tongue, but her aching stomach readily accepted the nutrients.

"Because they're going to capture Lonnie Lovingdove today. Before you go asking a hundred questions, relax. I have a plan to take care of everything." Bally smirked, pouring them both a glass of wine.

"Maybe we should take it easy on the drinking," Lonnie said. "You almost forgot to spellbind the servant. She saw me. I know she did."

"She saw a vapor in the steam," Bally said, handing Lonnie her glass. "Drink this and wash your pussy. We need to smell royal."

After Lonnie and Bally finished the bath, they climbed out and dried themselves with huge, fluffy towels. They also finished the food tray and wine. Drunk and lethargic, they returned to the hall outside. Lord Thomas slipped around a corner and met them with an impressed bow.

"The bath has treated you well," he said, bowing again. "Shall we go and meet the prince?"

"I'm afraid we must speak with the heads of the castle first," Bally said. "Bring the kingsguard, the king and prince, and anyone else of importance."

"Is there a problem?" Lord Thomas asked.

"A very grave one. As I said, we must address the castle at once." While Lord Thomas scampered off, Bally winked at Lonnie. Lonnie frowned, her mind heavy from the wine.

"What are—?"

"I've got everything under control," Bally said. "Just relax." She drew a bottle of tears from her necklace and swigged. Wincing, she tucked it back into her jacket. "Tastes like piss after sitting all night," she muttered.

"How long is everyone under the Occumancy spell?" Lonnie asked. "Like the kingsguard—will you need to re-spellbind him?"

"They'll see us as royalty for a few days. Although, it would certainly help if you started acting the part."

Lonnie stood tall, realizing she had drifted into a terrible slouch. She took a breath and tried to stay cool as distant footsteps fluttered about the castle. Despite the weight of the wine, she wished she had another glass.

"Princess Casper," Lord Thomas called. He rounded the corner, waving for them to follow. "Everyone is assembling in the throne room. If you'll come with me, please."

"Get the wand ready," Lonnie said quietly. "I'll come into the room after you so they don't see me. The king knows me."

"Everyone does," Bally said, pointing to another portrait of the castle's most-wanted women. "Come on."

And so they followed Lord Thomas, through halls and

courtyards, all the way into the hallowed King's Chamber of Castle Doane. Bally entered first. After the room flashed bright green, Lonnie drew a breath and wandered after her.

CHAPTER

FORTY-FOUR

The King's Chamber had a shorter ceiling than Lonnie expected, but what it lacked in height it made up for in extravagance. Brilliant tapestries hung across the walls. Between them, metal sculptures and weaponry glistened in the flaming torch light. A long green and gold carpet led all the way to the end of the chamber, where King Pollen Bane and the prince sat upon their thrones. A team of ornate men and women stood around them, all sharing the same bored countenance. Lonnie's nemesis kingsguard set a hand on the back of the throne.

"Greetings," shouted the king. He raised a jeweled scepter, sitting back as Bally marched up the carpet to meet him.

"Greetings, Your Highness," Bally said. She turned, smiling as Lonnie caught up with her.

"I hear you've come to see my son?" the king asked. He smirked, glancing at the prince. The prince looked more handsome than Lonnie remembered; his hair coiffed and tight, his beard neatly trimmed. He pursed his lips as he stared at Bally and Lonnie. Lonnie wondered what she actually looked like under the Occumancy spell.

"We have," Bally said. "But a more urgent matter has come to hand. I'm afraid it must be dealt with at once."

"Well," the king said. "Let's have it." He sat forward, setting both hands on his scepter. It slid out from under him and he snarled, handing it off to a staffer. "Speak, Princess," he said. "For the love of your king, get on with it."

203

"Your Highness, while taking our royal baths, we were served wine and vegetables by a servant. A young woman."

"Lord Thomas," the King said, turning to him. "Is this so?"

"Yes, my Lord," said Lord Thomas. "I believe it was Jessica."

"Are you sure?" asked the Prince. "You're certain it was Jessica?"

"Can we wait for some context before putting Lord Thomas on trial?" snapped the king. He shook his head and faced Bally and Lonnie. "Forgive the Prince."

"The Prince is forgiven," Bally said, sharing a smile with him. "I don't know what your servant calls herself, and it doesn't matter. She is not who she appears to be."

"And what exactly does that mean?" the King asked. "You confuse me, Princess."

"Yes, please explain," the Prince added.

"You heard him." The king rose from his throne, impatient wrinkles etching across his forehead as he stared down at Bally. "Explain your riddles. We have royal responsibilities to attend."

"I think it'll be easier to show you," Bally said. "Please summon this *Jessica* so I may show you what I see."

"Your Highness?" asked Lord Thomas.

"Go ahead," the king said. "Bring her here. While we wait, I'd like to learn more about our guests. Is your companion mute or simply tongue-tied?"

"I'm just tired," Lonnie said.

"Tired of *what?*" asked the prince, leaning forward with a suspicious glare.

"Tired from traveling. We've come a long way to see you, Your Highness." Lonnie's panic rose up and tampered her drunkenness, sending heat through her veins. She tucked her hand behind her back as it began to tremble.

"What I'd like to know is who you are," the king said.

"I am Princess Casper," Bally said. "Heir to the Kingdom of the Shrine. This is my cousin, Lady Pine."

"I've not heard of the Kingdom of the Shrine. It sounds made up."

"It does," said the prince. "Are you a new kingdom, or an inconsequential one?"

"*Watch your tone*," hissed the king. "These women came all this way to see you. Isn't that right, Princess?"

"Our kingdom is very distant, and yes, we've traveled all this way to meet the prince," Bally said. "We'd like to have a private conversation and discuss a possible union between our provinces."

"And you?" the king asked, turning to Lonnie. "What is your business?"

"I'm Lady Pine," Lonnie said, freezing under the pressure.

"I've seen sheep with stronger personalities," the king said. He smiled as he studied Lonnie. Around him, his heads of the castle forced a laugh.

"A tongue-less toad would offer more information," said the prince. With hesitation, one of the heads chuckled. To Lonnie's dismay, the king had no issues with the piggy-backed insult.

"I've come to assist the Princess," Lonnie said, her voice quaking. "We've traversed a great distance, and it's not safe for a princess to travel alone. I'm simply here to assist my cousin."

"She's invaluable," said Bally. "I'd ask you to show some respect."

"Respect is earned in this kingdom," the king said. He stifled a belch before turning to his kingsguard. "Where the hell is Thomas?"

"I don't know," the kingsguard said, throwing up a hand. "I imagine they're on their way."

"Tell them to come faster."

The kingsguard nodded before wandering out of the chamber.

"This mystery is making me hungry," the king said. He chewed on a fingernail, his eyes flickered from Bally to Lonnie. "Why are you staring at me?" he asked.

"Me?" Lonnie asked.

"Yes, you."

"You were speaking."

"Well, now I'm not." The king glared at Lonnie, who turned to her feet. "We're fighting a war, if you didn't know," he continued. "Please look at me when I'm speaking."

"Sorry," Lonnie said, turning back to the throne.

"At this very moment, my army is punching a hole through the southern defenses of our enemy. Victory will soon be at hand."

"They fall like butterflies in a windstorm," said the prince.

"No, they fall like men upon a sword," said the king. "This leads me to a question. Why would you choose to come all the way from wherever you came to court a prince who's engaged in a deadly war?"

"I wasn't aware of the war," Bally said. "And since you're winning, it doesn't sway my opinion of anything."

"What about you?" the king asked, turning to Lonnie.

"What?" Lonnie asked.

"Why would you choose to come all the way from wherever you came to court a prince who's engaged in a deadly war?"

"Because she wanted to." Lonnie tipped her head to Bally.

"Sire," Lord Thomas called from the hall. "I have Jessica. Shall I bring her into the Chamber?"

"For fuck's sake," the king said. "*Yes.*"

"Get ready to run if this doesn't work," Bally whispered, stepping in front of Lonnie. She lifted her wand and the tip turned brilliant green.

Everyone turned as Lord Thomas entered the chamber, leading a very nervous Jessica after him. She cowered as they walked the red carpet. The room fell deadly silent as she stopped before the throne.

"Jessica, did you serve them in the baths?" the king asked.

"Yes," Jessica said.

"And your name is indeed Jessica?" asked the prince.

"Yes." Jessica bowed her head to Lonnie and Bally, politely smiling.

"She lies," Bally said. "She's used a clever disguise, but I recognized her at once."

"Explain!" the king shouted.

"This is not Jessica." Bally pulled the servant forward, raising her wand as she forced Jessica into a spin. Jessica twirled beneath a flash of green light. When she stopped, facing the throne, a roar washed across the chamber. "This woman is no other than *Lonnie Lovingdove*," Bally announced, stepping back.

Lonnie, who hadn't closed her eyes in time, stared at a mirror copy of herself. Her stomach dropped as she gasped.

"Well, well, well," said the king, marching down the steps. He approached Jessica with unnerving satisfaction. "We meet again, *Lonnie Lovingdove*."

"Your Highness, it's me," Jessica said. "What are you talking about? I'm Jessica Pawn. I've served the castle for years."

"Your tricks no longer work on us," said the prince, joining his father on the floor. "You're caught in your own game."

"Take her into custody," the king said. "Bind her in a private dungeon with a dozen guards. Tell my torturers the time has finally come. I want her eyes gouged out and her anus ripped into a window. And that's just for starters."

"And split her nipples down the center," said the prince.

"*No!*" shouted the king. "Split them from left to right."

Jessica screamed as a team of guards rushed forward,

quickly binding her. She begged for mercy, pleading with anyone who would look at her, but the castle heads dared not speak against the king. Lonnie's stomach churned. No one deserved to have their anus ripped into a window, and to have another of her punishments passed to an innocent was a sickening reminder of the lashing she inadvertently passed onto Daniel.

"Maybe you should wait a few days," she said. "Let her feel the panic before you do anything."

"But this is the woman you've been waiting for, yes?" Bally asked. "Better to deal with her quickly, yes?"

"Correct," said the king. "Lock her up and wait for me. After I feast, I want to bear witness to the torture myself. And let's leave those long legs as they are. I have *plans* for them." The king met Bally, falling to a knee before her. "Forgive my lack of faith in your mystery," he said. "You are an honored guest of this castle, and you may stay as long as you wish. What can I give you?"

"I'd like some time with your son," Bally said, turning to the prince. "Private time, if I may be so bold."

"You heard her," the king said. "Pollen, take these ladies to your chambers and show them whatever they came to see."

"The pleasure will be mine," said the prince. He smiled, greeting Bally and Lonnie with cocked elbows. "Come on," he said quietly. "While he's still in a good mood."

Lonnie looked back while the prince led them through a back door. Jessica, entangled in a mass of kingsguard, wept with Lonnie's face, preparing to endure a torture devised for a wholly other innocent woman.

FORTY-FIVE

"Is there anything you can do for that poor girl?" Lonnie asked the prince. They moved with royal laziness through a velvet-lined hall, the torches leaving the room hot and smokey. "Her punishment seems rather harsh."

"I'm afraid my father no longer believes in mercy," the prince said. "Best we focus on our meeting. I must admit, I'm quite flattered to hear of your journey to speak with me. I'm quite interested in our conversation."

"But we come for more than conversation," Bally said. She smiled, setting a hand on the prince's shoulder. "I hope you have wine in your quarters, because we're quite thirsty."

"The finest in the kingdom."

"But what if you just delayed her torture?" Lonnie asked. "Just a couple days would work."

"But didn't she already escape once?" Bally asked.

"Yes, I'm afraid that's true," the prince said. "My father won't be taking any chances this time. Please, focus not on our housekeeping. It sounds like we have much to discuss."

"Oh, we'll be doing more than discussing." Bally grinned, her spell-emaciated face looking like a horse's asshole to Lonnie. But under the Occumancy, the prince giggled, releasing Lonnie to set his full attention on Bally.

"I think I like you," he said. "You're very bold, and *very sexy*."

"Even if you only let her be for just the night," Lonnie said. "You could use the time to think of better tortures."

"Please, Lady Pine. Don't trouble yourself with Lonnie Lovingdove. Her fate has no bearing on you."

The prince led them up a long, spiral staircase, where they finally came into a massive bedroom. Lonnie gasped at the posh luxury. Great purple and green silks draped across the ceiling and four-poster bed. An archway extended onto a stone balcony, which overlooked the whole of Doane. Golden sets of armor decorated the corners of the room, and paintings of the king and prince and the countryside filled most of the walls. It smelled of burned oil and sweet pastries. Lonnie turned around to find a table filled with stale trays of cakes.

"Forgive the mess," the prince said, tossing a silk over the table. "I wasn't expecting company—at least not such *beautiful* company." He smiled as he crossed the room, pulling back the curtain. The afternoon sun glowed over the countryside below. "Did you say you enjoy wine?" he asked, turning over his shoulder.

"We love it," Bally said.

"Then you're in good fortune." The prince walked onto the balcony and returned with a keg. He set it on the table and pounded a tap into the bunghole. In his cool, charming version of laziness, he filled three goblets and handed them to the women. "Sit," he said, motioning to the bed. "Tell me what you've come to hear. Or see. Or *taste.*" He crossed his legs tightly as he lounged back on the bed.

"I've heard stories of your beauty," Bally said, nestling beside him. "Stories that challenged me to leave all I knew in pursuit of you."

Lonnie remained on her feet, taking a deep sip of her wine.

"And do those stories hold true?" the prince asked. He leaned into Bally's greasy forehead, grinning as their heads connected. "Am I what you wanted to find at the end of your road?"

"And then some." Bally sucked down her entire goblet and dropped it onto the bed. She set her hands around the prince's neck, leaning in to kiss him.

"Should I leave?" Lonnie asked. She winced at the rising passion between Bally and the prince. "I'll go ahead and wait downstairs."

"Stay," Bally mumbled, kissing the prince a few quick times before turning to her. "Please, we may need your assistance."

The prince grinned at Lonnie, patting the unoccupied side of the bed. His beauty and the wine left Lonnie tempted, but even the suggestion of romance left her heart breaking for Daniel.

"I need more wine," Lonnie said. While Bally and the prince rolled back onto the bed, their kissing growing louder, Lonnie wandered onto the balcony.

The whole of Doane lay before her; the four hamlets stretching across the countryside like wicked wildflowers. From the tower on the hillside, it looked incredibly flat. Lonnie studied her old world as if it were a painting on a sheet of parchment. Everything she had ever called home sat in just a tiny corner of it all.

"Your breasts," the prince gasped. "I've never seen such perky perfection."

Lonnie turned, finding Bally topless on the bed. Her flat and bony breasts didn't so much as bounce as the prince pecked at them. Bally met Lonnie's gaze and waved for her to come.

"I'm still drinking," Lonnie said, lifting her glass. She took a swallow as she turned back to the kingdom.

It was a view very few people might ever see. She felt dizzy, although she suspected her incredible consumption of wine might have something to do with it. She wished Daniel could see what she saw; to feel the breeze and smell the air of royal privilege.

"Take that off," the prince commanded. "I'm tired of these games. Take it *off*." Bally giggled as fabric ripped. Lonnie turned, just in time to see the prince finish tearing Bally's dress away. He dropped the rags and chased Bally across the bed on all fours. They laughed and giggled, both completely naked as they romped in a circle.

"Come on," Bally said, waving to Lonnie. "We're having fun."

"Still drinking." Lonnie lifted her glass, but she nearly dropped it at the sight of Bally's wand, which lay upon the bed —right in the path of their raucous horseplay. "Stop," Lonnie cried, running into the room. "Be careful, you're going to—"

A bright *snap* came from under the prince's bucking knee. He paused, lifting the broken pieces of wood.

"What the hell is this?" he asked, turning to Bally. "Fuck!" he screamed, falling backwards off the bed. "*Demon!*" he cried, scrambling backwards across the room.

"What?" Bally asked.

"Your wand," Lonnie called.

Bally, an emaciated, greasy and wizened little creature, blushed to a mucus-like shade of yellow.

"Shit," she said. "We have to go. Lonnie, find me something to—"

A sword burst through Bally's stomach, pushing ribbons of wine-soaked guts across the bed. The prince shrieked as Bally crumbled, the sword falling from his hands. He stared at Lonnie with wide eyes.

"You," he breathed. "*You're* Lonnie Lovingdove. Witchcraft . . ."

"It was her idea," Lonnie said. "I didn't want to do any of this. I'd be insane to try and come—"

"*Witch!*" The prince pulled the sword from Bally, his chest heaving as he extended it toward Lonnie. "Now you'll die, *witch.*" He leaped forward and thrust. Lonnie barely managed to duck back in time.

"Please," she said, backing toward the balcony. "I'm not a witch, and I can explain everything. I'm not what you think I am—who you think I am."

The prince only doubled his grip. His fingers wound tightly around the hilt of the broadsword. He let out a growling scream and charged.

Lonnie splashed the last of her wine into his eyes. While he screeched, she ran to the balcony, finding the moat a few hundred feet below. She let out a yelp of self pity and leaped from the tower.

FORTY-SIX

L onnie managed to land herself into the moat, but as she crashed, all the air left her body in a hiss of bubbles. She floated through the water without breath or a sense of direction. The wine gave the world a strange tilt. One thought moved through her obliterated mind.

I'm getting tired of this.

Above, the sun rippled beyond a curtain of water, and she kicked her feet, stretching her arms to the light. Her head bobbed into the air just as the world started to blacken.

She drew a short breath and broke into a coughing fit. As she slipped back under the water, she bumped into the bank and dragged herself through the reeds and cattails. There, she took a minute to regain her breath. Her body throbbed and the wine still kicked like a jackass. She could remain on that bank for days, but the prince surely raced through the castle to round up the kingsguard, and Lonnie wasn't quite ready to die.

She wobbled as she stood, swaying before breaking into a crooked run down the bank. Déja vu and bad memories came of the repeated escape. She focused on hate, which helped her maintain control.

In hindsight, Bally had been a shit friend, and her idea of fun had been nothing more than magically seasoned insanity. Lonnie had somehow run off with the craziest person in the Shrine. Livid, she dumped the water from her bag and swayed into the woods.

She ran back toward the hamlets, figuring she could find

better cover in the city than the royal forest. The alcohol burned through her skin as she began to sweat. She sneered, wishing Bally were still alive so she could kill her. The anger kept her running for an hour.

But she ran out of energy soon enough.

She stumbled across an unknown neighborhood, still half-soaking wet. A few of the peasants glanced at her. Lonnie snatched a shirt from a clothesline and wrapped her head down to the eyes. She roamed until she found an old, covered wagon and peered into the back. A few dozen crates sat stacked across it, with a pile of old blankets on top.

She climbed inside and pushed the crates into a wall, giving herself a small lane behind them. Exhausted, she lifted the blankets, pausing to find the crates filled with water. She greedily drank two bottles and crawled into her hideaway. Wincing, she covered herself with the blankets. She barely managed to hide her feet before falling unconscious.

Her sleep was deep and heavy. It came without dreams, for her body had much poison to extricate.

She woke in a pleasant daze with a headache. To her dismay, the old wagon she hid within rocked and rolled beneath her.

FORTY-SEVEN

For the second time, Lonnie escaped the castle through the moat, and for the second time, she hid in a wagon only to find herself stowed away on a moving vehicle. She cursed as she lay in her wedge, listening to the labored breathing of horses. The sun had set and left her in near darkness. But a lamp at the front of the wagon cast light through the gaps in the wagon's frame. Lonnie quietly rose to her knees, peering over the water crates.

No human butchers rode in the back this time. Letting out a breath, she drank another bottle of water. She waited a while, figuring it would be wise to put distance between her and the castle, but then she realized she might in fact be on her way to the castle.

She climbed over the crates, nearly knocking one over as her foot snagged on the handle. She leaned out of the back of the wagon.

Swamplands surrounded her. The pools of endless muck stretched to the horizon, slightly glinting in the light of the crescent moon. A chilly wind roamed the wasteland. It carried a stench so foul Lonnie's nausea knocked on her belly button. She crawled back into the wagon, deciding she could wait a while. She had never seen or heard of such swamps, and that meant she was far from the Doane.

She wrapped a few blankets around herself and worked on another bottle of water. Outside, frogs shrieked ugly mating calls, solidifying her decision to not start anew in the watery desert. When a mosquito bit her on the nose, she climbed back into her hideaway.

While she lay, using Daniel's carving as a pillow, she decided she would never drink wine again. She would also take more time in choosing her friends.

The blurry memories of her fun with Bally played across her mind. Despite the passing moments of frivolous fun, it kindled her anger. She didn't know if Bally deserved to die, but society was certainly better off without her. Lonnie cursed herself for not breaking off from her sooner.

But at least she had survived.

Although, as she thought about it, she wondered just what survival meant. There was no longer a person to call her friend or family. She had no home. Since her rebellious decision to leave the house after curfew, she had drawn a plow of destruction across every life she crossed. Her curiosity had a part to play, but there was something else; something she could only see in the wake of her rampage with Bally.

She had yet to take personal control of herself.

As a child, her mother ruled with a wicker fist.

As a woman, Daniel did his best to lead their partnership.

As an escapee, Lonnie first submitted to Lahn, and then to Bally.

She clenched a fist, hating to admit the brutal truth.

How could she expect to find the life she wanted if she let other people choose her path?

And just what kind of life did she want?

Lonnie spent a while thinking about it. She knew she wanted love of some kind—everyone needed someone to walk the road of life with, but she had another need, and its primal hunger needed a director. If her spirit would only be fulfilled by the exploration of the unknown, then she must take charge of that expedition and find a safe way about it. A Head of Curiosity, so to speak.

Lonnie mused on this idea as the time whiled away. She decided she needed to start at once or someone else would once again assume control. Shivering at the idea, she pulled the blankets off and climbed out of her nest. The wagon rocked beneath her. She peered out the back, finding the endless mire. The horses moved with a sluggish gate, and knowing she could outwalk them, Lonnie climbed out.

She wandered along the cool mud behind the wagon, feeling a great energy in taking control of her escape. The earth felt good on her tender feet. She stayed close to the wagon, knowing she needed to lay eyes on the driver, but still not strong enough to do it outright. Finally, she veered to her left and found the shoulder of a tiny man. The swinging lamp backlit his face, revealing a thick mustache and a wide-brimmed hat. His thin arms gave her the boost she needed to approach him.

Her heart sped as she came up the side of the wagon, silently making her way to the driver. He idly hunched with the reins in his hand. Some kind of wheat or grass stem bounced from his lips. Lonnie inched herself forward until she came alongside him.

"Sir," she said. "Hello."

The driver shouted as he fell off the bench. He gasped, clutching at his chest.

"Are you all right?" Lonnie asked. She climbed onto the bench, finding a man far older than she expected on the floor. He breathed heavily as he wrestled with the breast of his shirt. His wide eyes glistened. "I didn't mean to scare you," Lonnie said. "Are you okay?"

"Help," the man breathed, laying back as his face flushed. "Need . . . help . . ."

After glancing across the wasteland, Lonnie took up the reins.

"I'll have to drive us," she said. "What kind of help do you need?"

"Doctor," the man gasped.

Lonnie whipped the team of mules into a light run, wincing at her lack of tact. The man gasped and groaned as he continued to wrestle with his shirt.

"Is there anything I can do now?" Lonnie asked. "I can get you water."

"Doctor," the man hissed. "My heart . . ."

Lonnie gave the mules a harder whip and stood, looking for a sign of the end of the swamp. She snuffed out the lamp and waited for her eyes to adjust.

"I'm really sorry," she said, turning to make sure the man was still alive. "I didn't mean to scare you."

"Where did you come from?" he breathed, wincing as they rocked over a rut in the road.

"I can't tell you. Where are we going?"

"I can't tell you." The man tried to sit and fell back. He grunted, pulling his hat behind his head. "I'm dying," he said, the distaste in his words clearly aimed at Lonnie. "You've scared me to death."

"I didn't mean to," Lonnie said. "And I'll get you to a doctor. Everything will be okay. How far are we from the next town?"

"Not close enough." The man slapped a hand onto the bench, finally dragging himself to a seat. He groaned with each exhale, his hand wrapped tightly around his shirt. "You've killed me," he muttered, shaking his head.

"Well, it wasn't on purpose," Lonnie said. "I was trying to do the right thing and introduce myself."

"Wait." The man leaned forward. "I know who you are. You're *Lovingdove*."

Lonnie blushed and kept her eyes on the mules.

"Were you in the back?" he asked.

"Maybe."

"Did you drink that water? I saw a few bottles missing."

"Maybe."

"For the love of . . ." The old man set a finger to his temple. "That was blessed water, you blasphemous git."

"Well, I didn't know. I feel fine."

"It's sacred," the man hissed. "It's blessed for anointing and *anointing only*. I expect you'll be struck down for drinking it."

"If you knew what I've seen and done over the past week, drinking blessed water is the least of my offenses," Lonnie said, growing tired of the man's attitude. "I want to help you, but if you don't tell me where we're going or how close we are to the next kingdom I can't do anything but drive these mules—which I don't really know how to do."

"We're a day out," the man said, his voice falling into a grumble. "There's no chance we'll make it before I finish dying. You scared me too good."

"I only said hello."

"You might as well have put a dagger in my heart." The old man sighed, leaning back against the wagon. "I never thought I'd end like this. And on a holy mission, too. God knows how many will die because I couldn't finish my delivery."

"You don't seem like you're dying." Lonnie turned to the man, but seeing the pale, deathly pallor of his face, she softened. "I'm very sorry. What's your name?"

"I was Grand Teacher Tomlin," he said.

"Tomlin, can you tell me where you're going?"

"I *was* going to deliver the blessed water to men in need of protection. Now? I guess I'm headed to the heavens."

"Let's not be so negative," Lonnie said. "I'm offering to

finish your delivery for you. If you tell me before you die, I'll make sure it gets to the men who need it."

"If you don't drink the rest of it," Tomlin said.

"I won't."

"Well . . ." Tomlin turned to the stars, his breath rasping with each draw. "If you mean what you say, then this water is meant for the men of Camp Aslin. This road eventually comes right into them. They're red."

"Red?" Lonnie asked. "What does that mean?"

"Finish what I—" Tomlin hissed as he sat forward, his hand bone-white as he clutched his shirt. "*If you mean to right your wrongs of killing me, then finish what I've started . . .*" He yelped as he sat back, his legs bucking and kicking. Lonnie scooted back and let the reins go. Tomlin huffed through his clenched teeth, his eyes wide and set on Lonnie's soul. He lifted an accusatory finger just as the light fell from his eyes.

Tomlin collapsed like a frail bag of bones.

Lonnie swallowed, taking up the reins.

"I'm very sorry," she breathed, keeping her gaze on the swishing mule tails. "I was just saying hello."

Her first attempt at decision making had gone poorly, but through Tomlin's death, she had at least made one righteous decision: to deliver cases of blessed water to the needy men of Camp Aslin. She sat a little taller under the responsibility. Tomlin hadn't been able to explain anything through his fixation with the negative, but he had at least given Lonnie the basic directions. She lifted her gaze as the sun began rising over the swamp.

And there, incredibly far but visible, she saw the stone outline of civilization.

FORTY-EIGHT

As the morning burned away, Grand Teacher Tomlin's stench began to magnify. Flies swarmed his corpse, and with hours before she came to the stone buildings, Lonnie made the decision to bury the holy man.

She pulled the mules off-road as they came into sturdier grasslands. She surveyed the field and found a beautiful lane between live oak trees. It took nearly an hour to dig the grave, but Lonnie didn't mind—it felt good to follow through with decisions.

She did her best to respectfully drag the holy man into the grave, but as he settled she frowned, realizing it was so shallow the tips of his boots sat a few inches above ground. Still, it was better than nothing. She raked the dirt over him and stepped back.

"Once again," she said, folding her hands, "I'm very sorry I scared you to death. I was just trying to do the right thing. I hope you're happy with your maker. Goodbye."

As Lonnie resumed the pilgrimage to Camp Aslin, she found a sense of righteousness. She sat tall as she drove the mules. The day looked to be a beautiful one, and she took it as a sign of spiritual growth. It felt good to have a task. The mystery of it only satisfied her, because she would soon have no choice but to learn the unknowns.

By noon, she came into the stone structures, which turned out to be a ruined village. Only ash and rats remained of what looked to have been a quaint community. She drove the mules onward, trusting Tomlin the road would end at Camp Aslin.

Her stomach rumbled by mid afternoon. She dug around and found a small pouch of dried meat underneath the wagon bench. Tomlin had salted it to oblivion, but she ate greedily, her body still ravaged by hunger. She finished it and a desperate thirst crawled out of her stomach. As her lips dried and cracked, she found herself glancing to the back of the wagon. The blessed water had been cool and pure as snow. She could easily drink another case, but she decided it would be wrong.

And her sacrificial decision paid off not ten minutes later. She came to a stream, where she and mules filled themselves with cool, delicious water. They moved with a new energy as they continued down the road. The fields thickened into a half-wilderness, with large brush and trees scattered about. It disrupted visibility and Lonnie kept an eye on her surroundings. She wished Tomlin had been more specific with how long the ride would take. His dying breaths had been wasted complaining.

But at dusk, the answer to Lonnie's questions appeared around a wide bend in the road. Nearly a hundred white tents sat scattered across the grass. Wagons and horses roamed between them, with a single raised flag bearing three red dots against white. Lonnie brushed out her hair as she approached. A few of the men from Camp Aslin were outside, and they waved at the sight of her. Thin, and wearing only linen long johns, they gathered at the entrance to camp.

"Hello," Lonnie called, pulling the mules to a stop. "Is this Camp Aslin?"

"It is," a man said. "And who are you?"

"I'm . . . Lonnie Lovingdove," she said, deciding it was time to be herself. "I've come to deliver blessed water for Grand Teacher Tomlin. Unfortunately, he died on the journey."

"I'm afraid you're too late," the man said. "Grand Teacher Raspin just arrived, and he's already brought us blessed water." The man held up a dusty bottle.

"Who's Grand Teacher Raspin?" Lonnie asked.

"Him." The man pointed down the road, where a white-haired old man in a long trench coat stood outside of a rustic wagon, grinning and shaking hands as he dispensed bottles of blessed water. Lonnie frowned.

"Wasn't Tomlin supposed to bring you the blessed water?"

"Well, Raspin got here first. Did you have anything else for us?"

"I don't think so."

The man grunted and wandered off. Lonnie, not ready to fail her death-wish to Tomlin, whipped the mules forward. She already didn't like Grand Teacher Raspin; the smug, condescending grin on his face; the way he clapped each man on the back as he gave them his blessed water.

If it even was real blessed water.

He turned as Lonnie pulled up, his bright smile slowly melting into a scowl. Lonnie climbed down to meet him.

"Good evening," she said. "Are you Grand Teacher Raspin?"

"Who's asking?" Raspin asked. "And where did you get that cart? I know those mules."

"It's Grand Teacher Tomlin's cart. I'm sorry to tell you, but he just passed away. I've come to make his blessed water delivery."

"The old bastard's dead?" Raspin relaxed, breaking into a chuckle as he studied the wagon. "What got him? Is he still in the cart?"

"Something went wrong with his heart," Lonnie said. "And no, I buried him on the road."

"You buried a grand teacher?" Raspin's grin turned manic as

he laughed. He paused, about to speak, then slapped his knee and went back into laughter.

"What?" Lonnie asked, hating how the camp men had started to gather around them. "What's so funny about burying a dead man?"

"Lady," Raspin said, wiping a tear. "You really don't know?"

"Don't know what?"

"A grand teacher has to be burned after death. It's the only way to the Maker." Raspin laughed again, shaking his head as he returned to his cart. "Old Tomlin's in for a real treat when he wakes up in hell. You might as well have dumped him in a gully."

"Then I'll go back and fix it." Lonnie seethed as Raspin headed back to his wagon. She hated the thought of backtracking to burn the holy man's corpse, but she didn't want to start her new life with such a horrendous blunder. "I'll leave the blessed water with you," she said to a few of the men from Camp Aslin. "You can save it for later."

But as she climbed into the back of the cart and started handing out bottles, Grand Teacher Raspin let out a shout.

Lonnie poked her head out of the wagon to find him storming up the road.

"What?" she asked.

"This is my camp," Raspin shouted. "Take that water back."

"I don't need it, and it won't hurt them to have extra."

"No." Raspin collected the bottles from the confused men and shoved them back into Lonnie's wagon. "This is my camp. You get out of here and take your *blessed* water with you."

"Grand Teacher Tomlin wanted me to deliver it. It was his dying wish."

"And you came too late," Raspin said. "You need to get out of here. You're throwing off the spirit of hospitality."

"Is there somewhere else I can take the water?" Lonnie asked, turning to the men.

"The next camp, maybe," one of them said.

"Absolutely not," Raspin said. "This is my route, now. I'm going through all three camps, and I don't need anyone to help me."

"Then you take the water," Lonnie said. "I'm going back to burn—"

"The water you just put your grubby hands all over?" Raspin barked out a laugh. "That water's as blessed as piss after you've touched it. If you don't want it, take it into the woods and dump it. This is holy business for holy *men*. Women have no place here." Raspin clapped his hands clean as he stormed off, waving for the men to follow him, and Lonnie decided she hated him more than Grand Teacher Tomlin.

"Where is the next camp?" she asked, turning to one of the camp men.

"Maybe a day's ride," he said. "They'll all along the road. You can't miss it. Camp Beetle's the next one, followed by Camp Cattail."

"Good." Lonnie climbed onto the wagon, her anger burning hot as she whipped the mules back into a trot. She squeezed past Grand Teacher Raspin's wagon.

"Where are you going in such a hurry?" he asked, walking alongside the wagon.

"None of your business," Lonnie said.

"It's exactly my business if you're doing what I think you're doing."

"Please, I have blessed water to deliver." Lonnie whipped the mules and left Raspin in the dust, feeling a great satisfaction to finally have the last word. She rolled out of Camp Aslin grinning.

But not an hour into her ride the mules started acting

nervous. Lonnie turned around to find Raspin's wagon in hot pursuit. He stood over his mules, whipping them violently. She gave her own team a whip and rose from the bench. The rocky road left her bumbling. She drove the mules for an hour, keeping her head start on Raspin, but they unanimously decided to walk again.

"Run," Lonnie said, whipping their broad backsides. The mules huffed as if only a fly had landed on them. Lonnie turned, her stomach dropping to see Raspin closing the gap. His eyes narrowed to match his growing smile. "Come on," Lonnie said, whipping the mules.

The rumble of Raspin's wagon rose like thunder. Lonnie could do nothing but stare ahead as he came alongside her, shouting and hissing at his mules.

"Women," he called, finally forcing Lonnie to turn. "Always getting into men's business." He cackled as he raced on, kicking up an awful dust. Lonnie pulled her dress over her mouth as the bastard officially pulled ahead.

But he only had the lead for a few minutes before his mules slowed, matching the comfy pace of Lonnie's team. She smiled as he shouted and whipped them to no effect.

Lonnie relaxed as they rolled into the night, the sky clearing to present a beautiful view of the stars. She eventually gave in and snagged a bottle of blessed water. She desperately wanted to win; to deliver the blessed water before Raspin could claim Camp Beetle for himself, but she was tired, and with at least the night to traverse, and the mules steadfast in their lazy collaboration, she grabbed a blanket and made herself comfortable. She lay on the bench and tried to rest. Her mind fluttered with memories of the past weeks, the insane living she had accomplished.

She was just falling asleep when the first strike fell.

FORTY-NINE

Lonnie jumped as something slapped the back of the wagon. She sat up, blinking through the dark. The mules moved at a painfully slow shuffle—as did Raspin's wagon. Lonnie stood just as a clot of mud slapped her in the face.

"Gotcha," Raspin cried, laughing like a maniac in the distance.

"What the fuck?" Lonnie said as she wiped the mud off her cheek. She scowled, her cheek throbbing from the blow.

Another clump crashed into her ear.

"Stop," she shouted.

"Give it up, *woman*," Raspin called. "You're out of your league."

Lonnie lay on her belly and leaned over the side of the wagon, scraping a handful of mud off the ground. She packed it into balls.

Another clump of mud splattered the wagon just beside her head.

"You fucking—" Lonnie wound up and threw a ball at Raspin's cart. It went wide and disappeared into the brush. Fuming, she climbed onto the top of the wagon with the rest of her mud. Raspin stood on the roof of his wagon, wagging his hands beside his head at Lonnie, and an incredible surge of rage came into her. She launched one of the mud balls as hard as she could.

When Raspin shouted and fell to his ass, she took up the second clump.

For two hours they packed and fired mud at one another. They had no clear way of winning, and every time Lonnie felt satisfied enough to leave it alone, Raspin hit her with a hard-packed ball that put her right back into the action.

By sunrise, mud covered her from head to toe. Her right shoulder burned, and her elbow had started to click. Raspin looked just as dirty. He knelt on the roof of his wagon with a massive pile of mud beside him. Lonnie too had built up a reserve, but as the sun rose and the heat fell upon the fight, the mud simply dried to dust.

"I win," Lonnie shouted as she climbed back onto the bench.

"You didn't even come in second place," Raspin shouted. He slipped over the front of his wagon, finally giving her a break from the sight of him.

Lonnie sighed and gave the mules a whip. To her surprise, they started to run. She stood as they raced up the road and gained on Raspin. He didn't notice her approach until she was right beside him, wiggling her hands beside her head.

"Men are lazy," she shouted. "I'll see you at Camp Beetle, *after* I deliver my blessed water." She laughed as she whipped the mules, pleased as they mushed harder, driving well ahead of Raspin.

With a racing heart, she stood and whipped the mules until a smattering of white tents appeared on the horizon. The sight filled her with a gloating pleasure. She climbed onto the roof of her wagon, wanting to throw some consolation mud at Raspin, but he had fallen so far behind she had no chance of hitting him. Grinning, she danced a little jig and wagged her fingers at the side of her head.

As the muled pulled into Camp, Lonnie climbed back onto the bench. The men at Camp Beetle looked just as displaced as the ones at Camp Aslin; tattered long johns, growing beards and a hungry look about them. They watched Lonnie's approach with apprehension. She lifted a hand to show her good intention, only then realizing she must look insane with mud covered every inch of her.

"I've come with blessed water," she called, pulling the mules to a stop in the center of camp. "Everyone, gather around. I have plenty." She parked the wagon diagonally, ensuring Raspin had no room to circumvent her.

"We've needed this greatly," one of the men said, offering Lonnie a hand off the wagon. "Thank you for coming."

"It's my pleasure," Lonnie said. She led the growing crowd to the back of her wagon, pleased to see their desperation for her help. It felt wonderful to dispense the bottles. The men bowed and praised her charity. Lonnie wished them well and gave them all a pat on the shoulder, ensuring they held the bottles tightly before she let go. A few loaded her cart with breads and dried meats, much to Lonnie's relief.

A short while later, Raspin came rumbling into the camp. He shouted for the crowd to move as he whipped his mules. By then, most everyone who wanted blessed water had it, and Lonnie grinned with a deep satisfaction as he forced his mules to a stop behind her.

"I've already blessed them," she said. "You might as well go home, old man."

"Move that claptrap of a wagon out of the way," Raspin shouted. He raised his whip, as if pain might drive his mules to fly over the barricade.

"I'm not quite done," Lonnie said. "Go around if you're in an emergency." She smiled as Raspin gritted his teeth, his face blackened with mud. She pulled a few more bottles from the wagon and satisfied the last of the camp's residents. They thanked her profusely and Lonnie took her time accepting the praise, laughing with the men as they exchanged names.

"Has he been bothering you?" one of the men asked, tipping his head toward Raspin.

"He's all bark," Lonnie said. "I survived last night, and I imagine I'll survive tonight. He's got to be tiring."

"It's dangerous on the road, though. Let me get you something. This way." The man led Lonnie into a nearby tent, where he handed her a bow and quiver of arrows. "Do you know how to shoot?"

"I don't think I'll need—"

"You nock the arrow, like this," the man said, setting the arrow on his knuckle, "and then you draw back to your shoulder. Hold steady and keep holding steady as you let fly. If he comes after you, an arrow in the chest or belly will kill him, and one in the leg or arm will disable him."

"I won't need this," Lonnie said. But she took it with her to the wagon. If anything, it would serve as a visual deterrent to any more shenanigans. She made sure Raspin saw it as she climbed back onto her wagon. "How far is the ride to Camp Cattail?" she asked, turning back to the men. They stood huddled with their bottles of blessed water in hand.

"A day's ride," one said. "Keep straight and you'll come right into it."

"Thank you, and bless you," Lonnie added, bowing to the men as she took up her reins. She let the mules take their time as they followed the road through camp.

Raspin cursed and crawled through the camp behind her, his mules inches from the back of her wagon. His whip cracked so often Lonnie wondered how it hadn't unraveled. She stopped the mules completely as she came to the end of the tents, selecting her food and arranging it on her lap. Raspin shouted a string of ferocious curses.

"Piss off," Lonnie shouted back, biting off a mouthful of petrified meat. She had barely started to chew when she heard feet slapping across the dirt. She leaned around the wagon to find Raspin running full sprint toward her. She whipped the mules and they took off.

"You bloody cunt!" Rapsin shouted.

Lonnie grinned as she climbed onto the top of her wagon, giving Raspin a little dance as he fell into her dust.

But he was the one who laughed, stepping out of a tent with his own bow and quiver of arrows. He climbed onto his wagon and whipped his mules into a run after her. Lonnie paled as they came tearing up the road, her lead diminishing by the minute. She dropped down to the bench and lifted the bow and arrows.

FIFTY

"This is insane," Lonnie said, trying to remember how to nock an arrow. She lifted her head over the wagon to find Raspin only fifty feet behind her. He never stopped whipping the mules, and after their extended rest in Camp Beetle, they responded brilliantly. They broke in and out of her dust trail like demons racing after sinners.

Lonnie stuffed some bread into her mouth as she kept an eye on Raspin. He focused solely on driving the mules, but his bow and arrows sat on the bench, within easy reach. Lonnie didn't know if he could shoot, but seeing how she had never done it, the fight didn't feel fair.

She debated pulling off the road and letting him pass; she had proved her point at Camp Beetle, but the thought of letting him win came with a bitter taste. She frowned as he inched ever closer. He looked mad enough to kill, but then again he was a holy man. Perhaps he hoped to scare her into submission—as he likely suspected a woman would do.

"Run faster," Lonnie called to the mules, giving the rein a gentle whip. She turned to the sky, where the sunset deepened, casting the dry grasslands in an overcoat of red and orange. The sight filled her with peace. Aside from the rumbling wagons, it could be a perfect evening. Perhaps she and Grand Teacher Raspin could start anew.

Lonnie stood on the bench, finding Raspin a dozen feet behind her wagon.

"We need to talk," she shouted over the din of the wheels. "This is crazy."

Raspin only glared at her, his face twisted into a disgusted scowl.

"Did you hear me?" Lonnie called.

Raspin stood and raised his bow.

Lonnie ducked as an arrow sailed beside her left ear.

She sat on the bench with her heart pounding.

"*Pull off or die,*" Raspin shouted.

Lonnie took the reins and was about to do as he asked when she paused, remembering her new promise: only she gave herself orders.

She turned to the bow and arrows, her hands trembling.

"Don't make me kill a woman," Raspin cried. "It's too easy." He somehow found a way to cackle loud enough for Lonnie to hear him, and it was the last push she needed.

"Fuck off," she said, taking up the bow. The camp man had given her twenty-some arrows and she nocked one, crouching against the wagon as she made sure her grip was right. She turned to the sky, wondering if it was safe to stand up. With self preservation in mind, she lifted her bag with Daniel's carving first.

An arrow knocked it out of her hand. The bag tumbled to the bench, with the arrow set perfectly into Daniel's heart.

"Shit," Lonnie breathed. She grabbed the bag and lifted it again, waving it until another arrow *thwacked* into the wood. Praying Raspin needed more than a few seconds to reload, she popped up and drew the bow.

Raspin stared at her, completely exposed, and she let her arrow lose. It swept through the air and embedded into his wagon, far wide of her scrawny target. Raspin lifted his bow and Lonnie ducked as the arrow flew over head.

She tried to think of a way out. Even if she gave up and pulled off the road, Raspin had every intention and ability to kill her. Biting her lip, she turned to the mules, who had started to slow in the dawning twilight.

"Keep running," she shouted. "Please." She whipped them hard, and thankfully they broke back into their steady trot. "Am I going to have to kill a holy man?" she asked herself, turning to the bow in her hands.

As an arrow sailed over the top of the wagon, she hung her head, fully aware of the answer.

Lonnie dumped her carving out of the travel bag and frowned at the two arrows embedded in it. She couldn't pull them out, and the desecration of Daniel's final work drove her into a rage. She stuffed a loaf of bread into the travel bag and set it on the bench. After knocking an arrow, she lifted the bread, giving it a wag over the top of the wagon.

When an arrow tore through the bag, she popped up, lining up her shot.

Raspin ducked behind the bench and she held steady. Her arms quaked as the time dragged out.

"You coward," she said, letting the arrow fly. It landed not far from her intended spot in the center of the wagon. She grabbed another arrow and nocked it. Raspin popped up with his bow drawn. He shot quickly and the arrow went wide. Lonnie returned fire and caught the edge of his jacket. She climbed onto the roof, hoping to find Raspin bleeding out, but he rose to his knees and let fly. Lonnie could only watch as the arrow flew into her thigh.

She shouted as it landed, burrowing into her flesh with a painful heat. She dropped back onto the bench and inspected the wound. The arrow hadn't gone deep, but it hurt. She dragged it free and set her thumb over the bloody hole. Raspin's arrows had only sharpened wood tips, yet hers were capped with metal.

"You women fight like children," Raspin shouted. "This is too easy."

"I'll show you easy," Lonnie said, setting the quiver around her shoulder. The sky continued to darken, and without knowing what the mules would do after dark, Lonnie lifted her sack of bread, desperate to kill the holy man before things could get any more complicated.

An arrow snagged into the bag and Lonnie dropped it. She popped up and shot an arrow as Raspin ducked for cover. It locked into his bench and she knocked another. She drew a long, steady breath as she aimed.

Raspin rose and Lonnie let fly, her eyes widening as her arrow sunk into the old man's head. She relaxed until Raspin pulled his own bait bag down. He swung onto his knees and sent his arrow loose. It struck the back of Lonnie's wagon and she returned fire.

Raspin ducked just in time.

They parried back and forth through the afternoon, until the day finally shifted into night. Lonnie's eyes grew heavy, but she dared not risk sleep with Raspin so vicious and spiteful. She munched on her snacks and pried a board out of the wall behind the bench. With some work, she fished a few bottles of blessed water out of the back and drank them. When she had to pee, she squatted over the side of the wagon and made water like a whore. She wondered what Bally might have thought of her adventure. Ironically, with Bally, she could have Occumanced Raspin into thinking she was a man and possibly avoided the whole conflict.

Lonnie stood on the bench and watched him, idly rocking behind the reins in the moonlight. He had wrapped a blanket around himself to fight the chill. It reminded Lonnie she had blankets in the back of the wagon. She climbed down and fished her arm through the hole, catching the fibers of a blanket.

She screamed as Raspin grabbed her ankle and bit it.

FIFTY-ONE

Lonnie spun to find Raspin climbing up from the bottom of the wagon, mouth wide as he lunged for another bite. She kicked him in the face and he grunted, but he had strength for an old man. He dragged himself up and tackled her into the bench. Lonnie pushed as he gnashed and bit at her throat. She kneed him in the stomach, causing enough pain to flip him onto the floor.

"Get out of here," she shouted, reaching for the bow.

"You first," Raspin said, grabbing Lonnie's arm. He thrust her over the side of the wagon and she flipped into the dirt. She rolled head-over-heels and smashed her shoulder on a rock. Gasping, she lay in the road. The wagons rumbled the ground beneath her. Raspin's triumphant laugh faded as he raced on in her wagon.

Lonnie rolled to her belly and faced the on-coming wagon. Raspin's mules either didn't see her or care about trampling her. She rolled out of the way, panting as she pushed herself up. The mules charged by with the ghastly scent of equine energy. Lonnie turned to the approaching wagon and made a desperate leap.

She caught hold of the bench. Her legs dragged along the road, grinding her bare feet. She pulled with all of her energy and got a foot onto the step. Grunting, she climbed to the bench and lay flat, unable to believe what had just happened.

In the distance, she could just barely hear Raspin cackling. She seethed, snatching his bow and arrow. She knocked and aimed at the wagon, but from the rear position, she had no chance of hitting him unless he peeked, and she had a feeling he didn't plan on peeking.

"Shit," she breathed, looking across the bench. Raspin left the bow and crappy wood-tipped arrows behind, but he had shot all but three of them. Only his blanket scarecrow remained.

But the cart did have a window into his cargo hold. Lonnie climbed through, finding a lifetime supply of blessed water. She slid the cases aside and discovered a bag of dried corn. One bite nearly cracked a tooth and she threw it aside, wondering what she might do.

In the dark isolation of Raspin's cargo hold, a dangerous, wonderfully devious idea came through her rage. She dragged the blanket scarecrow through the window and began to shred it.

FIFTY-TWO

Lonnie tore the blanket into dozens of strips. She carefully organized and braided them, making sure they were strong enough to handle her work. Once the makeshift ropes were ready, she dropped them onto the driver's bench and began passing bottles of blessed water through.

She climbed after the bottles and stared at her former wagon. It gently rocked as it rolled along the moonlit road. Still enraged but confident, she began tying the ropes around the blessed water bottles, thinking of Bally's bottles of tears. It took time, but after an hour she had two dozen of the bottles securely fastened to her body. She bounced from side to side to ensure they weren't going to fly off.

"Okay, she said, turning to the mules. "I'm coming up." With a careful hop, she leaped onto the right mule's back, stroking his mane as he adjusted to her. She checked to make sure all the blessed water survived the jump, and then frowned to realize she had left the bow and arrow on the bench. Unwilling to risk the climb back, she leaned down and began unfastening the carriage mounts, all the while whispering sweet praise into the mule's ear. "We're going to eat carrots, and oats, and drink lots of water. And fresh, chewy hay."

She stepped over the strap connecting the mules and unbuckled it. As it dropped, dragging along the ground, the other mule huffed under the brunt of the wagon's weight. He groaned as Lonnie unwound the last buckle between them. She lifted her mule's mount and guided him to the right, officially breaking free of the wagon.

The other mule stared at them with jealousy, his pace slowing under the weight of the wagon.

"I'm sorry," Lonnie said. "This is Raspin's fault." She kicked the mule and held on as he started to run.

As the mule came alongside the other wagon, something spooked it into a full-on sprint. Lonnie cringed as they came up on the bench, praying for her own divine intervention, and as they rode by, she managed to snag one of the arrows stuck in Daniel's carving.

Raspin let out a shout as they raced on. Lonnie grinned, turning over her shoulder. The old man stared at her with wide eyes. Like a warrior, Lonnie lifted Daniel's carving over her head and let out a guttural shriek.

Raspin cursed after her.

Lonnie hugged the mule as he galloped. A few arrows *thumped* into the mud, but Raspin couldn't hit the moving target at night, and they were soon driving across open country. Lonnie laughed as she leaned down to kiss the mule.

"Thank you," she said, holding him tight.

The mule kept running for another thirty minutes before he finally ran out of energy. Lonnie had no issues with it. He put miles between her and Raspin. She sat back and tied Daniel's carving into her tapestry of blessed water. The stars glowed from above, and she drank the sight, laughing again at her cleverness.

"We won," she said, patting the mule.

He huffed nervously.

When the sun rose, Lonnie and the mule both found a second wind. They rode through a lush country of broad fields and dark-green forests. A pleasant wind came with the sun and helped wick the heat away. They even came to a stream, where

Lonnie let the mule have his fill. She debated climbing down to wash herself and take a drink, but it was too risky. The only way to maintain control of the mule was to stay atop him.

As the morning drifted into afternoon, Lonnie set her sole focus on the horizon. She expected to see the white tents and red flag of Camp Cattail at any moment. The voyage would be her greatest accomplishment as an independently directed woman. When she did indeed spot the white tents, she lifted a bottle of blessed water in celebration. She drank it in one long chug.

"Do you see that?" she asked the mule, who she had taken to calling Brute. "That's the camp. We're going to rest and have a feast as soon as we arrive. Just a little further."

Brute, as if understanding, picked up his pace.

Lonnie switched to side-saddle on the other side, winching at the numbness in her left leg. She shook it out and wished she had some food. Her stomach hurt, and her head ached from the night of missed sleep.

In the distance, a light roll of thunder boomed. Lonnie frowned as she looked up at the cloudless sky. Brute grunted anxiously beneath her. As the thunder steadied and grew louder, a panicked tingle started in the back of her head.

Lonnie turned to find Raspin riding bareback up the road behind her. He drove his mule with a flailing whip, satisfaction wrinkling his face. He lifted the whip and pointed at Lonnie. Lonnie swallowed a dry lump.

FIFTY-THREE

"Run," Lonnie said, straddling Brute. "Run as fast as you can." She kicked him in the ribs and Brute did as commanded. Ahead, the tents looked to be no more than a few miles. Lonnie leaned down and gripped Brute's mane. Behind her, Raspin's whip cracked between trampling footfalls.

"*Death,*" the old man shrieked. "*Murder and pain!*"

"Come on," Lonnie said, bouncing atop the sprinting mule. The bottles of blessed water jingled like a windchime against her. She turned over her shoulder, jumping to find Raspin only a dozen paces away. He shouted as he kicked his mule. The desperate beast surged harder, pounding across the dirt like a rockslide.

"*Death,*" he screamed, cracking his whip. "*It comes for you, woman.*" He closed the gap and swung his whip at Lonnie. She let out a shout as it split the back of her dress.

"Stop," she cried. She ducked as Raspin repeatedly whipped her. Each strike came with a rash of searing pain. He accidentally whipped Brute and the mule surged forward.

"*Death,*" Raspin said, pulling alongside Lonnie. He rose tall on his mule, grinning as he drew back his whip. "*It's come for you.*" He cracked the whip and Lonnie lifted an arm, blocking the strike. The whip's tail wrapped her arm and she pulled it into her chest, almost toppling Raspin.

"Go away," she shouted. They tugged the whip back and forth. She hugged the mule to stay on his back. Raspin started to wind the whip around his own arm. The mules ran side-by-side as their riders pulled each other closer. Raspin kicked Lonnie in the leg and she shouted, quickly returning the kick. Brute let out a desperate grunt and turned Lonnie's attention forward.

They had trampled off road and sprinted toward Camp Cattail. A few men stood by their tents, watching the insane procession with raised eyebrows.

"Let go," Lonnie shouted to Raspin. "We're going to crash into the camp."

"You let go," he grunted. He kicked at Lonnie again, but she swung her leg out of the way. As the kick landed on her mule, he pulled ahead, turning the whole collection further off road.

Lonnie shouted as they closed the last dozen yards to camp. She and Raspin both pulled on the whip and created a clothesline between them. As the mules stampeded into the camp, the whip began ripping out tent stakes. Lonnie tried to pull it off her arm but it had knotted itself.

Men shouted as they dove out of the way, their tents collapsing around them. The mules charged in a panic and made a sharp turn.

"Watch out," Lonnie called, and soon other men began to echo the call. White canvas flew through the air. Tent poles snapped. Lonnie turned to kick Raspin in the face, but he slid to the far side of his horse. Tent's unrooted between them like grass against a sickle. Lonnie shouted for Raspin to unbind his whip.

"Suck shit," he shouted back.

"Turn off!" a man cried from somewhere in the camp.

Lonnie looked ahead. They ran full-speed toward the camp's flagpole. She pulled at the whip coiled around her arm. She didn't make it in time.

With a horrific yank, she and Raspin flew off their mules and swung around the flagpole. They crashed into each other like two clapping hands. Lonnie fell to the ground with a grunt. Raspin wheezed, flopping on his back.

A nearby tent collapsed, sending a puff of dust into the air. Lonnie sat up and brushed broken glass from her lap. A few of the blessed waters survived, and having sacrificed much to make the delivery, she climbed to her feet.

"No, you don't," Raspin said, wobbling to his feet. He raised his fists and glared at Lonnie. A huge gash on the side of his head dripped with blood, as did his eye, where she had gouged him with the bow.

"It's over," Lonnie said. "I won." She lifted a few of the unbroken bottles of blessed water, turning to spit blood. "Go home, old man."

Raspin shouted as he charged. Lonnie jumped out of the way and sent him crashing into a tent. A moment later, Raspin stumbled back out with a blade, his grin manic as he swept it through the air.

"Stop fighting," someone shouted. "This is a camp."

Raspin lunged at Lonnie, thrusting the knife at her throat. She ducked and punched him in the stones. Raspin gasped and slashed the blade. It nicked her shoulder, and as blood blossomed across her shirt, Lonnie had enough. She grabbed a tent pole and swung at Raspin, pushing him back as she repeated the blow. As he retreated, Lonnie pursued. She screamed and swung for his head. The blow landed and he spun around, racing into another tent.

Lonnie chased after him, seething to find him digging through a trunk.

"No," she shouted, clapping him broadside the head. Raspin crashed backwards, tearing through the tent wall. Lonnie stepped through the gap and Raspin tossed a handful of dust into her face.

The holy man laughed as Lonnie's world went black. He

grabbed her arm and swung her into a run. She rubbed at her eyes before crashing into another tent, which sagged as the poles came loose. Lonnie opened an eye to find Raspin holding a tent pole overhead. He brought it down like a hammer. She rolled out of the way just in time.

As the pole tore through the tent, Lonnie kicked Raspin. He flew headfirst into a tent and a man let out a shout. Lonnie took up the pole and chased after them.

Raspin lay beside a small cot, where a dazed man turned from one intruder to the other.

"What the heck is going on?" he asked.

"Death," Lonnie said, stepping over Raspin. She swung at him but he rolled away, slipping under the far side of the tent. "For fuck sake," she hissed, racing out the door.

Raspin stood beside a roaring bonfire, working a metal pole off the spit. He grunted as Lonnie came running. Just as he yanked the pole free, Lonnie came upon him. She smashed his nose with the broad side of the tent pole. Raspin spun and swung the spit wildly. He leaped onto a crate and parried at Lonnie. Blood ran from his nose. Teeth floated down the blood on his chin.

"High ground," he wheezed, smacking Lonnie's tent pole aside. He raised the metal spit and dove it upon her. Lonnie pushed it aside, managing to guide the end of the spit between her arm and chest before it sunk into the ground.

Raspin, in his haste, had not been so lucky.

He impaled upon the other end of the spit, groaning as he sank midway down the pole. Lonnie winced at the foot of metal extending out the back of his chest. Raspin turned, making one last lazy swipe at her. Lonnie kicked him in the face.

With a slow and lazy arc, the spit bent and dropped Raspin into the roaring bonfire. Lonnie stepped back as he screamed. His clothes ignited. And then his hair. Dozens of the camp residents watched in silence as the Grand Teacher burned. When he stopped screaming and his eyeballs boiled over, Lonnie finally relaxed.

"Sorry," she said, turning to the men. She patted across her body, finding the last remaining bottle of blessed water. She unwrapped the rope and held it out. "I brought this for you."

"Thank you," a man said, glancing toward his friends as he took the bottle.

"*You,*" another man grunted, grabbing Lonnie's shoulder. She turned to find a massive, muscular man standing over her. He scowled as he looked down at her. "Is this your mule?" he asked, pointing to Brute, who he had managed to rope.

"Yes," Lonnie said softly.

"Come with me." The man gripped her arm and dragged her across Camp Cattail. Lonnie, who had mostly heard the destruction, winced as they crossed the shambled remains. Whatever tents she and Raspin hadn't ruined had fallen under the mule's heavy hooves. Even the flag pole stood crooked, a clear crack in the spot where Lonnie and Raspin connected with it.

"I'm sorry," Lonnie said. "I didn't mean for any of this. It was all—"

"Shut up," the man said. "Show these men some respect."

Lonnie felt sick as they passed more torn-open tents, where shocked and terrified men lay in their beds, gaping at the destruction. Her escort dragged her to a large tent at the head of camp, which had only suffered a minor tear across the front panel. A bright red flag with three white dots decorated the entrance.

"Grand Teacher Raspin is responsible for this," Lonnie said as they stepped inside. "He was jealous that I was going to bring you blessed water. He's been after me since Camp Aslin."

"And yet somehow you, a thin and filthy woman, have

destroyed him." Her escort stepped around a table at the rear of the tent. He sat in a chair, curiously staring at Lonnie. "Who the hell are you?"

"I'm Lonnie Lovingdove," Lonnie said.

"Are you a Grand Teacher?"

"No."

"Then why the hell are you delivering blessed water to the camp?"

"I was riding with Grand Teacher Tomlin and he fell ill. Before he died, he asked me to finish his delivery." Lonnie turned to a chair in the corner of the tent, but her host made no invitation to use it.

"You came all the way from Camp Aslin with that man attacking you? Riding a mule bareback?"

"I had a wagon," Lonnie said. "He stole it, so I stole his wagon, and then to make sure I beat him here, I rode the mule."

"If you're not a Grand Teacher, then what the hell are you? Who trained you?"

"No one. I'm a peasant from Doane. I used to make bricks for the East Kiln."

"Don't lie to me," the man said. He set a dagger on the table, his eyes promising he wasn't afraid to use it.

"I'm not lying," Lonnie said. "Raspin started the fight, and luckily, I managed to finish it."

"You destroyed an entire refugee camp and murdered a Grand Teacher. You're telling me that was just dumb luck?"

"I don't know. I seem to always find myself in dangerous situations, but they usually work out. Well, not for everyone, but I've done okay. I'm really sorry about your camp. I'll help you rebuild what I can."

"Do you ever know what this camp is?"

"You said it's a refugee camp," Lonnie said.

"And you're from Doane?"

"I was, but I'm currently homeless."

The man scratched his head as he studied Lonnie. He swished his mouth, finally sitting back in his chair.

"Sit down," he said, waving to the chair.

"Thank you." Lonnie dragged the chair to the desk and sat, letting out an involuntary sigh from the pleasure of being off her feet. "What do you want to talk about?" she asked.

"Tell me your story. Everything that's taken you to this camp."

"It's a long story," Lonnie said.

"I don't care."

"Can I have some water, first?"

The man lifted a waterskin from beneath his desk and tossed it to Lonnie.

FIFTY-FOUR

And so, after a long, very wonderful drink of water, Lonnie went on to tell the man everything she could remember of her flight—from the night of the king's feast in the square, to the immolation of Grand Teacher Raspin in Camp Cattail.

"And then I met you," Lonnie said. "I still don't even know your name."

"My name is Commander Comley," the man said, taking back his dagger. "I lead the army of Castle Winston."

"Where's that?"

"You've never heard of us?"

"It sounds familiar, but I've never left Doane."

"We're on the other side of the war with your kingdom."

"You're the ones attacking Doane?" Lonnie asked, shocked she hadn't put it together sooner.

"Attacking Doane?" Commander Comley laughed without humor. "We've never thrown a pebble at your insane king's castle. This is his war. These men, all three of our camps, are the last of our army. We're nearing the end of our defenses. The women and children have fled. We can't even recover our dead to give them a proper burial. I thought it was out of cruelty, but it seems your king has only grown madder. How did my men's flesh taste?"

"They told us it was pork," Lonnie said, blushing. "I threw it up right away when I found out what it was. I'm terribly sorry."

"Apologizing won't bring back what we've lost," Comley said. "Neither will the blessed water. No, we have a monumental problem." His bright, intense eyes focused on Lonnie. "But I might have found a solution."

"What's the problem?"

"We've attacked this war from every angle, but our strongest tacticians can't come up with a strategy to defeat your king. He's not following the laws of logic, and it's working in his favor."

"What's the solution?" Lonnie asked.

"You," Commander Comley said.

"Me?" Lonnie looked over her shoulder, finding only the rustling tear in the commander's tent. "How am I the solution?"

"If your story is true, then you have a gift for survival. A *talent*."

"But so many people have been hurt," Lonnie said.

"Yet here you sit, covered in the blood of those who come against you. You've turned luck into a lifestyle."

"What do you expect me to do?"

"I need you to teach my men how to survive," Comley said. "And then I want you with us to take down the savage reign of Prince Pollen Bane. We need your good fortune; we need you to teach us how to be lucky."

"I can't help you defeat Doane," Lonnie said, frowning. "Yes, the king's mad, but he's just one person. Most of the kingdom is made of perfectly sane and kind people. And I know nothing about war."

"Yet you slayed a Grand Teacher—a man trained his whole life to defend himself."

"He was old. That was just luck."

"My point exactly. Lonnie, we need your luck. King Pollen Bane is going to destroy us, and his campaign won't end there. He'll take over the world."

"I can't help you destroy my city."

"I'm not asking you to destroy Doane," Comely said, his

gaze hardening as he leaned across the table. "I'm asking you to help us end the war. Once Bane is dead, it's over."

"What will happen to Doane? What about Prince Pollen Bane VI?"

"He'll have to die, too. The bloodline's too risky."

"But the kingdom will fall apart without a king," Lonnie said. "The peasants are starving even in good times. I can't help you destroy them."

"You're not understanding me," Comely said. "I have no ill will for Doane or any of its people. I want to kill your king and his bloodline so my kingdom can return to peace and safety. If you're so worried about Doane, you can take over once we kill the king."

"Me?" Lonnie asked, again turning over her shoulder.

"Why not?" Comely found a smile as he sat back. "You know what the kingdom needs—you've lived your life as a peasant. You could use the crown's purse and power to free the people. You could try capitalism, for all I care. With your luck, I bet it would work."

"I have no idea how to rule a kingdom." Lonnie frowned, but as her mind raced down a dozen narratives, she didn't hate the idea. At the very least, she wouldn't be bored for a long time. "But how do I know you're telling the truth?" she asked. "What if you're just lying to get me to teach your men how to be lucky?"

"How do I know you're not lying about being so lucky in the first place?" Comely asked.

"Would Doane even accept me as the ruler?"

"When we conquer them and put the man-eating king's head on a spike, I'll make sure they understand the rules." Commander Comely rose, offering a hand. "What do you say, Lonnie Lovingdove? Shall we put your luck to the test?"

"I can't promise anything," Lonnie said. "I've never taught anyone anything, let alone how to be lucky."

"At the moment, we're in no position to be choosey." Comely grinned as he took Lonnie's hand, violently shaking it. "Come with me. I have an idea that will either solidify your role as captain or kill you."

Lonnie, taking solace in the fact she had at least made the decision to join Castle Winston of her own volition, followed Commander Comley into the sun.

PART FIVE
IF YOU'RE ALIVE, YOU'RE ALREADY LUCKY

FIFTY-FIVE

Comley led Lonnie across the camp, slapping broken tent poles and canvas out of his path. The rest of the camp's residents were in the painful process of cleaning up the damage. To Lonnie, it looked easier to build a new camp. She kept her head down as she walked through the destruction, wishing everyone would stop staring at her.

"They don't seem too pleased with me," she said.

"These men are beaten dogs," Comley said. "They're tired, and they're scared of losing. Your entrance was probably a welcome escape from their thoughts. Did you know we get an average of three suicides a week?"

"That's terrible."

"Well, the way things are going, they're just jumping to the natural conclusion. We rotate active soldiers in and out of the camps to rest them. Everyone here will soon ship off, and we'll get whatever scraps survive the front in their place. But that's going to change, isn't it, Lonnie?"

"We'll see," Lonnie said. "Where are we going?"

"We're going to test your luck."

"You said that, but how?"

"Just relax."

Lonnie looked ahead, where a dark twist of smoke rose from the center of camp. As they drew nearer, she winced, smelling the involuntarily delicious scent of roasting man. She covered her mouth as Comley brought her back to the bonfire. Quite a few of the men remained surrounding the pit, watching as

Grand Teacher Raspin blackened into charcoal. Only his right hand had escaped total immolation. The flesh had roasted to a crispy golden brown, his long fingernails curling like wood shavings.

The thought of wood sent Lonnie sputtering. She patted her body to find only tatters of her rope harness.

"Shit," she breathed.

"What?" Comely asked.

"Daniel's carving—I need my carving. It's the last thing my husband gave me before he died. I had it on the mule, but I don't—"

"I'm sure it will turn up," Comely said, surveying the clearing. "Let's have you stand over here. Come on." He led Lonnie to the fire, right beside the metal pole the spit had once lay upon. "You stand right there," he said, placing her against the pole.

"What are you going to do?" Lonnie asked.

"Just relax—and summon your luck." Comely turned and called the men into a huddle. They leaned into one another, speaking softly, once in a while peering back at Lonnie. Lonnie swallowed a lump and tried not to smell the burning Grand Teacher beside her.

"I don't like this," she called to the men. "If you want me to help you, you need to tell me what—"

"This will only take a minute," Comely said. Two of his men raced into a nearby tent. One returned with a bow and quiver of metal-tipped arrows. The other came back with a half-rotten apple.

"No," Lonnie said. "You're not—"

"We'll have our best archer take the shot," Comley said, approaching her with the apple. "We need to have a test before we put our entire kingdom in your hands."

"I didn't want to hold any kingdom." Lonnie tried to run and Comley caught her, shoving her back into the pole. He wrapped his belt around her neck and bound her to the pole. "Please," Lonnie said. "Don't do this. I'm not a witch—I can't just make—"

"Quiet." Comely set the squishy apple on her head. "Just one shot and it'll all be over." While he walked the ten paces back to his archer, who had already knocked his arrow, Lonnie desperately rocked the spit pole. She tried to spin around it, but the belt held her skin in place.

"Don't do this," she shouted. "Please, there has to be—"

"Draw," Comely said. He stepped beside the archer, who lifted the bow. Lonnie began kicking at the stones around the base of the pole. "Fire," Comely shouted.

The arrow whizzed by Lonnie's head, the *whoosh* creating a terrible déjá vu from her race against Raspin.

"I said hit the apple," Comely grunted, handing the archer another arrow.

"But it just worked," Lonnie said. "My luck made him miss. That's perfect proof—"

"*Draw.*"

The archer drew the arrow back, his one open eye staring straight into Lonnie's soul.

Lonnie brought her feet off the ground and hung from her neck, grunting as the apple rolled off her head. The pole began to lean under her weight.

"Fix that apple," Comely called. "Lonnie, stand still or this is going to take all day."

But Lonnie had started to black out, and even as she set her feet back on the ground, the belt had cinched too tight. Darkness swelled across her vision as the pole came loose and began toppling to the ground.

FIFTY-SIX

"Lonnie," Comely said. He leaned over her with the brilliant blue sky at his back. "She's alive," he shouted, bringing on a swell of cheers. He pulled Lonnie to a seat, combing the hair out of her eyes. Lonnie drew a weary breath as she turned across the hazy wall of men surrounding her.

"What happened?" she asked.

"You've won the men, is what happened," Comely said. He laughed as he pulled Lonnie to her feet. Lonnie, still woozy, brought a weak hand to her head and felt for apple bits or arrow holes.

"What did I do?" she asked, turning to Comely.

"Come and see." Comely waved for the men to disperse. He guided Lonnie across the dirt, back to the heat of the bonfire. She found the fallen spit pole and belt laying at the fireside. Comely's outstretched finger directed her to the other end of the pole.

"No," Lonnie said, her legs going loose again.

"Yes," Comely said, guiding her forward.

The archer lay sprawled across his bow. The metal pin at the top of the spit pole had punctured deep in his head. A metallic, fly-infested puddle of blood surrounded him.

Lonnie wretched, unprepared for another death at her hands.

"No," she breathed.

"*Yes,*" Comely said. "Your luck is boundless. Lonnie, that man wasn't our best archer; he was our worst. He would have shot you in the foot before hitting that apple, yet here you stand, and there he lays."

"*Lady Luck,*" one of the camp men whispered, falling to a knee before her.

"Lady Luck," Comely said, snatching her hand. "Lady Luck," he screamed, lifting the hand over her head.

"Lady Luck," the men returned as they fell to their knees.

"Lady Luck?" Lonnie asked.

"Lady Luck," Comely said, nodding. He laughed as the men began to chant.

"*Lady Luck, Lady Luck, Lady Luck.*"

After a few minutes, Lonnie tired of the strange celebration.

"Commander Comely," she said, leaning into him. "I need to rest. I'd love a bath, but I need food and water. And sleep."

"You'll have everything you need," Comely said. "Lady Luck!" he cried, lifting Lonnie off the ground, twirling her before the men like a prize-winning pumpkin. Lonnie studied the praise, not hating it, but very unused to positive attention.

"For you," a man called, running to her side. He bowed as he offered a burlap sack.

"What's this?" Lonnie asked. She opened the bag to find Daniel's carving. The arrows and wine stains remained, as well as a new crack and hoof print.

"Well, look what turned up," Comely said. "Rather lucky, don't you think?"

"I guess it is," Lonnie said. She hugged the relic, tracing the knife lines, feeling the last work of Daniel's fingers. The men's chorus of *Lady Luck* continued to swell around her.

Lonnie, reunited with the carving, and feeling more love than she ever had since Daniel's death, broke into tears. She fell to her knees and tried to comprehend what came next.

"*Do you see?*" Comely whispered into her ear. "Do you see

the change you've already started? We're going to win, Lonnie. You're going to finish what we could not."

Lonnie could only bounce her jaw as she continued to weep.

"Let's get you that bath." Comely lifted her, guiding her back through camp. The men continued chanting her new moniker as they followed the procession like supplicants, their voices filling the air with hope and trust and love.

"*Lady Luck*," Lonnie whispered, tasting the words.

"Lady Luck," Comely agreed.

FIFTY-SEVEN

The commander took Lonnie into a new tent, where he had a team of men fill a bath with fresh water and soap. Lonnie picked at bread and dried meat while she waited. She wanted to stuff herself, but her stomach had been so neglected even the smallest amount of food caused it to swell with pain.

"I'll send a message to the main camp," Comley said. He stood over Lonnie, frowning at her neglected plate. "Tell me what food you like and you'll have it. We need you back at full strength before we march on Doane. What do you like?"

"Fruit would be nice," Lonnie said. "I usually only ate soup. Some pap would be nice."

"Take some time to think about it." Comely set a burly hand on her shoulder before wandering to the tub, where the men were pouring the last buckets of water into the soapy bath. "That's enough," he said, knocking his boot against the tub. "Let's give Lady Luck some peace and quiet."

The men bowed to Lonnie and scampered out of the tent. Commander Comely stepped to the door after them, turning back to Lonnie.

"There's some fresh clothes beside the tub," he said. "This is your tent, now. I'm going to have a guard keep watch to make sure no one bothers you. Take the rest of the evening for yourself. We'll start our training in the morning."

"What training?" Lonnie asked. She winced as she rose from the table, her back flaring with heat.

"The training where you teach us how to be lucky," Comely

said. "Good night, *Lady Luck.*" He smiled, taking a quick bow before backing out of the tent.

Lonnie fastened the tent ties and shuffled back to the table. She took Daniel's carving and dropped it into the tub, blinking as the water splashed her eyes. She untangled the ropes and tattered dress Bally had helped her steal. Her mind throbbed with a tornado of emotions. She slipped into the water, sighing as she finally sat back and closed her eyes.

Of all the strange surprises that came in pursuit of her curiosity, she had never foreseen herself coming to lead an army. She had always thought of herself as unlucky—especially when it came to the last few weeks, but Comely seemed to have a point, strange as it may be. No matter how dangerous of a situation she encountered, she always seemed to slip through the cracks unscathedish.

But being lucky did not mean one had a fountain of luck to rain on others. She had no idea how to teach the men to survive through luck. In her experience, everyone around her inversely became unlucky. She might lead the entire army into battle only to narrowly escape while everyone else suffered a horrendous death.

She lifted Daniel's carving, carefully taking a sponge to the dirt. It took a while, but she managed to wash it mostly clean. She didn't have the strength to pull the arrows out.

Daniel would never believe a word of what had happened since he died.

Perhaps her incredible feats of lucky survival could only happen in his absence.

Lonnie wiped her tears on the soapy sponge. She missed her partner dearly. While her adventurous side had been sated beyond believability, the part of her that enjoyed deep sleep in the arms of Daniel felt like a distant memory. She finally gave up on the bath and dressed.

Laying in bed, she did her best to accept Comely's charge. If he was correct and she happened to be supernaturally lucky, she had a duty to extend that luck to the righteous side of the war. If they somehow came out victorious, and Comely was right about her ability to take over as ruler of Doane, she could wield her luck to create a society as it should be; a place where anyone can be anything—where rewards come to anyone who puts in the work.

But first, she needed to teach luckiness to a camp of defeated, broken soldiers.

FIFTY-EIGHT

Lonnie woke to dull apathy. She lay in a strange bed, a glowing wall of white canvas before her. A layer of warm sweat covered her skin. She signed as she sat up, reality making a quick return through her memory. The camp was quiet. She took a piece of bread from the table, pleased to find it much more palatable after some sleep.

She ate a healthy breakfast and drank several cups of water. With no point in hiding any longer, she unfastened the tent and stepped into the sun.

The camp remained in shambles, but quite a few of the tents had been temporarily rebuilt. Lonnie turned to her left, where Commander Comely's tent sat with its long slit down the front. She only made it halfway before he stepped outside.

"Who knew you were so beautiful under all that muck," he said, meeting her. He tugged on her somewhat baggy shirt. "I know the clothes aren't ideal. I'm having the boys bring you some more lady-like clothes when they run to the main camp."

"They're actually nice," Lonnie said, kicking a leg out. "They'll be good for our training. It's difficult to look nice and still be able to walk."

"Are you up for training today? It's all right if you want to take the day to rest."

"No, we should get started. Luck works better when you're on the move. Where do you want to hold the training?"

"What do you want? We can gather around the fire, or take

it out into the fields. I'm giving you full authority over the camp. You're second in command only to me."

"Let's start at the fire," Lonnie said. "Luck is more spiritual than physical, so I imagine we'll mostly be talking."

"Good. When do you want to get started?"

"Now. Like I said, I've come this far by keeping moving."

While Comely went through camp to gather the men, Lonnie headed to the ashy remains of the bonfire. She sighed as she found the charred skeleton of Grand Teacher Raspin. The poor holy man had no idea how much raw luck he had challenged. Lonnie at least took comfort in the fact she had immolated him. She didn't know what kind of Maker would be proud to meet a man like Raspin, but at least they had the opportunity. She cringed to think of Grand Teacher Tomlin, whose shallow grave had most likely already been excavated by buzzards and wolves.

"Lady Luck," a man mumbled, bowing as he came into the center of camp. He sat on one of the many logs surrounding the fire pit.

The rest of camp drifted into the circle over the next half hour, all paying their respects to Lady Luck. Lonnie stoically nodded to the praise and stood by the re-planted spit pole. She waved to Comely as he followed the last group of stragglers in. He joined her at the fire, calling for everyone to quiet.

"We're standing on a precipice," he said, his gaze sharp as he surveyed the hunched and sallow men of Camp Cattail. "If we continue doing what we're doing we'll all be dead within the month. Worse, King Pollen Bane and his army will officially break our last stronghold and take all of Winston. Their corruption won't stop there, either. They'll conquer until there's nothing left to conquer. They'll paint this planet red.

"But there might be another way," Comely said, his voice softening with emotion. "She stands beside me now."

"*Lady Luck*," a man in the front row whispered. The words echoed like cicada chirps across the camp.

"Her name is Lonnie Lovingdove," Comely said. "With her official agreement to join our fight, she is now in charge of this camp. She's agreed to train all of us in the ways of luck. With her strategies, we can combat the insanity of Pollen Bane and his army. We'll not only push them out of our home, we'll pursue them to theirs. We'll wipe them from the face of the earth, and Maker willing, we'll give peace to generations."

The men twitched a little as they looked from Comely to Lonnie. A few nodded, but most seemed to be stuck between terror and drowning depression. It reminded Lonnie of the crazed residents of the Shrine.

"Your training will start immediately," Comely said. "Any man who disrespects or questions the ways of Lonnie Loving-dove will be hanged. Am I clear?"

"Yes, sir," the men shouted, sitting a little straighter.

"Good." Comely turned to Lonnie. "They're all yours, Lady Luck." He stepped back and sat on the log with the men. Lonnie, fighting a nasty swarm of butterflies in her stomach, cleared her throat.

"I'm not a teacher," she began. "So . . ." She froze as she stared at the dozens of eyeballs; the quivering jaws and fidgeting fingers. "So, you'll have to be patient while I figure this out," she said, audibly swallowing a lump. "So, we need to get you all lucky." Again, she froze under the gaze of her audience.

Comely stepped to her side and leaned into her ear.

"Don't worry about them," he whispered. "Just relax."

"They're all staring at me," Lonnie said. "It's making me really nervous."

"Men, stop staring at Lonnie. Look at her feet, or the fire. She'll tell you when to look at her."

The men shifted their gaze in unison, as if something extremely interesting just bloomed within the flames. Lonnie took a breath.

"Thank you," she said. "So, let's see. I don't really think about luck, so I'm trying to come up with a good way of explaining how it works. Honestly, I don't really know. I just do whatever the situation calls for. Maybe I should tell you some of my story."

Lonnie turned to Comely, who nodded.

"I'm curious by nature," Lonnie started. "It's just how my brain works. I don't want to sit in the square and enjoy the breeze, I want to study the strange people passing by; I want to follow them home and see what they're eating for dinner—or hear what they talk about behind closed doors. That's what started my journey. I wonder if curiosity might be part of luck. In fact, it has to be." Lonnie frowned, feeling a cool clarity move into her mind. "When you're curious, you have to take a risk to properly investigate whatever's got you interested. You have to do abnormal things. To learn something new, I mean. You have to *be* something new to do something new. Does that make any sense?"

"Yes," Comely breathed, his eyes fixed on Lonnie.

"So, that's the first step then," she said. "Each of you has to find a sense of curiosity. Get interested in things that are different from what you normally do. The key is to pursue that curiosity. It's scary, because you don't know where it's going to take you, but you need to get so curious you don't care. Find something you don't understand and risk everything to figure out what it is."

The men mused on Lonnie's words as they stared at the holy man's skeleton in the fire. Lonnie mused on the words too, because she had never thought of curiosity in such terms. She wondered if she might be making a good point. Curious to see where her mind might go with it, she continued down the rabbit hole.

"When you chase curiosity, you're going to get into trouble. I've almost been killed a dozen times in the last few weeks. Right now, the entire kingdom of Doane is hunting for me. That dead man in the fire went after me with everything he had, and he almost got me, but I was running toward something new; something I didn't understand but risked everything to learn."

Lonnie's butterflies moved out of her stomach and into her heart, sending it thrumming against her chest.

"And that's where luck lives," she continued. "It's not about guessing which side of a coin will land; it's a spirit that favors the curious. If you stay at home carving blocks of wood by the fire, you're going to be comfortable, but you're not going to be lucky. Why would luck spend any of its energy in such a boring place?

"No, luck is a restless spirit. It favors the curious. It wants to see how far you can go, and it rewards those who push it to the limits. Because luck can bend the rules. It can throw a bird into the arrow speeding toward your head. It can wash you down stream instead of into the nest of poisonous snakes. You don't see half of what it does—I never even realized I was getting lucky until Commander Comely pointed it out. But he's right. I am lucky, because I'm very fucking curious, and I persue that curiosity with ferocity. When you push it like I do, luck apparently really likes that."

"Lonnie," Comely said, turning to the men at his sides. "Will you teach us how to be curious?"

"That, I can do," Lonnie said. She found herself smiling. "Everyone, get up. We're going on a walk."

CHAPTER

FIFTY-NINE

Lonnie led the men to the entrance of the camp, where the road curved into the horizon. On one side, long and wandering fields humped across the landscape. To the other side, dark woods led into the hazy Seregile Mountains.

Lonnie turned from the sights, focusing herself on the task at hand. The men awkwardly huddled before her. Some shielded their eyes from the sun, and others squinted.

"How long have all of you been here?" Lonnie asked.

When none of the men replied, Commander Comely said, "This pack has been here for three weeks, give or take."

"Good." Lonnie nodded as she studied the men. "In those three weeks, have any of you ever taken a walk through the forest?"

The men shook their heads, including Comely.

"Have you explored the fields—or ever wondered what kind of creatures or plants might live in them?"

Again, the men stood still.

"What about the road? Do travelers ever pass by?"

"Some," a man said softly.

"When those travelers pass, do you ever wonder who they are and where they're going? Do you wonder if they have families, or if they're running from trouble, or if they're following a dream? Do you ever think of what their parents might have looked like, or if they were kind or cruel?"

As the men shook their heads, Lonnie let out a sigh.

"Don't any of you want to know more than what you already do?" she asked.

"We learn plenty," Commander Comely said. "We study combat strategies and the on-going war campaign. Personally, I spend a good deal of time wondering how things are going on the front lines."

"But that's not curiosity," Lonnie said. "That's fear. You don't want to learn anything, you want to hear good news."

"Then what is curiosity?" a man asked.

"That," Lonnie said, pointing to him. "You just had it."

"Had what?"

"Curiosity."

The man frowned, glancing at the men beside him.

"Let's try an exercise," Lonnie said. "I want everything to look around for a moment. Find something strange or weird. Maybe it's that crooked tree in the forest, or maybe it's someone in camp. Think of three different secrets that person or thing might have. Think deeply about them."

"How do we do that?" Comely asked.

"I'll give you an example," Lonnie said. She waved Comely to his feet, who reluctantly rose. "This is Commander Comely," Lonnie said. "He leads the camp, and he put me in charge. I don't know much else about him, but I have all kinds of curious ideas. Did he always want to be the leader of an army? Is he married? Does he have children? If he does, is a kind father, or does he treat his children like soldiers? What does do for fun when not in war time? Does he know he's the most handsome man in camp?"

Lonnie blushed as Comely turned to her.

"Don't answer my questions," she said, turning back to the men. "Those are just a few curiosities I have about the commander. Let's have another example. Do you see that tree? The tall one at the edge of the forest?"

"Yes," Comely said.

"I'd like to know why it's so much bigger than the others. Did someone plant it? Is there a stream running over its roots? Is it made of hard or soft wood? Are there more trees like that, or is it the only one of its kind in the world? Did a bird fly by and plant its seed? Can you climb it? Did lovers carve their initials in the trunk? Did someone bury treasure at its roots, only to die before they could retrieve it?"

"It's an oak tree," one of the men said. "They're all oak trees, that one's just older."

"You're missing the point," Lonnie said. "I'm trying to show you how a curious mind works. If you want to get lucky, you need to start by changing the way you think. Let's get back to the exercise. Everyone, find something you don't understand, and then start exploring the possibilities. Take a few minutes."

While the men broke off, wandering around the road to study the world through a new lens, Lonnie met Comely.

"Do you think this will work?" he asked.

"Not if their leader doesn't learn," Lonnie said. "Go get curious, Commander."

Comely blushed, nodding as he wandered off in the direction of the forest. Lonnie, unable to not think in questions, looked across her body of students.

She wondered how much combat they had seen. Did they know King Pollen Bane found their brothers in arms delicious? Would telling them make them work harder at learning to be curious? Did they even have the capacity to learn new tricks at this late stage in their lives? How many of them had wives and children? How many, despite having wives and children, secretly lusted after men?

And what was the deal with the blessed water? How did one go about blessing water? What did the soldiers expect it to do for them? Did they drink it, or sprinkle over their heads? Was faith in a blessing enough to manifest one?

"Ms. Luck," a weathered man said, coming up beside her. He poorly hid his trembling hands.

"Yes?" Lonnie asked.

"I think I did it."

"You found something?"

"You," he said, nervously rubbing at the back of his neck.

"Good. So what are you curious about?"

"I've been wondering what you'll say when I fail your test."

"Oh," Lonnie said. "But that's not curiosity. Like Commander Comely's idea, that's only fear. Curiosity would be wondering where I came from—how I managed to become a deliverer of blessed water. If I were you, I'd wonder how the war might change if the entire army learns to be lucky. If I'm Lady Luck, what other tricks might I know? Why do I carry a wooden heart with me?" She leaned into the soldier, meeting his eyes. "Do you understand? Curiosity is when you wonder something and *want* to know the answer. But even more than that, it's when you *need* to know the answer. Take a few more minutes and try again."

"Okay," the man mumbled, nodding as he wandered back to the others.

After a few more minutes, Lonnie called the men back to the huddle.

"Let's hear some of your curiosities," she said. "Raise your hand if you'd like to share."

A few hands went up, and Lonnie pointed to the closest one.

"I thought about the sun," the man said.

"Good," Lonnie said. "What about it?"

"It's very bright. And if you're out too long, it can burn you."

"And?" Lonnie lifted her eyebrows.

"And everyone can see it, but no one can touch it."

One of the other men clapped him on the back, nodding as if he had uncovered a new science.

"That's good," Lonnie said, "but not quite right. You're getting philosophical, which is the right direction, but you're not asking the proper questions. Thinking about that isn't going to drive you to action. If I look at the sun, I might wonder *why* it burns our skin. If everyone can see the sun, *why* can't anyone touch it? What if there was a way to touch it? What if there's a mountain somewhere in the world you can climb right onto the sun and drink its golden heat? Who else might be studying the sun? Would they teach me their secrets if I found them?"

"Brilliant," Comely said, stepping beside Lonnie. "Boys, we have to do better."

"Hush," Lonnie said. "We've barely started to discuss everyone's thoughts. Who's next? Let's hear some more ideas."

An older man tentatively raised his hand.

"Go ahead," Lonnie said.

"I thought about the grass," the man said. "Why can animals eat it but not us?" He turned to the ground, frowning. "Why is it green, of all colors? Why hasn't anyone found a way to make clothes out of it? Why does it only burn when it's dead?"

"*Yes*," Lonnie said, her eyes wide. "Now *that's* curiosity. Those are real questions, and if you think about them long enough, you're going to need to find the answers. Really nice job. Who else? Come on, there's no wrong answer."

With praise on the table, more hands rose.

"Commander Comely," Lonnie said. "What did you think about?"

"I'm wondering why the main camp left us with only two horses," he said. "What if Doane comes after us and we have no way to retreat? What if those horses die and we can't send messengers for supplies?"

"That's fear," Lonnie said, trying her best to remain patient. "You're asking questions based on worry."

"I have something," a younger man said, stepping to the front of the men.

"Let's hear it."

"Why did we camp out in the sun—right on the road? What if we moved into the shade in the forest, where we can stay cool? What if there's water nearby? And game? What if we went all the way to the top of the mountain, where we can watch the entire road? What if we sent a lookout to keep an eye on things from up there?"

"Excellent," Lonnie said. "Does anyone see the difference? The commander's questions generate fear, but this man's questions create more questions. If he continues thinking about them, he'll soon be in the woods, possibly finding us a superior campsite. What if he goes out and discovers a whole grove of blueberries and apples trees? What if he discovers a tree that can help us build better bows?"

"Wait," Comely said. "I think I understand." Grimacing, he turned to the men. "Why is Doane beating us in the war?" He glanced at Lonnie, and with her approving nod, continued. "We know the enemy's soldiers aren't any bigger or stronger than us. What are they doing that we're not? What do their war counsels look like? Is the king even really in charge? Would it be possible to get a spy into their chambers?"

"That," Lonnie said, grinning as she set her hand on Comely's back, "is how you do it."

For the next two hours, the men shared their thoughts and questions. Most picked up the concept, and those who didn't were challenged to rethink until they did. By the time they finished, everyone was starving so they returned to camp for lunch. Lonnie ate by herself to focus on the subject of her next lesson, which was anyone's guess. She came up with a few ideas but decided to play it by ear. Comely met her with an extra helping of grits, which Lonnie happily received.

"Thank you," she said, scooting down the log to make room for him.

"I didn't know what to expect," Comely said. He picked up a twig and began picking at the bark. "You're a good teacher."

"I'm still learning."

"At this rate, how long will it take to get the men lucky?"

"I have no idea. We've only just scratched the surface on curiosity. I think the men are starting to understand it, but until they can permanently think in questions, we're not ready."

"I don't know how much time we have." Comely tossed a strip of bark into the wind, his confidence falling as he faced Lonnie. "This group returns to the war front in a week, and then we'll be starting from scratch again."

"Let me continue with the lessons," Lonnie said. "I'm getting better, as are the men."

"Good," Comely said, rising from the log. "And to alleviate one of your many questions: Yes, I know I'm handsome. I've been wondering if you know how beautiful you are." He smiled as Lonnie blushed, giving her a nod before he returned to the fire.

CHAPTER
SIXTY

Late that afternoon, Lonnie assembled the men in the woods, where they could think outside of the uniform blandness of camp. She stood beside the old tree she had questioned for her curiosity example. The men sat cross-legged on the forest floor.

"We're making progress," she started, smiling to prove her approval. "This morning, we uncovered the first step to luckiness: intense and persistent curiosity. I want everyone to continue to think in questions. This means you're going to have to lift your heads and pay attention to the world around you. Look for things that are out of the norm. Look for things that confuse you, because that's the next step to getting lucky."

"Confusion?" Commander Comely asked.

"No," Lonnie said. "Well, not exactly. What I mean is, you need to find curiosities that are so interesting you're willing to risk everything to explore them. It's how almost every couple meets. Many people are interested in each other, but the ones who are so interested and curious that they'll risk embarrassment and rejection to introduce themselves are the ones who get lucky. Have any of you married?"

Half of the men raised their hands, some more proudly than others.

"Let's talk about it," Lonnie said. "You, in the front. How did you first meet your wife?"

"We were young," the man said, nervously glancing across the circle. "She and I worked in the fields."

"And when did you realize you liked this lady as more than just a coworker?"

"She liked to make me laugh. She would scare me with the sickle." The man fought a grin as he blushed.

"So how did you go from co-workers to man and wife?" Lonnie asked.

"I asked her to dinner with my family," the man said.

"Were you nervous?"

"I threw up on the way to ask her."

"But you did it anyway?"

"Eventually, yeah."

"Why did you push through being nervous? It sounds like it was pretty serious."

"It was. I didn't sleep the night before. My heart felt like it was going to break out of my back. I get nervous thinking about it now."

"What made you push through all that?" Lonnie asked.

"Because I loved her," the man said. "I would have died for her—before she even knew I wanted her. I couldn't lose the chance of loving her."

"That's beautiful," Lonnie said. "And that is exactly what I'm talking about. This man was so driven to know and love his wife that he pushed himself through very uncomfortable feelings just for a chance of loving her. Do you know what happened by taking that chance?"

"I got lucky," the man said at once.

"What about me?" another man asked, his face drawn tight with content. "I've loved many girls, and here I am, unmarried and fighting a losing war. I've never had a spot of luck in all my life. Do you really think asking questions is suddenly going to change what I am?"

A few of the other ugly men agreed with grunts.

"You're unlucky?" Lonnie asked.

"Very unlucky," the man said. "Women and children are scared of me. Despite working hard, I've been poor my entire life. My brother drowned when I was six. My father was crushed by a wagon wheel on my fifteenth birthday. You tell me what's lucky about any of that."

"You're a fool," Lonnie said, pleased to see a wave of shock roll through her audience. Even Commander Comely raised an eyebrow. "That's right," she said, smiling. "Just like curiosity creates luck, poor thinking creates bad luck."

"So my brother drowned because I'm bitter?" the man asked, anger flushing his cheeks.

"Of course not. Pain and accidents are part of life. My very own husband was murdered only a couple weeks ago. I loved him dearly. But you know what I've done since then? Why I'm now leading a camp of soldiers instead of complaining about how poor my life has become?"

"You've been curious," one of the men said.

"I know no other way," Lonnie said. "But let me set something straight right here and now. If you're alive, you're already lucky. You need to understand that immediately. Your brother might have drowned, but you didn't. Why are you still here? Why did your father get crushed and not you? You may not be rich, but I bet you're good at working. Why has life decided to keep you around and build you into a hard worker? Is it just a cruel joke to torture you?"

The man frowned as he stared at Lonnie.

"Of course it isn't," she said. "Life is a gift. And I'll say it again: if you're alive, you're already lucky. There are a thousand ways to die each day. The fact any of us even survived childbirth has shrouded us in luck. I don't want to hear anyone else tell me they're not lucky, because the very breath in your lungs is proof of the opposite. If you want to be lucky, you need to know that you already are and embrace it."

Everyone quieted as Lonnie's word sunk in. She herself had never thought of life in such a way, but she had indeed lived so. She tried not to be too proud of herself.

"Let's have a quick exercise," she said. "Everyone take a minute and think of three times you were lucky."

"Three?" one of the uglier men asked, frowning.

"You should be able to come up with a million," Lonnie said. "If you can't come up with three reasons, then I'm going to have Commander Comely hang you."

A quiet rumble rose through the men at Lonnie's shocking statement. But they quickly went to work, staring into space while they brooded on their luck. Lonnie thought of a few of her own lucky moments to keep her mental inertia moving.

She had managed to keep possession of Daniel's carving through a whirlwind of adventure.

She had lost Daniel, but she had many wonderful years with him, and thousands of memories to carry for the rest of her life.

She had finally taken charge of herself, and by doing so, she had quickly moved into a leadership role within a real army. Not only that, she had become a teacher. She had never taught anyone anything before, yet here she stood, teaching a losing team how to be lucky.

And she didn't think she was doing a half-bad job.

But the greatest luck of her life was being born with a supernatural curiosity. She had always been told to ignore and avoid it, but it was not a force one could affect by will alone. Yes, it had taken her down long and twisted roads in her life, but it had allowed her to find secrets and opportunities that would have never come from the safe and predictable paths. It had made her a partner with luck, who had been following her all along. If luck consumed curiosity, he grew fat at Lonnie's side.

"Let's hear it," she said, turning back to the men. Under the threat of hanging, everyone raised their hand. Lonnie pointed to the ugly man whose father had been crushed by a wagon wheel. "When have you been lucky?" she asked.

"On the front lines," he said. "I came into combat with a big knight last go around. He had me cornered and disarmed me. He was laughing as he brought his sword up, but he tripped on another body. I was able to escape before he could get back up again."

"What else?"

"I'm not allergic to bees. I've been stung many times, and it never killed me."

"And your third?"

"My mother's still alive. Through all the chaos of the war, she's still with me. She's always been with me."

"It sounds like you're one of the luckiest ones here," Lonnie said. "Even I don't have a mother."

"She's the greatest thing in my life," the man said, breaking into literally ugly crying. As the other men shifted away from him, Lonnie redirected the conversation.

"What about you?" she asked a younger man.

"I caught a wild horse once," he said, smiling. "I also managed to break it, and that horse lived for twenty years."

"I'm curious," Lonnie said. "How did you find a wild horse?"

"I heard they were out there, and I wanted a horse."

"Curiosity." Lonnie grinned, glancing at the other men. "This man grew curious about wild horses, so he risked his life and time to go looking for one. What did he find on that journey?"

"Luck," a few of the men said.

"Louder," Lonnie said.

"Luck," everyone replied.

"And was this man born lucky, or did he put himself in a position where luck had no choice but to meet him?"

As the men agreed, Lonnie nodded, her energy rising with

every word. She turned to Commander Comely and lifted her finger.

"And you, Commander," she said. "When have you been lucky?"

"It's interesting," he said, climbing to his feet. He joined Lonnie in front of the men. "I've taken this exercise very seriously, and I too didn't ever think of myself as lucky. But I've been wrong. Lonnie's opened my eyes; I'm ashamed at the way I've lived. Luck has been with me all the way. I just never took a moment to notice her."

"There's no need to feel shame," Lonnie said. "I don't want anyone to feel bad about what they're done. We're all starting new. Right here and now."

"My wife died just a year after our marriage," Comely said, his jaw flexing. "It made me *hate*. I wanted to kill and punish everyone for what disease had taken from me. It led me into the army. The army led me to the battlefield. I've taken hundreds of lives. The fact I stand here is a testament to unfailing luck. Do you know how many blades I've dodged? How many wounds I've survived?"

Comely lifted his shirt, revealing a patchwork of scars. Lonnie gasped, her attention shifting to the stunning muscles beneath his skin.

"Just a few months ago," Comely continued, "I was scheduled to lead the fight at Scutter Bridge."

Around him, the men gasped.

"And I wanted to lead that fight." Comely's lip buckled and he grunted through the emotion. "But I had come down with a fever. They wouldn't let me go. I fought with leadership all the way until they rode off to battle. I was still fuming the next day when we received word: not a single man had survived the fight.

"At the time, I thought I could have changed the tides. It

wasn't until today that I see the truth." Comely turned to Lonnie, a tear slipping down his cheek.

"It's okay," Lonnie whispered.

"*You* are my third luck," Comely said. "When you came riding into this camp, I saw something I had never seen before. A tiny woman destroyed an entire camp and slayed a trained fighter all on her own. Even stranger, she seemed to have done it by accident."

The men laughed, as did Comely as he wiped her cheeks.

"But I was wrong. You did nothing by accident because luck is your partner. And you aren't lucky by birthright, you're lucky because you've become the embodiment of curiosity. Everything in my mind is changing because of you, Lonnie. *I'm* changing. I didn't get that fever just so I could survive Scutter Bridge. I got that fever so I could find you."

Lonnie took Comely's hand as he extended it.

"And you're not here by chance, either," he said, turning to the men. " Lonnie Lovingdove has blessed us with a power far greater than magic and weaponry. It ascends strategy itself. Luck has brought her to our doorstep, and by our curiosity, it has come into us. We are not another camp of men waiting to die. No, not any more. We're the camp of men who are going to end this war and bring peace to the nation."

Comely roared, lifting Lonnie's hand over their heads. He howled with incredible emotion, the noise racing through the forest, lifting the hair on the nape of Lonnie's neck.

The men stood as they too broke into a roar.

When they eventually quieted, they stood not as the broken spirits of old, but a true army of warriors. To Lonnie, they looked lucky.

"I think we're about ready," she said, her smile unbreakable. "Let's get back to camp and rest for tonight. We'll go over this some more tomorrow, but I don't want to wait too long. Like food, curiosity and luck and best when hot."

They were halfway back to camp when Lonnie realized she still held Commander Comely's hand.

She turned to him.

He turned to her.

They walked a little more.

"I don't know much about fighting," Lonnie admitted. "But I'm very curious about it."

"I'm curious to see what you'll do," Comely said, smiling. He started to speak and froze, blushing as he turned back ahead. Lonnie continued to stare at him, silently willing him to do what she knew he must.

And finally, at the outskirts of town, he turned to her.

"Lonnie Lovingdove," he said, taking both of her hands. "Would you like to have dinner with me?"

"Of course I would," Lonnie said. She stared into his eyes, through his pain, to the curious boy he had once been.

They met each other with a gentle kiss.

SIXTY-ONE

Commander Comely took Lonnie to his tent, where she sat at the table while he personally prepared their dinner. A lamp burned from the tent pole, filling the space with warm light. The rest of camp quieted as the sun made its way to bed.

"Can I help with anything?" Lonnie asked.

"No, I'm hosting," Comely said, organizing dry goods at a small table against the tent wall. He smiled as he turned over his shoulder. "Tell me something I don't know about you."

Lonnie swished her mouth, wondering what might be of interest to the commander. She had only been able to focus on the tingling in her belly since their kiss at the edge of camp. Their connection had come like a thief in the night. She watched him cook, his broad shoulder turning as he mixed pap and water. He was so different from Daniel, yet something about him reminded her of him; perhaps his constant certainty.

"Well?" Comely asked.

"I told you all of my adventures to get here," Lonnie said. "Those are the most exciting bits."

"Are you telling me Lady Luck can't think of a single story to tell me?"

"Of course not. I just need a moment to think."

Lonnie spent little time in the past, and she frowned as she pushed into the barricade of her memories. She didn't want to share any of her childhood—the dark and frightening brutality of her mother. But as the silence grew uncomfortable, she could think of nothing else.

"I told you I was born a peasant?" she said, sitting a little taller.

"I assumed as much," Comely said, "after you told me you were a peasant."

"I had a very difficult mother. From her perspective, nothing in the world had ever gone right for anyone. Even I was just a by-product of her pleasing my father. She told me that. Pretty often, too. But I never cared what she thought. I saw the world as a way out of her cruelty. For everything she hated, I found something to love. She lied and told me what a dangerous and despicable place the world was, but I crept through the shadows and found something wholly other."

"My mother was a cunt, too," Comely said, now chopping a head of cabbage.

"It's weird how things work out. I'm the complete opposite of my mother, despite being part of her. I married a very kind man to make sure my home never had any of that awfulness. But that wasn't what I needed, either. Daniel was so content he had no interest in anything. I couldn't even get him to take a walk with me. He would just sit at the fire and carve. He didn't have a curious bone in his body."

"Have you ever carved?" Comely asked, carrying the pap and cabbage to the table.

"No. It's incredibly boring."

"My brother used to carve. He sold lots of pieces to knights and the royals. I was never good at it, but I loved to watch him."

"Why?" Lonnie asked.

"Because he wasn't just shaving wood; he was uncovering a mystery. He told me he never set out to create something in particular. He just started carving, and soon he'd find a shoulder, or a wing, and then he had to work carefully to uncover the rest of it."

"Daniel usually shaved a block down to a toothpick and moved on to the next one."

"Maybe he never had the right piece of wood," Comely said. He carried a plate of dried meat to the table and sat. "That heart is one of his, isn't it?"

"The last one he ever made," Lonnie said. "He actually finished it, which is why it's so important to me."

"Perhaps that was what he's been looking for all this time." Comely spooned pap onto both of their plates. "Not all curiosity has to take you across the world, right?"

"No, I guess not." Lonnie dabbed at her eyes with the napkin. "It hurts to talk about him. So much has happened, but it still feels like yesterday when I came home and found him."

"I didn't mean to upset you." Comely reached across the table and took her hand. "Lonnie—"

"No," she said. "It's okay. You're right; I guess he was curious, just not in a way that brought luck." She stared at the pap, her mood sinking. "Before I came here, I never thought I was lucky. My life's been one painful event after another, with only long and boring stretches between them. I was convinced curiosity had cursed me. Honestly, if I had just stayed home, Daniel would still be alive."

Comely faced her from across the table, his hand tightening on hers.

"So how does that make sense?" Lonnie asked. "I'm out here telling everyone to chase curiosity and expect it to change the world, but I'm no better than any of them. I have no business teaching anyone how to get lucky. I've gotten at least three people killed. Last night, I kicked a holy man into the fire. I murdered him."

"Nothing makes sense," Comely said. "That's how the world works."

"Then what's the point?"

"I don't know."

"What if I lead your men into a battle and kill all of them?"

"If it's not you, then it'll be me." Comely leaned across the table and took Lonnie's other hand. "I don't know if luck will help us win this war, and I don't care. I'm confident for the first time in months. I'm *excited*. You excite me, Lonnie Lovingdove. Your spirit is bringing life back into my blood. Maybe I'm selfish, but I think it's more than that. I think your entire life has come to this point for divine purposes."

"No," Lonnie said.

"*Yes*." Steely determination hardened Comely's gaze. "You've had incredible losses, and yes, you kicked a holy man into our fire pit, but do you understand what we're going against? What your king has done? Doane's army has been ordered to kill everyone in their path. They've burned through peaceful villages. They've murdered our women and children. I've watched them bash children's heads against rocks. They're not on a crusade of defense but domination. Your losses have been nothing compared to those in the path of your king."

Lonnie turned to the table as disgust washed through her heart.

"Let's look at this with curiosity," Comely continued. "What if you've been stripped of all ties so you can become what you've always been meant to be? What if you're the last chance to stop Doane before they destroy the world?"

"No," Lonnie said, spitting the word out.

"What if you don't stand up for what's right?" Comely sat back, releasing Lonnie's hands. "What if you sneak out of the camp tonight and hide in the depths of the forest? What if the men lose faith in curiosity?"

"I made all of that up to begin with," Lonnie said. "You're the first person to ever call me lucky in my entire life."

"What if I'm the first person to see you for what you are?"

Tears fell down Lonnie's cheek. She buried her face in her hands, crashing into the table as she broke into sobs. Comely stepped to her side and set his hands on her shoulders.

"I've lost, too," he whispered, taking hold of her. "Lonnie, the world doesn't make any sense until it does. Long ago, I gave up on building a home and finding love. And then I found you."

Lonnie faced Comely and buried her head in his chest. He held her tight as she wept. A dangerous heat formed between them. Lonnie squeezed, holding Comely so fast she expected his back to break. He only held her tighter.

"I'm scared," she breathed. "I'm terrified of what might come next."

"I am, too," Comely said. "But I promise you; it will be far less terrifying if we face it together."

They held one another. The lamp flickered and sizzled, the pap solidified into a gelatinous goo.

"I'm sorry," Lonnie said when she finally gained control of herself. "You made us dinner and we haven't even touched it."

"Well, good news," Comely said, smiling as he returned to his side of the table. "It looks like it survived the wait."

Lonnie found her appetite in the catharsis of their conversation, and she ate all of the pap and cabbage in a few minutes. She chewed through the dried beef while Comely refreshed their drinks.

"I have some wine around here somewhere," he said, digging through a crate.

"We shouldn't," Lonnie said. "The last time I drank wine I drank it for three days straight." She smiled as she turned to Comely. Despite the depths of her emotional unloading, his confidence in her seemed only to increase. He ran a hand over her shoulder as he returned to the table. "What about you?" she asked.

"What about me?" he asked, pouring water into Lonnie's cup.

"Tell me something I don't know about you." She smiled, hoping he might choose a lighter topic.

"Bram." Comely grinned as Lonnie stared. "It's my name; Commander Bram Comely. I don't think I ever told you."

"Bram Comely," Lonnie said, tasting the words. "It's a nice name."

"Not as nice as Lonnie Lovingdove. What's the story behind your surname?"

"I guess someone in my line really liked doves."

Comely burst into laughter, which soon infected Lonnie. They howled as they sat at the tiny table in a tent in the middle of the road, a long way from home, far from normality. The unhinged laughter came with incredible euphoria. Lonnie swelled as she stared at Comely; the cracked lines around his eyes, the veins jutting from his neck. She had found herself upon a foreign planet.

And she didn't hate it, despite the hell she had crossed to find it.

"Bram," she said, finally composing herself. She climbed out of her chair and rose into the lamp's heat. He watched her, the smile remaining in his eyes. "I'm very glad to have found you."

"As am I," he said, standing. They met in the middle and kissed, holding one another tight, the passion expanding through every inch of Lonnie's body. Comely carried her across the room. He stopped at the bed, panting as he met Lonnie's gaze. "Lonnie," he breathed. "May I—"

"Yes."

SIXTY-TWO

Lonnie woke at daybreak. Comely lay behind her, his heavy arm draped across her bosom. At first shame washed over her, but as she lay, feeling the soft expansions of Comely's broad chest, an incredible sense of peace and safety took hold. She rolled over and kissed him. His eyes shuttered open and he took her by the neck, pulling her back for a superior kiss.

An hour later, covered in a fresh layer of sweat, they quickly dressed.

"So, what's next?" Comely asked, taking great pleasure in watching Lonnie tie off her pants. "Any ideas for today's lesson?"

"I just want to make sure everyone gets it," Lonnie said. "I don't think I can stretch it any more than I have. How soon could we join up with the rest of the army? How will that even work? Do I have to teach everyone how to be lucky? How much time do we have?"

"It's our responsibility to make those decisions," Comely said, his thinking scowl returning. "If you think you can finish your teaching today, then we can leave as soon as tomorrow. We'll send word to Camp Aslin and Beetle and have them meet us at the main camp. It won't be that much harder to teach the full army. Besides, you'll have all of us to help you. The most important thing will be making sure all the other commanders understand the principles of luck. We—"

A great scream came from outside the tent, followed by a

trampling of horses so fierce Lonnie ran to Comely. The ground trembled as if a hundred bulls stampeded across the tent. Comely took up his tunic and tied a sword around his waist. He drew the blade, his eyes frantic as he turned to Lonnie.

Outside, shouting rose with the stampeding thunder.

Comely ran to the front of the tent and pulled the door open. Lonnie raced to his side.

A cavalry of soldiers charged through camp, their swords drawn and hacking. Lonnie trembled at the sight of Doane's green and gold colors wrapping the horses and soldiers.

"They've come," Comely said, pulling Lonnie back. "They've come while we're down. Stay inside—"

"Get me a bow," Lonnie said. "I'm not great, but I can shoot."

Comely kicked open a trunk and handed Lonnie a bow and quiver.

"Stay alive," he said, taking hold of her. "We will not mourn tonight."

Comely raced outside. The tent entrance waved after him as if saying goodbye. Lonnie nocked an arrow. The shouting and ruckus of war left her hands trembling. She took a few breaths to steady herself, doing her best to keep hold of the fact luck had chosen her.

The Doane cavalry had kicked up a dust storm, and Lonnie could hardly see fifteen feet in front of her. Men shouted from all directions. Horses trampled and wood snapped.

Lonnie turned as a rider came through the dust, his face wrinkled with rage. He slashed a half-collapsed tent open and leaned down to find it empty. His horse spotted Lonnie and grunted, drawing the rider's attention.

He faced Lonnie as she drew her bow to her shoulder. At first he smiled. But upon closer inspection, he frowned.

"*Lovingdove?*" he called.

Lonnie let fly and the arrow landed in the soldier's belly with a wet *thump*.

The soldier gasped as he looked down, taking hold of the arrow. When he lifted his gaze the second arrow found him in the chest. He groaned and took hold of the arrow, yanking and pulling on it. Lonnie's third arrow hit him in the leg. The soldier ignored it and ripped the arrow from his chest. A trickle of blood followed it. He took a last desperate glance at Lonnie and rolled off his horse.

Lonnie winced as he crashed head-first into the ground. His left foot remained in the stirrup, and his horse grunted, trying to shake him off.

"It's okay," Lonnie called, taking the black stallion by the reins. She gave him a pat as he backed into a collapsed tent. "Stay still," she said. "I'm trying to help." She carefully stepped to the horse's side and slid the dead soldier's foot from the mount. The man died with a horrid realization across his face. Lonnie used him as a stool to climb onto the beautiful horse.

From up high, she could see over much of the dust. At least thirty other riders roamed the camp. They hacked at the already destroyed tents and shouted to one another. Lonnie couldn't see any of her own men.

She followed the outskirts of camp with her bow across her thigh, an arrow nocked and ready. Ahead, swords chimed as they clashed. Lonnie lifted her bow and urged her horse through the gray dust cloud.

Commander Comely tumbled backwards into the lane. He jumped to his feet as two Doane soldiers pursued him, both hacking as they screamed. Comely parried and slashed one's leg. He blocked a killing blow and kicked the other into a tent. With a grunt, he speared the downed man and then the other. He turned to Lonnie, blood decorating his face, his chest heaving.

"Where is everyone?" Lonnie shouted.

"I don't know," Comely said. He stiffened as someone shouted, and without a word, raced back toward the center of camp.

Lonnie turned to the action and creeped down a tight lane between tents. Shadows raced beneath the dust before her. She squeezed the bow tightly, turning to the riders roaming the rest of camp. None of them were close enough to take an accurate shot on.

She jumped as a man raced out of the dust cloud before her. He held up a hand, his face pale. Lonnie lowered her bow as she recognized the ugly man whose father had been crushed by a wagon wheel.

"Lonnie," he said, panting as he stopped in front of the horse. "Are you all right?"

"I'm fine," Lonnie said. "Where is everyone?"

"They're fighting, but not like we did."

"What?"

"We're doing what you said." The man smiled despite the horrendous tension. "We're looking for interesting opportunities." He carried a sword, but it remained in his holster. As a man shouted nearby, he turned, twitching like a watchdog. Before Lonnie could ask another question he took off.

Lonnie set her horse forward and turned across the camp. To her surprise, the mounted men from Doane started climbing off their horses. She squinted as the dust continued to settle. A team of the camp soldiers huddled behind a tent, all carrying bows and whispering to one another. Not two tents ahead of them, three of the dismounted Doane soldiers hacked open tents only to find empty beds. They scowled as they huddled to regroup.

Three arrows flew through the dust and decorated the men's backs. They shouted and ran for their horses, one stumbling to the ground. The other two were only halfway into the saddle when a rain of arrows turned them into porcupines. The camp's soldiers quickly secured the horses.

A trumpet sounded from the road.

Lonnie turned, spotting another team of Doane's riders in the distance. She kicked her horse around and took a wide sweep to the outside of camp, where she could escape the dust. But not for long. As she came into the field, smoke joined the battle. Within a minute, the entire camp came to flame.

The fire raged and black smoke billowed into the air, twisting toward the clouds. Lonnie used the cover of smoke to get closer to the road. Her stolen horse fidgeted under the heat, but she held tight, soon coming to the road.

Another thirty Doane horsemen gathered outside the camp, watching the rising fire. They blew the trumpet and shouted to one another. Nothing came of the call. A few tried to push forward and their horses nearly kicked them off. The men dismounted and drew their swords. They entered the burning camp and became one with the smoke.

Lonnie turned her horse and rode for the backside of camp. There, a dozen of her men stood outside of the smoke, each steadying a newly acquired horse. One held a torch to a tent and smiled as it went up in flames. Lonnie raced to meet them.

"Lady Luck," one of the men said.

"Why are you burning the camp?" Lonnie asked.

"I'm following my curiosity." The man smiled, his eyes flickering with the firelight. "The soldiers came in to slaughter us, but when they saw the state of the camp, they thought another crew had already done it for them. I'm making sure they think we're already dead."

"Where's Commander Comely?"

"I haven't seen him."

Lonnie turned to the raging fire, the entire camp putting off a dizzying heat.

"Where's everyone else?"

"We don't know," another man said. "We saw these horses and wanted to get them out before the fire killed them."

"There are more riders on the road," Lonnie said. "A few of them just went into the fire on foot, but at least thirty are out front. They all have horses."

"I wonder if we might have those horses," a man said. "I wonder what it would take to get the rest of those bastards into the fire."

"We have to find Comely," Lonnie said.

"The commander's a fighter."

"But this is an ambush."

"And the commander has never been killed in an ambush. Lonnie, can you help us get the rest of Doan's men into the fire?"

Lonnie frowned, unable to focus with Comely somewhere inside of the inferno. She stood in the saddle, but the smoke and flames had risen. Her heart pounded as she turned back to the men.

"They need to think we're dead," she said. "Come with me, and bring those horses."

SIXTY-THREE

Lonnie led the men down the hillside, where they slipped into a small thicket of trees. After tying off the horses they gathered, each holding out their weapons. Six of the twelve had bows, five swords, and the remaining were left barehanded in the heat of the ambush. The archers quickly distributed their arrows.

"We need to be quick," Lonnie said. "Is there any way back into the camp without burning ourselves?"

"Should be," the arsonist said. "The fire's still young."

"Then let's go." Lonnie led them back up the hill, toward the stinking offering that was Camp Cattail. They ducked beneath the hill as three Doane riders came trotting along the outskirts of camp. The riders stood in their saddles, surveying the smoking wreck.

"Luck is with us," one of the men said. "If we waited another minute, those bastards would have come right upon us."

"We need to get those horses," Lonnie said. "Quickly, before they ride back around. Who can shoot?"

"We're trained archers," another man said. "Let them get ahead and we'll run up and take our best shot."

The team let Doane's riders cross the midway line of camp and started to run, creeping through the high grass behind them. With a silent signal, all five archers knelt and nocked.

"Let fly," one hissed.

The arrows sprung from the bows. All but one struck its

target. The Doane soldiers shouted and kicked their steeds, one slumping as the arrow caught him in the neck. The archers drew a second round and landed two more arrows.

"Run," a camp soldier said, waving for Lonnie to follow. "Before the horses drag them back to the others."

The team raced across the field, finding the first horse with its rider dead upon his back. A soldier dragged him off and mounted.

"I'll take him to the hollow," he said, kicking the horse into a run.

The rest of the group continued forward, finding the last two horses just around the corner of camp. A sole rider desperately tried to stay conscious as he dragged the other horse after him.

"Nock," one of the archers said. The men at his side let fly as if controlled by a single mind.

The last rider slid clean off his horse.

The team carefully approached the horses, not wanting to spook them. Two men climbed into the mounts and raced for the hollow.

"Luck," a man breathed, anxiously grinning as he turned to Lonnie.

"Don't think about it," Lonnie said. "Just keep doing what we're doing."

Ahead, a Doane soldier flew out of the burning camp, screaming as he slapped at his flaming jacket. Commander Comely stepped after him, shirtless, sweat rising from his skin as steam. He speared the burning man and turned to find Lonnie and the others.

"Comely," Lonnie said, racing to meet him.

"I can't find any more of them," Comely said. He grunted with every breath, his flesh hot to the touch. "I killed a dozen. Maybe more. What's going on?"

"We're burning the camp," a soldier said, smiling. "And we're stealing horses. We've already got about twenty."

"There's at least two dozen other mounted men on the road," Lonnie said. "We're going to try and draw them off their horses and into the camp."

"There's ten more horses trapped in the fire," Comely said. "A few others ran off into the field. What's your plan to get the riders into the flames?"

"We don't have one." Lonnie winced as wind blew over the camp. The heat of it stole her breath away, simultaneously stoking the inferno. "Where's the rest of our men?"

"I looked," Comely said. He met Lonnie's gaze with a pained grimace.

"Riders," one of the men shouted, pointing to the road.

Five mounted Doane men turned the corner. At the sight of the camp's survivors, they kicked their mounts into a run. They drew swords and shouted as they raced down the side of the burning camp.

"Nock and draw," Comely shouted.

Lonnie and the archers pulled the arrow fletching to their shoulders. The approaching riders ducked low on their horses, their eyes crazed as they closed the gap.

"Fire," Comely screamed.

The arrows flew, but only one hit its target. Comely raced to the flames and took a burning tent stake. He swung it like a mace as the Doane riders came upon them.

The horses reared from the heat and whinnied. Their riders leaned forward and helplessly swung their blades, but they could not reach their targets. Comely didn't need to tell the archers to knock and fire.

The riders bounced as the horses grounded. A pair of arrows sunk deep into each of their chests. While they groaned, hacking wildly, Comely ran up and speared one under the ribs.

The rest of the camp's men dragged the others to the ground and tossed them into the fire.

"Easy," Comely cooed, holding two of the bucking horses. The men secured the third as it tried to run into the field. They climbed into the mounts and raced for the hollow, a vivid excitement in place of their once-desperate misery. "Lonnie," Comely said, stumbling as he met her. "Come on. We can't ease up."

He dragged her toward the road with the rest of the camp soldiers at their rear. Lonnie kept an arrow on her bow string, still feeling sick from the heat.

"Why are they attacking?" she asked between breaths.

"Because we're weak," Comely said. "This is how Doane fights." He slowed as they came toward the end of camp. Grunting, he creeped to the roadside, laying on his belly as he turned the corner. Lonnie crawled after him.

Only a dozen riders remained out front of the camp. Their horses grew restless, huffing and pacing before the swelling flames. Two of the most decorated soldiers stood in the front, animatedly conversing. They waved their swords and pointed into the flames. A man in the rear blew his trumpet to no effect.

"They're scared," Comely said. "They thought they won before it started." He looked up, studying the sky, the grove of trees on the other side of the road.

"How can we get their horses?" Lonnie asked.

"We can't." Comely turned to the men over his shoulder. "Fall back. I have a plan." He led Lonnie to the rest of the men, bringing them all together. "I want our swordsmen right on the corner, and I want the archers back here. Strike on sight. We're finishing this now."

"What about me?" Lonnie asked.

"Nock."

Comely ran into camp, the smoke and flames swallowing

him in an instance. Lonnie started to call out when he returned, holding a flaming section of canvas. He tossed it to the grass and began wrapping it around a charred tent stake.

"Get ready," he shouted, holding out the torch as the flames rose into a handheld sun. "For Lady Luck."

The archers fell to their knees and set their arrows on the line. Lonnie joined them, her heart thundering as Comely and his swordsmen raced to the road. The swordsmen paused as Comely rounded the corner. He shouted and lifted the torch over his head. For a moment Lonnie could hear only the crackling incineration of Camp Cattail.

Commander Comely came sprinting around the corner, pumping his arms as grass flew from his feet. He lifted the flaming torch as he screamed.

"Fire!"

All twelve remaining Doane riders galloped after him. They stood in the saddles and hunched over their mounts, victory and flame twinking in their eyes.

Comely's swordsmen sprung up and speared two of them clean off their horses. A third took a deep gash and lost his hold, tumbling to the ground. The soldiers dispatched him at once.

The archers let fly and peppered the riders. The front four broke into the field, leaving the middle of the pack exposed. Comely turned and hurled the flaming torch at the horses. They reared back, sending two riders from the saddle. Comely dropped to his belly as another round of arrows flew from the bows. The swordsmen raced from behind and slashed at the men.

The ugly man whose father had been crushed by a wagon wheel took up the flaming torch and waved it at the horses, laughing as they reared back. Only two of Doane's riders remained upright, and arrows hung from their bodies like shriveling appendages. They desperately extended their swords as the camp soldiers surrounded them.

"You're done," the ugly man said, lifting his sword. "The luck's on our side, now." He slashed at a rider's belly, but the rider dove clean off his horse. He crashed into the ugly soldier and lunged at his neck. Comely and the rest of the soldiers rushed in, but they were too late. The Doane soldier came up with a mouthful of the ugly man's throat. He screamed in triumph as the others speared him lifeless.

"Get him down," Comely shouted, waving to the last mounted Doane rider.

The soldiers yanked him off the horse and dragged him through the grass. Comely set him on his knees and sneered, taking a sword from the man's own belt. He took no break before slashing the blade across his neck. The man fell with spurting blood across the grass. Comely took him by the belt and easily tossed him into the flames.

He watched the man convulse for his last few seconds of life.

Lonnie fell to her hands and knees and vomited, the trauma of the battle finally infecting her spirit.

"Gather those horses," Comely shouted. Lonnie lifted her gaze as Comely climbed onto one of the larger horses. He found her with sorrow in his eyes. "I'll make sure we're finished here. *Boys, get those horses.*" He kicked his mount and raced toward the road.

SIXTY-FOUR

Lonnie had little to offer the veteran soldiers in the wake of her first real battle, but she did her best to look strong, nodding and following the men as they chased the rest of the horses around the field. After half an hour they gathered them in the hollow with the others. Lonnie did a rough head count, numbering their cavalry at thirty-one.

While victorious, the men couldn't sit still. Most went running back toward camp, assisting Comely in the search for living enemies. Only two remained with Lonnie, who did her best to keep the stable of horses calm.

She pet her black steed, her gaze locked on the Doane crest wrapping his neck. She felt sick to have come from a place that preyed upon the weak. It still twisted her mind: the soldiers had stormed right into a camp, expecting to spear the men in their beds.

But they had not succeeded.

Lonnie bitterly smiled, thinking of all the luck that had come their way.

Her accidental destruction of the camp had confused the soldiers and slowed their attack.

And the persistent heat and drought had caused a terrible dust storm. Lonnie suspected some of the camp's soldiers had escaped in the dust.

The most lucky thing, though, was the men's attitude. They had not only remembered her lessons, but found a way of working them into war tactics. She didn't know how they might translate to an offensive attack, but they certainly succeeded in defense.

The sky grew increasingly darker over the next hour. Soldiers slowly returned to the hollow as it began to drizzle. A few rode back out on mounts, but most congregated in the center of the horses, wildly relaying their stories of the fight. Lonnie kept her eyes on the steaming camp as the rain began to extinguish the fire. She hadn't seen Comely since he rode off, and despite their victory, she grew painfully nervous.

"Lady Luck," a man shouted, waving her to the big huddle. "*Lady Luck*," he repeated when she didn't come.

"Has anyone seen Comely?" Lonnie asked as she stepped into the huddle.

"*Lady Luck*," a man announced, lifting Lonnie's arm over her head. The men cheered as they rushed Lonnie, desperate to touch her; even just to brush the hem of her tattered shirt. They shouted and buzzed about like school boys. Soon, they came into a unison chant of *Lady Luck*.

Lonnie smiled for them, waving off the praise, but as soon as they drifted back into chatter, she slipped away and climbed onto her horse.

"Stay," a man said, taking hold of her mount. "No need for you to get wet, Lady Luck. The battle's been won."

"It's okay," Lonnie said. "I'll be right back." As the man stepped aside, she sent her steed into a trot.

She climbed up the hillside, wincing as she came upon the camp. The fire had chewed it into a black graveyard. Charred tent poles and fabric lay everywhere. Splintered beds and broken tables lay between, equally charred and shattered. Lonnie rode her horse into camp and winced at the unfortunately familiar scent of burning human flesh.

The thrill of victory fell away as she saw the death—dozens of camp soldiers, laying hacked apart and smoked to blackened mummies. She could only tell the Camp soldiers from the Doane soldiers by their inferior boots. The air tasted of acrid smoke and death. Lonnie looked ahead to the empty road; to the few camp soldiers riding out of the woods on the other side. She galloped to meet them.

"Where's Commander Comely?" she asked, looking from one pale face to the other.

"We can't find him," one replied. Rain ran down their faces, as it did Lonnie's. The water prickled her with a chill and she shivered. "We found some tracks in the woods, but the rain's mussed them."

"He said he would be right back." Lonnie turned to camp—across the fields. The steadying rain destroyed her visibility. "I'm going to look for him."

"It's slick," a man said. Mud covered him and his horse, echoing the warning.

"I'll be careful," Lonnie said. "Keep looking for survivors in camp." She clenched her jaw as the men turned to the blackened square of earth. "That's an order," she said. "Go through every tent."

"Yes, Lady Luck," the men said, kicking their horses to action.

Lonnie rode into the woods and searched through the dim light, making her way for the tree where she held her lesson on luck. A horrible feeling filled her gut. She called for Comely, but nothing but battering rain returned the charge.

As best she could, she turned her horse up the hillside. The steed could only manage the sloppy bank on an angle, but eventually they came to a level precipice, where Lonnie could see for miles in every direction. She stood in the saddle and searched for her partner.

The camp loomed as a black rectangle in the field; smoke rising from the remaining pockets of cinder. Her men rode through the rubble, looking like toy soldiers in the expanse of ruin. Lonnie studied the road in each direction. In the rain, she could hardly see more than a mile, even at her vantage on the precipice.

"Comely," she shouted with cupped hands. The rain increased in response, dropping visibility to a dozen yards. She turned to the continuing rise into the mountain, but the idea had no merit—Comely had not ascended. He had left to look for men.

Lonnie walked alongside her horse back down the hill, half of the time using him to keep from slipping. She returned to the hollow drenching wet.

In her absence, the men had salvaged cornmeal and a decent pile of dried meat. They stretched a half-charred piece of canvas between trees to build a small cooking station. Lonnie watched them fail to light a fire. Every peripheral movement sent her head whipping to the field, hoping to find Comely.

But the day passed without his return. As Lonnie huddled around the fire, chewing on brittle jerky, the sun fell and left her in starlight. Everyone was perpetually damp from the rain. Lonnie wrapped herself in a blanket and tried to be curious. She brooded on the battle and the war that must come. Her heart broke to know the killing would only continue.

Late in the night, she realized she didn't have Daniel's carving. Consumed by fear, she climbed to her feet, battling the wet blanket off.

"Is everything all right?" one of them asked, starting to stand with her.

"I just need to check something," Lonnie said. "I'll be right back." She found her horse, but with the sloppy ground and lack of light, she didn't want to risk breaking his leg.

She climbed out of the hollow and walked along the grass, moving for the place that once held Commander Comely's tent.

Her hands trembled as she moved through the still-smoking remains. Heat nipped at her ankles. The rain had washed ashes across everything, turning it all into a black quicksand.

Lonnie stopped outside of the tent's footprint. The poles had fallen and the canvas melted into a black webbing. She crouched and took hold of the corner, wincing at the weight of it. Still, she yanked and pulled, peeling the canvas back. After ten minutes she exposed what had been the place she found love again. She stared at a dark lump beside the broken table; two charred arrows curling from its side. With a tear falling down her cheek, she lifted Daniel's carving.

A great portion of it had been burned. She brushed away the ashes, finding a faint trace of her and Daniel's initials. It no longer looked like a heart but an homage to rotten fruit. She knelt beside a puddle and wiped the ashes off, but each stroke only took more of the wood away.

"Lonnie," Comely said.

He stood five feet behind her. Mud covered him like skin. He limped forward, staring down at the carving between her hands.

"I'm sorry," he said, surveying the rest of his tent.

"Where were you?" Lonnie sneered as she rose, wanting to slap him across the face. "I thought you were dead. You've been gone all day, and I've been—"

"Please." Comely held out his hand, his eyes bright with a pain Lonnie had not seen before.

She ran to him, breaking into tears; hating herself for doubting his return.

"I'm sorry," she blubbered, burying herself in the heat of his chest.

"I tracked a rider down the road," Comely said. He gripped Lonnie, his fingers pulsing around her shoulder. "I questioned him before I killed him. Lonnie, they came for all of us. They attacked Camps Aslin and Beetle. I rode all the way out to Beetle. They massacred the men; no one survived."

Lonnie stepped back, her self pity feeling blasphemous.

"Both camps?" she asked, the words falling from a shallow breath.

"And the main camp," Comely said. "We are all that's left of Castle Winston's army." He let her go as he eyed the corner of the tent. With a grunt, he kicked a pile of charred wood aside. There, he found a bag of dried meat.

"What happens next?" Lonnie asked. "There's only thirty of us. We have horses, but—"

"We finish it," Comely said, his eyes reflecting the starlight. "Our only chance is to ride into Doane and finish this. Lonnie, it's time to kill the king."

Lonnie stared at Comely, unable to believe it, but knowing with all of herself the decision was right. She took his hands as they met.

"How?" she asked. "How will we kill the king?"

"With luck," Comely said. No smile fell across his face, for the comment was not hopeful but true. "We're going to need all the luck in the world."

PART SIX

IF THIS IS LUCK, THEN WE'RE PRETTY WELL FUCKED

CHAPTER
SIXTY-FIVE

Comely took Lonnie's hand and led her back to the hollow. Neither had words to speak. The night continued cooling, nearing a downright chill.

The men cheered for their commander's return, but upon hearing his report, silence quickly retook its hold. Comely stood before the sallow collection of men. Lonnie sat beside him with a damp blanket around her shoulders. The fire's heat seemed determined to avoid her.

"We're all that's left," Comely said, surveying the men. "We're the last fist of Castle Winston. Our only chance—*the world's* only chance of survival, is to do what we just did today." Comely turned to Lonnie, gently nodding. "Despite our losses, we've come into some luck today. While the rest of our brothers were slain in their beds, we managed to escape with not only a third of our men, but enough horses to take us into Doane.

"And that's exactly what we're going to do." Comely's gaze hardened, the firelight a swirling ferocity in his eyes. "Our only chance is to kill the king himself. We can't beat their army, but we can infiltrate the castle, and with luck, we will succeed."

A few nodded, one verbalizing his agreement with a grunt. Most just stared in the stunned exhaustion of surviving the ambush. Even Lonnie couldn't will herself to rally.

"I won't force anyone to come with us," Comely said. "If you're scared, or you're tired, take a horse and go find your peace."

When the men didn't move an inch, Comely nodded.

313

"We'll sleep tonight. When we wake, we'll ride straight to Doane. We'll collect what weapons we have, and we'll pick up what we need along the road. Our team is small, but that will be our edge. We're not going to look like an army. We're not going to fight like an army. Curiosity will guide us, as will Lady Luck. Lonnie knows the kingdom, and she knows the castle. We'll either succeed or die trying."

"I'm curious to see how this goes," one of the men said. "If they think we're whipped, I wonder if we might catch them off guard."

"I wonder if all of the kingdom's soldiers are out on the campaign," another said. "I wonder if we'll find a soft guard at the castle gates."

"I know a back way in," Lonnie said, lifting her head. "I wonder if we can come into the castle without anyone knowing we're there."

"This is why we're alive," Comely said, a stolid pride on his face as he looked across the survivors. "This is why we will not only succeed, but why every event in our lives has led us to this very moment. Luck has chosen us, men. We must feed her and ensure we do not disappoint."

The mood in camp didn't quite shift into celebration, for even with inhuman luck many of the men would not live to see another full moon, but the spirit of curiosity possessed the dark hollow.

As things quieted, Comely made a bed out of salvaged canvas and lay with Lonnie. She clutched the ashen carving of her old partner. With Comely's plan in motion, she let her curiosity loose, exploring all the possibilities that might come of penetrating castle Doane.

Sleep came without warning.

It left just as mercilessly.

Lonnie stood on the edge of the hollow as the rising sun

turned the skyline pink. The men were up and about, foraging for weapons and supplies in camp. Comely and a team inspected the horses to identify the strongest ones. Lonnie had been given a single instruction, and she used her silent magic with all of herself.

She wondered how they would find weapons for their final stand, for burned arrows would not secure anything.

She wondered how long it might take to return to Doane. Perhaps their small troupe might find a road less traveled, cutting off large corners of the crusade.

She wondered what it might feel like to kill a king— to end a reign of madness.

The rising sun turned the dew into golden honey. Comely called the foragers back to camp, where they settled for whatever they had found. They packed out and mounted the horses. Lonnie climbed atop her black steed, turning to Comely, who rode a dapple gray. He nodded and led the army across the field. To Lonnie, they hardly qualified as an army, but she had found success with an army of one, and she had no room to doubt them.

They rode for a few hours and came upon a shaded gulley where a stream crossed their path. The day had grown hot, and the horse drank deeply, as did the men. Comely allowed everyone a small ration of dried meat before they continued.

Their trail crossed endless humping fields and wild woods. Lonnie kept an eye out, hoping they might come across a lone wolf blacksmith, or a retired veteran who hoarded crossbows and broadswords, but they had no such luck. They rode deep into the night and camped in an open field. Comely assigned shifts for sleeping, wanting someone to keep an eye on the horses at all times. Lonnie volunteered for the first watch.

It felt good to walk after the day of riding, and she spent the time pacing around the grazing horses, letting her mind run free with every curious thought it crossed. Her fear had lessened after the physical assault of bouncing across a horse for nearly twelve hours. She wasn't quite optimistic, but she certainly wondered how they would survive.

They might find some other men to join their party, if they looked in the right places.

With only thirty mouths to feed, they only needed to find a single elk or cow to keep them fed for the rest of the journey.

And they were moving at an incredibly brutal pace. If Doane had sent a sizable portion of their soldiers to commit the massacres of Castle Winston's camps—which they would have if they took out all three refugee camps and the main war camp simultaneously—they probably thought the war was over.

Comely and Lonnie's last stand might just make it to the castle before they arrived.

And if they did?

The challenge might not be too big for luck to mantle.

Lonnie smiled when Comely met her, pulling her behind the horses for a much-needed kiss. He lifted and held her. Soon, they rolled through the grass in heated love. Their passion came through desperation. They poured into one another as if testing the bounds of physical affection. Lonnie lay with him when they finished, staring up at the stars.

"We're no more than a day's ride," Comely said. "With this small of a troupe, we're making good time."

"I'm scared," Lonnie said, feeling better for finally admitting it.

"Don't be." Comely sat up as he faced her. "We only need you to lead our curiosity."

"I'm so tired of running. I've created so much death."

Comely took her hand, bringing it to his whiskery lips for a kiss.

"When we finish our mission, you'll have as much rest as

you can handle." He leaned forward and kissed her cheek, tucking her hair behind her ears. "Go and lay down," he said. "Sleep if you're tired."

Lonnie kissed him and rose, making her way to the dark huddle of bodies on the other side of the horses. Her head felt empty and dull, and she wished she could splash herself with cold water. She hadn't been herself since the attack.

She was just picking out a blanket when a glittering light in the distant tree line caught her eye. It shone only for a moment, but in the dark of the field, Lonnie could not ignore it. She glanced at the sleeping men and wondered if she should tell someone. Frowning, she watched the trees for a few more minutes.

The flash came again. A bright, silvery light.

Lonnie started walking, keeping her head low as she creeped along the field. She fought through knee-high grass and gopher holes. The trees didn't seem to get any closer. She barely blinked in hopes of finding the light again, but all remained dark.

She came to a pond at the end of the field, the crescent moonlight allowing her view of the muddy banks. On the other side, fresh foot and hoof prints textured the mud. Lonnie froze as she turned to the woods beyond the pond.

The flash of silver light returned.

Lonnie kept her eyes on the spot as she walked around the pond, taking great care to remain completely silent. She understood the danger of chasing phantoms in unknown country, but she needed to know; to uncover the secret of the light. As her curiosity rose into a force, she crossed the last dozen feet and came into the woods.

Lonnie gasped as she fell back to her bottom. A dozen knights hung from the trees, their armor twisting in the wind.

She crawled backwards until her eyes adjusted to the light, and then she rose, frowning as she stepped closer.

They were not knights but a dozen suits of steel armor hanging from the trees. Lonnie ran her hand over the cold metal, fingering the Doane crest upon one's breast. She turned as the wind carried a whiff of smoke through the woods.

The chilly night sent a shiver up Lonnie's spine. She followed the smoke and wandered deeper in the forest. Her breath became visible and the smoke intensified; its body smelling of pine and greenery.

At the end of the trees, Lonnie came into another field, where a dozen fires glowed across the barren expanse. What looked to be five hundred soldiers lay between them. Some huddled around the fire, others lay on blankets. A massive pack of horses stood on the outskirts of the camp, grazing in the high grass.

Lonnie could hardly breathe as she stared at her find; what must be a significant piece of Doane's army. Many men were still awake, but the majority slept. While fear left her frozen, she couldn't help but survey the army's supplies, all stacked neatly in the corner of camp: swords and bows and arrows and crates. Curiosity mated with her fear and created a whirlwind of thought.

She ran back to camp.

Comely stood with his dapple gray, absentmindedly scratching the beast between its ears. He turned at the sound of Lonnie's frantic breathing.

"What?" he asked, running to meet her.

"Doane," Lonnie said. She stumbled to catch her breath. "There's a camp just on the other side of those trees. It has to be half of their army."

"Do they know we're here?" Comely asked, his eyes bright.

"No, they're resting. They have fires. A lot of them are sleeping."

"Watch the horses." Comely raced off, but Lonnie ran after him.

"What are you doing?" she asked.

"I want to see what we're facing. They may have scouts. We won't stand a chance if they come after us."

"That's fear," Lonnie said, taking his hand. "This isn't bad luck but good." She forced Comely to face her, feeling more awake than she had in days. "Bram, if a few of us can sneak into their camp, we can take all the supplies we need. There's so many soldiers they wouldn't notice a few strangers."

"But if they realize—"

"No," Lonnie said. "We've come too far to lose faith in luck. We need weapons and food. If we're really a day's ride from Doane, this is our only chance."

Comely drew a long breath, his eyes shifting as he thought.

"How will we do it?" he asked.

"With confidence. Come on." Lonnie took his hand and led him to the men. "We only need two or three to go into the camp. The rest of us will wait in the woods while they bring us the supplies. They hung some of their armor in the trees, so it won't even look strange if someone's walking about."

Comely stared at their weary soldiers, their sleep deep and heavy. He let out a breath and nodded.

Lonnie and Comely woke all of them, telling them to keep quiet as they assembled for an emergency meeting. The men, still riding the shock of war, were fully awake within a minute.

"What's going on?" one asked as he tightened his boots.

"We have an opportunity," Comely said. "Lady Luck got curious, and she found Doane's army camping just beyond those trees." He pointed to the dark swath of woods. "This is luck, boys. They have the weapons and food we need, and we're going to take it right out from under them."

"Now?" a man asked.

"The timing is perfect," Lonnie said. "Most of them are sleeping. They won't even notice us."

At Comely's command, the men headed to the woods, anxiously weaving through the suits of hanging armor. They all brought a weapon. Lonnie led the way, waving for everyone to quiet as they came to the end of the trees.

"On the right corner of camp," Lonnie whispered as she crouched. "Their weapons and supplies are all sitting on those carts. Two of you go down and start bringing up anything we can use. The rest of us will watch from here, and we'll take whatever you find back to camp."

"Weapons and food," Comely said. "That's what we're after. Good steel, and quality arrows. Who will come with me?"

"You should stay," Lonnie whispered as she leaned into Comely. "We need you here."

"Who will come with me?" Comely asked again, facing his men.

"I'm quite curious to see what we can find," a man said. He smiled, but its twitchy nature confessed to his panic. "I'll go with you, Commander."

"Then we go." Comely dressed down to his plain tunic, as did the volunteer. They stepped beyond the trees and watched the camp for a few minutes, leaning into one another, nodding and discussing their plan. Lonnie drew a shaky breath as they turned right and followed the trees until they left her sightline.

Lonnie crawled a few feet out of the woods to get a better view of camp. The Doane soldiers had covered what looked to be a hundred acres. They arranged themselves into factions of twenty-five or so men, with a campfire between every few factions. Lonnie followed the conscious soldiers. No one seemed to be on the lookout, but they sat straight, talking to one another with an energy that suggested they had no plans to sleep.

Comely and his man started down the bank a hundred yards to the right. Lonnie watched them, glad to see them move with confidence in place of creeping. They marched down the hill and approached the carts of supplies. Lonnie surveyed the nearby factions, but the few waking men paid no attention to the shadows beyond the fire.

Comely led the way into the stable of carts. He leaned into wagons, lifting box lids, stepping up on wagon wheels. Finally, he found a crate he liked and heaved it over the side. He and his partner walked it back out of camp with the same confidence they had entered. Lonnie breathed as if she were still running for her life.

It took fifteen minutes to complete the round trip. As Comely and his man returned, they simply set the crate before the rest of the soldiers.

"Tipped arrows," Comely said. He pulled the lid off to reveal hundreds of perfectly straight arrows, the fletching thick, and the tips sharp as needles. "We'll be back."

"Be careful," Lonnie said, but Comely didn't hear her.

While a team carried the arrows off, Lonnie turned back Doane's camp.

Soon, Comely and his man once again strode into the supplies. They took longer than before, but this time came away with a large pack on each of their backs. Comely's bag caught on the back of the wagon as he left camp, snapping a piece of the wood off. Lonnie heard the snap from all the way up on the hill. She held her breath as she turned to the nearest camp fire. A few of the Doane soldiers turned, but no one bothered to investigate.

"They heard you," Lonnie said when Comely returned. "That's enough. We can't risk—"

"Meat," Comely said, dropping his massive pack before the men. "Enough dried meat to last us a winter." He smiled as his partner dropped the other bag. "And corn. Take it back and start feeding the horse. Pour it out and make sure they all get to eat."

"Bram," Lonnie said. "This is enough. They heard you."

"What did they do?" Comely turned to the camp, which looked exactly as it had before they began to pilfer from the supply carts.

"They turned their heads," Lonnie said. "They heard the snap."

"It was that stupid bag," Comely said. "The wagons are on their last legs."

"Ready?" his man asked.

"There's a box of swords," Comely said. "We'll be quick, and then we'll be gone. Everyone else, head back to camp and start packing. We'll meet you with the swords and ride out tonight. This is our chance to get ahead of them." Before Lonnie could protest, Comely took hold of her. "This is how we'll win," he said, his fingers tight across her shoulders. "You said we have to take luck as it comes, right?"

Lonnie said nothing as they left, once more marching through the woods before taking the trail down to the camp. She perched on her knee and wished her hands would stop shaking. The chilly night left her entire body trembling. She held her breath as the men strode into the supply wagons.

Her eyes bounced from the wagons to the soldiers at the nearby fire. The Doane soldiers continued what looked to be a hilarious conversation, laughing and slapping their knees. Comely and his man shuffled a long wooden crate toward the back of a wagon. They worked slowly to avoid making any more noise, but as time dragged on, Lonnie began muttering under her breath.

"Just leave it," she whispered. "If it's so difficult, don't bother with it."

But the men had not returned to the wolf's den to give up. They finally brought the case to the ground between wagons and paused, visibly heaving to catch their breath. Lonnie shook her head as Comely's man stepped aside to relieve himself.

She turned to the campfire, her chest tightening as one of the men rose. He stretched and said something to his men. They laughed. He started walking, looking to the stars as he headed straight for the storage wagons.

"*He's coming,*" Lonnie whispered, trying to will the message into Comely's mind. "*He's coming. Either run or find a good place to hide.*"

The Doane soldier started to whistle, and in the great clearing, Lonnie could hear the tune from all the way up in the woods. To her relief, Comely heard it, too. He waved to his man and they crouched into the shadow between carts.

The Doane soldier came to one of the carts and stepped up on the wheel, digging around for a moment before coming away with a waterskin. He uncorked it and started chugging.

On the other side of the wagon, Comely crawled on hands and knees, trying to get eyes on the soldier.

"Just stay down," Lonnie said. "He doesn't know you're there. *Stay down.*"

When the Doane soldier started back for the fire, Lonnie let out what might be the biggest breath of her life. She almost laughed as Comely and his man heaved the massive crate out of camp. They stumbled under the weight, swaying as they moved up the hillside.

"*Evening,*" a man said from behind Lonnie.

Lonnie turned to find a stranger grinning at her. He lifted a crossbow, and behind the bolt, the Doane crest glistened across his chest.

SIXTY-SEVEN

"May I ask what you're doing in our camp?" the man said, wrapping his finger over the crossbow's trigger. "Start talking, cunt. Come on."

"I was just out for a walk," Lonnie stammered, her mind falling to pieces in her terror.

"You live out here?"

"I do."

"And you go walking in the woods this late at night? Alone?"

"I smelled smoke and worried there might be a forest fire."

"It rained buckets yesterday." The man's mock smile fell away. "Let's try again. *What are you doing in our camp?*" He pressed the tip of his arrow into Lonnie's forehead. A shock of pain crossed her body. Blood trickled down her nose. He lowered the bolt, moving it in line with her right eye. "Speak, you *fucking cunt.*"

Lonnie hyperventilated as she stared at the arrow. She wanted to scream and bring Comely or the others to her rescue, but screaming would also bring the entirety of Doane's army.

"Please," she whispered. "I'm sorry. I didn't know you were an army. I was just curious and wanted to see what was going on."

The man's eyes drifted to Lonnie's cheap shirt and pants; the loose white of Castle Winston's refugee camps. His gaze met Lonnie's.

"I figured we missed some of you," he said, "I didn't realize there were women. Do you know we killed the rest of them?"

"I don't know what you're talking about," Lonnie said.

The soldier slapped her with the back of his hand, sending her crashing to the forest floor. The slap echoed across the field.

"Castle Winston's finished," he grunted, kicking her in the stomach. "You're lucky I don't rape you before I kill you. Well, I suppose the others might want some fun." He grabbed Lonnie by the hair and lifted her off the ground. She screamed, unable to stop herself.

As the soldier turned her toward camp, dozens of Doane's soldiers rose from their beds. They turned to the woods as the soldier marched her onto the hillside.

"A cunt," he shouted, lifting Lonnie. He laughed as the camp went into a frenzy, the men racing to meet them, others rousing from the beds. Lonnie took a desperate swipe at the man's crossbow and he dropped her, bringing his elbow into her face.

Lonnie grunted as her vision flashed with new stars; dazzling constellations. Her keeper only laughed and dragged her forward.

Footsteps came from behind.

Lonnie turned just in time to see the moon glint off Comely's sword.

The soldier let go of her hair as the blade burst through his chest, blood and steam rising from the steel. He slumped to his knees and a roar came out from Doane's camp.

"Come on," Comely said, throwing Lonnie over his shoulder. He raced up the hill and into the woods. Arrows *knocked* into the trees after them.

"I can run," Lonnie said. "Let me run. I'm okay."

Comely set her down and they raced out of the woods, nearly straight into the pond.

"Mount the horses," Comely shouted, pulling Lonnie around the muddy banks. "They're coming. Mount the horses!"

They dashed across the field. In camp, the men swarmed like flies on a three-day corpse. Lonnie found her black steed and leaped into the stirrup, gasping as she clawed her way onto his back. The rest of the men battled to strap supplies to their horses.

"Leave it," Comely shouted, mounting his dapple gray. "They're coming and we can't fight them. Leave it and ride with me."

A shout came from across the field. Lonnie turned as her horse grunted, pacing in the swelling panic.

"Fire!" came another call.

Seconds later, a hundred arrows rained upon them.

"To me," Comely shouted, turning his horse. "Ride!" Lonnie chased him across the field. Another bath of arrows fell upon them. Two landed not six feet ahead of Lonnie's horse's thundering hooves. She lay low as they raced, taking a wide sweep to the right. Comely moved with purpose as he led the flight. He cut around a few trees and turned back in the direction of Doane, moving on a slant to put them well away from Doane's camp.

In the distance, horns blasted.

A few of Castle Winston's soldiers came alongside Lonnie as they followed Comely down a narrow trail, moving into a field adjacent to Doane's army. They sprinted through the midnight with fear and terror on their breath. Lonnie gripped the reins so hard her fingers went numb. She wished she had never found the armor—led the team to a temptation far too great to dismiss.

But after an hour of riding, they heard no pursuers. Comely had led them on such a twisted and breakneck pace only a savage could have followed them. When he finally slowed to let the horses rest, Lonnie came alongside him. He turned to her with a pale countenance. Sweat glistened across his face.

"We're okay," he said, his voice charred from shouting. "Are you all right?"

Lonnie nodded and turned to the rest of the party.

But only four horsemen stood behind them.

"Where are the others?" Comely asked, kicking his horse to meet them. "Where are the rest of them?" He panted, turning from one face to the other.

"They didn't make it onto their horses," a man said, battling to keep himself upright. "I barely made it myself." He turned, revealing six inches of arrow shaft in the back of his shoulder.

Comely stared down the trail they had followed, his confidence breaking with each passing second. He rubbed at his leg and Lonnie realized he too had taken an arrow. It hit the side of his thigh, buried down to the fletching.

"Bram," Lonnie said, pushing her horse to his. "Your leg."

"It's fine," he grunted. His eyes remained on the trail. "I have to look for them."

"The army's coming for us."

Comely's jaw flexed, his hands tight on the reins.

The four remaining soldiers slumped on their saddles beside them, looking from Lonnie to Comely.

"Did anyone else make it out of camp?" Lonnie asked.

"A few," one of the men mumbled. "But they fell off soon after we started. They were hit."

Comely kicked his horse into a run, the hooves knocking over the hard-packed earth. He soon faded into the shadowy trail.

"Do we need to take that out?" Lonnie asked, turning to the man with the arrow in his shoulder.

"Better to leave it in," he said. He blinked as he surveyed their dwindled group, his face gray in the moonlight.

Their horse's heavy breathing filled the ensuring silence. Lonnie could hardly stay upright in her exhaustion, but her troubled thoughts kept blood thundering through her veins. She only prayed Comely would return.

In a strange sense, she could feel the twenty-five missing men. It was as if their ghosts had come to ask why they had survived one assault only to fall to a second.

And the answer was simple.

Lonnie Lovingdove did indeed have a supernatural amount of luck. Unfortunately, it only guaranteed her personal survival. With her new family of soldiers nearly wiped from the earth, it also proved her luck's tertiary effect: everyone she knew would soon die. It was as if her luck fed on the souls of her companions.

She wanted to cry, but the numbness in her mind left her unable to do so.

As the waiting turned into torture, Lonnie also realized she had left Daniel's carving behind in camp. It had become an unrecognizable thing after her travels, but to know it was gone and that she would never see it again . . .

Lonnie climbed off her horse and wiped away his foamy sweat. He grunted, pulling away to graze on the softer grass.

"How long should we wait?" one of the men asked, his words falling on dry breath.

"Where are we going?" another asked.

"I don't understand," a third said. "I thought we had luck? What's happening, Lonnie?"

Lonnie stared down the dark, twisted trail, praying for Comely to return.

"Lady Luck," the fourth asked. "What do we do now?"

"Don't call me that," Lonnie said. She seethed, wanting to

scream and hurt someone. "I'm not what you think I am." She walked to her horse and took hold of the saddle. Part of her wanted to climb on and ride away—to escape and save the rest of the men from her curse, but a dapple gray horse came racing down the trail.

CHAPTER

SIXTY-EIGHT

Comely returned looking moments away from collapse. He had wrapped his arm around the reins to keep himself on the saddle. Lonnie ran to him. The rest of the party only turned their heads, looking to the empty trail behind him.

"It's just us," Comely breathed, his horse wheezing beneath him. "I didn't see anyone, so at least Doane's not coming this far."

"They're dead, then?" one of the men asked.

Comely confirmed with a grim nod.

"Well," another man said. "If this is luck, then we're pretty well fucked."

No one denied the statement. Lonnie, still afoot, turned to the wilderness.

"Did we do something wrong?" one of the men asked. "Lonnie, did—"

"Shut up," she snapped.

"Quiet," Comely said. "We're still too close. We have to keep riding."

"For what?" Lonnie turned to him, her tears finally breaking through the gates of her anger. "What do we have left to ride for?"

"We still have a war to finish. Get on your horse." Comely's stare could melt iron, but Lonnie remained where she stood. "Get on your horse," he repeated. "I'll tie you to the saddle if I have to. This isn't your fault."

"Then whose is it?" Lonnie asked. "Who sent our men into that camp? Who let the whole army know we were there?"

"The same scout who found you would have found our camp," Comely said. "The same scout who would have had the whole of Doane's army surround and murder all of us if we weren't awake. If we didn't do what we did, none of us would be here." Comely let out an exasperated breath. "Get on your horse, Lonnie. I'm not telling you again."

Lonnie clenched her teeth as she mounted, her legs and bottom painfully throbbing from the day's ride. She turned to Comely, who set back down the trail.

They rode for three grueling hours. Lonnie wondered how a single night could last so long. She switched to riding sidesaddle as they started into another bumpy section of woods. Comely led them in silence. Lonnie wondered what he really thought of her. Did he regret his brash decision to place her in charge of the men? Did he regret loving her before understanding what happened to those she loved?

Comely paused as they came into another clearing. Lonnie and the others rode up alongside him. They slouched as they lay eyes on a glowing cabin. Lonnie frowned, recognizing the long clothesline running from the back of the house.

"I've been here," she said. "When I escaped the cult with Bally, we stopped at this place." She frowned, trying to recall the man's name. "Kegan, I think."

"Is he friendly?" Comely asked. "Will he feed and water us?"

"He might." Lonnie thought back to her last visit, when Bally had talked the man into a deadly despair. "At the least, I don't think he'll hurt us."

"Come on." Comely rode into the clearing, leading the way toward the glowing cabin. It looked like something out of a fairytale. Lonnie stared at the clothesline as they neared the house, pausing to find a large dress hanging at the end of the line.

They came to the house and tied the horses to a mounting post. With Lonnie in front, the men stumbled to the door, brushing mud from their shirts. Lonnie knocked on the door and tucked her hair behind her ears.

A door thumped from inside. Something flashed in the window, but by the time Lonnie turned the shade fell back into place. The door squealed open.

Kagan loomed over them, his gaze hard, the door only open enough for half of his enormous face.

"What's this?" he asked. A wooden handle crossed his leg. Lonnie couldn't tell if it was an ax or a mallet.

"Kegan," Lonnie said, drawing his eye. "Do you remember me? It's Lonnie Lovingdove."

"Aye," Kagan grunted. "Have you brought more friends to insult me, or are they just going to kill me this time?"

"We're soldiers for Castle Winston," Comely said. "Sir, we've been attacked and need water. If you have food, I promise we can repay you as soon as we've finished our mission. We need rest."

"Any friend of *Lonnie Lovingdove* is no friend of mine." Kagan scowled as he stared down at Lonnie. "What happened to your charming little friend?"

"She's dead," Lonnie said. "I'm so sorry for what she did to you."

"Key, who is it?" a woman asked.

"Go back to bed," Kagan said. "It's just some beggars."

"Please," Lonnie said. "We need water." She could smell the same intoxicating stew she had stolen with Bally, and her stomach audibly rumbled.

"Is that a girl?" the woman asked. Heavy footsteps crossed the house.

"Stay in the bedroom," Kagan said, turning over his shoulder, but his friend didn't accept the order. She pulled the door the rest of the way open and stared right at Lonnie.

Lonnie frowned, recognizing the woman but having no memories to explain their connection.

"Lonnie?" the woman asked.

"Yes?" Lonnie said, throwing on a polite smile.

"Key," the woman said, pushing his ax down. "This is Lonnie Lovingdove. This is the girl who told me about you. She's the reason I found you."

"This is one of the girls who broke into my house and insulted me," Kagan said. He frowned, turning back to Lonnie. "You're the one who told Naples to find me?"

"I think so," Lonnie said, the memory starting to return. "Were we in East Ballick?" she asked.

"Of course," Naples said as she smiled. "We were a bit drunk, and there was some magic going on. What's happened to you? Key, let them in, for god's sake. Look at them."

"Come on, then," Kegan said, stepping aside. "I've got some water, and stew, if you can stomach it." He glanced at Lonnie as he said it, but his anger didn't last long with Naples' glowing approval of her.

Soon, the army sat at the massive table with cups of water and big bowls of stew. They feasted without saying a single word. As Naples set the stew back over the fire, she joined Kegan in the kitchen, frowning as she noticed the arrow in their soldier's shoulder.

"You're hurt," she said, reaching for a towel. "What's happened to you?"

"We were ambushed," Comely said. He looked deathly pale in the firelight.

"We have to take the arrow out," Naples said.

"Do you know how to do it?" Comely asked.

"No, but I understand how to tend to a wound. I worked in the East Ballick medical office as a girl. We need to keep the blood inside of your body." She shuffled to the counter and gathered towels and a bucket of water.

"What the devil have you been doing?" Kagan asked Lonnie.

"I joined Castle Windston's army," Lonnie said.

"We're making the final push against Doane," Comely said.

"Where's the rest of the army?" Kegan asked.

Comely swallowed a mouthful of stew, hesitantly splaying a hand across the table.

"This is it," he said, taking up his spoon.

"You're an army?" Kegan frowned as he surveyed the dying men.

"We only need to kill the king," one of the soldiers said. "It doesn't take much to kill an old man."

"Key, help me," Naples said, coming alongside the man with the arrow in his shoulder. "I'm going to wash this, and then I'll need you to take the arrow out."

"Easy," the soldier said, wincing as Naples cut away the shirt around his arrow. "Fucking hurts."

"Well, it's not going to feel better like this." Naples poured water over the arrow and wiped it away. Kagan stepped beside her, eyeing the thin arrow.

"Is there a tip on that?" he asked, turning to Comely.

"Yes," Comely muttered, tucking his leg further under the table. Lonnie leaned into him.

"We have to get your arrow out, too," she whispered.

"It's a bolt," he breathed. "It's down to the bone."

"Bite this," Kegan said, handing the soldier a wooden spoon. The soldier's teeth chattered as he chomped down, already splintering the outer layers of the wood. "I'll go slow," Kegan said, "but you might pass out."

With Naples' signal, Kegan began extracting the arrow, squeezing and pulling so hard his massive arms trembled. The soldier screamed into the spoon. Comely and the others gathered to hold him in place. The arrow came out a little bit at a time, breaking its way through the soldier's flesh. When it finally came loose, a torrent of blood ran from the hole. The soldier passed out and nearly landed in his stew.

"Turn his head," Naples said, pressing a towel to the wound. She pinned the man's shoulder to the table and held him steady.

As Comely backed beside Lonnie, wincing as the sight, Lonnie took him by the arm.

"We have to get your bolt out," she said.

"Not until we're done," Comely said. He turned to Lonnie, the warning glare so severe she dared not press the matter. "Kegan," he said. "How far are we from Doane?"

"The castle?" Kagan asked.

Yes."

"A few hours ride. Are you really going after the king?"

"We have to."

"And then what?"

"When the king dies, so will his insane war."

Kagan and Naples shared a wary glance.

"If we can rest," Comely said. "It would be very helpful."

"I can set out some blankets," Naples said. "Are you cold?"

"Yes," Lonnie said, afraid Comely might refuse the fire.

A short while later, all six members of the army lay before the heart on a cushy blanket. Kagan and Naples went back to bed. Lonnie nestled into Comely, careful to avoid the crossbow bolt in his leg.

"We can still win," he breathed into her ear. "We've come this far, right?"

Lonnie laced her fingers in his, afraid to speak her mind on the matter. She lay down and the heat of the fire fused her to the warm blanket. Between the crackling coals and Comely's rising chest at her back, she fell asleep within seconds.

When they woke, a terrible omen awaited them.

SIXTY-NINE

"Geoff," one of the soldiers said. "Geoff, wake up."

Lonnie lifted her head, her entire body flaring with pain. She turned to find one of the soldiers on his hands and knees over another. The man on the ground lay pale as chalk, his eyes and mouth permanently open. Blood had soaked through the blanket around his shoulder.

"Fuck," the soldier said, turning to Comely, who sat up behind Lonnie. "He's dead, Commander. Ice cold."

Comely grunted as he twisted himself free of the blankets, staggering to get on his feet. His face looked nearly as pale as Geoff's. He walked with a terrible limp across the blanket, staring down at him.

"Take him outside," he said, turning to the men. "We'll bury him and be on our way."

Lonnie wanted to bury herself in the blankets and drift back unconscious, but she could not hide from the day. She stood with Comely, who leaned on the kitchen table to take weight off his leg.

"You don't look well," she said, running her hand across his chest. "Are you sure we shouldn't take the bolt out?"

"It didn't work so well for Geoff." Comely limped to the table and filled their glasses with fresh water. Kagan and Naples came out of their bedroom a moment later.

"I thought you'd sleep through the day," Kagan said, yawning as he crossed the room. He paused at the bloodstain in the blanket. "Is that from—"

"Yes," Comely said. "They're burying him outside."

Naples quickly collected the blanket and carried it into the bedroom.

"When are you leaving?" Kagan asked.

"As soon as they're done," Comely said. "If we can trouble you for one last bowl of—"

"Of course," Naples said. "I'll give you some dried game to take with you, too."

A dim quiet fell over the house while Naples prepared breakfast. Lonnie stared at the blood-stained floorboard, adding another notch to her metaphorical kill belt. She estimated thirty people had died in the wake of her luck. The way Comely looked, it was only a matter of moments before he too fell into the afterlife.

"I don't think we should do this," she finally said, drawing everyone's attention.

"Do what?" Comely asked. He stood tall, fighting the pain in his leg.

"Go to the castle."

"We don't have a choice." Comely scowled, glancing to Kegan and Naples as if Lonnie's suggestion had been an unforgivable embarrassment. "It's piss on the grave of everyone who died for us to get here," he added.

"It's suicide," Lonnie said. "You're not even going to make it to Doane with that bolt in your leg, let alone into the castle."

"Bolt?" Naples asked, leaning around the table.

"The rest of the country will fall if we don't do something," Comely said. "I'll gladly kill myself to give them a chance."

"We don't even have any weapons," Lonnie said. "I'll give my life for the country, too, but there has to be a chance of winning. I've killed too many, Bram. I'm not the lucky charm you think I am."

"Then stay." Comely lifted his bowl, drinking the last of his stew. "Kegan," he said, finding their great host. "May I borrow your ax?"

Kegan turned to Naples, who didn't have an answer.

"Once I kill the king, I'll bring you a wagon of axes," Comely said. "*Please.*"

After a long, groaning sign, Kagan nodded.

"Fine," he said, heading into the bedroom to fetch it. "But you might want something lighter." He returned with his ax and a long carving knife.

"Thank you," Comely said, turning to Naples. "Both of you. I'm sorry to disturb your home, and I hope to live and make it up to you." He turned for the door, pausing as he faced Lonnie.

"Bram," she said. "We can't win this fight on our own."

"But what if we can?" he asked. "What if your entire journey has led us to this day, and this place, with these men? Aren't you curious to see inside the castle?"

"I've seen the inside of it," Lonnie said. "It's filled with men who want to kill me."

"And what if our tiny little army is quick enough to outwit them?"

Lonnie broke into tears as she took hold of Comely.

"Please," she whispered. "I can't lose you, too. We can run and find another life somewhere else. It's okay to admit we've lost."

"This is how it ends for you?" he asked. "Lonnie, we've come so far."

"I've only helped Doane kill another army."

Comely clenched his jaw, turning over his shoulder to Kegan and Naples. He started to speak and stopped himself.

"Good luck, then," he said, brushing past Lonnie. He stormed outside and whistled for the men.

"Bram," Lonnie called as she chased him outside. He battled

to climb onto his horse, wincing as he swung his bolted leg over the saddle.

"We're riding out," he said, turning to the soldiers, who had come running to his whistle. He wrapped the reins around his wrist and settled himself on the saddle. With a grunt, he pulled a travel back off the side of his horse and tossed it to Lonnie's feet. "I grabbed the wrong bag on the way out of camp," he said. "Was it a mistake, or did you get lucky?"

As the men climbed on their horses, he kicked, sending them into a run across the clearing.

Lonnie broke into tears. They raced away, their death inevitable, her heart breaking for the umpteenth time. She fell to her knees and pressed her head to the earth. Kegan and Naples stood in the door behind her. Lonnie remained frozen until the running hooves faded into the wind.

She sat back on her knees and wiped her tears, finding the army travel bag on the dirt before her. Frowning, she dragged it to her lap and pulled it open.

Daniel's desecrated carving lay inside.

Lonnie lifted the burned, crumbling thing. She fingered the faded initials, where the tiniest of wine stains remained through the charring like freckles.

Naples set a hand on her shoulder, seeming to have come from nowhere.

"You're not wrong," she said. "It's not easy to kill a king in his own castle. They'll need all the luck in the world to pull something like that off. It looks like the lot of you've run out."

Lonnie could only stare at the miraculous carving.

No matter what forces came against it—what cruelty defaced its beauty—it had always found its way back to her. She had thought of it as her last piece of Daniel, but she now saw something else.

It was a reflection of her. Life had crushed her, mutilated

her heart into an unrecognizable lump, yet she continued to exist. She was not the beautiful and innocently curious woman she had been, but nothing finished life intact. Her curiosity had come out of a desire to find something new. To *change* her surroundings. Did she not realize changing those surroundings might in turn change her?

A cold pit formed in her stomach. She climbed to her feet, tucking the carving back into the travel bag.

"Come inside, Lonnie," Naples said. "You need to rest. You've come far enough."

"No." Lonnie turned to her horse, who stared back at her. "I have to help them. They need me. They don't even know how to get into the castle."

"Lonnie," Kegan said. "They won't survive."

"You don't know that." Lonnie breathed heavy, her heart racing within her ribs. "What if we can do it?" she asked. "I've been to the castle twice. I know a back way in. I know where the prince sleeps."

"Lonnie," Naples called after her, but Lonnie had already started running for her horse. She leaped into the stirrup and climbed onto the saddle. With a kick, she sent her black stallion into a sprint and prayed she could catch the men in time.

SEVENTY

Lonnie raced along the forest trail, doing her best to track the men. She wanted to curse herself for letting fear take hold of her, but to fulfill their impossible mission, she needed to practice what she had preached; to do what she had done her entire life.

She found herself smiling as she galloped through the morning haze. A hundred questions sprang across her mind, and any of them could be the answer. She wondered if the staff entrance still remained wide open. She wondered if the posters of her face still hung across the kingdom and castle. She wondered what the king might say when she rammed a knife into his heart.

She wondered what Comely would say when they finished the deed—how passionate their love would bloom in the shadow of success.

"Go," she cried, kicking her horse. He galloped out of a wooded trail and into a wide, vast field. Lonnie panted as she lay eyes on the castle, far off in the distance, but finally in sight. The grass before her had clear signs of horse travel, but she still couldn't see Comely or the men. "Run," she shouted, kicking the horse again.

They raced across the field, leaping over a downed tree and following the tracks into another wooded glen. Lonnie ducked branches and battled to stay in the saddle. Mud splashed from deep puddles formed from the rainstorm. Daniel's carving banged against her knee like a hammer.

It dawned on Lonnie she had no weapon, but she turned her mind, shifting back to the curiosity she would need to succeed.

How might they use the castle moat to their advantage?

Did they still keep a wagon of Castle Winston's dead outside the castle?

What would the kingdom say if they learned of the dead king's proclivity for long pork?

Lonnie came alive with proper thinking.

Where would the trail bring her into the kingdom?

Did anyone know she was still alive?

How many kingsguard were actually in the castle? There had been no more than twenty running about when she escaped the prison. Did any of them question their loyalty to the twisted crown?

Lonnie couldn't help but wish she had Bally's magic to assist them. She had every chance in the world to kill both the king and prince on her last visit, but instead Bally used the tears to romp around the prince's bed.

The prince who seemed rather terrified of his father. Lonnie wondered what he might say to an abbreviated succession. Perhaps he was already in the throes of a coup to kill the king.

The idea made Lonnie laugh.

Just as her horse stepped into a gopher hole.

His front leg snapped like a stalk of celery, throwing Lonnie into the air. She crashed into the grass and tumbled a dozen yards before thumping into a tree. Her horse whinnying and grunting from somewhere nearby. Lonnie gasped, unable to breathe. The world seemed to quake beneath her. She crawled across the grass, drawing sweeping breaths into her lungs.

Up the field, her horse desperately tried to get back on its feet. Each attempt ended with a pained whiny before crashing back to earth. Lonnie climbed to her feet and found him, weeping as she knelt to pet his head.

"I'm so sorry," she breathed, kissing him.

The horse only grunted, flailing to get back on its useless legs.

With no weapon to put the horse out of its misery, Lonnie took the travel bag and shouldered it. She found the castle on the hill. Only a few miles stood between them. She ran, hoping she could catch Comely and the men before they came up with a plan.

Horrible thoughts came into her head: the horse—just another victim to her luck—but she chose curiosity; to move forward.

She had no other choice.

After what felt like an hour of running, she came to the end of the final ring of woods, where she found Comely's dapple gray and the rest of the horses tied to a tree. The horses swayed as they found Lonnie. They were still out of breath, which meant they hadn't been resting for long. Lonnie turned to the hill, which held the castle like a crown of its own over the land.

She ran with curiosity burning her mind.

SEVENTY-ONE

With no sign of guards on the castle walls, Lonnie climbed the hill toward one of the front left corner turrets, wanting to stay out of view of the main gates. Ticks swarmed across her ankles as she waged through the waist-high grass. Her heart stirred, but energy overpowered her fear. She climbed the last hundred feet and finally stood at the banks of the moat.

The moat stretched thirty or so feet across, but it came to a steep bank, which rose into the sheer castle walls. Lonnie wondered if she might climb the stones. They looked pronounced enough. She glanced to the castle entrance, where the sun silhouetted the gate house. The drawbridge stood high over the water. She saw no guards, but that didn't mean they weren't hiding in the shade of the house.

With no sign of Comely or the men, she slid down the bank and into the moat. Her eyes continued to drift to the castle walls. With curiosity as her guide, she swam across the dark water. Daniel's carving floated in the travel bag beside her. She came to the castle-side bank and dug her fingers into the mud. It held her enough to climb a few steps, but quickly dropped her back into the moat.

Lonnie found a tangle of grass roots a few yards down, but they too broke as soon as she pulled with her full weight. Growing tired from treading water, she began swimming along the bank toward the rear of the castle. The filthy water chilled her to the bone. In the castle's shadow, she couldn't help but shiver.

She made her way to the back of the castle where another, smaller raised bridge stood over the moat at its center. Lonnie tried to remember where she had come through the staff tunnel on her first visit. She could see nothing but the castle and sky from the water, so she climbed up the outside bank, getting a view of the hamlets below.

A long cobblestone road twisted out of them, riding into a closed gate in a smaller wall around the moat. Inside that wall, the road led to the drawn bridge and a small, gated-off tunnel: what must be the staff tunnel.

Lonnie turned to the castle, freezing at the sight of two archers leaning over the wall, absentmindedly talking to one another. She quickly slipped back into the water and swam toward the wall, where they would have to lean all the way out to see her.

She wondered where the hell Comely and the men had gone. They surely wouldn't attempt to walk in the front gate. Lonnie couldn't remember if she mentioned the staff tunnel, but even if she did, it was locked. She frowned as she paddled toward the drawbridge. Chains hung from each side of it. They didn't reach the water, but she thought she might have a chance at making a jump for one—if she could get a footing on the bank.

With no other option, she swam beneath the bridge. Rust had formed a red paint along the thick chains. Lonnie sunk her fingers into the bank, hating the warmth inside the mud. She set a foot in the bank and rose up. Water drained from her clothes and she waited, wanting to drop every pound she could. When her arms began to buckle, she kicked her foot into a higher hold, slowly lifting herself toward the chains. They dangled just out of reach. As the mud loosened beneath her foot, she kicked a higher hold and used it to jump.

Her fingers kissed the corroded chain before she bounced off the bank, splashing like a boulder into the moat. She cursed and pulled herself under the bridge's shadow. Through a small gap in the bridge, she watched the archers lean over the castle wall. They frowned as they stared at the settling ripples in the moat. Lonnie didn't dare move. She waited five minutes and the men didn't turn away.

"*Move*," she muttered, knowing every passing second put Comely and the men at further risk of death.

Finally, the archers turned away.

Lonnie watched the wall for a few more minutes, making sure they were gone, and quickly swam to the outside bank. She ran up and over it, making her way toward the tunnel entrance. At any moment she expected an arrow to fly into her back.

But she made it, taking hold of the cast-iron gate. A lock the size of her head held it shut. She jiggled it but made no progress. Glancing to the wall, she cringed to see the full view of the archers. She quickly slipped around the backside of the tunnel.

With privacy, she took a moment to let her heart settle. She closed her eyes and put her curiosity to work. Never in her life had she needed luck more.

She thought of what she wanted—to find the king and stop his heart.

She thought of her options—to climb the wall or break into the tunnel.

But where the hell had Comely and the men gone?

It was the only question that mattered, and it led her gaze back to the castle walls. She turned to the far side of the castle; the only wall she had not yet laid eyes upon. With a glance to the archers, she followed the backside of the tunnel. It took her most of the way across the back wall of the castle until it turned inside, where she followed it once more to the moat.

Lonnie paused to find a few sets of muddy footprints along the top of the tunnel. She set her fingers between the stones. With a grunt, she climbed into a foot hold.

She worked her way up, the job getting easier as she came closer to the top. Finally, when she could stand, she rose to find four sets of muddy footprints leading straight across the moat. They trailed off to the left, where the wall turned to the sunny-side of the castle.

Lonnie raced across the tunnel and slid down the thin shelf of grass on the castle-side of the moat. With her back to the wall, she worked her way to the corner. As she came around, using the corner to get herself facing the castle, she finally lay hand on the rough stones making up the castle walls. She blinked as dust fell into her eyes. After wiping it away, she lifted her gaze to find four shadowy figures halfway up the wall. They looked like ants from her vantage, but she didn't need a looking glass to know it was her army; the last good men of Castle Winston.

They moved at a crawl, taking great rests between climbs. Lonnie waved and silently screamed for their attention, but they seemed to have decided against looking down.

And so she set her fingers between the stones, taking the first step of many.

SEVENTY-TWO

Lonnie had no experience in climbing. After only fifteen feet her arms and legs burned. Panting, she found a half-comfortable position and rested. With what looked like a mile to go, she didn't rest for long.

Her gaze bounced from her hand holds to the men, who were nearing the top of the wall. She desperately wanted to cry out and let them know she was coming; to finish the mission as they had started—together, but they stubbornly refused to look back.

Lonnie found it helped to brush away the petrified grout between stones to deepen her holds. The game of it kept her distracted from the sharp pain settling into her muscles. When she did look down to track her progress, she gasped to find the moat a hundred feet below. She turned back up, where her spidery companions were making the final ascent to the top of the wall.

Lonnie blinked as more dust fell into her eyes. It burned, and she cursed her inability to brush it away. She climbed another ten feet and found a groove she could fit her entire fist inside. Gasping, she rested her depleted body.

She lifted her gaze to find the wall empty; her men racing onto the next leg of their suicidal journey. She opened her mouth to call to them, her tongue pressing to the roof of her mouth, but a strange conversation fell across the eerie quiet of the castle wall. Frowning, Lonnie turned to her left. It sounded as if the speakers were only a few feet away.

"Then he can cook the fucking skanks himself," someone shouted. "No, I'm done with it. Call it what you want, but it's not cooking."

"Then you tell him," a man said. "I'm not getting killed because you're afraid—"

"Afraid? *Afraid?* No, I'm not afraid. I'm disgusted. In fact, I'm repulsed. How many men have you skinned? Do you know how long it takes to pickle a penis? Because I do. How many arms have you blanched and plucked?"

"I have the distinct pleasure of watching our king devour the filth," the other man said. "But if you're set on quitting, then go ahead and tell him yourself. See how long it takes before you're on the menu."

Lonnie thought she recognized the second voice. It sounded like Lord Thomas, who had happily welcomed her and Bally into the castle while under the Occumancy spell. Lonnie leaned back to discover a small window a dozen feet to her left. Curious, she inched horizontally along the wall.

"I will," the other man said. "I'll march down to the throne right now."

"Then go ahead."

After a silence, the man cursed.

"What the fuck did he want?"

"A braised back strap," Lord Thomas said, sighing.

"Fucking fucker."

"Send it down when it's done."

A door thumped shut.

Lonnie stopped three feet from the window. She could smell smoke and cooking oil. The window was tiny, but after weeks of starvation and vomiting and physical abuse, so was she. She drew a breath before shuffling the last few inches to the window. A breathtaking heat flowed from inside.

A small, stuffy kitchen lay within the window. Stoves sat

along the left wall, piled with dirty pots and pans. On the other side of the room, a fat and greasy cook hacked at a corpse, wincing as he filleted a strip of meat off the dead man's spine.

Lonnie set an arm through the window and tried to pull herself through, but she couldn't get any leverage on the wall. She squirmed and pushed but simply had nothing left. She clung to the window frame, panting, hoping she had chosen wisely.

"Can you help, sir?" she asked, causing the cook to jump so badly he dropped his knife. He gaped at the woman in the window. "Please," Lonnie breathed. "Pull me in."

The cook ran across the room and took Lonnie's hand, his thick, greasy fingers wrapping her like blunted claws. He twisted her into the window. Her travel bag caught with her hips, but with a good pull, she came flying into the kitchen. The cook let her fall to the ground as he lifted his knife.

"Who the hell are you?" he asked. Curiosity filled his face, but Lonnie saw the moment of recognition as his eyes flashed. "*Lovingdove*," he breathed.

"Unfortunately, yes," Lonnie said.

"Then you're as stupid as they say."

"I'm not stupid at all." Lonnie smiled, enjoying the shock on the cook's fat face. "Listen to me. I need you to help me, because I'm here to help you."

"And how's that?" the cook asked, leaning back on the table with the mutilated corpse. Somehow, he managed to find a smile.

"I'm here to kill the king," Lonnie said. "I just need a good knife."

"The king?" The cook's humor fell away. "*Regicide?*"

"And treason. I'm going to end this insanity today."

The cook turned to the door, which Lord Thomas had closed on his way out.

"No one has to know about this," Lonnie said. "I just need a knife. If you happen to know where the king is, it would help me chances."

"There's a reward for your head. I'll be a rich man if I turn you in." But the cook trembled as he spoke, turning from Lonnie to the corpse on his table.

"I heard you talking to Lord Thomas," Lonnie said. "I know what the king makes you do. That can end today—if you help me."

"No." The cook lifted his knife and turned back to the body. "No, I have too much work to do." He resumed trimming the back strap, taking great care with his work. "I would never let you take one of the knives from that top drawer," he said, giving the bench beside him a kick. "Those are the sharp ones. It would be very bad if you got one of those."

Lonnie opened the drawer and took a long, glistening blade.

"And I can't tell you how to find the king," the cook continued. "I'd be hanged if I told you his bedroom is upstairs, on the front right corner of the castle."

Lonnie stepped to the door and took the handle.

"And I certainly wouldn't tell you to watch out for the kingsguard. The king's so paranoid he has them patrolling the castle at every hour."

"Thank you," Lonnie said as she pulled the door open.

"Here I am, talking to myself again," the cook said, shaking his head as he set the backstrap on a cutting board. "Next thing you know, I'll be wishing ghosts *good luck*." He turned, catching Lonnie's eye. They shared a mutual nod before she slipped into the hall.

SEVENTY-THREE

Lonnie stepped into a cold, stone corridor. She turned down both sides of the hall, frowning at the darkness. Only one torch burned along the entire wall. Flickers of yellow light at the corners suggested the same cheap lighting for the rest of the floor—what appeared to be staff quarters.

Lonnie thought for a moment and put herself on the center-right side of the castle. The cook suggested she would find the king upstairs, on the front right corner, so she headed to the left. She pressed her ear to the closed doors along the hall.

Behind the first, a pair of women complained while splashing clothes through a wash bin.

The other was silent, and upon opening it, Lonnie found only a small bedroom with four sets of bunk beds. The window-less room stunk of body odor.

As she came to the front-right corner of the castle, Lonnie expected to find an entrance to a spiral staircase—as she had ascended to the prince's turret—but she found only a right-angled corner. It came to a hall so long and barren it made her dizzy. A few tiny windows spat natural light into the hall every dozen yards. On the other end, she could see the staircase that led to the prince's turret; a dark shadow against the corner.

Lonnie held the knife tight as she marched, wondering where Comely and the men had gone. She imagined they were still alive—the castle would buzz with the announcement of intruders—but then again she stood on a decrepit floor, where neglect had left a visible layer of dust across the stone.

As she came to the first window, she peered out, finding the vast forests and fields she had traversed not long ago. She could just barely see the horses tied at the edge of the tree line. Beyond them, the intermittent fields and forests stretched all the way to the horizon.

Lonnie's stomach dropped as the sight of a dark swarm in the distance. It looked like ants, but she had never seen ants who could ride horses.

"Shit," she breathed, breaking into a run. Doane's army didn't look to be in a rush to return, but with their mission accomplished, they were indeed on their way back. She had no more than an hour before her extremely difficult mission became unpossible. She moved into a full-on sprint.

On her right, odd doors lined the hall. Lonnie's mind begged to know what mysteries hid behind them, but she had no time for extracurricular curiosity. She needed to find Comely and the men. If she couldn't, she must find the king and strike him dead.

The knife grew heavy as she considered cold-blooded murder. She switched it to her left hand, finally coming to the left-front corner of the castle. The stairwell spilled a cool, damp musk into the hall. Lonnie stepped into the shadow and listened; her skin tingling with excitement. A stir of voices came from below. The words were muddied and indecipherable. As her eyes drifted skyward, she began to climb.

She tripped over the uneven steps. They carried through two loops before coming to the next level of the castle.

Lonnie leaned out, finding another short-ceilinged hall. The dusty floors suggested she keep climbing.

So she did.

Before she made it halfway to the next floor, the sweet smell of perfume and pine met her. She crawled on hands and feet into the hall.

A bright green carpet ran the length of it, illuminated by large, arrow-shaped windows in the wall. The ceiling stood double the height of the staff floors. Lonnie studied the tapestries along the wall as she stepped out, finding portraits of the king and his deceased queen; triumph at a hunting party; glorious proclamations before the kingdom. The further Lonnie walked, the sadder the story became.

The king wept over the white and lifeless body of his partner.

Hand in hand, he strode through a shadowy grove with the toddler that would become Prince Pollen Bane VI.

The last mural stopped Lonnie in her tracks.

King Pollen Bane stood before a war counsel, with a gaze so fierce and lucid Lonnie barely recognized him. He set his long and muscular finger on a map. His guard stood at full attention, their hands resting on their swords. A portrait of the queen looked down on the war table from the mantle behind the king. She too held an expression that suggested agreement with the coming fight.

Lonnie had been a child when the queen died and couldn't remember the circumstances. Her mother hadn't cared, and that was the end of the conversation. Lonnie stared at the king, noticing a flower-print scarf wrapped around his hand.

As a door banged in the distance, she raced down the rest of the hall.

At the end, she found the spiral staircase she had been looking for; the one that could only lead to the bedroom of King Pollen Bane. As she stepped onto the base of the stairs, she frowned to find a portrait of herself—the same stupid look the king's artist had captured as she peeked through the window; when she realized her king had become a cannibal.

Only this portrait had been abused. Dark, dripping stains ran down her face. Lonnie guessed the king had made a habit of spitting on her during his comings and goings. She turned to the rising stairs, the knife starting to feel heavy again.

"He'd eat me for breakfast," she whispered, assuring herself she could go through with it. With a nod, a few steps to get her blood pumping, she started to climb.

The king's stairs were wonkier yet. Some rose a foot and half, and others only a few inches. Their length varied just as greatly. Lonnie again crawled on hands and feet, knowing one slip would be loud enough to cost her life. She wound around and around the castle. The heat came to head and sweat broke across her back. She started to grow dizzy, wondering how anyone could stand to live atop such a treacherous climb.

But around the next corner, she found the open doorway. Her hands trembled as she slithered up the last few steps. The king's bedroom looked to be twice the size of the prince's. From her low view, she could only see the massive bed, which hid behind a series of green and gold drapes.

Lonnie climbed to her feet and stepped to the door frame. She held her breath, as if it might slow her pounding heart.

The king's bedroom reeked of rotting meat. Lonnie leaned inside to find a full dining table swarmed with flies. It looked like a week's old wedding feast. Platters of bones and gristle lay at the center, with decomposing fruits and veggies surrounding them. A dried flower bouquet completed the scene. Lonnie covered her mouth at the sight of a skeletal hand. All but the thumb had been sucked clean of meat.

A knock came from the bed.

Lonnie stiffened, swinging the knife between her and the king.

The bed curtain rusted as something brushed across the inside of it. Lonnie drew a massive, silent breath and creeped forward, thinking of all the killing; all the innocent lives that had come at the king's hand.

In a way, every death on her conscience had been a byproduct of his corruption. The thought steadied her blade as she walked heel-to-toe across the sticky floor. The stench of human death concentrated—preluding to the coming regicide. Lonnie lifted the blade as she came to the bedside curtain.

Again, a foot or hand bumped the bed frame.

Lonnie braced herself as she took hold of the curtain slack, knowing her blow must fall between the ribs to be deadly. She drew one last breath and ripped the curtain open.

CHAPTER

SEVENTY-FOUR

The curtain rings squealed over the frame. Lonnie gripped the knife with both hands, drawing it over her head. She let out a gasping whelp as she leaped onto the bed.

A fat dog rolled over, finding Lonnie with little interest. She barely had time to divert the killing blow into the mattress.

The dog gave her a kick in the back of the head as he stretched out, nestling back into the sheets. Lonnie lay face-down with her heart punching against her ribs. She rolled to find the dog, who gave her a sandy kick in the chin.

"Fuck," Lonnie said as she shuffled back. She yanked the knife from the sheets, sending a few feathers into the air. The dog grunted and rolled into the center of bed. He turned to Lonnie, his intense gaze suggesting she was still in his way.

With her body still throbbing from the attempted killing, Lonnie paced across the room, confirming the king was not there. She cursed as she stepped onto the balcony. Below, she scanned the woods and planes to find the army. They were still miles away, but drawing ever closer.

Lonnie winced as she turned to the feasting table. If she did manage to kill the king, all she had to do was walk the kingdom through the room to prove her actions righteous. Feeling calm enough to try again, she headed for the stars, taking one last look at the lazy dog.

"You're lucky I'm nice," she muttered.

The dog pawed at the bed, letting out a burp as he settled into the sheets.

Lonnie stepped into the stairwell and sighed at the long and dangerous descent. She had no idea where to look for the king. Perhaps the cook might offer more information, but that meant crossing many halls, and she had already been lucky to make it as far as she did. She debated just waiting in the king's bedroom, where he would surely eventually return, but the soldiers would be there well before nightfall.

Voices came from downstairs. They were low, but close enough to back Lonnie into the bedroom. She stood dead silent as the voices stopped. Soon, soft and determined footsteps came in their place. Lonnie turned across the room and spotted a closet. She raced to it, but the door refused to open. Panting, she leaped back into the bed, getting a kick in the leg as she whipped the curtain shut.

She crawled to the pillows and pulled back a sliver of the curtain, laying eyes on the stairwell door. The dog pawed at her leg, his pads as rough as splintered wood. Lonnie gave him a kick back and held her breath.

The footsteps were clean and practiced, perhaps one of the kingsguard making the rounds. Lonnie held the knife tight as she shuffled to her knees. She felt less than optimistic about fighting a burly kingsguard, but she had little choice in the matter.

The dog picked up on the approaching stranger and stood, wagging his tail as he padded to the end of the bed. He made a sloppy jump to the floor. Lonnie cursed as his nails click-clacked over the stone floor, his bottom wobbling on his way to the stairwell.

And then he barked.

He barked again, backing from the stairwell as he growled.

Lonnie looked up just in time to see Comely dive into the room, tackling the dog across the floor. The rest of Castle

Winston came rushing into the room as Comely ran a knife through the dog's soft belly.

"Comely," Lonnie said, slapping the curtain aside.

Comely looked up as the dog's guts flopped over his hand. He frowned and shoved the dog away.

"How did—?"

Lonnie crashed into him, holding him so tight she herself couldn't breath.

"I'm sorry," she said. "I was an idiot, and—"

"Quiet," Comely said. He managed to smile as he held her back, meeting her eyes. "How the hell did you beat us here?"

"I got lucky," Lonnie said. "I left right after you, but I couldn't catch up. I was on the wall behind you. I found a window and climbed inside. A cook helped me. He gave me this." Lonnie held out her knife. "He told me the king would be here, but I only found the dog. How did you get here?"

"We came over the wall," Comely said. "We were able to slip into a stairwell, and we've been slowly making our way across the castle. We got stuck in a closet hiding from a few guards. They're patrolling. We counted three groups of three, but we've only been on two floors. Have you seen anyone else? Has anyone seen you?"

"No," Lonnie said. "Just the cook. But the soldiers are coming back. Look." She led the men to the balcony, where they grimaced at the sight of the on-coming warriors. "We don't have much time. And even if we kill him, what's going to stop—"

"One thing at a time," Comely said. "Where was the king the last time you visited?"

"I've only ever seen him downstairs. Either in the throne room or his feasting hall." Lonnie couldn't help but glance at the table of rotting meat. Comely followed her stare, scowling as he led the men to the table. He pushed a horribly gray plate of meat with his knife.

"These are our men?" he asked, turning to Lonnie.

"It could be pork." Lonnie blushed as one of the men lifted the skinless hand. "But it's probably your men, yes."

Comely sneered as he turned to the stairwell.

"Let's find the fucker," he breathed. He moved straight down the stairs, not stumbling for a moment on the asymmetrical architecture. Lonnie allowed the men to go second and braced the wall as they wound round and around. The stairs were easier from the top, which she suspected to be the point of their design. They returned to the next floor quickly.

"How do we get downstairs?" Comely asked.

"That stairwell on the other side of the hall," Lonnie said, leading the way. "That's how we came to the prince's bedroom last time. It goes all the way down."

"Do you think the prince is in his room?"

"The prince is usually with the king."

As they crossed the hall, Lonnie again found herself lost in the last painting of the king, where he stood watch over the war table. She pointed it out to Comely.

"Do you know how Queen Cassima died?" she asked.

"Aren't you the one from Doane?" Comely asked. He smiled, giving Lonnie a gentle prod with his elbow. "She died giving birth to what would have been your king's second son. She was in Winston at the time, visiting her cousin. You really don't know the story?"

"My mother hated politics."

"Queen Cassima died on the birthing table, as did her son. Your king thought she could have been saved. But our best healers did everything possible to save her. I don't know if it started the war—it happened twenty some years ago—but it certainly didn't build any bridges."

Comely quieted as they approached the stairwell, his eyes shifting into slits, as they did when his mind moved. He leaned into the wall and listened.

The stairwell served as an amphitheater, carrying distant mumbles and shuffling. Lonnie listened for a full minute and deciphered nothing.

"Now or never," Comely said, turning to her. "For luck." He gave her a quick kiss, and together, they started down the stairwell.

SEVENTY-FIVE

They moved quickly, their feet making only a soft rustle as they unspooled the stairwell into the heart of the castle. Lonnie studied every passing floor. The ceilings grew higher, and the decorations grew brighter and more luxurious. She stiffened as Comely and the others slowed, a wash of daylight illuminating the end of their descent. They crowded into the shadow of the final arched door frame.

They stood outside the courtyard, where Lonnie had once innocently creeped about, a foolish woman with no idea of the journey soon to overtake her. She carried a knife this time, but her hands still trembled as she crowded over Comely's shoulder. Heat radiated off his skin, and his face looked far too pale. He held up a hand.

"Someone's coming," he whispered, leaning back into the shadow.

A heavy clop of boots filled the air. Lonnie turned as four long shadows grew solid against the wall. Mercifully, the soldiers continued past the stairwell. They carried swords but lazily, looking to be on one of many fruitless patrols. Comely leaned back as they continued along the wall, finally fading through the depths of the castle's main entrance.

"Lonnie?" he asked.

"What?" she asked.

"Take us to the man-eating king."

Lonnie turned to all four members of their army and nodded. With a breath, she led the way into the hall. It felt like a thousand years, yet it felt like a day since she had ventured across the castle. Her eyes shifted over the courtyard. She passed the outer stone walkway and into the grass, leading the men to the center of the ground floor, to the place where men literally devoured their enemies. Heat washed over her body. Fear came as a cold finger along her spine.

A section of pillars and stone benches marked the midway point of the courtyard. Lonnie crouched behind a shrub, waving for the others as another patrol came up the left side of the room.

The guards mumbled to one another as they marched, their conversation looking far from enjoyable. One held a look of desperation. The others frowned and shook their heads. They too carried long, sparkling swords. Lonnie and her army lay on their bellies until the guards circled all the way around the courtyard, finally following the last patrol into the entrance hall.

"Where is it?" Comely asked.

Lonnie lifted her head, finding the wall of windows looking into the feasting hall. With a nod to Comely, they swept across the grass, all stiffening at a distant shout Lonnie knew all too well.

"Forks and fish and *frankincense*," the king shouted. A loud clatter followed the expulsion. "Shall I marry a pumpkin? Will vines drink seed from a mallet?"

"He's here," Lonnie whispered. "This is where I first found him."

And he found me, she thought, shivering at the sight of the window.

"Let's see what we've got," Comely said, assuming the lead. He winced as he crouched, the crossbow bolt still stuck in his leg. They gathered beneath the windows and readied their weapons.

"They say mid-winter holidays are for suckers," the king continued. "Well, I'd like to see them throw a feast when rations are thinning. Do they still sing in the pools? Do the prophets cast shadow before taking their shits?"

Comely frowned as he turned to Lonnie.

Lonnie swirled a finger beside her head.

"Perhaps you should take a nap, father," the prince said, his voice meek and tired.

"And perhaps I should set you on a sharpened tree," the king said. "Let's see just how long it takes for *you* to taste bark."

As Comely rose to the window, so did Lonnie, squinting at the glow of a dozen torches.

The king and prince sat at the ends of the long table, as they had before, but the scene came with a new definition of sanity. While the prince wore a sensible tunic and pants, the king wore a bright green dress. He also traded his crown for a tall and pointy hat; one a flamboyant magician might wear. His hands glistened with the reflection of a dozen rings. The ill-fitting dress left great patches of his skin exposed, revealing dark, reddened veins.

"I swear to the river I'll rape a fish," the king said, turning to his cup bearer. He laughed until the servant laughed, and then he leaped to his feet, wrapping his hands around the trembling man's throat. "Are you the one who ate my backstrap?" he shouted. "Is it you who drank the pickling juice?"

"No, Your Highness," the man wheezed.

"*Breathe.*" The king pressed his nose to the man's, not seeming to understand breathing was not possible without airflow.

"Your Highness," the prince's cup-bearer called. "I'm sure the cook's just making sure your backstrap is perfect. Shall I go check?"

"Does marble bleed salt?" the king asked, dropping the cup-bearer.

The cup-beared turned to the prince for help, but the prince only stared at the hearth, which blazed from the back of the feasting chamber.

"Yes," the king said, straightening his dress. "Please, my good man, go and see how the cook's coming alone." He returned to his seat and sighed, taking up a long and meaty bone. "I do wish the dolphins had our confidence," he mused, tickling a dangle of sinew on his plate. "If not purple, then why green? That's what I need to know."

"Touché," said the prince. "Besides, whatever happened to blue?"

"Why, blue's been retired since he married yellow, but it's orange that keeps me up at night."

Comely pulled Lonnie back behind the wall.

"What the hell is happening?" he asked. "He's gone beyond mad."

"It wasn't this bad last time," Lonnie said.

"Some good news, at least. Only two guards at the door." Comely waved for the rest of the team to crawl into a huddle. "With that cup-bearer out of the way, we're evenly matched," he continued. "Heath, take the other cup-beared. Jagger, you're on the prince. Luke and I'll handle the guards—we'll go around front and catch them from behind."

Lonnie, understanding where Comely was headed, said, "I—"

"Yes," Comely said. "You, Heath and Jagger are going in this window. While Heath takes the guard, you put that sad prick out of his misery. It has to be you, Lonnie. It's your luck that's taken us this far."

Lonnie searched for a reason to protest, but she saw the logic. With a pained nod, she turned to Comely.

"You want me to kill him?"

"As fast and violently as you can," Comely said. "Luke and I'll go to the corner. On our signal, drop in. We'll handle the guards, you three take care of the royals and cup-bearer."

"Do you want me to kill the cup-bearer?" Jagger asked.

"Only if you have to. He's a boy, and I doubt he's here because he wants to be." Comely took Lonnie's hand, squeezing it tight as their eyes met. He nodded and crawled along the wall, Health right behind him, their knives in hand.

"Who planted water warts in the livery?" the king asked. When no one replied, he pounded a fist against the table. "Black tartar and the whore's mustache, *that's* who. I'll fuck his cousin if I see her again. I'll teach sleeping possums to bridle haggis, and if the bouncing cunt still wants a fight, *well*" —the king laughed, a condescending ejaculation of sound— "*then* we'll know who stepped on the apple's womb. We'll write a song and sing it to the milk of starlight."

Lonnie shared a glance with Jagger and Health. They turned to Comely and Luke, who crawled the last few feet to the end of the wall. After glancing around the corner, they turned to Lonnie and crew, who nodded back.

Comely held up a hand, the coming signal pulling Lonnie's nerves like a marionette's string. She swallowed a lump and re-gripped her knife. The blade sparkled in the corner of her eye. She ignored the distraction, keeping her attention on Comely.

With a wave, he and Luke dashed around the corner.

SEVENTY-SIX

Lonnie and the men hopped into the windows as a roar came from below. They dropped to the stone as Comely and Luke battled the guards. Their swords crashed and chimed, the men grunting and dancing across the foyer.

"Go," Jagger called, racing off with Health. He lunged into the cup-bearer and pinned him to the floor. The prince backed himself into a wall, his hands raised as Heath raced forward with Kegan's ax.

Lonnie turned to the king, who watched the scene with a crazed stare, his eyes wide, his mouth swishing as he chewed his food. He remained in his seat.

"Go," Comely shouted.

Lonnie started for the king, her skin prickling as she lifted the knife.

He turned and found her. His shock melted into a fiery recognition.

"*Lovingdove,*" he breathed, hopping from his chair. He dragged a ten-foot lance from beneath the table. Lonnie backed up as he waved it toward her.

A wild scream came from the hall.

Lonnie turned, just as Comely lowered his kingsguard to the ground. Luke rolled across the floor with the other guard in hand-to-hand combat. Comely dragged the guard off him and slit his throat.

"*No,*" the king shouted. "This is not how we do our dinner!" He turned his lance from the men to Lonnie, grunting as he cut a Z through the air. "*My wife's not for sale.*" He screamed as he leaped forward, nearly slicing Lonnie's ear off. She stepped back as Comely and Luke rushed to her side.

"It's over," Comely said, still fighting to catch his breath. He waved Luke around the table.

The king swung the lance and widened his defense.

Comely walked to the wall of windows, officially surrounding the king.

"Drop that lance," he commanded. "You're finished."

The king grunted like a wild pig, thrusting the obnoxious lance back and forth. Comely easily caught it when it came his way. He dragged it out of the king's hands and tossed it aside. The prince broke into tears.

"Get on your knees," Comely said to the king. He turned to Lonnie and waved her forward.

"If you want me to bend, you'll have to break me," the king said. "I've palavered with many men, and few know how to do it." He laughed and turned to the empty wall. A great and dark vein stood out on his neck like a lighting bolt. Lonnie deigned it her target and creeped forward, the knife tight in her hand.

"Go," Comely shouted. "Kill him before—"

A rumble of bootsteps filled the air. The hall trembled as two dozen kingsguard raced into the room. They surrounded Castle Winston's army of five. Half of them raised crossbows, the others lifted their swords.

"Stand down," a guard called, stepping forward. Lonnie met eyes with her nemesis kingsguard. He sneered, taking in the scene; his fallen brothers in arms. "Drop your weapons," he growled.

Lonnie dropped the knife, and with hesitation, Comely and Luke dropped their blades and ax. They huddled as the guards tightened their perimeter.

"*Well,*" said the king, chuckling. "Just in time, boys." He stepped around the table, smiling as he found Lonnie. "Our great bird has finally returned," he continued. "I feared she may have been lost. To celebrate this momentous occasion, I declare tonight a national holiday."

"He's insane," Comely said, focusing his attention on the guards. "This man can't rule his own mind, let alone a kingdom. You can't—"

"Break that man's jaw," the king said.

Two guards stepped forward and took hold of Comely. The nemesis kingsguard stepped forward and tightened his gloves.

"No," Lonnie shouted. "Don't hurt him. Break my jaw if you have to break one."

"Oh, don't you worry," said the king. "I'm having you skinned and fileted alive. Get your knives out boys. We'll do it here and now."

When no guards stepped forward, the king slapped a platter off the table.

"Start *skinning,* or I'll have your wives and children burned at the stake," he snarled. "I'll start with you, Tony."

The nemesis kingsguard paled as he turned to Lonnie. He took her by the arm and guided her to the center of the room. Lonnie fought and kicked against him. Comely and the men shouted, but they could do nothing to stop him from placing her on her knees.

"There we are," the king said, humor returning to his eyes. "It's funny, I was just thinking of you, Lonnie. A wedding bean had fried my hat rack, and I told him to spread cheeks. I bent three trees into the pitchfork, but still" —he pressed a fist to his mouth as he stifled a tremendous burp— "it's the blood that makes the pudding. I thought Roger Benton might have poisoned the cheese, but you know how stuffy the cupboard gets after sundown."

Everyone stood in silence, taking in the king's streaming gibberish with weakly veiled disgust.

"He's lost it," Comely said, still wrestling his holders. "You have to—"

"And he'll be desert," the king said, turning to Comely. "He'll make a fine rabbit stew. Look at those ears. I bet he came pre-salted." The king jumped into the air, as if someone had just stuck a hot poker into his behind. "Why is she still wearing skin?" he barked, snarling as he rounded on the nemesis kingsguard. "Why is your blade still clean?"

"You shouldn't have come back," the kingsguard whispered to Lonnie, setting his blade on her shoulder. "Why the hell would you come back?"

"Someone has to stop him," she breathed.

"You had no chance." He slid his knife hand down Lonnie's dress, taking hold of her wrist. "Not with that little blade of yours." Quietly, he slipped the hilt of his sword into Lonnie's hand. "*Try this*," he breathed, leaning into her ear. "*End this fucking shitshow.*"

Lonnie rose over her nemesis kingsguard—Tony, as the king had called him. She lifted the massive sword, finding the king. The color left his face and dark bags pooled beneath his eyes.

"She has a sword," he said, looking across the room.

The kingsguard stood still.

"She has a sword," the king repeated, taking a step back.

"And you're insane," Lonnie said. She walked the room, following the king as he backed behind the table. "You've killed hundreds of innocent men. You've eaten the dead, and you've tricked the people you swore to protect into joining your sin."

"I sang with the piglets," the king said, his jaw quaking, his eyes welling with tears. He backed another step as Lonnie rounded the table. "I breached a place only the monkeys can see."

Lonnie charged the king—screaming, lifting the blade, the weeks of pain and death and suffering driving her forward.

But the king ran, too. He turned and sprinted for the back of the room. As he crossed the carpet runner, he stumbled. His ankle cracked and he yelped as he flailed for balance. He tripped over his own boots and flew forward. No one moved a muscle as he crashed face-first into the hearth.

With an awful, mushy crunch, his head found the rack of iron pokers.

Lonnie winced as she came to the king's side.

Blood ran from the eye socket, where the pocket had found a new home, and the king, with a last gurgling breath, finally escaped his flesh.

"He's dead," Lonnie breathed, turning to the army of men.

Well," someone said from the back. "That was lucky."

Lonnie found Comely's eyes. Both froze in disbelief.

"You know what's even luckier?" Tony said as he crossed the room. "The poor prince tripped and died in almost the same way."

"What?" the prince asked, coming out of his cower.

Tony waved the guards back and grabbed the prince by the ankles. The prince screamed as Tony lifted him clear over his head. With a grunt, Tony swung the prince to the ground like an ax, but instead of splintering wood, he shattered the prince's skull like a soft-boiled egg.

As blood pooled across the floor, Lonnie rushed to Comely's side.

"What just happened?" she whispered.

"Quiet," Comely said.

"We've had a serious accident," Tony said, facing the rest of the kingsguard. "We've lost our cannibal king and his foolish son." Behind the soldiers, other castle staff crowded into the room, all gasping at the grizzly sight.

"What is this?" Lord Thomas asked, pushing his way to the front of the room. "What has happened?" He went white at the sight of the prince.

"A terrible accident," Tony said. "Our king and his prince are dead."

Lord Thomas smiled but quickly shifted into a very fake-looking frown.

"How terrible," he said. "How shocking."

The room fell silent again. As the guards released Jagger and Luke and Heath, they stepped to Lonnie and Comely's side.

"So, what do we do now?" a kingsguard asked.

"Now," Comely said, glancing at Lonnie as he stepped forward, "you bow to your new queen."

"Queen?" Lord Thomas asked. "What the devil are you talking about?"

"Did the prince not tell you?" Comely stepped forward, addressing the curious faces. "Not one of you knows what happened?"

"Explain," Tony said.

"Do you recall Lonnie Lovingdove's last visit to the castle?"

"She brought a witch who used magic to disguise them," Lord Thomas said. "We nearly killed an innocent servant because of it."

"On that very visit," Comely said, casting Lonnie a look the demanded she shut up and play along, "your dear Prince Pollen Bane VI had a private wedding with his guest. That guest stands before me now, and her name is Lonnie Lovingdove. Or should I say, *Queen Lonnie Pollen Bane.*"

"No," Tony said, stepping forward. "God, no. We can sell the accident, but we're not putting a peasant on the throne."

"Well," Comely muttered as he stepped back to Lonnie's side. "I tried."

"Succession will be decided in private," Lord Thomas said. "Everyone but the heads of the castle must leave."

As the kingsguard shuffled out, Lonnie turned to Tony.

"We can go, too?" she asked.

"I don't care," he said, taking his sword from her.

"But what about Castle Winston?" Comely asked. "And the war?"

"It was the king's war, and the king is dead."

"What about the false treason charges?" Lonnie asked.

"I just said you can go," Tony said. "Fuck off. You're free, we're not interested, and we don't care who you are or what you did or want to do. Good bye."

Lonnie grinned, feeling as if a thousand-pound sack had just fallen from her shoulders. She turned to Comely and kissed him. He lifted her off the ground and held her tight, spinning as he kissed her.

"Fuck off with that, too," Tony said.

So they did, racing through the halls and out the door into the light of freedom.

LET'S DO SOMETHING FUN (AGAIN) (AND THIS TIME WITHOUT OCCUMANCY)

Three months passed.

SEVENTY-EIGHT

Lonnie lowered the bucket into the stream, wincing as the icy water kissed her fingers. A wind swept through the woods and rustled her fur coat. Despite the brutal elements, she smiled. A perfect layer of white snow capped the trees and forest path. She lifted the bucket and marched back up the Seregile mountainside.

Comely had the fire roaring by the time Lonnie returned to camp. She handed him the water and he kissed her. His beard, a new accessory since the war, tickled her every time.

"You should shave that," Lonnie said. "It makes you look so old."

"In the spring," Comely said, setting the bucket beside the fire. He lifted a string of skinned squirrels and set them over the flame. The meat soon began to brown.

Life for Lonnie Lovingdove had changed dramatically after the death of the king and prince. She and Comely fled Doane, having no interest in the ensuing war for the crown. After returning Kegan's axe and knife, they headed into East Ballick, where they spent the next month licking their wounds. After settling in, Comely had the rest of the army return home to announce their victory, and a few weeks later, the king sent Comely a bucket of medals and a chest of gold coins.

They fattened up and enjoyed copious couplings in their inn. When they tired of sex and food, and reliving the glory of their adventure, they found an unsettling side to their newfound peace. Comely wondered if they should search for another war. Lonnie couldn't find anything exciting enough to be curious about. She enjoyed the boredom for a time, but like all artists who abandon their calling, she began to lose her identity.

She took to taking long walks at night. There was always something happening in East Ballick, but even the drunken parties at the taverns seemed tame after her time with Bally. The city itself was a constant reminder of the dead witch. Lonnie refused to miss her, but she did find herself wishing to feel the overwhelming chaos that followed her.

Late one night, after a particularly brutal round of coupling with Comely, Lonnie again found herself thinking of Bally.

Not as a witch, but when she had been called Fest Doe Raymo. Their time at the Shrine fell like a long-forgotten dream, but as Lonnie dove into those naked, uncomfortable memories, she found she did have something worth her curiosity.

It only took a few days before she convinced Comely that they must pursue the idea. Comely, enthralled by the danger of it, didn't need much convincing.

So there they sat in the Seregile mountains, huddled around a fire in the dead of winter. Lonnie didn't worry about the cold with their tent and thorough provisions. They had so many fur blankets they usually left the tent open at night.

"I think today might be the day," Comely said, holding his hands to the fire.

"I think so, too," Lonnie said. "Did you ever write the note?"

"There's no point."

"It could save someone's life."

"It might just as easily send someone into a fit of curiosity that all but guarantees their death."

"Assuming we die," Lonnie said.

"Assuming we die," Comely agreed. "If you want to leave it,

then go ahead and write. I'm going to get started. Watch the squirrels."

Once Comely set out, Lonnie crawled into the tent and set a fresh sheet of parchment on her lap. She took a long time to assemble her thoughts in a way she felt good about leaving behind, but her third draft was solid. After some hesitation, she signed the note, figuring whoever found it had a chance of knowing her growing legend.

She folded the note and returned to the fire, cursing to find half of the squirrels burned. After scraping the char off, she brought one to Comely, who happily accepted a moment of rest. They ate in silence, as they usually found themselves on work days.

"How's it coming?" Lonnie asked.

"We're just about there," Comely said, meeting her gaze, his eyes fierce and bright in the whitewash. "Another hour and we'll be able to squeeze right through."

"Good."

"You're sure about this?"

"No, but that's the whole point. I have a very high tolerance for excitement, and this might be the last chance I have to feel something."

"You can always feel me," Comely said, smiling as he tossed his squirrel bones aside.

They fell to their knees and coupled right there in the snow, their passion an ever-expanding star.

"I have to set up the letter," Lonnie said when they finished, still catching her breath.

"Then set it," Comely said. "I'll see you inside."

Lonnie jogged back to the tent, opened her trunk and found the travel bag with Daniel's carving. The carving had fallen off a table a few weeks after the king's death and split right down the center. While just rubble, Lonnie still couldn't let it go. She shouldered the travel bag and stepped back outside.

A light snow started to fall across camp. Lonnie studied the cliffside, taking a cool breath of air. The rising fear in her heart came with a welcome familiarity. After snapping the tent shut, she pulled the letter from her pocket and pinned it to the top. With a nod, she headed to the mountain with the travel bag swaying against her belly. She wondered if anyone could take her letter seriously.

"You've found yourself in a dangerous place. Whatever curiosity brought you here, know that you stand at the door to another dimension. This place was once called the Shrine. Now, it is only a graveyard.

But do not mistake death for the end. My partner, Commander Bram Comely and I, have ventured here in pursuit of our own curiosity. There is a cave within the mountain. A witch once murdered a god with a single punch inside of that cave. A wise and naked man once told me there is a portal to another dimension inside of that cave, and the Commander and I have decided we must investigate.

I don't know what we will find, and that is why we must pursue it. If you find this letter, we have died or been trapped inside. Do not attempt to follow our quest unless you are prepared to make the same sacrifice (if you do, bring some food and water, because we might be alive and very hungry). If negativity and poor luck plagues you, I beg you to consider simpler curiosities. The path we walk is only for those who have already turned every rock this earth has to offer.

Best of luck,

Lonnie Lovingdove."

AFTERWARD

There are infinite entries to a story, and like most of mine, Lonnie Lovingdove came through the door of curiosity. What started as a silly idea about a cannibalistic king soon evolved into a much deeper story about luck and the fuel that creates it. I hope you had as much fun exploring Lonnie's world as I have.

If you did, I would be ever so grateful for a review!

You can also stay up to date on all of my up-coming stories by subscribing to my newsletter.

If you'd like to hear the soundtrack to Lonnie's story, the playlist is on Spotify. https://tinyurl.com/3xrmxzcd

If you have any questions or want to reach out directly, feel free to send me an email (matt@matthewscura.com).

-Matthew

ABOUT THE AUTHOR

Matthew Scura is an avid reader, writer, musician, podcast host, and business owner living in the Philadelphia suburbs. He writes for both adult and YA audiences—primarily psychological thrillers, speculative fiction and grounded fantasy.

When not with his family or writing, Matthew works for Edge of Cinema, an international video production and digital marketing agency he co-founded in 2009. He also love running, cooking, ripping the occasional Pokemon pack, working on handyman projects, and producing original music out of his home studio.